AMITHIA RAINE

Should The Sky FALL

WHO WE ARE BOOK 1

Copyright © July 2023 by Amithia Raine

Beta-read by Saga Nansen and Katie

Editing and proofreading by Ryn McLean

Cover and title page by GetCovers.com

ISBN: 978-0-6457348-1-2

The contents of this book may be triggering to some people. Major triggers include: sexual assault, domestic abuse and alcohol addiction. For a detailed list, please visit

https://amithiaraine.com/should-the-sky-fall

Contents

Acknowledgements

This book would've never seen the light of day without all the people who supported me through the ~~self-inflicted pain~~ process.

Huge thank you to Saga for holding my hand the whole time and letting me rant. You're my guardian angel (and the devil on my shoulder making me do bad, bad decisions).

Katie, you're a gem. Thank you for stepping in when I needed you, and for being such a great cheerleader and gentle with your edits (you know I cry easily).

Ryn, your edits are not gentle and they do make me cry, but they also made this book into the best version of itself, so thank you for keeping me on my toes.

Finally, big thanks to Em and V for putting up with me and answering my incessant questions about amnesia, surgeries and rehab. You guys really saved my ass.

Prologue

Soon.

Impatience is such an illogical concept. Time doesn't even exist. Things simply are, or they are not. And if they are meant to be, they will be. The *when* doesn't matter.

Except it does. This time, it does.

He doesn't know what lies beyond the threshold. None of his kind do, destined to tread the edge of the precipice. Seeing the horizon, but never further. It's perfectly possible there's nothing there at all, just an endless void sucking everything in like a black hole.

He hopes not.

He'd much rather believe the good old tales that speak of heaven and hell, of bringing justice that failed to be delivered on the plane of the living.

But better late than never.

Until now, he never cared what's out there. His job is easy and straightforward, beautiful in its ruthless simplicity. Just take, hold, and deliver. Then do it again. And again. And again. Like a perfect machine, doing what it was created for.

And he *is* a machine, a pawn among many. Most of the time, at least. And sometimes, once upon an eternity, he feels it. A surge of something that should be foreign and wrong but is uncomfortably familiar. He's only able to put a name to it because he's been watching humanity succumb to the same force for as long as he can remember.

Emotions are such a silly thing. They're also, to his grief, seemingly imperishable.

He doesn't know what lies beyond the threshold, but as he watches Caledon Reeves wash drying blood from his knuckles, watches him sway as he takes another swig from the rapidly emptying bottle of whiskey before stumbling over to the sofa and collapsing onto it like a pile of worthless filth...

Yeah, he really hopes there's a heaven and hell. And he really hopes that, when he finally rips Caledon's rotten soul from his disgusting body, he will be delivering him to the hellfire where he'll burn forever. If he had a heart, it would be fluttering in excitement at the prospect of dragging the monster from this plane.

Soon.

Until the time comes, he'll be following the man like a dark shadow, lurking beyond the veil, awaiting the moment he'll finally get his hands on him. It will be so, so sweet.

He'll have to think of a way to make it last, to drag it out with excruciating slowness. The exact opposite of what he always does. One touch, and it's all over, like severing a thread. Painless. Absolute.

Not this time.

He will rip Caledon open, seam by seam, until there's nothing left but fear and agony.

It's the quiet sobbing that pulls him out of the well of hatred and rage he's been sinking into. Calling out to him.

He shouldn't. He knows that. There's nothing forbidden about it, but Caledon is his job. He shouldn't allow any distractions.

As if an invisible force has taken hold of him, he follows the anguished sounds, passing through the door like a ghost. He knows what he'll find there, but that doesn't stop him. Nothing could stop him.

The rage he just escaped pulls him under before it's replaced by something else. Something quieter, softer, and unfathomably more powerful. It doesn't matter how many times he reminds himself what he's come here to do; the sight of Dawson strips the rest of the world away, making everything else insignificant.

Dawson's hands shake as he cleans his face, running a damp, red-stained cloth over the open wounds. Blood drips from his bottom lip into the sink, flowing faster the more Dawson cries, the more he trembles. His left eye has started to swell, the skin around it turning darker as seconds tick by. Who knows what violence can be found under his shirt sprayed with crimson droplets.

Dawson lifts his gaze, looking at his reflection. His face hardens, disgust flashing over his features. He grips the edge of the counter, leaving two bloody handprints behind.

Maybe it's because he can't stand the sight of himself, or maybe he's just tired, but he allows his legs to cave, sliding to the tiled floor. Leaning against the wall, he pulls his knees to his chest and buries his beautiful, hurt face in his palms. A violent sob is torn out of him, sending ripples through his body.

His haunted eyes shoot towards the door when his own pain-filled sound reaches his ears. When nothing happens, when no monster comes barrelling in, the tremors resume.

He pulls in a hiccuping breath. And stills. When he looks up, his face is tear and blood streaked, and hauntingly blank. Light flickers out of his honey-colored eyes, leaving them hollow.

Unable to stay away, he gets closer to Dawson and kneels at his side.

"Soon," he whispers into Dawson's ear. He wills himself not to read anything into Dawson's soft gasp, the sharp intake of breath.

He never thought he'd have to fight so hard to not break the rule—the only rule. But the sight of Dawson's battered face tries him, tempts him to return to the living room and take Caledon with him right now.

"Soon, you'll be free. He won't hurt you anymore. I promise you."

He wills himself not to read anything into it when Dawson's eyelids flutter and slide shut. Or into the ghost of a smile that tugs on his still bleeding lip, serenity smoothing out his features.

He drags his gaze over Dawson's wounds and wants nothing more than to reach out and trace those nasty bruises and cuts until they're gone, like they were never there.

He doesn't do that, of course. His touch doesn't heal—it destroys.

He can't heal Dawson, but he can take away what is hurting him. The wounds will close, the bruises will fade, until they're nothing but an ugly memory.

He just hopes that when his job is finished, when the threat is finally gone, it won't be too late for Dawson's soul to remember its light, to reclaim what Caledon has stolen from him.

He'd give anything to make sure Dawson's soul shines again.

He'd give anything to show Dawson how much he deserves to be loved. Utterly, completely.

He'd give anything.

Chapter 1

"I'VE MADE A RESERVATION for 6.30."

Dawson's hands still, his shoelaces only halfway tied. A knot forming in his stomach, he looks up.

Cal's expression is unreadable—or it would be to anyone else. He taps his fingers against the mug of coffee in his hand before bringing it up to his lips. There's a hint of challenge in his eyes as he watches Dawson over the rim of the mug.

Gaze dropping to his shoes, Dawson finishes up with the laces and slowly rises to his feet.

"That sounds nice, but I'm not sure I'll make it in time." He grabs his jacket and throws it over his shoulders. Since September arrived, the weather's been getting warmer, but the mornings are still a bit chilly for his tastes. Definitely no dipping into the ocean for at least another month.

A lump grows in Dawson's throat when Cal doesn't say anything. There used to be a time when he dreaded what Cal might say, but if the past six years taught him anything, it's that silence is so much worse.

"What do you mean?" Cal asks, voice smooth and cool, like the edge of a knife.

Okay. So, they're talking.

"I mean, it takes over two hours to drive to Toowoomba. I'd have to leave at four at the latest–"

"So do it."

The lump turns into a giant rock, cutting off his voice. He glances at Cal, seeing his expression hasn't changed.

Dawson makes a show of looking at his phone. "It's ten o'clock already. It's Olivia's birthday, Cal. I haven't seen her and the kids in months." He resents how desperate he sounds. "I'd just like to spend more than a few hours together."

A muscle in Cal's cheek jumps. He hates canceling plans, hates steering away from routine.

This one is on Dawson. Stupidly, he'd thought that when Cal agreed to let him visit his sister, he wouldn't make any other plans that day. Dawson shouldn't have assumed. He knows better.

"We always dine out on Saturday," Cal says, a ghost of darkness in his tone.

We eat out most of the time, Dawson almost points out, but his sense of self-preservation keeps his lips sealed. Sliding his hands into his pockets so they don't shake, he summons a sheepish expression. Depending on the situation, that tends to do the trick.

"Maybe we could do Sunday this time?"

Cal watches him for a long moment, then finishes his coffee in one big gulp and turns away with a grimace, as if Dawson's suggestion had been outrageous. Heading to the kitchen, he makes a beeline for the coffee machine and turns it on. It makes a churning sound as it heats.

"Cal?"

Fuck, he hates this. Being the center of Cal's attention makes him uneasy, but being ignored isn't much better. Maybe to other people silence equals agreement, but that's not the case here. He can't just up and leave until they've come to some kind of compromise. He'd never hear the end of it, and who knows how long he'd end up paying for this stunt.

The coffee machine beeps half a minute later, signaling it's ready. One can't expect any less from state-of-the art equipment. *Cal* wouldn't be satisfied with anything less. Patience isn't his virtue.

He slides his empty mug under the two spouts, the smell of coffee reaching Dawson's nose a moment later, drawing a rueful sigh from him. He loves when the smell fills the whole apartment. It's as close as he can get to drinking coffee, since he'd found it triggers his migraines.

Opening the overhead cupboard, Cal pulls out a half-empty bottle of Paul John and pours an inch into the mug. The coffee has barely stopped dripping when he removes the mug and takes a sip. That's how he likes it; steaming hot and black, unless the whiskey is supposed to smooth out the bitterness.

Leaning his hip against the counter, Cal gives Dawson an unnerving look.

"What time do you plan to get back?"

Dawson's shoulders droop with relief. He does a quick calculation. "Uh, eight or nine?" When Cal just looks at him, he says. "Eight should be fine."

When Dawson called Olivia to let her know he'd be there today, she insisted he stay the weekend. That could never happen. Cal would lose his shit, and even if he could somehow be convinced to let Dawson stay for that long, he'd keep bringing it up for months. Like when Dawson and Kieran flew over to Adelaide because Kieran's dad was in hospital after suffering a stroke. It killed Dawson to have to fly back to the Coast the next day and leave his best friend to deal with that shit alone.

It wasn't even two full days, but all hell broke loose when he got home. The upheaval happened mostly because Dawson had taken off without discussing it with Cal first, but he hadn't had time for that. Kieran hopped onto the first available flight and Dawson happened to snatch the last ticket on the same flight.

Despite the shitshow that followed, he never regretted it. He'd do it all over again if he had to. He'd just rather...not. And since neither his sister nor his nieces are on their deathbeds, the few hours will have to do.

He looks at Cal expectantly, hope flickering in his chest when Cal seems to mull it over.

"Fine." Cal walks away without another word.

The relief is overwhelming. The knot in Dawson's stomach unravels, leaving him a little nauseous and unsteady. He has one foot over the threshold when he remembers Olivia's present and dips back in to retrieve the gift bag.

He walk-runs to the lifts, worrying that if he's not fast enough, Cal might catch up with him and say he's changed his mind. It wouldn't be the first time.

He's still looking over his shoulder as he waits for the lift and doesn't relax until he's in his car and putting the key in the ignition. Even as he drives off, he can't shake the feeling that he'll hear about this when he comes back, and likely a few more times after that.

He sighs. It's fine. He gets to see Olivia and the girls. He'll worry about making this up to Cal later.

A normal person would probably feel ecstatic at the prospect of seeing their family after nearly half a year. To be fair, Dawson did see Olivia two months ago when she had to run some errands in the city, but he hasn't seen his nieces for even longer. He forgets how quickly children grow. The last time he saw them they barely came up to his mid-thigh. Now, they easily wrap their deceptively strong arms around his waist as they ambush him the second he steps out of the car.

"Uncle Dee!" Chloe and Leia scream.

It's not like Dawson isn't happy to see them, but he could do without the guilt that pours over him like an avalanche.

Blinking rapidly, he musters a grin and kneels in front of the girls, spreading his arms wide to envelop them both. Normally, he'd grab and lift them up, do an airplane with them. But they've definitely grown, and Dawson had noticed a headache starting to form deep in his eye-sockets shortly after he passed Hatton Vale. It's not too bad, just some annoying pressure and dizziness, but he's not in any shape to play the fun uncle today.

The girls don't mind; they throw themselves at him without hesitation, and god, two four-year-olds shouldn't make him feel like he's being hit by a lorry. He falls back on his backside with an amused *oof*, making the girls laugh. They climb on top of him, giggling as they try to pin him down. Dawson lets them, ignoring the growing pit of guilt in his stomach. The world won't implode if he enjoys himself for a bit.

"Do you need to be rescued?" comes an amused voice. Dawson lifts his head, finding Ray standing a few feet away and watching the ambush with a smirk.

"Yeah, I do." He groans theatrically. "They're *so* strong."

The girls laugh, doubling down on their efforts to immobilize Dawson, but don't resist when Ray comes to fetch them.

"Okay, goblins, leave your uncle alone. He just spent hours driving here."

Two hours isn't awful, but given his headache Dawson will happily take the excuse.

After he ushers the girls inside, Ray turns to Dawson, offering him a hand.

"Sorry about that. Liv has been running around all morning, so they're a little bored. It's good to see you." He pulls Dawson into a lightning quick one-armed, back-slapping hug.

Dawson grins, patting his shoulder in return.

When Olivia met Ray, Dawson had already been living with Cal, so he never really had the chance to get to know his brother-in-law. This has resulted in their interactions being a little awkward and stilted, but he knows Ray is a good guy and Olivia won the lottery with him. His sister and nieces are happy, and that's all that matters.

"Good to see you too. And don't apologize. You know I adore them."

Dawson loves kids, always has. They're so honest and uncomplicated. Not easy by any means, but uncomplicated. He still remembers what it felt like holding Chloe and Leia when they were just cute, ugly bundles, so small he could fit them both in his arms at once. The memory is bittersweet, filling him with longing. He'd be a crappy dad, he knows. There's no way he could ever take responsibility for another human being. He can barely take care of himself.

He shakes the thought away. There's no use brooding over it. Cal doesn't want kids—that, he made perfectly clear from the start. Hell, he won't even be talked into adopting a dog. It's for the best, anyway. Cal isn't exactly the nurturing type, so Dawson would end up worrying about one more thing on top of the bunch of shit he already loses his sleep over.

Ray huffs, though he's smiling. "We'll see what you say when the day is over."

Dawson snorts. "That bad?"

"Worse." Grinning, he claps Dawson on the shoulder and steers him inside the house. "Maybe seeing you will finally make Liv sit down and relax."

"'Relax' and 'Liv'? Those two words should never be used in one sentence."

Ray throws his head back, laughing. "Good point. Anyways, everyone else is here and they've got their drinks and nibbles, so it should be smooth sailing from now on."

Dawson bites his lip. "How many people are we talking?"

"Just a couple of Liv's friends and their kids."

That's not too bad. Dawson will just say hi, introduce himself, and steer clear of unnecessary human interaction.

"Okay, then."

After Olivia has thoroughly greeted him—in other words, hugged him tight enough to make his spine crack—and introductions were made, Dawson withdraws to play with the girls. Whoever says kids are loud has never been witness to a group of women gossiping about god knows what. Having pretend afternoon tea with his nieces sounds much more appealing. He already popped two Panadol, so hopefully they'll kick in soon.

Spoiler alert—they don't. An hour later, Dawson is forced to join the toast and sing happy birthday while convincing himself to stay upright. He reluctantly accepts a slice of red velvet cake which he doesn't touch, pretending he doesn't notice the way Olivia's watching him, a perpetual furrow between her brows.

"You look like shit," Olivia says after she's dragged him to the kitchen under the pretense of needing his help with plating up.

"Thanks. You look great, too." He doesn't take it personally. Hard to look as fresh as a daisy when you feel like you're dying inside.

Olivia isn't impressed. "Seriously, Dee." Oh, no. Not that tone. "Are you okay?"

Dawson shrugs, but it feels all wrong, like even his shoulders can't relax enough to do that. "Just a headache."

That's not what she's really asking, but Dawson wouldn't know what to say. They don't talk anymore, not like they used to. Dawson knows it's his fault, but that doesn't make up for shit, and it sure as hell can't turn back time.

As an older sister, Olivia's always been overprotective of him, even more so after their parents passed away when Dawson was sixteen and she became his guardian. The overprotectiveness didn't go away when Dawson hit not-so-sweet 18, and blew up when Dawson met Cal shortly after turning 20.

Olivia has never liked Cal. She finds it suspicious that a man like him showed interest in someone like Dawson—a kid twelve years younger, who had his head in the clouds and dreamed of becoming an artist. Yeah, he knows—super original.

Her suspicions didn't ease even after Cal gave him a ring. Dawson remembers getting angry when she tried to talk him out of it, remembers not talking to her for several months after that, not until she turned up at the wedding to call a truce.

He'd been so stupid and naive. And now, he's too ashamed to admit the truth.

Olivia knows enough about Cal to hate him with abandon, but what she knows barely scratches the surface. Dawson could never tell her, not in a million years.

Olivia frowns, her lips forming a firm line. "You're not happy, Dawson." Yeah, no kidding. "I can't handle seeing you like this."

"You don't have to look." He regrets the words immediately. Olivia's eyes widen a fraction, the corners of her mouth turning down. Jesus, he's such a dick. "I'm sorry. I'm just tired."

Fucking exhausted, to be precise. He gets Olivia's point. If their situations were reversed, he'd fuss just as much. But they're not. Olivia might not like what she sees, but she's subjected to it only a handful of times a year. Dawson sees it every time he looks in the mirror, this pathetic version of himself that he's become and has no one to blame for but himself.

She's quiet at first, studying him. At last, she closes the gap between them, sliding one arm around Dawson's waist and the other around his neck, pulling him into a hug. It feels strange, different from the bone-crushing welcome hug, but also kind of good. Olivia's never been very touchy-feely, and losing their parents just hardened her, forcing her to grow up quickly.

Sometimes Dawson wonders if this touch-starved part of him is responsible for his poor decisions—like latching onto the first person who showed him affection and attention. The saddest part is that Cal isn't even an affectionate person. Just how desperate must Dawson have been?

He returns the hug hesitantly at first, then more firmly. His eyes sting, so he squeezes them shut.

"You don't need him to sign," Olivia says into his neck. "If you stay apart for a year, they'll divorce you either way."

He suppresses a groan. No matter how many times he tells Liv that divorce is not an option, she always comes back to it, like a dog with a bone.

"I can't just leave, Liv."

She pulls away to look at him, and there's a sense of urgency in her eyes. "Why? Don't tell me you still love him."

Has he ever? It's hard to say. What he felt for Cal in those first months, maybe years, seems like a case of infatuation in hindsight. It would be easier if he had something to compare it to, and he doesn't think that his crush on Timmy Robbins in sixth grade is a great point of reference.

It doesn't matter anyway. Whatever he felt for Cal back then has gradually disintegrated as years went by. But things are more complicated than that. It's not about whether Dawson loves him or not.

"No, I don't think I do."

"Then leave, for Christ's sake!"

If only it was so straightforward. "Where would I go? I have nothing." For nearly six years he's been Caledon Reeves' husband. He's nothing if he's not that.

He was no one before he met Cal, just a boy with a bunch of dreams and no direction. Naively believing there was someone out there looking for him just as he was looking for them. Someone made just for him.

And even though he always knew, deep inside, that Cal wasn't the one, at least he was *someone.* Someone who looked at Dawson and saw him, who said all the right things and was willing to keep him.

Olivia opens her arms, as if to encompass the whole space of the house. "You have *us.* You have Kieran."

Kieran has his own relationship drama to worry about. Not to mention that his current girlfriend hates Dawson's guts and would throw a fit if Kieran suggested Dawson stay with them for a bit.

"So, what? I'd just move in with you?" In the middle of nowhere, pretending everything is nice and dandy?

Olivia rolls her eyes. "It's not like you have any other obligations."

The words hit him like a sledgehammer.

Olivia freezes, her eyes widening a fraction. She lifts a hand, maybe to reach for him, but he takes a step back.

"Dee..."

He shakes his head. Olivia isn't wrong. He has no friends besides Kieran, no life purpose. He doesn't even have a real job. He'd taken the job at the dog shelter knowing it'd be a voluntary position. If he was getting paid, he doesn't think Cal would have been okay with him working there.

"Why would you want a job? I can pay for everything you need," Cal had once told him.

Dawson won't lie—he found it incredibly attractive at the time. After years of struggling to make ends meet, and with Olivia juggling two jobs while studying to be able to pay rent and all the bills their parents had left them, the idea of being provided for had made him agreeable to anything Cal might've wanted.

How had he ever confused this with love?

"I..." He turns away. "I forgot your present in the car. I'll be right back."

"Dee, wait."

He all but runs for the car, throwing himself in and burrowing his face in his hands. Bile burns at the back of his throat and he swallows it down. The pressure behind his eyes builds, reaching new heights and promptly morphing into a throbbing sensation that spreads across his forehead and to his temples. It doesn't take long before he has hundreds of needles stabbing into his skull.

Shit. This isn't a headache. But he hasn't had a migraine in weeks and didn't bring his pills with him. Fucking figures it had to make a comeback today.

Soon, a high-pitched noise fills his ears, similar to the echo that's left behind after a fire alarm has stopped beeping. Except this noise doesn't stop, just keeps on going and growing in volume. The sky is overcast, but he squints against the daylight, wanting nothing more than to hide in a dark, silent room and stay there.

Resigned, he grabs Olivia's present and heads back to the house, his stomach churning and threatening to empty its contents on the welcome mat.

Olivia's on him the second he walks in. Whatever speech she's prepared dies on her tongue with one look at his face. He must look like something chewed him up and spit him out.

She takes his hand, and this time he lets her. "Come with me."

"I don't think I can take the stairs," he says when she leads him to the staircase.

"One of the rooms upstairs is nice and dark. It'll be better for you. And the bathroom is just next door."

Weighing the pros and cons as much as his fogged-up mind allows him, he opts for the stairs. After the miserable trip up, Olivia opens the first door on the left. She wasn't lying. The room has no windows and is blissfully dark.

Inside, he collapses onto the single bed. The blanket is a bit thicker and warmer than he'd like, but he drags one over himself anyway, needing to feel surrounded. Contained.

A gentle hand runs through his hair. It feels so good.

"I'll bring you some water, okay? Do you need a bucket?" She knows the drill. Dawson's migraines were a regular occurrence when he was a teen. They'd happened further apart as he got older, but never went away completely.

"An icepack, if you have it."

"Sure do. Do you have your pills?"

"Left them at home."

She sighs. "Okay. I'll be right back."

He can't tell at which point she actually comes back with the water and an icepack because he starts to drift off seconds after the door clicks shut behind her.

Just before he sinks under completely, he hears it again, the same thing that's been echoing in his mind for a while now. Every time he feels like he's drowning, whenever things get so much that it's hard to breathe, it's there. Just one word, whispered in the silence, so close he swears someone is there with him, speaking right into his ear. Like a secret. Like a promise.

He lets the darkness envelop him, pull him under, chasing away the pain and leaving behind only a blissful void.

Soon.

Chapter 2

Olivia's sitting on the bed when he wakes.

"Hey." Her smile is sad. "How you doing?"

He rolls onto his back with a groan and throws a hand over his eyes. "My head doesn't feel like a ticking timebomb anymore." Now it's just a good, old splitting headache. "What time is it?"

"A little after six."

Fucking great. Visiting his sister once in a blue moon only to sleep through it. Way to go, Dawson.

He pinches the space between his eyes, hoping to alleviate some of the tension. "I slept through your birthday. Liv, I'm sorry—"

She waves a hand, making a dismissive sound. "Nothing to celebrate about getting old. I'll take the presents, though. Speaking of, thank you for the tapestry. I love it." He knew she would. She loves covering the walls until there's not a single inch of space left. "Although I'd have preferred a Dawson original. I miss hanging up your stuff."

Dawson closes his eyes, turning away. Thinking of his art always awakens that hollow ache in his chest. "I haven't painted in a while." It's been years, all of his paint long since dried out. "Haven't felt inspired."

"That's a shame. You're so good at it."

His eyes burn. He can't even pretend it's from the headache. "I..." As the fog clears from his mind, something else clicks. Dawson shoots up, horror dawning on him. "Shit. Oh, fuck."

"What's wrong?"

"I'm late." Kicking the blanket off, he throws his legs over the edge of the bed.

Olivia stops him with a hand to his chest, lifting an eyebrow. If he wasn't used to her teacher-face, it'd intimidate him. Who's he kidding—it still scares the crap out of him.

"What do you think you're doing?"

"I have to—" He points a trembling hand at the door.

"No fucking way." She stands up, her hands on her hips. "You look like you're gonna keel over if you try to stand up. If you think I'm letting you drive, think again."

"You don't get it," Dawson pleads with her. "We had a deal. I need to be back by eight."

"What deal?" she asks derisively, anger flashing in her eyes. "Are you fucking kidding?"

He cringes at the volume. "Liv..."

"You're not a fucking slave. He can't order you around." Her eyes stormy, she looks around the room. "Where's your phone?"

"Why?" A quick pat around his jeans reveals the phone's still in his pocket.

Olivia zeros in on Dawson's hands like a hawk. "I'm gonna have a talk with that fucker." One second she's standing there, fuming, and the next she's battled off Dawson's hands and extracted the phone from his own jeans.

"Olivia, no!" In his attempt to make a grab for the phone, he shoots to his feet, then instantly collapses back on the bed when the room spins. "For god's sake, don't," he manages through a bout of nausea, swallowing several times in a row.

Olivia swears, glaring at the offending device in her hand. "It's dead."

Dawson could cry from relief. He never thought he'd be grateful to have forgotten to plug his phone in overnight. He stretches out his hand. "Give me the phone."

She watches him suspiciously, pointing the phone at him. "You're not leaving today. Are we clear? You're in no state to drive."

Swallowing down a protest, Dawson says, "I could order an Uber." Except he can't leave his car behind.

"All the way to GC? Don't be ridiculous."

At the moment, he couldn't care less how ridiculous it is as long as it gets him home today. Anything is better than the alternative.

"Please." When all he gets in return is an unwavering stare, he finally admits defeat. "Can I borrow a charger?" His throat clogs up with what he's about to say next. "I need to let Cal know I won't be back until tomorrow."

She watches him mutely, then sighs and walks out. When she's back, she hands Dawson the charger and jingles what he recognizes are his car keys at him. He must've left them in the car.

"I'm keeping these." The tone of her voice brooks no argument. "You'll get them in the morning if you don't look like death warmed over."

"Okay."

After she leaves him be, Dawson relaxes for all of five seconds before it occurs to him what he needs to do next. Panic claws at his insides as he connects his phone to the charger and plugs it in, barely breathing while he waits for it to wake up. It doesn't take long. The phone is almost brand new—a birthday present from Cal, even though Dawson preferred his old one.

The screen lights up, the reception being restored bar by bar.

Dawson goes to the texts and opens a new chat window. Cal only ever calls. He's not going to be happy with a text—definitely not with its content—but Dawson isn't brave enough to talk to him.

Typing out the message, he thanks the gods of autocorrect when he screws up every other letter.

Dawson: *Got a migraine from hell. Can't drive. Be back first thing in the morning. I'm sorry.*

The *sending* status turns to *delivered*. Seconds later, it changes to *read*.

Dawson waits.

A quick glance at the time tells him he's been staring at the screen waiting for ellipses to appear for eight minutes. Five more minutes pass, each of them feeling like an eternity.

Twenty minutes after he sent the text, Dawson breaks. He leaves the phone next to his pillow and pulls the blanket up to his chin. Whatever happens, it's not going to be good.

Olivia and Ray's bedroom is on the same floor, and Dawson has been listening for the sound of a door opening since four. When it finally does just before seven, and footsteps echo in the hall, he waits a couple of minutes before running downstairs, hoping it's Olivia who's up, and not Ray.

The odds must be in his favor for once. He finds Olivia standing in the kitchen in her SpongeBob pajamas, scooping ground coffee into a Moka pot.

She turns when she senses him there, but doesn't seem surprised. "Shower first. Then you'll eat."

One look from her makes him swallow down the protest. What does it matter? He's fucked anyway.

He means to make quick work of showering—the last thing he should do is take even more time than he already has. His good intentions last only until he steps under the hot spray. The water pressure is amazing and feels like a balm on his muscles, stiff after hours of fitful sleep.

When he feels his fingers pruning, he regretfully steps out of the shower. Olivia must've planned to bully him into the shower, because there's a fresh towel hanging on the rack among a few that are clearly in use.

He dries off, scrunching his nose as he reaches for yesterday's clothes. He'd sweated through them last night, but he isn't going to ask to borrow something from Ray. He can survive a couple of hours in sweaty clothes.

After he's finished dressing, he collects his phone and heads downstairs. Olivia's already sipping her coffee, an eyebrow raised in expectation.

At the thought of food, Dawson's stomach rebels. "Not sure I can hold anything down at the moment."

"You haven't eaten since you got here," Olivia points out and opens the cupboard. "Toast or Weetabix?"

Like talking to a brick wall. "Toast." Not as hearty as Weetabix and he won't have to wait for it to soften enough to eat.

With a curt nod, Olivia snatches a couple of slices from the pack and shoves them in the toaster. Knowing Dawson's preferences, she plops a chunk of salted butter and a jar of marmalade on the table.

Pointedly ignoring Olivia's searing gaze burning holes in the side of his face, he polishes off the toast before brushing the crumbs off his hands and taking his plate to the dishwasher.

He looks at Olivia expectantly.

With yet another sigh, she heads upstairs and comes back with his car keys. Before he can pluck them from her hand, she fixes him with a look.

"Drive safe. Text me when you get back."

"I will." He's both annoyed and touched by the mother-henning. "I'm sorry it was such a bust."

Giving him a sad smile, Olivia hands over the keys. "I'm just happy I got to see you. And that you got to see the girls."

Dawson's first instinct is to get defensive—is she trying to guilt-trip him?—but her expression is open and genuine. He feels like a dick for being so touchy.

"They grow fast," he concedes, sparing a mournful glance upstairs. He won't have time to wait for the girls to wake up and say goodbye.

Olivia huffs, grinning. "Tell me about it. My bank account is crying. You try shopping for new clothes every few months." Her smile fades. "Don't be a stranger, okay?"

"I won't," Dawson says, praying it's not a lie. He's thankful when Olivia walks him to the door but doesn't hug him. He's not sure he'd be able to hold it together.

"Think about what I said, okay? Just think," she stresses, when she senses Dawson wants to argue. "You don't *need* him, Dee. You're stronger than you realize."

He has no idea what to say to that, because nothing could be further from the truth.

He gets into the car without looking back, knowing Olivia's watching him. The remnants of the headache keep buzzing at his temples, making the drive back to the Coast more miserable than it was already going to be.

The two hours go both excruciatingly slow and all too fast. Despite having spent the night and the entire ride giving himself a pep-talk, Dawson's hands shake as he unlocks the door to the apartment.

"I'm home!" His voice cracks only a little. "Cal?" he tries when there's no response.

Cal must be home—his car was in the garage, and he rarely walks anywhere. On the other hand, it's not even ten. If Cal drank last night—highly probable—he might still be asleep.

Leaving his shoes at the door, Dawson heads to the kitchen. He forgot to drink anything and he's parched. Pulling a glass from the cupboard, he fills it with tap water and nearly chokes on his first sip when he spots Cal from the corner of his eye.

He clears his throat. "Oh. Hey."

Half-sitting, half-leaning on the arm of the sofa, Cal is watching him with cold, calculating eyes, a tumbler of something in his hand. Dawson doesn't have to guess what's in it.

"How nice of you to show up," Cal says, an edge to the words that has Dawson backing away and hitting the counter. The island between them creates some kind of barrier, at least.

"Sorry." He sets the glass on the countertop to avoid spilling it. "I sent you a text—"

"I got your fucking text," Cal hisses and pushes away from the sofa. "What of it?"

"I couldn't drive with a migraine."

"Sure you couldn't." Cal throws back whatever remains in the tumbler. "How convenient for you to get a 'headache' when you went to visit your sister and her brats."

Dawson bristles. "Don't call them that."

For the first few seconds, the silence is so thick Dawson nearly chokes with it. Everything after that happens in a blur.

Cal stalks forward, slamming the tumbler onto the island as he trudges around it, his gait uncoordinated. The tumbler doesn't shatter, though it must be a close thing. The sound snaps Dawson into action, forcing his legs to move, to get away. It's an instinct, a useless one, bound to only make Cal angrier.

He barely makes it two steps before Cal grabs him by the collar of his shirt, yanking him back.

"Say that again," Cal growls. He presses Dawson against the counter, the edge digging into his lower back.

Dawson grinds his teeth. On a deeper level, he's made peace with the fact that he won't be walking away from this unscathed. Since he's already doomed, he might as well grow a backbone for once.

He catches Cal's gaze. "I don't want you to call them brats. You've never even met them." In retrospect, Dawson's grateful. He doesn't want someone like Cal around his nieces.

Cal's smile is slow and cruel. "I'll call them whatever I want. Brats," he enunciates. "What else could they be, born into your pathetic little family. Fucking spineless, spoiled brats. Just like you." His fingers wrap around Dawson's throat and squeeze. "Look at me when I talk to you."

Dawson opens his eyes. He wasn't aware he'd closed them.

Cal's fingers tighten, cutting off Dawson's airway. His stomach lurches, his head throbbing with renewed vigor.

"I... I don't feel so good," he chokes out. "Can I just—"

"Drop the fucking act, will you? No one's falling for that bullshit."

His heart threatens to beat out of his chest. "Cal, seriously. I can't do this now."

"Oh, you can't?" he says snidely. "In that case, let me make it swift and clear."

Cal lets him go, and Dawson can breathe again. His vision swims from the lack of oxygen, and before he can wonder what Cal meant, he's being spun around and crowded against the island. With one hand on his back, Cal presses him flat onto the island and pins him between it and his body.

The reality doesn't fully sink in until Cal starts undoing Dawson's jeans one-handed.

Dawson freezes at first, then starts thrashing against the hold. Cal is bigger and stronger than him, but he's inebriated. Maybe Dawson could—

Rough fingers grip his hair and slam his head against the counter. The impact makes him black out for a few seconds, and when he comes to, he's dizzy and his jeans are around his thighs.

"Wait. Cal." He can hear the panic in his voice.

Clearly, so can Cal, because he chuckles darkly. "You paying attention now?"

The sound of a zipper opening sends a fresh wave of panic through Dawson.

"Cal, please, don't do this."

This can't be happening. Cal's gone off the rails countless times, especially after he's had a drink, but it's never come to this. He has never stooped so low.

"Can we... Can we go to the bedroom?" He might not want this, but at least he could pretend. Just a spouse trying to please his husband even though he's not in the mood himself. It's not like he hasn't done it before. People do that all the time. "Please, Cal, not like this."

The fingers in his hair tighten, jerking his head up.

"You don't make the rules here, sweetheart," Cal growls into his ear. Dawson can smell alcohol on his breath. "You follow them. And if you don't?" He pushes Dawson's face into the counter, making him cry out as his cheekbone collides with the hard surface.

In a haze, he hears Cal spit into his hand, and, for some reason, that's the thing that makes all the fight leave him. The thing that drives it home.

This is really happening.

There's pressure against his entrance, blunt and dry.

"If you don't, I'll make sure to remind you of your place."

Dawson closes his eyes, a few tears spilling free. White-hot pain flares through his pelvis when Cal forces his way in, so intense he can't breathe. Cal pulls out before thrusting back in, crueler and harder than before. He lets go of Dawson's hair to grip the back of his neck, keeping him immobilized. Dawson's bruised cheek is still pressed against the counter, but he barely feels it. Every nerve in his body is focused on the point where Cal is forcing his way inside him, reducing him to ugly sobbing and hopeless pleas.

He didn't know it could hurt this bad. He's always struggled to relax during sex, needing thorough, patient prep before he felt confident enough to allow anything inside his body. Cal isn't a patient man, and over the years, Dawson has learned to make do with as little as possible.

This is something utterly different.

His perception of time becomes distorted, making it impossible to tell how long this hell lasts.

When Cal thrusts in a few more times before he finally stills, Dawson's body doesn't feel like his own anymore. He can feel Cal's release spilling inside him, and the sensation has bile rising in his throat. He's never minded before, but knowing he'll be carrying proof of what just happened inside him makes him want to shed his skin. He's never felt so disgusting, so humiliated in his life.

Cal's front covers his back. "I own you, Dawson. You better remember that, unless you want another reminder."

With that, he pulls out and steps away, leaving Dawson there like a filthy thing he used.

Even with nothing restraining him anymore, Dawson continues to lie there, sobbing quietly as come runs down his bare thighs.

An unidentifiable time later, he finds the strength to pull himself up, tug up his jeans, and stumble to the bathroom. He's aching to step under a scorching hot shower and wash everything away, but his stomach has other ideas. He collapses onto the floor and has the presence of mind to grip the edge of the toilet before his body purges out the little he managed to eat this morning.

Flushing the toilet, he makes it to the sink on unsteady legs to rinse his mouth. He doesn't dare to look in the mirror. He slides back to the floor, leaning against the cabinets under the sink. A morbid part of him wants to laugh at how familiar this feels. He remembers sitting here just like this only a few weeks ago, after Cal drank himself stupid and beat the shit out of him because Dawson confided in him that he'd like to try and get a job.

He hadn't gone to the hospital the next day. He never does. Even drunk, Cal is always mindful not to do 'too much damage'. Using Dawson as a punching bag isn't something he gets off on; control is. It's something that became apparent to Dawson over the years, something that he, disturbingly enough, always found comfort in. Comfort in knowing that Cal would never go too far, would never cross the line.

Until now.

His pocket vibrates. He contemplates not checking the message, but then remembers that he promised Olivia to text her when he got back. If he doesn't reply, she'll call him.

Pulling the phone out, he checks the thumbnail. *Get back OK?*

He laughs. The sound feels wrong and ugly on his tongue. He stares at the message until the letters begin to blur.

"Soon."

His head snaps up. He looks around the large, sterile-looking bathroom. What the...

He strains his ears, checking if Cal is at the door, but hears nothing. He must be losing his mind.

Returning his attention to the message, he stares at it some more. As if in a trance, he watches his fingers type out one word and press send.

Dawson: *Fine.*

He drops the phone to the floor, staring blankly ahead. His throat burns with the remnants of stomach acid, and Cal's come is drying on his skin. He should get up, take a shower, check if he's bleeding.

For some reason, it's that thought that has him reaching for the phone again.

Dawson: *About what you said...*

Chapter 3

DAWSON CHECKS THE CLOCK for the millionth time, getting progressively more nervous.

"What time did you say the asshole should be back again?"

Dawson huffs, half in annoyance, half in amusement. Leave it to his best friend to make him smile while he's sick with nerves.

"About half an hour ago." He licks his lips, guilt simmering under his skin. "You don't have to stay." As if asking Kieran to stay by his side like a guard dog when he presents Cal with divorce papers isn't humiliating enough, he's wasting his time, too.

"Oh, shut up, will you?" Kieran sounds almost offended. "As if I'd leave you alone."

Dawson thumbs the corner of the documents in his hands. "It could get ugly."

No *could* about it. It *is* going to get ugly. To what extent, Dawson can only guess. Just to cover all bases, he's packed some essentials and had Kieran load it into his car. He doesn't think that packing up his shit and leaving it in clear view as people always do in the movies would be wise. There's no need to taunt Cal on top of everything.

"Another reason for me to be here. I've taken Krav Maga classes." Rolling up his sleeves, Kieran clenches his fists and flexes. Or attempts to. The biceps of his left arm makes a feeble attempt to buff up but ends up twitching instead.

A starlet laugh bursts out of Dawson, and it keeps going when he gets a glimpse of Kieran's scowl.

"Well, fuck you too."

Wiping a tear from the corner of his eye, Dawson grins.

"I love you."

Kieran's eyes narrow further. "Don't think you can slap that band-aid on everything. I'm hurt."

"You're full of shit, is what you are."

Like magic, the metal vise that's been closing in around Dawson with each passing second releases its hold. For a moment, he forgets why they're both here, forgets about that morning nearly two weeks ago that's driven him here in the first place. It's not the *only* thing that's brought him here, but definitely the one that drove the point home.

"Are you sure Jess won't bite your head off for letting me stay with you?"

Kieran's expression darkens. "If she does, she can pack her shit and get the fuck out."

Dawson's eyes widen, and Kieran laughs. "Bros before hoes, Dee. Those are the rules."

Dawson doubts it's that simple, or that Kieran is as unbothered as he pretends, but the sentiment pulls at his heartstrings. Dawson has received way too many drunken calls from him that resulted in an hour long rant to be convinced otherwise.

"I don't want you two to fight because of me."

"Please," Kieran huffs. "As if she wouldn't find something to fight over."

Dawson's tempted to ask why Kieran stays in a relationship that clearly makes him miserable, but he's not about to call the kettle black.

Dawson's phone vibrates on the table, followed by the ringtone.

"Is it him?" Kieran asks, as Dawson reaches for it.

"No, it's..." Unfamiliar digits stare at him. "I don't recognize the number." The code is from NSW. Probably an insurance scam, as usual. He gets one every other day. Under normal circumstances, he'd let it go to voicemail, but a foreboding feeling prompts him to pick up.

"Hello?"

"Dawson?"

He recognizes the voice, but can't place it. "Yes?"

"It's Ellis."

"Oh. Hi?"

Kieran taps his shoulder, showing his palms in a *who is it?* gesture.

Dawson covers the speaker. "My brother-in-law."

Kieran frowns, but Dawson isn't much wiser, so he just shrugs. He could count the number of times he and Ellis talked to each other on one hand. And why does Ellis have his number?

"I just got a call from Cal's PA," Ellis says, pausing for a second before he continues. "Are you already at the hospital?"

Dawson blinks. "The hospital?"

"Yes, the hospital," Ellis says irritatedly. "Did they give you any information on Cal?"

What information on Cal? And who are *they?*

"Ellis, I don't know what you're talking about. And how did you get my number?"

Ellis goes completely silent for a long moment. "The hospital didn't call you?"

"Uh, no? Why—" Wait. Hospital. Information on Cal. "Cal's at the hospital?"

He feels Kieran stiffen next to him.

"He was in a car crash. He's in surgery as we speak—GC University Hospital. How did they not tell you?" He sounds angry, but it doesn't seem to be directed at Dawson. He continues before Dawson can reply. "I'm already at the airport, but won't be there sooner than two hours." A pause. "Dawson?"

The sound of his name drags him from his spaced-out state.

"Y-yeah. I'm here." He stands up, Kieran doing the same. "I'll be at the hospital in half an hour."

There's a shaky exhale on the other side of the line. "Thanks. Keep me updated. I won't have reception on board, but I'll get back to you once I land."

"Okay. Uh, see you there."

The call disconnects. Dawson stares at the dark screen in a daze.

"Cal's in hospital?"

"Yeah," Dawson says, still not quite able to believe it.

"Okay." Kieran gently pries the phone from his fingers and takes his hand. "Come on. I'll drive you."

Dawson lets himself be dragged to the door.

"You might want to leave these here." Kieran nods towards Dawson's other hand, where he's clutching the papers.

The divorce papers. He was about to drop the D-bomb on Cal, stressing over it ever since he'd decided it was the right thing to do. Jesus, he'd even asked Kieran to hold his hand while he did it.

And now Cal's in the hospital. Because he was in a car crash. He's in surgery.

What if the surgery doesn't go well?

What if it does?

What will happen now?

He leaves the papers in the kitchen and follows Kieran to his car.

They walk into the ER exactly 34 minutes later and head to the front desk. A kind-looking young woman behind the desk smiles when she notices them; her name tag says Claire.

Claire's eyes do a quick scan of them both, probably assessing if they're in need of medical assistance. "Can I help you?"

"Hi. I'm Dawson Reeves. I got a call that Caledon Reeves was brought here for surgery?"

Her smile slips off. "Ah, yes. And you're..."

"His husband."

She turns her attention to her computer and types something. She nods solemnly and looks at Dawson. "Ambulance brought him in at six-oh-five, unconscious and with shallow breathing. He was triaged and diagnosed with hemopneumothorax." With a sad smile full of sympathy, she adds, "The surgery is still underway, but we'll let you know as soon as the doctors finish."

At a loss as to what he should do, Dawson just gives a single nod. "Okay. Thank you. Um, any estimate on how long it'll be?"

Her features twist in a grimace. "It all depends on the extent of his injuries."

Great. Very specific.

"Thank you."

"Come on." Kieran steers him towards the cheap-looking plastic chairs lining the wall. "Let's sit down. It could be a while."

Dawson collapses into the nearest chair, feeling his insides twist and squeeze like they're trying to tear themselves out of his body.

"Dawson?"

"I was about to ask for a divorce," he says, stupefied.

"What?"

"He's in surgery. And I was about to ask for a divorce."

"What does that have to do with anything?"

"I don't know," Dawson chokes out, hiding his face in his hands. "I don't know. Just... I feel like the worst kind of scum."

"Oh, no. Fuck that." Kieran pries Dawson's hands off, forcing him to look at him. "Don't you dare go there. This has nothing to do with you. He was in an accident. Shit happens. It could happen any time, to anyone. You want a divorce because you're miserable, and not wanting to be miserable doesn't make you scum."

Dawson's eyes well up. "But—"

"No," Kieran grits out, his expression contorted into a stern mask. "I won't let you do this to yourself. It's enough that I feel like a useless shit when I see how he treats you and can't do anything about it. But I *can* do this, and I won't let you blame yourself."

Taking a shuddering breath, Dawson nods, letting Kieran pull him into a hug.

"It's gonna be okay, Dee."

It doesn't feel like it.

Closing his eyes, Dawson leans into Kieran, wrapping his arms loosely around his waist. It helps a little.

"Oh. I told Ellis I'd keep him updated." He pulls away regretfully, reaching for his phone. He shoots off a quick message to let Ellis know Cal's still in surgery. Ellis responds in twenty seconds.

"What did he say?" Kieran asks.

"Thanks and that they're about to take off."

"You never mention him."

"Ellis?" Dawson shrugs. "I don't really know him. The first time I met him was at my wedding."

And it was awkward as hell. Ellis basically spent the duration of the ceremony with a resting bitch face, then dished out some off-hand comments during reception. When Dawson asked Cal what he should do, he was told to ignore Ellis. It wasn't hard. Ellis made it clear he had no desire to engage in chitchat.

They've met a few more times over the years when Cal would drag him to functions and some pretentious get-togethers, but they never really talked. In fact, Cal and Ellis barely talked either, reserving their exchanges to work-related topics.

"I don't think he likes me."

Kieran snorts at that. "Is he a corporate asshole like Cal?"

It draws a small chuckle out of Dawson. "He runs the Sydney office."

Kieran's brows furrow with a thought. "If he lives in Sydney, why did Cal put him as his emergency contact?"

"He didn't," Dawson says, not quite able to keep bitterness from his tone. "The hospital called Amanda, his PA. And she called Ellis."

Because of course, Cal would want the company to be the first to know if he, God forbid, couldn't make it to work the next day.

Kieran looks flabbergasted. "He put his PA as his emergency contact?" His confusion kind of pleases Dawson. It's nice to know he's not being unreasonable for finding it debasing that his husband wouldn't even want him to know if something happened to him.

"The company is all he cares about, so..."

"What a dick," Kieran says, and the no-nonsense tone makes Dawson laugh. "It's true!"

"I know. But it was funny."

Kieran huffs. "So, back to my question. Is this Ellis a lot like Cal?"

"Not really. I mean, they kind of hate each other." Hard to say since he and Dawson have barely interacted.

Kieran looks dubious. "I don't know. I wouldn't jump on the first plane for someone I hate."

Yeah, it had taken Dawson by surprise too. "Family is family, I guess. Cal runs the company because he's older and he was the golden child, but the two of them have been at each other's throats ever since their dad passed away and Cal took over."

"Ah, sibling rivalry. How original."

"Mr Reeves?"

They both stand up. "Yes?" Dawson says to the woman who must be a doctor if the scrubs are anything to go by.

"I'm Doctor Connelly." She smiles, offering the hand not holding a clipboard for a shake. "You'll be happy to hear your husband is out of surgery. All went well, considering. We just transferred him to the ICU."

Dawson exhales. Something shifts inside him, but it doesn't feel like relief. "Thank you."

"We're keeping him sedated for now to keep him comfortable. He had low blood oxygen due to a collapsed lung when he was brought in, and there's bleeding in his chest. He'll need a chest tube for a few days to drain any leakage and inflate his lung. We'll run a few tests, check everything's in order. "

"Jesus," Kieran breathes out. Dawson doesn't speak.

"If you want to see him before we start on those tests, I can give you five minutes, but no more," the doc says, even though Dawson didn't ask to see Cal.

That's because any normal person would want to see their spouse if they were hurt.

His stomach threatens to turn itself inside out, but he manages a nod.

Kieran must pick up on his lack of enthusiasm. "I'll go with you." To the doc, he says, "Is that okay?"

"Are you family?"

"A friend."

She hesitates, but when she looks at Dawson, something in her expression shifts. He must look like a mess. "Five minutes." She turns around, cocking her head.

They follow her to the ICU and she stops before she lets them in, speaking mostly to Dawson. "Just a fair warning; the machines and everything will look scary, but it's a standard procedure. We had to intubate him because of the sedation. He has some cuts and bruises, but nothing serious."

Dawson nods. It seems to be the only thing he's able to do.

"When is he going to wake up?" Kieran asks.

"Depending on the test results, we'll take him off the sedation in a day or two. It's mostly just to keep him from causing more damage to himself. The chest tube can be very painful."

"Right."

The doc gives them a strained smile and opens the door.

Chapter 3.5

"YOU'RE REALLY GOING TO do it, aren't you?"

He glances at Sienna briefly, before returning his attention to the body lying in the hospital bed. The sight of Caledon disgusts him to his core.

He knows that the human body is nothing but a vessel. It could carry anything, anyone. It's no reflection of what resides inside it. Yet, the mere idea of having any of Caledon's parts close to him is repulsive.

"I am."

His feelings about Caledon don't matter. His inhibitions don't matter. There's only one thing that does and it lies on the other side of here. And he'll do anything to get there, even if it means becoming what he hates.

"Do you know what you're getting yourself into?"

In spite of her words, Sienna doesn't sound worried. Of course she doesn't. She never worries, none of the harvesters do. Probably. Sienna is the only other of his kind he's ever interacted with. The rest? They just pass by, aware of each other but feeling no inclination to seek any sort of connection.

Not Sienna. In another life, he might've called her a friend. She definitely seems to enjoy sticking her nose in his business. That's his doing, though. He was the one to confide in her about his agenda.

"Not a clue," he admits.

She laughs softly, and it gives him the courage to ask what's been on his mind since the idea started to form.

"Do you think it will work? What if..." He turns his gaze back to Caledon, revulsion battling with yearning. *What if his body isn't able to hold him in?* "What if I can't pass through? What if they don't let me?" Whoever *they* are.

There's only ever been one thing on his mind; do your job and follow a single rule. It's inherent knowledge deep inside him, in all of them. Like newborn babies who take their first breath without knowing *how.*

"Why wouldn't they?"

"Because it's..." *Forbidden.* But it's not, is it? There's no mention of it at all. "Unheard of."

Sienna rolls her eyes. "Everything is unheard of here. We aren't exactly an adventurous bunch."

His lips twitch with an attempted smile. "It almost sounds like you're prompting me to do it."

"I'll miss you," she says. "But if it's something you have to do, you should."

"I don't *have to* do it." *Liar.* "I *shouldn't* do it."

"Says who? Have you ever spoken to anyone besides me?"

She knows he hasn't. "*You* have. Tell me, how many harvesters have you met who ever thought about doing anything else but their job?"

Something in her eyes softens, and her hand reaches up to cup his face. "You're not like the others."

If that's supposed to comfort him, it has the opposite effect. "You're not helping."

She laughs again, exasperated and a little affectionate, so unsuitable for someone of her designation. "You big baby." She grins when he scowls. "What's the worst that can happen?"

He opens his mouth to respond, but nothing comes out.

It's not like he can die. He could be punished, though he has no idea what kind of punishment it would be. How do you punish someone who doesn't feel pain?

The machines keeping Caledon alive beep over each other, the sound high-pitched and constant. He's watched humanity for long enough to know what that sound does to them, how much they hate it. Hate what it represents.

But not him. He revels in it, feeling a rush of excitement every time Caledon's tainted heart beats a little out of sync.

"I could cease to exist." It's the only thing he can come up with.

A thoughtful expression on her face, Sienna gives him a small smile. It feels sad. "Would that be so terrible?" is what she says, but what he hears is, "How much do you actually like this life?"

"I don't know."

The door creaks, opening wide. The air seems to be sucked out of the room when Dawson walks in, wide-eyed and scared and ethereally beautiful. His soul feels small but shines bright, like a beacon in a dark night.

A man close to his age follows behind him, shutting the door once they're inside.

Dawson approaches the bed with slow, careful steps, his eyes never steering away from Caledon. He looks like a feral animal expecting to be attacked at any moment, always alert, always scared. The other man stays by his side, his expression gloomy when he looks at Caledon.

Stopping by the bed, Dawson breathes heavily as he takes in Caledon's state, the multiple tubes inserted into his body and the scratches and bruises on his face.

Dawson doesn't move, doesn't speak. He stands over Caledon, watching him, his hands balled into fists.

"I don't know what to say," he says, voice barely above a whisper.

The man places a hand on Dawson's back, rubbing it. "You don't have to say anything. But if you want to call him names, I'll join in. Can I take a video?"

Dawson lets out a shaky laugh, pressing himself closer to his friend. "Thanks for being here."

"Of course." He slings an arm around Dawson, joining him in the silence. It feels like it drags on forever.

They both start when the door opens, the doctor who was there before with the nurses appearing in the doorway.

"Sorry, gentlemen. Time's up."

Dawson gives a clipped nod and with one last look at Caledon, he follows the doctor outside, his friend by his side.

It's quiet again, the sound of the machines filling the room.

He feels Sienna's searing gaze on him. There's a silent question in her eyes when he looks at her. This time, he knows the answer like he knows the sun will always come up in the morning.

The consequences don't signify.

He will go through with his plan, and he might get what he wants or he might crash and burn, vanish out of existence.

Whatever happens, it will happen after Caledon has disappeared from Dawson's life. Whatever happens doesn't matter, because Dawson will finally be free. He'd love to be there, to stand guard to Dawson's heart and soul for the rest of his days. But if he can't, that's okay too. It's okay as long as Dawson is safe. As long as he's happy.

"How much longer?" he asks. It's a redundant question; he'll know when it's time, as always. Impatience has never been an issue, not until now. His fingers twitch with the desire to reach out and rip Caledon's soul out.

Sienna's eyes darken. She smiles, slow and sinister.

"Soon."

Chapter 4

HE'S FALLING. AT LEAST he thinks he is. There's nothing but darkness around him, weightless and cold. There's no sound but for his racing heart as it hammers against his chest.

He's falling. He must be. Sinking deeper into the darkness that seems to grow thicker, suffocating him. When he tries to scream, the words halt in his throat, making him choke.

He wonders how long he'll be falling for and if there's an end to it at all. Maybe he'll spend eternity like this, suspended in the void with no way out.

Even as that thought forms, something changes. The darkness seems to shrink. There's no light, but it's not as heavy anymore, not as oppressing. And the voice...

He can't decipher it, but it's there. Calling out to him.

The sensation of falling stops. Now it feels like he's floating, suspended in the air by an invisible force. Only it's not. Something's holding him. Someone. There are arms around him, strong but gentle. Their touch is just as cold as the surrounding darkness, but it sends warmth through his body all the same. His heart slows down, his lungs expand with a breath. God, it feels like he hasn't taken a breath in years.

"Soon," the person holding him says. It sounds strange, distorted, like listening to one of those really old stereos filled with static.

"What?" he asks. He has no idea what's going on and doesn't care. If only he could stay like this, held and protected.

"It will be over soon. I promise." The arms around him tighten, making him sink deeper into the embrace with a sigh. "I will always keep you safe."

The words bring a smile to his face even if he doesn't understand them.

"Dawson."

His heart skips a beat. "Yes?"

"Dawson. Dawson."

A foreign touch jerks him awake. He blinks against the brightness, shielding his eyes. Peeking through his fingers, his gaze falls on a familiar figure.

"Ellis?"

Someone groans next to him. Dawson turns, seeing Kieran blinking his eyes open, red creases on his cheeks. Right. The hospital.

"Hey," Ellis says, his signature frown firmly in place. "Sorry to wake you." He doesn't sound sorry.

Dawson runs a hand over his mouth to check he didn't accidentally drool in his sleep. "It's fine. We were waiting for you anyway. This is Kieran," he says when Ellis fixes a calculating gaze on Kieran. "My friend."

Kieran gives him a nod that only seems semi-conscious. "Hey."

"Hey," Ellis says with disinterest and looks at Dawson. "Did they let you see him?"

The image of Cal in the hospital bed, at least three different tubes protruding from his body, flashes in front of him. "Yeah, for a bit. He's in the ICU and they're running a bunch of tests."

Ellis nods, like it all makes sense. "What did they say?"

"Something about a collapsed lung, bleeding, and low oxygen." The doctor must've given him the watered-down version. "They want to keep him under for a couple days."

Ellis frowns at that. "But he's okay?"

"They said the surgery went well."

"Okay. Fuck. Okay." Ellis runs a hand through his hair. He must have been doing it a lot today because it's in disarray, gelled strands sticking out on the sides in all directions. Dawson feels a pang of sympathy for him. At least he didn't have to jump on a plane and fly all the way here straight from work.

"I'm sorry," he says, because it's the only thing that comes to mind.

Ellis eyes him critically. "For what?"

Dawson shrugs. "All of it."

"Don't be stupid. Cal is an idiot."

Dawson's eyebrows shoot up. Ellis was pretty much having a mental breakdown just seconds ago. Now he's back to insults. Is this a sibling thing? Dawson and Olivia aren't like this.

"Why?"

Ellis' shoulders sink. Sighing, he grabs the chair next to Dawson and turns it so he can sit in front of him, ignoring Kieran completely.

"I don't think it was a coincidence it happened today. Shit went down at work, he lost us a lot of money and—" He huffs, shaking his head. "It doesn't matter. Bottom line is Cal must've freaked out. He probably wasn't in his right mind when he was driving."

"Oh." Dawson can definitely see that being the case. Cal's always had a short fuse, but nothing makes him more prone to losing his temper than stress from work. Dawson's been tip-toeing around him for months. It just keeps getting worse.

Ellis goes on. "I'd have to come here either way to iron shit out, but I didn't expect to spend time at the hospital."

That's right. Depending how long Cal will be out of commission, Ellis will have to take over for the time being. Poor guy.

"Mr Reeves?"

Dawson jumps up. Ellis rises to his feet with way more grace, even tired as he looks.

"Yes?" they say as one.

Doctor Connelly raises an eyebrow at Ellis.

"I'm Cal's brother," he says, unprompted.

"Ah. Alright." She pinches the corner of the papers in her hands, her lips forming a thin line. That can't be good. "The blood results just came through. They revealed Cal had alcohol in his blood." A pause. "In quite a high concentration."

"Fuck," Ellis says under his breath. While he might've expected it, it must hit different when faced with a confirmation of his fears—especially if he doesn't know that finding Cal with a bottle is not a rare occurrence.

"Okay," Dawson says carefully. He can't quite feign surprise at the revelation, he's not that good an actor, but the fact that Cal sat behind the wheel while drunk off his ass is surprising. He's usually more careful than that, being a control freak and all. "Will that complicate his healing?"

"Nothing you have to worry about," the doc says. "But we have to notify the police."

"The police? But no one else was hurt, were they?" Oh God, please, don't let there be casualties.

"Not to my knowledge. But the police are involved every time there's an accident. It's a standard procedure. And we're obligated to release the test results since they're likely the reason why the accident happened."

Ellis steps forward, determination oozing from him. "I'll take care of it. I'll give you my contact details if you could forward me the information."

"That can be arranged."

"Can I see him?"

She shakes her head. "I'm sorry. We're still running tests. You can see him tomorrow. And if all goes well, we might take him off the sedation then."

Sensing an argument incoming, Dawson puts a hand on Ellis' arm to get his attention. "Ellis, you're tired. Cal's unconscious. There's nothing either of us can do. We can come back tomorrow." He really doesn't want to come back here. God, what if Cal is awake when he comes back?

Ellis seems to mull it over. Maybe chewing it over is a better expression, given how hard his jaw works. "What if something happens?"

"We're continuously monitoring him. If something were to happen, we would respond immediately. There's no better place he can be."

"Fine," Ellis begrudgingly agrees after a long moment of teeth grinding. "I'll leave my number so you can contact me directly."

"Of course." The doctor nods, smiling tightly before she walks away.

"They're just trying to help," Dawson turns to Ellis after she's out of earshot. "You don't have to be rude."

Ellis' eyes flash. "Yeah, well, my brother almost died because he was drunk driving. Forgive me for being on edge." He must see the way Dawson flinches and closes in on himself, because he takes a step back and an apology passes across his face. "Sorry. I'm just tired." He grimaces. "I forgot to book a hotel."

Ignoring his fight-or-flight response, Dawson says, "You can stay at Cal's apartment."

Ellis' brows shoot up. "With you?"

Dawson would be insulted if he didn't know that the Reeves family has the emotional range of a rock. What on earth did he marry into?

He gives Ellis a look. "It's up to you if you wanna be looking for a place at this hour?"

Ellis watches him for a moment. "Fine. Just tonight." Could he sound any more inconvenienced?

Dawson goes to fetch Kieran to tell him they're leaving.

"Definitely brothers," Kieran says, his expression disapproving.

Dawson chuckles. "He's tired. He doesn't have a hotel, so he'll be staying with me."

Kieran's eyes almost pop out of his skull. "With you?!"

"Relax. He's fine."

Before Kieran can protest, the lady behind the desk—was it Claire?—calls for Dawson.

"I might as well give you this now." She pushes a sealed plastic bag across the desk. "Mr Reeves had these on him when he was brought in."

Dawson takes the bag, scanning the contents. Cal's wallet, his phone—which now has a smashed screen—and his Rolex, which seems to have made it out without a scratch.

And a ring identical to Dawson's.

"Thanks," he mumbles, making a mental note to have the phone repaired before Cal wakes up and asks for it.

"Does it make you wonder what the car must look like?" Kieran asks, sounding dismayed.

"Not really." He saw the one his parents were in. That will do for one lifetime. "Let's get out of here."

"I'll wait for you in the lobby," Ellis informs him when Kieran parks in front of the apartment building, probably still salty that Dawson convinced him to ride with them.

"Okay. I won't be long."

"You sure you don't want me to stay over?" Kieran asks after Ellis is gone.

Dawson shakes his head with a smile. "You've been a huge help already. And you have work tomorrow."

"I can call in sick."

"It's okay. I promise."

"Okay," Kieran relents after a moment. He points a finger at Dawson. "I'll be checking in with you though. Assholery runs in the family."

Dawson rolls his eyes, though he appreciates the concern, as misplaced as it is. "Okay, Dad."

"Shut up, brat." Kieran slaps the back of his head, but his mock-scowl softens immediately. "I love you."

"Love you too." They hug it out and Dawson has to extract himself from the embrace since Kieran seems determined to lock him inside and drive away with him.

"Don't forget your suitcase."

Ah, shit. He forgot about that in all the mayhem. He fetches it from the trunk, coming to a halt when it hits him that he can't take it upstairs with him unless he wants Ellis to ask questions. He makes a quick run to the garage and leaves the suitcase in his car. He rushes to the lobby where Ellis is already waiting for him, arms folded across his chest and an irritated look on his face.

"Sorry," Dawson says, sheepish. He waves in the general direction of the street. "Kieran gets overprotective."

"That's...nice," Ellis says, as if the concept of caring for someone is foreign to him. Hell, maybe it is. Although he was plenty concerned about his brother who he doesn't seem to even like.

Dawson presses the lift button and the door opens right away. They step inside, standing as close to the opposite walls as possible.

"How was your flight?" Dawson asks, cringing. He's terrible at small talk.

Ellis gives him a long-suffering look. "We don't have to do this, you know?"

Well, that's a relief. Even if it's awkward. "Right. Sorry."

Ellis lets out a groan. "No, I'm sorry. I'm grumpy when I'm tired."

Dawson snorts. "Only when you're tired?" He wants to take the words back just as they leave his mouth. He shoots Ellis a skittish glance, but to his shock he doesn't look pissed, only a little amused.

"Fair point."

"You never told me how you got my number."

"From Amanda." Right. Cal's PA. "I thought the hospital called you first, and then you called her and she called me. Thought I'd talk to you directly, since I assumed you'd already be at the hospital." He shifts, looking uncomfortable. "I had no idea they never called you."

"They wouldn't, since I'm evidently not Cal's emergency contact." It shouldn't upset him as much as it does.

"Yeah. Clearly, I'm not either."

Ellis can at least blame it on living in different states.

"Do you think it's going to be okay?" Dawson asks. "With the police and stuff?"

Ellis thinks it over. "I can get a good lawyer. I assume Cal had car insurance..." He waits until Dawson nods. "So we should be good." Not that money would be an issue anyway. "No one else but Cal got hurt, and as far as I know it's his first transgression?" Another nod from Dawson. "We should be fine. If it goes really well, he might not even have to go to court."

The lift stops and as they step out towards the apartment, an overwhelming mixture of relief, gratitude, and guilt sweeps through Dawson.

"Can I help? I mean, you already have to take care of the work stuff." He has zero idea of how he could be of help, but he'll take anything that won't make him feel like a waste of space. It's not fair to unload that all on Ellis who, under normal circumstances, wants nothing to do with Dawson and Cal's life, apart from working for the family company.

To his credit, Ellis doesn't laugh in Dawson's face. And is that a smile?

"I'll manage. Thanks for the offer, but I'll manage."

Keeping disappointment at bay, Dawson unlocks the front door and unnecessarily adds, "This is it."

They toe off their shoes and hang up their jackets. Ellis leaves his suitcase by the door, then sweeps his gaze over the kitchen and the living room, and snorts.

"What a dump."

Dawson's eyes nearly pop out. "What?" He's not exactly in love with the place, but he wouldn't call a luxury two-mill apartment a dump.

Ellis takes a walk around the place, undoing his cufflinks and rolling up his sleeves. He stops in front of the large glass doors leading to the balcony and overlooking the ocean. There's not much to be seen at night, but it's easy to tell the view must be beautiful.

"Typical Cal. All shiny on the surface, but no substance."

"Yeah. Doesn't feel very homey," Dawson agrees. The apartment itself is beautiful, but Cal keeps it strictly sterile-looking.

Ellis turns to him, surprise—no, disbelief written in his face. "Thought you liked shiny stuff."

Dawson balks like he's been slapped. Is that how Cal talks about him? After all Cal's done to him, it shouldn't hurt so much. "What gave you the impression?"

Ellis snickers. "You married my brother."

"What—" Hurt slices through him. To his horror, he feels the familiar sting in his eyes. "You think I married him for the money?" He can admit that Cal's financial situation and status made him feel secure and cared for, but that was more of a byproduct of their relationship. A perk. Sure, Dawson liked it. It was new and exciting, and he'd never been around someone of Cal's caliber before. But it was never about the money.

"Are you saying you didn't?" Ellis eyes him skeptically. Suspiciously. "You got married less than a year after you met him. A guy twelve years older than you."

The age-difference was one of Olivia's arguments too, but she was reaching because she hadn't liked Cal from the beginning. But Jesus, she had never even implied that Dawson was marrying his bank account.

The hurt quickly turns into anger. "Fuck you," he bites out, surprising himself and, by the dumbstruck look on his face, Ellis as well. "You know nothing about me. Last time I checked, I wasn't the one who was fighting over who gets to run the company."

It's Ellis' turn to be taken aback. It only lasts a second before the impenetrable mask is back. He lets out a humorless chuckle.

"That's what he told you, huh. That I want to be in charge."

He did, in fact. Dawson didn't question it because what does he know about business? It explains why Cal never talks to his brother unless it's work related.

"I don't care. That is between you and your brother. But I won't just stand here and take shit from you when you have skeletons in your own closet and don't know a thing about me."

Ellis opens his mouth to say something, but changes his mind. He huffs and heads to the kitchen. "I need a fucking drink. Cal have anything here?"

Dawson almost laughs. Kieran was onto something when he said assholery runs in the family. "Oh yeah. Help yourself." He gestures towards the cupboards, making himself sound as sarcastic as possible. "I'm sure you'll find something among the dozen whiskey bottles."

Ellis stops in his tracks and looks at him. "What did you say?"

Dawson squares his shoulders. "You heard me."

Ellis doesn't move straight away. He stands there, his mouth opening and closing. He turns to the cupboards, eyes them, then begins to open them. He stills when he opens the third one.

"Jesus. Fuck." He pulls out one of the bottles, staring at it like he just found poison. He gives Dawson a wide-eyed look. "He drinks?"

This time, he does laugh, putting as much deprecation into it as humanly possible. "Just a little."

All defensiveness seems to leave Ellis, and he looks at Dawson with that pitying look he hates so much. "Dawson..."

"You know what? Maybe you should find that hotel for tonight."

If the abrupt change of mind shocks Ellis, he doesn't show it. He nods, putting the bottle away and studying the cupboards for a while before finally closing it. He turns to Dawson to say something, but his gaze falls onto the kitchen island.

"What's this?"

Dawson puts two and two together too late. By the time he does, Ellis has the divorce documents in his hand and is reading the first page.

"Are you getting a divorce?"

Dawson looks away. "I don't know."

"You don't know," Ellis echoes flatly.

No, he doesn't know. He doesn't know anything anymore. He thought he could do it, he almost *did*. But throwing this in Cal's face after he nearly died? What kind of person would do that?

Yeah, carry on making excuses for being such a wuss.

The cosmos clearly hates him, because the one time Dawson finally decides to grow some balls and stand up to his abusive asshole of a husband, life throws him a curve ball. *Oh, you think you're leaving? Guess again, loser.* "It doesn't matter. I can't leave now, anyway." *Serves you right, too. You've been one pathetic wuss your whole life, so you might as well stay one.*

"Dawson, look at me."

He jumps when Ellis is suddenly in front of him, a look on his face Dawson would've never imagined him capable of. "Is there anything else?" He lets the question hang in the air for a moment. "Anything besides the drinking?"

Does he know? Can he tell because he knows Cal's temper, or is Dawson just that obvious?

After a small eternity of battling with himself, Dawson gives a defeated nod, unable to look him in the eye.

Ellis lets out a shuddering breath. "Okay. I'm gonna get you some water." He speaks slowly, like one would to a child. "Then we'll sit down, and you tell me. Okay?"

He doesn't want to air his dirty laundry, but, more than that, he wants to finally tell someone. Someone who doesn't know him, who won't be disappointed in him for enduring this shit for so long and never standing up for himself.

"Yeah, okay."

"Fuck," is the first thing Ellis says when Dawson finishes giving him the run down on the past six years of his life. "I can't believe... Dawson,

I'm so sorry." He takes Dawson's hands between his, surprising him. "I never knew."

"No one did. No one else does."

Ellis frowns. "Why didn't you tell anyone?"

For a million different reasons. "They'd tell me to leave." He laughs self-deprecatingly, pulling out of Ellis grasp. He doesn't really want to be touched right now. "I don't even know who I am."

"You *were* about to leave."

As if he needs a reminder. There's no way to explain it to Ellis and not sound completely pathetic, so he keeps his mouth shut.

Ellis isn't finished, though. "You can't stay. You know that, right? It will only get worse. Especially with everything that's just happened."

Right. Add a major injury on top of the shitstorm at work, and you got yourself a very pissed, very stressed alcoholic.

"It never would've worked anyway." He was just lying to himself. He thought he had it figured out, but realistically, Cal would never let him go. He'd find him—it wouldn't be hard—and drag him back, kicking and screaming. "The papers were just to prove a point, to show him I'm serious. But no one will divorce us unless we've been separated for a year."

Ellis' jaw works, anger simmering in his eyes. He knows Dawson is right. "You could report him. If you're afraid he'll try something, you can get a restraining order."

Dawson lets out a humorless laugh. "No one will believe me." When Ellis wants to protest, he says, "I'm gay. I'm a gay guy and my husband is the rich owner of a company. No one will believe me." The odds are not in his favor. It's already hard for women to escape an abusive partner. He doesn't stand a chance. Who'd give a shit about him? "And don't tell me you can help. He's your brother, you don't want him to go to jail."

"He's an asshole," Ellis says matter-of-factly. It makes Dawson want to smile. "Him being my brother doesn't change what he's done to you." He sighs when he senses Dawson's reluctance. "You should really apply for a restraining order."

Dawson raises an eyebrow. "You think that would actually help?"

Ellis hesitates. "As you said, he's the head of the company. He can't afford a scandal."

"That didn't stop him from beating the shit out of me for years."

Ellis flinches, his hands clenched into fists. "Dawson. You're not alone in this. Your sister will help, Kevin will help."

"Who?"

"Your friend?"

Dawson chuckles. "Kieran."

"Yeah, whatever," Ellis says, blushing a little. It looks hilarious on him. "*I* will help. You can come to Sydney with me if you want."

Dawson can't help but laugh. That's even more ridiculous than living with his sister or Kieran. "You hated me all this time and now you'd have me live with you?"

Ellis makes a face. "I never hated you."

"No, you just thought I was a gold digger."

Ellis lowers his gaze guiltily, so Dawson knows he hit the nail on the head.

"I'm sorry. It's..." He sighs in frustration. "You wouldn't be the first." There's something painful in that statement.

"Personal experience?"

Smiling wryly, Ellis shrugs. "Comes with the territory."

Sympathy wells inside Dawson. He never worried too much about being seen as a gold digger, simply because Cal never worried about it in the first place. Is Ellis used to people just taking advantage and leaving when they get what they want?

"I'm sorry, that sucks. For your information, Cal had me sign a prenup."

Out of all the things they talked about, this is what makes Ellis' jaw drop. "And you still married him?"

"I thought it made sense. As you said, we got married quickly. I wouldn't want to throw half my assets at a guy I just met either." Looking back, he should've questioned it. He should've questioned many things.

"I'm—"

"Stop." If he hears one more 'sorry' today, he's gonna throw himself out of the window. "It doesn't matter. Water under the bridge, yeah?"

Ellis is reluctant to agree. "Yeah. Promise me you'll think about this?"

Dawson bites his lip and smiles. "You sound like my sister."

"Yeah?" Ellis gives him a grin that looks strange on him, because it changes his whole face. "She seeing anybody?"

Dawson laughs. "Her husband."

"Shucks."

They go quiet for a bit, but it's not heavy or uncomfortable. More like they're testing the waters of where they are now that they're not virtual strangers anymore.

"We should sleep," Dawson suggests, fighting a yawn.

"Yeah." Ellis stands up. "Get some rest. I'll see you tomorrow."

"Where are you going?"

"A hotel?"

"No, that's..." Dawson waves a hand. "Forget I said that. You can stay. Of course you can stay."

"Are you sure?" He watches Dawson carefully. Assessing. "It's not an issue."

"I'm sure. It's late. You'd be dead on your feet by the time you found something."

"Okay," Ellis finally says. He licks his lips, looking a little lost. "Thanks."

Dawson nods and gets to his feet. "Here. I'll show you the spare room." It's a four-bedroom apartment, but Cal turned one into his office and the other is for storage, leaving only one available in case someone sleeps over. Which never happens, anyway.

After he shows Ellis around, he goes to take a shower, washing the day away. Even though he's tired, he doesn't think he'll get much sleep, not with his brain going into overdrive and analyzing everything that happened and will happen.

Ellis was right when he said things will only get worse. With Cal healing from the injury and dealing with the aftermath of the money-loss at work, it's bound to become ugly. Ellis was right about other things too. Dawson can't stay here. Maybe this is the right time. Take off while Cal is too busy worrying about his health—as cold as that sounds—and the company, so he doesn't have time to worry about Dawson.

He can't stay with Olivia. She has enough on her plate as it is, with raising two kids and working full-time. And there's no way he's going to Sydney with Ellis. That's ridiculous. Plus, he doesn't even like Sydney. It's too busy, too hectic, and the weather is more unpredictable.

This leaves Kieran. He knows the man would do anything for him, but the idea of causing trouble for Kieran doesn't sit well with him—what with his constant arguments with his girlfriend. Dawson doesn't have his own money either, so he couldn't pay Kieran half the rent. Fuck.

Okay. Step one: find a job. He used to work in hospitality before he met Cal. Surely, a restaurant or a cafe would hire him. There are plenty along the Coast. Except it would have to be close-by because he'll lose his car. Well, not his—Cal's. Everything he has doesn't actually belong to him. Not even his life feels like it's actually his.

He'd hoped the shower would make him feel better, but he feels even crappier by the time he gets out and wanders to the bedroom. He wants nothing more than to fall into bed and black out. Except when he looks at the bed, all neat and large, he can't bring himself to lie in it.

He hates this. This bed, this room, this apartment. He hates this life that he's fallen into and has been too scared to find a way out of. In the end, he grabs his phone, a blanket, and his favorite pillow and goes to sleep on the sofa. It's fucking uncomfortable and stiff, but it's better than the alternative. He just needs to be somewhere else.

Once he's somewhat settled in, he does a quick survey of his phone only to find Olivia's been trying to reach him for hours. He contemplates calling her in the morning, but he knows she won't be able to sleep until she hears from him. She's been worried sick since Dawson had told her he was going through with the divorce.

He takes a deep breath and dials her number. It's going to be a long night.

Chapter 5

THE MORNING IS STRANGE. Dawson comes to slowly, his mind hazy as if he's been asleep for years. Waking up in an almost unfamiliar environment doesn't help, and it's not until he tries to move and gets a crick in his neck that he's reminded where he is. And why.

"Did you sleep here?"

Dawson startles and rolls off the sofa, tangling himself in the blanket and landing with a loud thud. "Shit."

"Jesus," he hears, and then the blanket is being pulled off him. "You okay?"

"Yeah. Just woke up."

Ellis is standing over him dressed in yesterday's suit but a fresh shirt, his hair styled immaculately. Looking at him, no one would be able to tell he's been through the meat-grinder in the past 24 hours.

"Why did you sleep here?"

Standing up clumsily, Dawson trails to the kitchen to get some water into him. "Couldn't sleep in the bedroom. Are you headed to the office?"

"Later." He hears Ellis move around. "After I've stopped at the hospital. I don't even want to anymore, but..."

"But he's your brother," Dawson finishes for him, turning to face him, a glass of water in his hand.

Ellis makes a sour face. "Unfortunately."

An unexpected wave of affection fills Dawson's chest. Ellis nearly raised all hell when the doctor refused to let him see his brother, but after what Dawson had told him last night, he's been acting strangely protective.

Summoning a reassuring smile, Dawson says, "I get it." And he does. He'd be a hypocrite if he gave Ellis grief.

Ellis studies him. "Do you want to come?"

Dawson averts his gaze. Even though Ellis knows now, it doesn't stop Dawson from feeling guilty for not wanting to stay by his husband's side after he's been in an accident. Are the nurses and doctors going to talk about him when they notice how little he's invested in Cal's well-being?

"Not really. It's not like it'd make a difference." That's what he's been telling himself. What good would it do if he spent day and night at the hospital while Cal is sedated? "I have a shift starting in two hours."

"I never asked what you do."

Dawson laughs bitterly. "I don't *do* anything. I volunteer at a local dog shelter."

Ellis' face softens, not with pity, but something else. "That sounds nice. We had a dog when we were kids," he says, his tone nostalgic. "A border-collie. Teddy." His lips twitch. "He was such a crazy fucker. I loved him."

Dawson smiles at the admission. Cal never mentioned having a dog when he was younger. "Cal never let me have a dog."

Ellis huffs in amusement. "Teddy liked peeing in his shoes. Guess he never got over it."

A giggle bursts out of Dawson unexpectedly. Jesus, he can't imagine. Well, he can imagine it a little, and it's hilarious.

Dawson just now notices Ellis has a suitcase with him. "What's with the suitcase?"

Ellis looks at it like he's forgotten it's there. "I found a hotel. Thank you for letting me stay but I think it's better if I get out of here." He looks around the apartment with distaste. "The place is giving me the creeps."

Dawson tries not to look disappointed. He was kind of looking forward to getting to know Ellis and, well, not being alone. "Fair. How long are you staying for?"

"Well, the shitstorm at work will take a few days to blow over. And I'd rather not go back until I know that Cal's out of the woods."

Poor guy. He has his work cut out for him. "That could be a long time."

"Yeah, well." Ellis shrugs. "It's what you do for family."

"You want coffee before you go?" Dawson points at the five grand coffee machine.

Ellis makes a face like Dawson just offered him dish water. "Yeah, no. I'll just get one from a coffee shop on the way to the hospital."

"Jesus, you really are brothers." Spoiled brats.

"Excuse me, I'd never have a coffee from something that pretends to be a coffee machine,"

"It's literally—" Dawson cuts himself off. "Nevermind. Go visit your equally privileged brother."

Ellis glares at him. "I will not dignify that comment with a response."

Dawson snorts. "Just get out already, before I kick you out."

"Fine." Ellis throws the door open, but before he disappears, Dawson gets a glimpse of a grin.

It's weirdly quiet when Ellis is gone, and the apartment seems to close in on Dawson. It's not the first time he's felt claustrophobic in the open space, but for some reason, it's more pronounced this time.

He makes quick work of brushing his teeth and dressing, then grabs his keys and phone and leaves the apartment like he's on a schedule. He's not, he just needs to get out. He still has two hours before his shift starts, so he heads to *Lost and Ground*, the only place that, ironically, doesn't make him feel so lost.

For eight o'clock, the place is unusually quiet and Zeke notices him before the door even closes behind Dawson.

"You look like crap," Zeke says in lieu of a greeting. "Wild night?"

"Not the way you think," Dawson says with a sigh as he approaches the counter. "Flying solo today?"

"Nah. Gabe's in the kitchen. Wanna say hi?"

"No, no, don't disturb him from the important task of washing the dishes."

Zeke laughs. "Baking, actually. What can I get you?"

He gets his usual–an almond milk chai latte with some 'enchanted' mushrooms, as Zeke insists on calling them. Dawson's pretty sure it's just reishi powder, but he never argues. If you ask him, the whole cafe is magical. He's already starting to feel better just by being inside.

He pays for his drink and heads over to his favorite corner table by the window. Damn, he should've brought a book or something. He has over an hour to kill, after all. Nevermind. He can spend it reminiscing about all his bad decisions. That should entertain him for long enough.

Evidently, the cosmos doesn't want him to identify all the ways his life has gone wrong, because the door to the kitchen flies open and Gabriel strolls out, a smear of flour on his cheek and pieces of dough stuck to his apron. He makes a beeline for Dawson's table.

"Hi, Gabe."

"What's wrong?" Gabe goes straight to the point. Dawson must look a mess. "You made my head spin over there."

"I thought that's a good thing." He attempts to waggle his eyebrows suggestively, but doesn't quite pull it off, if Gabe's unimpressed face is any indication.

"Not quite what I meant."

"Am I pinging your superpowers?" It's what Gabe calls it. Dawson calls it 'being good at reading people'. Yeah, the place sure feels magical, but that's just because Gabe and Zeke are lovely people.

Dawson isn't a pure-blooded skeptic. He believes in stuff. He's scared of ghosts, for one. And when he accompanied Olivia to a fortune telling session the lady who did the reading was scarily accurate—about Liv's marriage, her work. She even predicted Liv would have two girls. Then again, she also told Dawson that the man he'd marry wouldn't be from here and he'd be the love of his life, his soulmate.

He found out it was bullshit pretty quickly, considering that Cal is a born and bred Australian. As for him being the love of Dawson's life...he sure as hell hopes not, otherwise he might as well throw himself off a bridge.

Gabe flings his tea towel over his shoulder and wipes his hands on his apron before folding his arms over his chest. "Joke all you want, I know I'm right and you know it too." His eyes bore into Dawson, as though trying to stare into his soul. "What's up?"

Superpowers or not, Gabe does have a penchant for smelling bullshit, Dawson will give him that.

"Cal's in the hospital. He was drunk driving and crashed. Collapsed lung. Internal bleeding. Something like that."

Gabe's mouth falls open. "Shit." He doesn't offer any condolences—aside from Kieran and Olivia, he's the only other person Dawson ever confided in with what's going on at home. Nothing detailed, just bits and pieces. Just enough to make him dislike Cal without ever meeting him. "When did that happen?"

"Last night. His brother flew over from Sydney. He went to see him today."

Gabe raises an eyebrow. "Do Cal and his brother have a lot in common?"

Dawson chuckles, hearing the hidden meaning loud and clear. "Well, they have similar looks." His smile falls at Gabe's solemn expression. "Ellis is fine. I didn't really know him before yesterday, and he sure is an entitled prick, but he's not a bad person."

"Hmm." Gabe looks dubious. "Not sure how much I should trust your judgment."

Dawson rolls his eyes. "Maybe I'll bring him here and you can use your powers on him."

Gabe lights up. "That would actually be—"

"I was joking."

Gabe's excitement turns into a scowl. "You're the worst."

"Yet, here you are."

Gabe watches him. Slowly, his annoyance gives way to concern. "What is it?"

Dawson blinks at him. "What?"

"There's something else."

Dawson scoffs. "Something else besides my husband being in the hospital?" Gabe doesn't buy it. He knows about the hell Cal's put Dawson through, and shit, he's really good at reading people. "How are you doing this?"

"It's a gift," Gabe says simply. "What is it, really?"

Weighing his options, Dawson decides to spill the beans. He has a feeling Gabe will be like a dog with a bone until he gets his answers. "I want to ask him for a divorce. And I feel like shit for doing it now."

Gabe seems shocked but recovers quickly. "That's a lot to process," he concedes. "But you have to do what's right for you. He's alive, yeah?" Dawson nods. "He'll be fine. He'll get out of it in a few weeks and he'll be good as new."

"Yeah. Maybe," Dawson relents, knowing full well it's not going to happen. People like him always get the shittiest of luck.

The physical work at the shelter helps take Dawson's mind off things, at least for a while. Is there a better therapy than doggie cuddles? If only he could take one of them home. Or all of them, preferably.

He doesn't check his phone until his shift ends at two, and panics when he sees several unread messages from an unsaved number. He only needs to read the first one to realize it's Ellis, and calms down.

Ellis: *Leaving the hospital now. He looks like hell but everything seems fine. They'll start waking him up tomorrow.*

Dawson's fingers hover over the screen. His emotions are a mess and he has no idea what to reply. Maybe he doesn't have to? Ellis isn't asking anything.

No, that feels weird.

Dawson: *Thanks for the heads-up. Headed to work?*

He wants to smack himself a second after he hits *send*. Ellis sent the message hours ago, obviously he's gone already.

Ellis: *Already here. It's mayhem.*

Dawson: *Sorry.*

Ellis: *I should've been an astronaut.*

A small, genuine laugh bursts out of him. He's starting to appreciate the dry sense of humor.

Dawson: *lol*

He pockets the phone and starts towards his car. Now that he has nothing to do, guilt makes a vicious comeback. Should he visit again after all? Out of courtesy, if nothing else.

What courtesy? He's unconscious and he wouldn't want you there anyway.

Tomorrow. He'll go tomorrow. Just for a little while in the morning, when Cal is hopefully still sedated. He's not ready to face him yet.

Maybe he should've asked Kieran to come with him again. It feels really uncomfortable to be at the hospital by himself. He almost turns on his heel and runs, but controls himself.

He approaches the front desk with a stiff smile. "Hi. I'm here to see Cal Reeves?"

The middle aged man behind the desk nods. "Are you family?"

"He's my husband." His body rebels at the word. It always does. He always ignores it.

"I'll get one of the nurses to show you in."

"Thank you."

A nurse picks him up a few minutes later and leads him to Cal's room. It doesn't seem like anything's changed since he was here two days ago. The tubes are still sticking out of Cal's battered body, and his face plays out in three different colors. The machines are the worst, the sound terrifying even though everything is clearly okay, the beeping nice and regular.

Dawson lowers himself into the uncomfortable-looking plastic chair by the bed. Just a few minutes, then he'll go. He doesn't want to stare at Cal like last time, in silence. He'd already shaken the shock off. Mostly. Maybe he should try talking to him? He heard it helps.

"Ellis was here yesterday," he starts. "He's different from what I imagined. Then again, he thought I was someone else too." He understands what made Ellis think of him that way, but it stings all the same. Probably because Cal never tried to convince his brother that Dawson is better than the picture Ellis had of him. Has Cal always thought Dawson married him for the money? Does he care?

"You're lucky to have him," he goes on. "You always talked so ill of him, I thought you hated each other's guts, but he cares." An unbidden thought forms in his mind. "Is it strange that it makes me feel better knowing I'm not the only person close to you who you treated like crap? I always thought I was the problem. Always wondering what I'm doing wrong. I think I get it now."

It's kind of freeing, to be able to say these things to Cal's face, even if it's pretend, but that's fine. He's been pretending this whole time, most of his life, really. Pretending he's okay, that he's stronger than he looks, braver than he feels. Now he'll just need to pretend that he's scared for his husband's well-being. Not for long, though. Soon, he'll be back to where he started. Alone and lost.

"I wish I never met you."

The deafening, high-pitched sound of the machines going haywire sends his heart racing. He springs to his feet, looking around in panic. What's happening? Did he do something? Should he call for someone?

Everything happens too fast. Two nurses storm in with a doctor in tow that Dawson has yet to meet. They push Dawson aside, barking out medical terminology he has no hope of understanding until he hears 'Code blue'.

He stays rooted to the spot, his ears filling up with the violent sounds of the machines. Rough hands grip him by the arms, trying to move him.

"Sir. You need to leave," someone says, then he's being escorted out of the room. He moves mechanically, frozen in place as the door is shut in his face.

A nurse passes Dawson, asking him questions, checking on him. He tries to answer, his mind fuzzy. He lets her lead him back to the waiting room, taking one of the chairs and accepting the cup of water she fetches for him. She's trying to talk to him, but her voice sounds like it's coming from a distance, the words not making sense.

He sits there and waits for what feels like hours, even if realistically it's probably just minutes.

"Mr Reeves."

Dawson lifts his head. The figure in front of him is vaguely familiar. Is he the doctor who was in the room when Cal coded?

"Yes?"

The doctor's inscrutable expression breaks, turning grim. He takes a chair next to Dawson, turning to face him. "I'm sorry," he says, voice full of empathy. "We did everything we could, but—"

The intercom crackles to life with another call for *code blue*.

Code blue for Cal's room.

The doc' face drains of color, his mouth agape. He shakes himself impressively quickly, springing to his feet and mumbling a brief "Excuse me" to Dawson before he takes off.

Dawson stares after his disappearing form, his chest hollow and feeling like it's being crushed in an iron fist.

His eyes close and, finally, he lets himself fall apart.

Chapter 6

HE'S NOT SURE HOW much time has passed when Ellis barges into the waiting room. He strides towards the front desk but halts when he sees Dawson. He lets out a relieved exhale and starts towards him.

"What happened?" he asks as he drops into the chair next to him.

The hospital must've called him, because Dawson doesn't remember doing it. He would feel bad about it if he was able to feel anything other than the suffocating void.

"I don't know. I was there when he coded. They made me leave, and then, I don't know after how long, a doctor came to tell me they lost him. But then..." He takes a shuddering breath. "They managed to bring him back and took him to surgery."

Ellis pulls at his hair none too gently. He's been doing it a lot. If he keeps it up whenever he feels stressed, he'll go bald by the time Cal is out of the woods.

"Shit. Way to scare the crap out of everyone."

"Yeah, he's good at that," Dawson says, uncaring how bitter he sounds.

Ellis eyes him carefully, but he doesn't seem mad. "You don't have to be here. I know this is a lot, especially when..." His expression is strained, the words hard to get out. Dawson doesn't blame him. Hearing about the side of his brother that he'd never known existed must've shaken him. "I'll stay. You go home. I'll let you know if something changes."

Dawson doesn't even have the strength to protest. Honestly, it sounds good to him, even if leaving Ellis to deal with everything by himself—again—makes him feel like crap. He doesn't want to stay here. His brain is already playing tricks on him, making him feel like the walls of the waiting room are closing in on him. Kind of like when he's at the apartment.

So he nods, searching his pocket for the car keys. He might need to sit in the car for a bit, make sure he's fit to drive. Ellis wouldn't be impressed if Dawson ended up in a car wreck too.

Before he can leave, one of the doctors who was in the room when Cal coded approaches them. Dr Wells, his name tag says.

"Mr Reeves?"

Dawson stands up. "Yes?"

Ellis stands next to him. The doctor gives him a glance, but turns his attention back to Dawson.

"We just finished the surgery." A hint of a smile. "Your husband will be alright. He'll need to stay in the ICU for longer than we intended. We'll keep him sedated for a couple more days, but—"

Dawson's thoughts begin to wander. He's vaguely aware of what Dr Wells is saying, catching a word here and there.

"Missed bleed... happens sometimes... seat-belt syndrome..."

They don't always make sense, and honestly, it makes no difference. Cal is alive and he'll be up in a few days.

And things will go back to the way they were.

"We had to perform exploratory laparotomy. We opened up his abdomen to stop the bleeding," he explains when he sees their blank expressions. "It will require some extra post-op rehab and home care, but if you follow the instructions everything should heal with no issues."

Dawson nods absently while Ellis asks questions. Dawson just tunes him out. He should probably pay more attention, but he's not sure it would stick.

"You should go home, too," Dawson says when the doctor leaves. "You heard him; Cal is sedated."

Ellis sighs. "Yeah, I know. And I do have a shitload of stuff to iron out. It's just…"

"I know."

Ellis eyes him with concern. "Will you be okay?"

Unlikely. "I could ask you the same thing."

"It's not the same. You know that."

Swallowing hard, Dawson looks away. Ellis' gaze is way too intense, not unlike Cal's. They both have the ability to make a person feel like they're a bug under the microscope. For Dawson, who hates being the center of attention—positive or not—this is really uncomfortable.

"I'll be fine. I might stay with Kieran for a bit." He doesn't want to impose, but he wants to stay at the apartment by himself even less. Hopefully, Jess will survive his company for a few days.

Ellis nods. "Good idea."

They walk towards their respective cars. Dawson takes five minutes to put himself together, using the time to shoot a text to Kieran.

Dawson: *Could I stay with you for a few days?*

The response is instant.

Kieran: *Pack your stuff. I'll pick you up in an hour.*

Dawson smiles, tearing up a little. He really should give Kieran more credit. He's made it clear to Dawson several times that friends come first. If only Dawson could say the same for himself. He's the shittiest friend one can have. Hopefully there's still time to make up for it.

Dawson: *My suitcase is still in my car. I can head straight over.*

He laughs at Kieran's message.

Kieran: *Then put your phone away and get your ass over here.*

Dawson puts his phone away and gets his ass in gear.

"Sorry about the mess," Kieran says as he opens the door to his apartment. "I would've cleaned up if I knew I'd have a guest."

Dawson snorts. "No, you wouldn't." He doubts Kieran even owns cleaning products. "That's fine. I don't care."

The place is such a startling change from Cal's meticulous apartment that he welcomes it. Plus, Kieran isn't really that dirty, more like...untidy. Clothes strewn everywhere and all kinds of crap dotting every surface. The kitchen is spotless, though, probably because Kieran's never cooked anything but water. From what Dawson's seen, Kieran's girlfriend doesn't seem like the cooking type either, even if her nails could easily substitute a filet knife. Speaking of...

"Where's Jess?" He really hopes Kieran's told her Dawson would be staying over. He'd hate to witness her reaction in person.

"We broke up."

"What? When?"

Kieran purses his lips, thinking. "About half an hour ago."

Oh no. "Wait. Is it—"

"Nope," Kieran doesn't let him finish. "It's because she's a horrible, toxic person and I'm fed up with her shit."

Accurate, but it can't be a coincidence that they broke up today, just a while ago. And while Dawson is glad that his best friend can finally relax a little, he doesn't want to be the reason why they broke up. He doesn't need to add yet another thing to his growing pile of *Things that Dawson has screwed up.*

"Kieran..."

"Don't Kieran me." He steps towards Dawson and grips his shoulders. "You're my best friend. I'd do anything for you." He pauses. "Except drink kombucha. I draw the line there. That shit is vile."

The easy banter brings a smile to Dawson's face, and his eyes well up. It hasn't occurred to him how much he's missed Kieran. He never sees him as often as he'd like, because Cal would have something to say about Dawson spending so much time with another guy, no matter if the guy is straight as an arrow. He knows it's just an excuse. Cal doesn't want him to spend much time with anybody.

Something must show on his face, because Kieran lets out a curse and pulls Dawson into a tight hug. He's not a big guy, but he's taller and his long arms envelop Dawson easily, and he allows himself to enjoy the comfort. He really needs it today.

"I know this will make me sound like a total hypocrite," he says when Kieran lets him go. "But why were you with Jess if she's so bad?"

Kieran gives a sheepish shrug. "The sex was pretty hot. The woman was willing to try anything." He winks.

Dawson punches him in the chest, making a face. "You're disgusting."

Kieran laughs. "And yet, here you are."

"Seriously, though."

Kieran spreads his arms and flops down onto the sofa. "Look, I don't know what I want. I thought I did. Turns out I know squat." He laughs. It sounds bitter this time.

Jess was just the tip of the iceberg. Dawson's known him long enough to notice Kieran tends to gravitate towards a certain type of woman.

Dawson joins him on the sofa, pressing their shoulders together. "Maybe you should try something you never have before."

"Like what?"

Dawson shrugs. "I don't know. Just the opposite of what you alway do."

One of Kieran's eyebrows rises up slowly. "Are you propositioning me?"

Dawson gives him a flat look. "You're an idiot."

"Well, excuse me, you were the one talking about trying something I never have before," Kieran laughs at him.

"I didn't mean *that*!"

"You don't have to sound so outraged. I'm a catch."

"Uh-huh." Dawson gives him a quick once-over. "Sorry. Not my type." It's true, even if he didn't necessarily mean the looks. He's always been attracted to men older than him. Men who had their shit together and radiated confidence and security. He thinks about Cal, and almost laughs. That blew up in his face spectacularly.

Kieran huffs, sounding offended. "Sure. Too young for you, huh?" he taunts. He always liked taking the piss about the age difference between Dawson and Cal.

"You're definitely immature."

"You'd be talking differently if you saw my dick."

Dawson scrunches his nose. "I've seen your dick. You're not that impressive."

Kieran gapes at him. "When did you see it?!"

"Your birthday five years ago. You took off your clothes and danced on the table singing *I touch myself*. Everybody saw it."

"Oh! I remember!" Kieran grins. "Good times."

"For you, maybe."

Kieran's dick aside, Dawson hates being around drunk people. Not drinking also means being the only sane person who remembers everything and is responsible for the rest of them. He used to enjoy a glass or two himself, but living with Cal kind of put a damper on everything. He can't remember the last time he had cider or beer.

Slowly, Kieran's grin disappears, as though he can sense the shift in Dawson's mood.

"Well, now that you've unsuccessfully tried to change the topic, let's come back to you. How are you feeling?"

He'd pay money for someone to tell him what it is he's feeling.

"Like...like I'm watching this happen from the outside. Like it's happening to someone else."

"Technically, it's happening to Cal," Kieran says, chuckling. He sobers up when Dawson doesn't laugh. "Sorry. Too soon?"

Dawson shakes his head. It was a little funny. "It's fine. I'm feeling...lots of things I shouldn't feel." Things that would earn him a one-way ticket to hell, if he believed in such a thing.

"Dee." Kieran slings an arm over his shoulders and kisses the top of his head. "You can't control how you feel. There's no right or wrong—"

"I wished he didn't survive."

Kieran freezes. "What?"

Dawson closes his eyes, pulling away. He can't look at Kieran as he admits something so horrible to him.

"After Cal coded...when the doctor came out to tell me..." His voice cracks.

Kieran shifts, closing the distance Dawson so desperately tried to put between them. "What?"

"I knew it was bad news. The doctor had that look and then he started to apologize and..." He can't do it. The mere thought is abhorrent; he can't actually let the words out.

"And?" Kieran prompts gently. "It's okay Dee. You can tell me."

It takes a small eternity before he finds his voice. "I was...I was relieved." He looks at Kieran with wide eyes, unable to believe he's admitting this to someone. "I was relieved when I thought he died, Kieran. And then...then they called out *code blue* for Cal's room again and I..." He hides his face in his palms, fighting a bout of nausea. "Fuck. Fuck."

"Come here." Kieran's arms are around him, pulling him up and into an embrace. "It's okay."

"It's not okay. What kind of monster wishes for their husband to die?"

Kieran holds him tighter, his voice quiet but firm. "Someone who was hurt a lot. There's nothing wrong with what you feel, Dee. It's not your fault he's an asshole." He trails off for a moment. "Honestly, I've wished so many times that he would end up dead in a ditch. I hate the guy."

An unexpected laugh escapes Dawson. "Really? I couldn't tell."

He feels rather than hears Kieran's answering chuckle. Another kiss lands on his forehead. "You're okay, Dee."

He's far from okay, but at least he doesn't feel like he's being swallowed by darkness anymore. He might not deserve a friend like Kieran, but he sure is grateful for him.

When he feels marginally more put together, he sits up straight and wipes moisture from his eyes.

"I think I need a shower. Do you have a spare blanket and a pillow?"

Kieran looks at him. "You don't think you're sleeping on the sofa, are you?"

Dawson looks at the sofa. That was, in fact, what he thought. "Well..."

"Nuh-uh. You're sleeping in the bed with me."

Dawson makes a face. "Really? Do I have to?"

Kieran rolls his eyes. "I'll change the sheets, okay?"

Dawson is dubious.

"I will!"

"Okay, okay. I'll sleep in your bed with you. But I'll pinch your nose if you snore." It might be nice not having to be alone with his thoughts for once.

Two days later, Dawson is questioning his life choices yet again, although this time for a different reason. If he'd thought that staying with Kieran would be preferable to being alone in the empty apartment, he's sorely mistaken. And when he said Kieran wasn't that dirty? It couldn't be further from the truth.

He could get over finding wet towels on the bathroom floor, or the bathroom mirror sprayed with toothpaste, but why does he have to find Kieran's *used* underwear on his side of the bed, or a half-eaten container of food left on the table overnight? Also, people who leave a used butter knife on the sink's edge have a special place in hell reserved for them.

He's barely got any shuteye in the past two days, because his dear friend snores like a chainsaw and talks in his sleep. Not to mention he's a damned blanket hog. That's one good thing about Cal—he sleeps like the dead.

Jesus, straight guys are gross. He might end up taking the sofa in the end. The lesser of two evils.

Since he's been up most of the night, he watches the minutes on the clock tick by. At six, he can't take it anymore and decides to go for a run. Kieran's place is further from the beach, not just a street over like Cal's, so he'll need to go through streets and crossings, which he hates.

He brushes his teeth first and washes his face before going through his suitcase. He didn't bring his running clothes, so he just throws on a plain white shirt and the joggers he was wearing yesterday. He doesn't have his running shoes either, but that's fine. He'll run barefoot once he reaches the beach. If he's quick enough, he might still catch the sunrise.

Spoiler alert: he's not quick enough. He doesn't mind. The sky is absolutely stunning, playing out in shades of orange and purple.

Dawson loves this; the beach and living on the East Coast. It's one of his favorite things, just listening to the sound of waves and seagulls (and occasionally being attacked by them), and feeling the sand slide between his toes. Whenever he's here, he can pretend he's living a different life. He should've married a surfer, then he would have a good reason to spend most of his time on the beach. Before work swallowed up his life, Cal used to surf too.

While the morning run doesn't miraculously make his problems go away or his gloomy mood disappear, he does feel a little better when heads back to Kieran's half an hour later. He considers steering his course towards *Lost and Ground* to grab a quick bite, keep the endorphins pumping through both exercise and carbs, but he hasn't brought his wallet nor his phone with him, and he forgot to put his watch on after he showered last night. Gabe and Zeke would probably try to make him get whatever he wants for free, or let him pay later, but he'd feel awkward doing that. Although he could convince Kieran to go with him before he has to leave for work.

Kieran's already up and in the shower when Dawson gets back. Knowing his friend doesn't tend to bring clothes with him to the bathroom (ask Dawson how he knows), he steers clear of the bedroom and waits in the living room, chugging down a glass of water.

"Wanna go to the cafe with me?" Dawson asks when Kieran emerges—fully dressed—a few minutes later.

"Oh yeah. I haven't been in a while. Now?"

"I need a shower." Dawson pulls on his sweaty shirt. "But then I'm good to go."

"No rush. I've got plenty of time."

They get to the cafe just after eight, and this time it's decidedly not quiet. Gabe manages a quick chat with them while Zeke pumps out drinks.

"Are you staying?" Gabe asks after Dawson paid for them.

"Yeah, we have time to kill," Kieran says.

"Cool. Just take a seat, I'll find you."

"Of course you will. Hard to miss this pretty face." Kieran bats his eyelashes, and Gabe giggles.

"So gay," Dawson stage whispers, getting the honor of seeing Kieran stick his tongue out. "And we can wait here. You're busy enough as it is." He thinks Gabe wants to argue, but in the end he just smiles.

"Such a gentleman. Damn, Dawson, if you weren't married..."

Dawson laughs, and Kieran with him. Gabe is a flirt; it's no secret. He flirts with everyone, but it's just harmless fun. Well, mostly harmless, if Dawson doesn't count the people who are so enamored with Gabe, men and women alike, that they come to the cafe daily just to see him. Gabe thinks it's sweet. Dawson thinks it's bordering on stalking and obsession.

They collect their pastries-slash-breakfast and move out of the way and to the end of the counter, exchanging a few words with Zeke while he works on their drinks.

"This is nice. It's been a while since we were here together," Kieran says as they take their seats, balancing the plates and drinks.

Guilt fills Dawson's veins with ice. "I know. Sorry."

"What? Why are you apologizing?"

Dawson starts pulling his cinnamon roll apart to have something to do with his hands. "I'm usually the one to come up with excuses when you wanna do something together."

"They're not excuses. I'm not stupid. I know Cal gives you shit when you make plans with other people. God forbid you have a life outside of him." Kieran rolls his eyes for emphasis, then fixes Dawson's with an uncharacteristically solemn look. "You're still going through with the divorce, aren't you?"

Dawson's throat tightens. He's not sure what to say. Or do.

"I–"

He's saved by an incoming call. He reaches for the phone, sucking in a breath when Ellis' name flashes across the screen.

"Who is it?" Kieran asks, sipping his mocha.

"Ellis." It's not even nine, why is he calling so early?

"You gonna take that?"

He has to. It must be important. He presses accept.

"Ellis? What's wrong?"

"Nothing," Ellis says, but Dawson doesn't quite relax. "The hospital called." Right. Dawson didn't leave his number, so of course they called Ellis. "They're taking Cal off sedation, but it might be hours before he wakes up. Just wanted to let you know." He's quiet for a moment but Dawson feels like he's not done, so he waits. "You don't have to be there when he wakes up. Maybe it would be better if you weren't."

Dawson takes a moment to think it through. It sounds tempting, but also wrong. After what he told Kieran the other night, there's no pretending he's the worried, loving husband everyone would expect him to be. And he's already told Ellis about what Cal is like. He doesn't need to force himself to pretend anymore, at least not in front of them.

His conscience will let him have it, but he decides to take the offered escape route. "Will you let me know when you go?

"Of course."

"Thanks. How's work?"

"It's...improving." Ellis lets out a frustrated groan. "With a bit of luck, I'll sort it out before Cal gets back so he doesn't end up back in the hospital with a stroke or something."

Dawson chuckles. "Well, you have at least a few weeks before he's able to work, so..."

"Yay me," Ellis says, very dryly. Someone speaks in the background. Ellis says something back, then tells Dawson, "Gotta go. Talk to you later."

"Yeah. Bye."

"Bad news?" Kieran asks.

Depends who you ask. "They're waking Cal up today."

"Oh." Kieran frowns, making a sour face. "Do they have to?"

Despite himself, Dawson laughs. "Probably. I'm not gonna ask."

"Shame."

"What's a shame?" comes Gabe's voice. They look up to see him approach the table with a curious expression.

"Nothing. Just a joke," Dawson says quickly. Not everyone would find the dark humor funny.

"Nothing, huh?" Gabe says with a healthy dose of sarcasm. "Then why did your aura just get all gloomy?"

"Aura?" Dawson and Kieran say in identical, skeptical tones.

Gabe laughs. "Kidding. I can't actually see auras. You're just projecting a really strong yuck emotion."

Uh-huh. He must be pinging Gabe's 'superpowers' again. Or maybe Gabe just took one look at him and deduced it from his miserable face. "Okay, Sherlock."

Gabe doesn't seem offended. He never does, simply brushing off any skepticism he receives.

He doesn't let Dawson off the hook, though. "What is it?"

Dawson sighs, twirling the phone between his fingers. "That was Ellis. My brother-in-law," he clarifies. "They're taking Cal off sedation. He should wake up soon."

Gabe looks at him, his eyes overflowing with empathy. "And you aren't ready."

"No." The admission fills him with shame. "I know, I'm a horrible person."

"No, you're not," Kieran and Gabe say in unison.

Gabe takes a chair from the free table next to them and drops into it. "It's a fucked up situation, it makes sense that you have conflicting emotions about this." He drums his fingers on the table. "You know, if you need to talk about it with someone..."

Dawson shakes his head. "I appreciate it, I really do, but you didn't sign up to listen to me vent on the regular. Pretty sure they don't pay you for that."

Heaving a sigh, Gabe reaches across the table slowly, as if to not startle Dawson, and wraps his hand loosely around his forearm. His hand is warm and gentle, and the contact causes a strange sensation in Dawson's body. It's as if all the tension that's built up over the past few days loosens its hold, some of it leaving when Dawson exhales. He can feel his shoulders relaxing and his next breath comes much easier.

Jesus. What is that? Is he so touch-starved that the simplest, most innocent touch will awaken such a reaction in him?

"First of all," Gabe starts. "You can vent to me anytime you want. I'm happy to listen and share my wisdom." His lips twitch, and so do Dawson's. "Second, that's not what I was getting at."

"Huh?" What were they talking about again?

"I meant, you might want to talk to someone unbiased."

"A therapist?" Dawson takes a guess.

Kieran lets out a groan that leaves no doubt about his opinion on the matter.

Gabe shoots him a glare, but mostly keeps his attention on Dawson. "You get to vent all you want without feeling guilty because you'd literally be paying someone to listen."

"I mean, I'm not *against* the idea." That's true. "I just wouldn't know where to start looking, *how* to start. The last thing I need is someone watching with pity as I unload all my shit. I don't want to hear about loving myself or dissecting my childhood, and being told how I have mommy or daddy issues."

Gabe smiles like he knows something Dawson doesn't. "Lucky for you, I have someone who'd be a perfect fit." He lets go of Dawson and stands up. Even after he stops touching him, Dawson feels much better than he did before.

He watches Gabe disappear in the staff room. He comes back a minute later, holding up what looks like a business card. He hands it to Dawson.

"Ashley Cleaver," Dawson reads out loud. "Is that your therapist?"

"That's my cousin." He holds up his hands. "I promise I'm not biased. Ash can be a bit unorthodox, but I guarantee there won't be any pitying looks or hand holding."

Someone who'd let Dawson vent while not treating him like a snowflake. Okay, that doesn't sound too terrible.

He pockets the card. "Thank you."

"Don't mention it." Gabe smiles, then makes a face when a small group of people flows into the cafe. "There we go again. Sorry, guys, I'll catch up with you later."

"Don't let us keep you," Dawson says, finally digging into the cinnamon roll while it's still warm.

"Really?" Kieran asks incredulously when Gabe's gone.

"Hey. I'm desperate."

Kieran blows a raspberry. "Okay. Fair."

"Why do you hate therapy so much, anyway?"

"Because the only reason people go into the field is so they can feel superior to everyone else."

Dawson senses a history there, but he doesn't want to pry.

"Okay, fair," he repeats Kieran's previous words, earning a stink-eye.

"What are your plans for today?"

"Work. I took extra shifts at the shelter this week just to escape reality."

"I approve. Especially since furry four-legged creatures get to benefit from it."

"Yup. It's a win-win." It's not a secret that the volunteer work is as much for his benefit as for the dogs. He always feels better when he's there.

If only dogs could solve all his problems.

Chapter 7

"OKAY, DONUT." DAWSON KNEELS and scritches behind Donut's ears. As a reward, he gets a gust of dog breath in his face as Donut pants happily, craning his head to show where he wants to be scratched. Dawson is more than happy to oblige. He loves all the dogs at the shelter, but he and Donut just bonded from the start. "I'll see you tomorrow, you little monster."

Donut whines in protest when Dawson pulls away and shuts the kennel door. His heart breaks as it always does when Donut lifts up his paw, his claws hooking into the door like he's trying to reach for Dawson.

"Don't make it harder than it already is," he begs, placing his palm over Donut's paw. "Be good. See you soon."

"Heading off?" Aubrey, one of the employees, smiles at him on his way out.

"Yeah." He'd rather stay here, make himself busy with cleaning the kennels and playing with the dogs. "I'll be back tomorrow."

"Right," Aubrey says. "You took on extra shifts this week."

"I might do the same next week." He's not sure how long Cal will stay at the hospital, but he wants to take advantage of the time he has. Once Cal is awake and back home he won't be happy with Dawson spending all his time away. He'll probably need help when they discharge him, but in the meantime Dawson can keep himself busy instead of agonizing over what's going to happen next.

Aubrey perks up. "Oh, that would be great, actually. Two of our volunteers are on a holiday. We can make do without them, but an extra pair of hands always comes in, well, handy."

"I'll try to make it, then." He likes being useful. And if he gets to spend more time with the dogs that's just the cherry on top.

In his car, he checks his phone before leaving. There's a text from Ellis and the notification has Dawson's heart galloping into his throat.

Ellis: *I'm at the hospital. Call me.*

His thumb is so shaky he nearly misses the dial button.

Ellis picks up immediately. "Dawson."

"Hey. I'm sorry. I was at the shelter and I can't have my phone on around the dogs and—"

"Dawson, it's fine," Ellis puts a stop to Dawson's nervous rumbling.

Taking a few breaths to calm himself, Dawson asks. "Did he code again?"

"No. It's..."

The silence tells Dawson all he needs to know.

"Is he awake?"

"More or less. He's been in and out." Ellis sounds weird, so there must be something else.

"Okay. But that's good, right? That's normal."

"Yeah. That's not...There's something else," he confirms Dawson's suspicions.

"What?"

"I think it'd be better if the doctors explained. In person."

Well, that's not ominous at all.

"Alright, yeah." Dawson puts the key into the ignition. "I'm on my way."

He finds Ellis outside the waiting room, talking on his phone. He only catches a few words that tell him it's work related and not good.

"Yes. Yes, I'm aware, believe it or not, but I just went to see him and—" He breaks off when he spots Dawson. "I'll call you back," he says and pockets his phone. "Hey."

"Hey." Dawson studies him. He looks like he hasn't slept in days, which probably isn't inaccurate. "Work?"

Ellis sighs, pinching the bridge of his nose. "Just when I think things can't get more complicated." Before Dawson can ask, Ellis points at the entrance and says, "Let me get a doctor."

Inside, he speaks to the receptionist who nods amicably and makes a call. Shortly after, Doctor Connelly comes to see them.

"Mr Reeves," she says to Dawson only, so she must have already talked to Ellis.

"Just Dawson is fine." He hasn't been called by his last name as many times in five years as he has in the last few days, and it's getting under his skin.

The doctor nods. "As I explained to Mr Reeves..." She glances at Ellis, "Cal started to regain consciousness today. We've been testing his responses to various stimuli. He's fully responsive to auditory and visual stimuli, obeys commands, and his motor control is remarkable, considering he's been in an induced coma and undergone two surgeries."

"But?" Dawson prompts when she doesn't continue. Next to him, Ellis shifts on his feet.

"Cal struggles to recall events and facts."

Dawson lets the words sink in. "Are you talking about amnesia?"

"That's the conclusion we've come to, yes."

"He doesn't remember the accident?" That's not unusual, is it? It makes sense that the brain would want to spare you the trauma.

"Not just the accident," Ellis says, his tone sending a chill down Dawson's spine.

"Like, short-term memory loss?" It's called retrograde amnesia, he thinks. That's what they call it in the movies. But how come no one mentioned the possibility to Dawson? There must be something in all those tests they did. Something in the brain scans.

Just how much has Cal forgotten? Is it weeks, or maybe months? What if it's years? The mere idea makes Dawson's head spin. But when he looks at Ellis and notices how pale his skin is and how all the energy seems to have been sucked out of him, he has a feeling that reality is even worse.

"Cal doesn't remember anything."

Dawson frowns. "About?"

"Anything."

"What?" A nervous chuckle spilling from his lips, Dawson's turns to the doctor. "I don't understand."

"Cal doesn't seem to be able to retrieve any personal information. He doesn't know where he is, what year it is. He doesn't recognize his name."

"How's that possible? You didn't say anything about a brain injury."

"The initial tests only revealed cerebral hypoxia. We ran a CT and MRI again after the surgery. Cal *was* clinically dead for over a minute, but the results came back clear. There's no visible injury. It's possible the event, or the hypoxia impacted specific centers in the brain that store long-term memories. He has no issue retaining new memories, though. So far."

"Does that mean that he'll start to remember, eventually?" Ellis asks.

"There are no guarantees. The brain is a complicated thing. Most people experiencing amnesia begin to regain their memories to an extent, usually within the first few weeks post trauma."

"To an extent," Ellis echoes.

"I'm sorry I can't give you all the answers," the doctor says, genuinely apologetic. "I've shared with you everything we know."

"What happens now?" Dawson asks, feeling strangely hollow and numb. Shouldn't he be freaking out? Asking more questions? What's the protocol here? This is huge. This changes everything.

"We'll keep monitoring him. Test him every few hours. He'll need to start rehab and continue with it after we discharge him."

Dawson meant what happens now that Cal has forgotten who he is. How do you treat someone like that?

"How long until he can go home?" Ellis asks.

"Given he's been unconscious for almost four days and that he had two invasive surgeries—one week, minimum. It all depends on how well he's healing and if there are any complications." She looks at Dawson, smiling a little. "You can see him now if you'd like."

Right. That's what any normal person would want if their spouse woke up from a coma, right?

Apathetic, Dawson merely nods, looking over at Ellis when he doesn't follow. "You're not coming?"

"I've already seen him. He didn't recognize me." It's impossible to miss how much it bothers him. "Go," he tells Dawson when he hesitates.

Unsure, he follows the doctor, feeling as though he's walking to his execution. How does he act around Cal? He was unsure how to behave around him when Ellis told him they would be waking Cal up, but now? How do you act around someone who has no idea who you are, when you remember every single thing?

"We're not going to the ICU?" Dawson asks when the doctor leads him to another wing.

"My apologies, I forgot to mention. Cal has been moved to a private room. Since he's fully conscious and able to breathe on his own, there's no reason to keep him in the ICU."

Dawson nods absently, then braces himself when they stop in front of the room where Cal must be. His stomach churns threateningly and he forces himself to breathe through it. It wouldn't do if he threw up on the doctor's shoes.

Doctor Connelly pushes the door open.

Cal is lying in the hospital bed, his upper half slightly propped up with a pillow. There's no tube sticking out of his chest anymore, just an IV drip in his left hand which a nurse is changing the bag for. The bruises on his face have faded to yellowish-green, the abrasions partially healed now.

"Is he awake?" Dawson asks, because Cal's eyes are closed.

"He dozed off again a few minutes ago," the nurse says, taking the empty bag and putting it on a trolley before leaving the room.

"You can stay if you want," Doctor Connelly says. "Or we can call you when he's awake."

He doesn't want to stay, doesn't want to be here at all. But he can't say that, can he? He knows what everyone must think, what the doctors and nurses must think. What do they expect him to be doing? Bawling his eyes out? Have a breakdown because his husband lost his memories? Because he probably doesn't remember their time together?

"I'll stay." Better to rip it off like a bandaid.

The doctor nods and steps out, shutting the door behind her.

Dawson watches Cal for a long while before biting the bullet and sitting down by his bed. It's a strange sight, seeing him like this. His face has never been so serene, not even in his sleep. There's always this perpetual hard edge to it. Dawson likes to refer to it as Cal's personal resting bitch face—in his mind only, of course. The sharpness is usually exaggerated by the strong cut of Cal's jaw, always visible because he never lets his facial hair grow past a five o'clock shadow. After four days at the hospital, he's sporting a short beard. It makes him look softer, if a little older.

Dawson must make some kind of noise, or maybe Cal just senses someone in the room with him. A soft groan comes from him, his face no longer so peaceful. The space between his brows pulses, and his eyelids move without opening.

Straightening in the chair, Dawson leans forward, watching Cal's face.

"Cal?" It comes out barely a whisper but Cal hears it. Opening his eyes, he blinks several times, his head lolling towards Dawson. He looks at him through half-lidded eyes, the blue of his irises darker and deeper than Dawson remembers.

Cal sucks in a sharp breath, his body visibly locking up as the machines go off. A sense of déjà vu overtakes Dawson, making him freeze. Oh God, why does this always happen when he's here? Forcing himself to snap out of his stupefied state, he jumps to his feet, set on getting help. He doesn't need to, in the end. The nurse who was here before walks in, taking in the scene before her.

Part of Dawson expects to be yelled at and chastised, the nurse demanding what he did. He swallows up his apology and frivolous explanation when he sees the nurse's unperturbed expression. In a trance, he watches as she strides past him, giving Cal's vitals a quick glance before doing something that makes the monitors go quiet. She checks the IV, adjusts it slightly, then turns to Dawson.

"I'm sorry. I didn't mean—" Dawson stammers, trying to calm his own racing heart.

"Not your fault," the nurse says, the picture of calm. "His BP just went up for a moment. He might be a bit jumpy at first, so go easy on him."

When Dawson looks at Cal, he finds his eyes on him already. Carefully, he lowers himself into the chair again, trying to maintain eye contact. There's something in Cal's gaze—not recognition, not quite, but he's not looking at Dawson like one would at a complete stranger. The nurse is watching them, Dawson can feel it.

"Cal? Do you know who this is?" she asks, speaking slowly.

Cal doesn't reply, just continues looking at Dawson. His chest rises and falls quicker with each breath, but the machines don't go off again. What happens is much worse.

Cal's fingers twitch, and then he's moving his hand, inching it towards Dawson until it reaches the edge.

Dawson just stares at it like Cal's offering him a gun instead of his hand.

What should he do? What will the nurse think if he doesn't take Cal's hand? What will Cal think? Or do?

It's fine. He's just overthinking it. He can hold Cal's hand, can't he? The world won't end.

He raises his trembling hand and gently slides it into Cal's open one. He's careful not to dislodge the BP monitor or the IV, but Cal doesn't seem to care. His fingers curl around Dawson's, and he gives them a gentle squeeze. Feeling like he's going to throw up, Dawson pulls away, beyond caring what anyone will think of his strange behavior.

"I'll give you some privacy," the nurse says, sparing them both another look before leaving.

"Do you know who I am?" Dawson asks when he can't bear the staring contest any longer.

Cal studies his face, and his expression shutters. "I'm sorry."

The relief is unexpected. Why is he relieved that Cal doesn't recognize him?

"It's okay," he says. "I'm Dawson. Your..." The word burns a hole in his throat. "We are married."

He would've expected some kind of reaction—shock, surprise. Anything, really. But Cal's expression doesn't change.

"Are you hurt?" Cal asks in a raspy voice, raising his hand and reaching for Dawson's face. Before he can touch him, Dawson draws back so fast the chair screeches with it, close to toppling over.

Cal's eyes grow wide.

"I don't..." He lets his hand flop back and winces. "Sorry. I can't...Everything is blurry." His voice is hoarse, barely recognizable. It must hurt to be talking after being intubated this whole time.

Trying to get his racing heart under control, Dawson says in a tight voice, "Just take it easy. You've been under for days." It's okay, he tries to assure himself. Cal isn't going to hurt him. He's just confused and in pain, dosed up on morphine and who knows what. He couldn't hurt him if he tried.

"I saw you," Cal says. "You were hurt."

What does he mean he *saw* Dawson? Did Cal dream about him? Maybe had a flashback? But he said he doesn't remember him. He tried to touch Dawson's face—does that mean he saw him being injured there? That would be ironic, since the only reason for Dawson to be hurt like that would be thanks to Cal.

"I'm fine, as you can see," he says, a rush of resentment filling his chest. He needs to get out of here. Now. "Sorry. I...I should let you rest." He flees—there's no other word for it. It's not until he shuts the door, knowing Cal is on the other side, that he can breathe again.

"What do you mean he saw you?" Ellis asks, looking like he can't decide whether he's worried or happy that Cal might be remembering something.

"I don't know. Maybe in a dream?" That would make the most sense. "He said—he said I was hurt. When he saw me." Doesn't exactly narrow down which occasion he was referring to.

Ellis frowns. "But he didn't remember you?"

"I don't think so." He doesn't tell Ellis about Cal wanting to hold his hand.

Ellis studies him and something shifts in his gaze. "Were you hoping he wouldn't remember you?" It doesn't sound like an accusation, but Dawson goes still. Ellis must notice his reaction. "It's okay. No one can blame you. I certainly don't."

Unsure what to say to that, Dawson asks "What are you going to do? With the company and everything? He can't work like this."

Ellis lets out a groan so loud the floor nearly shakes with it. "Oh, shit. I didn't even..." He runs a hand over his face. "Fucking great. Just what I needed, on top of everything."

Dawson winces in sympathy. "I'm sorry. Did you speak to the police?"

Ellis nods. "And to a lawyer. The police will want to know Cal's awake, but..." He waves a hand in the general direction of the ward. "This changes things."

To put it plainly. How do you take a statement from someone who doesn't remember anything?

A wave of gratitude washes over Dawson. God, he has no idea what he'd do if Ellis wasn't here. He could never do this alone. Sure, he wouldn't be completely alone. He has Kieran and he had to spend a full hour the other night convincing Olivia that no, she doesn't have to come down to GC and make sure Dawson isn't having a mental breakdown (which he kind of is, but he doesn't need his sister to witness it).

He rakes his gaze over Ellis, noticing not for the first time the shadows under his eyes and the tension rolling off him.

He makes his decision.

"You should go home. You're exhausted. I'll stay."

Ellis barks out a laugh. "Don't be silly. What for? He's gonna be in and out of it for a while."

"I'd feel like crap if I went home." He'll feel like crap if he stays too, but at least he can convince himself he's not being selfish.

"Well, don't. You don't owe him shit," Ellis says, voice stern.

"But—"

"Dawson." Dawson shuts up. "This doesn't change anything. He's the same person he was before he arrived at the hospital. I know seeing him like this is pulling at your delicate heartstrings, but don't be fooled. He's no poor bastard. He got himself into this mess."

As harsh as that sounds, it lifts a heavy weight off Dawson's chest. He probably needed to hear it from someone else, someone who actually cares for Cal.

"I could come back tomorrow."

Ellis sighs, but doesn't push it. "Sure."

Chapter 8

At 10 o'clock sharp, the door to Cal's room flies open, signaling it's time for a torture session. This isn't fair. He already had one yesterday. Why does he have to do this every day? Three times a day, actually, if he counts the times he has to do it on his own.

"Good morning!" Eddie beams at him, unbothered by the scowl that must have overtaken Cal's face. "Well, aren't you glad to see me?" he teases, sauntering over with a grin. Does he like seeing people in pain? That must be it.

"I think I prefer the nurse who came to change my dressing," Cal says dryly.

Eddie gasps, placing a hand over his chest. "Rude." He winks, dropping the pretense, "Come on, I'll go easy on you." The glint in his eyes says otherwise. "Okay, sit up straight."

Bracing himself, Cal places both palms on the bed and pushes himself up, gritting his teeth as the movement makes the foot-long wound running down his belly sting like hell. At least he's mostly upright already, like he's been since he woke up. The position makes sleeping uncomfortable, but the nurses said he has to stay like that until his lung is fully healed. He's sure that by the time he leaves the hospital, his ass is going to be flat as a pancake.

"Good. Now, deep breath," Eddie instructs, inhaling deeply to demonstrate as if Cal doesn't know how breathing works.

Inhaling carefully, Cal pushes past the discomfort and fills his lungs with as much air as he can. Jesus. Why is breathing so important, anyway? He can function with one lung, no?

"There you go," Eddie praises. "Hold it. Aaand out, nice and steady. Again. That's it. Great."

He makes Cal repeat it ten times, then brings his palms together with a clap. "Alright, let's warm up your muscles a little."

Groaning miserably, Cal pulls his blanket off. Suspecting what's coming, he shimmies down the bed until he's mostly flat. It actually feels good to lie down like this. He should cherish it before he has to sit up again.

"Put your hands under your lower back," Eddie says. "We'll do some pelvic tilting."

Sounds riveting. "You mean *I* will."

Eddie's grin nearly splits his face in half. Yeah, he definitely enjoys seeing others suffer. "I'm your emotional support. Now, suck your belly in."

Letting his expression speak for him, Cal does as told. Eddie drags him through three different abdominal exercises that leave him sweating and shaking. This is ridiculous. He's barely done anything, but it feels like he's climbed a mountain. The human body is stupid.

Halfway through his knee rolling exercise, someone knocks on the door.

"Come in!" Eddie calls out.

The man from yesterday. He was one of the first people Cal saw after he woke up, the first altogether if he omits the staff. Cal's brother, as the man told him. He tried to hide it, but Cal could see the hurt when he admitted he doesn't remember him.

And now he can't even recall his name. Way to twist the knife.

"Oh. Hey." The man—his brother—says, eyes flicking between Cal and Eddie. "I can come by later—"

"That's okay. My job here is done for today," Eddie says, turning to Cal and raising an eyebrow. "How often are you going to do these?"

Cal sighs. "The breathing exercise every hour, eight to ten times. Three times a day for the rest."

Eddie smiles, pleased. "And?"

"A short walk every hour.".

"Atta boy." Eddie grins. "See you later, Cal."

As much as he likes seeing Eddie go, he's not sure what to do with his brother.

"Hey," his brother says, shifting awkwardly on his feet. Cal feels for him. It's kind of comforting to see him as out of his depth as Cal is.

"Hi. Eli?" he tries, knowing he got it wrong when not-Eli's face shutters.

"Close. Ellis." He walks over to the chair by the bed and sits down.

"Right. Sorry."

"Do you need help?"

Cal pushes until he's almost upright and leaning against the pillows. "I'm fine, thank you."

Ellis nods stiffly, interlacing his fingers and looking like he'd rather be anywhere else.

"Thanks for stopping by," Cal says. He figures it's the polite thing to say. "Is Dawson with you?"

He hasn't been able to get the man who claimed to be his husband out of his mind. The second Cal opened his eyes and found himself looking at Dawson, everything in his body just...shifted. Came to life. Like someone set him on fire, but instead of pain he only felt warmth spreading into every cell of his being. He had no idea who Dawson was, not logically, but he ached to be close to him, to touch him.

But Dawson had left in a hurry. It must've been something Cal said, or did, that upset him.

"No," Ellis says, something dark in his tone. "He might stop by later. This whole thing shook him pretty bad."

So he *is* upset that Cal can't remember. "I'm sorry. I wish I could remember you." Remember anything, really. "The doctors say it might come back to me eventually."

"Yeah, maybe." He doesn't seem comforted by it. "How are you feeling?"

Physically or otherwise? "I'm alright." When Ellis gives him a look full of skepticism, he admits, "Everything hurts, even with morphine. They assigned me a physiotherapist, and it's torture."

Ellis' face softens. "Two surgeries and a huge-ass scar. No wonder." He leans back in the chair, looking like he could fall asleep.

Now that Cal takes the time to look him over, it's clear Ellis is exhausted. There are shadows under his eyes, and he seems to be struggling not to let his eyelids droop. His skin is paler than Cal's, but not by much. Would people say they look alike? They have the same dark hair and blue eyes, though Ellis' are a lighter shade. His cheeks are shaved, his nose straighter. There are some similarities, but not enough that the sight of him causes some visceral reaction in Cal.

Unlike yesterday, when the sight of his own reflection in the bathroom nearly made him lose his balance. And it wasn't because of how haggard he looked, or because he didn't recognize his own face. Because he did. Kind of. A single glimpse made him want to put his fist through the mirror. He had to look away because the sudden surge of anger and hatred made him so dizzy he barely managed to keep himself upright.

He didn't recognize himself, but his subconscious did, somehow. Does his reaction mean that he's a bad person? If he is, how had he lived with himself for this long? But he can't be too bad, right? Bad people don't have other people visit them at the hospital. Right?

"So, what have the doctors told you?" Ellis' voice brings him back to the present.

"That I was driving and crashed, then brought here with a collapsed lung and shallow breathing. That I was sedated for a few days. That my heart stopped beating during surgery and that's why I might be confused and having issues remembering stuff," he parrots what he was told.

There were other things, of course. They told him his name and gave him a brief rundown on his bio, none of it ringing any bells. Caledon Reeves, 38 years old, lives here in Gold Coast with his husband.

"Drunk driving," Ellis says.

"What?"

"You were drunk driving. That's why you crashed."

"Why would I drink if I was about to drive?"

Ellis lets out an ugly snort. "Well, it seems to be your Achilles' heel."

That's... No one told him, no one's even *mentioned* that. Isn't it something he should know about?

"I'm sorry. I don't remember," he repeats like a broken record. "I don't feel like drinking." Is it because of the meds they're keeping him on? Or just because his body is too tired to summon up the craving?

"You're probably high on morphine and shit, so..." Ellis says, adding to Cal's theory.

Cal watches him closely, noticing the clench of his jaw and how Ellis can't quite meet his eyes. "You're angry with me."

Ellis exhales harshly and fixes him with a hard look. "You've done some stupid shit, Cal, but this..." He gestures vaguely towards Cal. "I didn't even know. Dawson had to tell me."

A chill runs down Cal's spine.

Dawson.

He was so...skittish yesterday, barely able to look at Cal. And the way he took off so suddenly...

Of course this is hard for him. To see his husband like this, knowing Cal has no idea who he is or what they are to each other...

Well, that's not quite true. Even without his memories, Cal can feel it. The connection he has with Dawson. He must love him very much, even if he can't remember.

Ellis, on the other hand... He gets nothing when he looks at him.

"We're not close?" Cal asks.

"You could say that." If they're not, then why is Ellis here? Why was he here yesterday? Why does he care? "We own a business together. You took over when our dad passed away, stayed here. I moved to Sydney to run the office there."

So that's why. It's all business for him.

Cal should probably ask about their dad, but it's hard to care when he can't remember caring in the first place.

"I...don't think I'll be able to work anytime soon." More like ever. Where would he even start? And he's supposed to be in charge? There's no way.

"Yeah, I figured," Ellis says, looking more exhausted by the second. He sighs and smoothes down his suit. "Don't worry, I'll take care of it. As usual." Cal winces. "I have to go. I have a meeting."

"Thanks again for coming to see me," Cal says quietly as Ellis walks to the door. "And for sorting things out at work."

Giving him a stiff nod, Ellis opens the door and walks out.

Cal's body feels like one giant bruise when he wakes up from a nap. Despite the stitches in his abdomen and chest, it's his lower half that feels the worst. His ass has gone numb, and his legs are heavy as though infused with lead.

As much as he hates the exercises Eddie has given him, he has to, rather begrudgingly, admit that they make him feel better, especially when he's so stiff. Figuring he might as well get it over with, he slides down the bed until he's lying flat and starts doing them one by one, even adding two repetitions for each as Eddie encouraged him to do. It makes his wounds sting, but he can feel his muscles warming up and relaxing, so he pushes through. The more effort he puts in, the easier it will get and the quicker he'll heal. He can't wait to get out of here and go home with Dawson.

He tries not to be too cranky that Dawson hasn't come to see him in two days. He's aware that Dawson likely has more important things to do, as Ellis does, than to sit at Cal's bed and hold his hand. Plus,

Ellis said Dawson is still coping with the whole situation, and no one can blame him. But it's hard to employ logic when he misses him so much.

He knows it doesn't make sense—how can you miss someone who's a virtual stranger? Except Dawson doesn't feel like a stranger. On the contrary. He feels like home.

Finishing the last exercise, Cal rests for a bit before getting out of bed. This morning, he managed to walk without help for eight minutes. If he can make it ten this time, he'll be happy.

He walks around for five minutes before he notices his bladder is trying to get his attention. With a sigh, he heads over to the en-suite bathroom. He pointedly ignores looking in the mirror, keeping his gaze downcast and watching his steps. After relieving himself and washing his hands, he heads back to the room. His heart stutters when he opens the door.

Dawson stands in the center of the room, looking confusedly at the empty bed and rumpled sheets.

"Hello," Cal croaks out.

Hazel eyes flick towards him, widening as Dawson takes him in.

"Oh. Hi." His gaze rakes over Cal, making him feel a little self-conscious about his appearance. "Sorry for barging in. There was no answer when I knocked and..." He trails off, licking his lips. "How are you?"

It takes Cal a minute to formulate an answer. He can't take his eyes off Dawson, fighting the urge to stride over and do...something. Caress his face, take him in his arms, make sure he's okay. It's the same urgency he felt when he first saw Dawson sitting there by his bed, looking small and vulnerable and startlingly familiar.

"I'm good." *Now.*

"Do you need help?" Dawson offers, probably because Cal keeps standing there and staring at him like a weirdo.

He's about to politely decline but changes his mind. If he has an opportunity to be close to Dawson, he sure as hell is going to take it. "I was about to take a walk down the hallway." Eddie said not to walk down the hallway unsupervised, but if Dawson's with him, it should be fine, right? "Maybe you could come with me?"

Panic fills Dawson's features. "Is that safe? I mean, shouldn't you have someone keeping an eye on you?"

A fluttery feeling expands in Cal's chest, the desire to reach out and touch Dawson intensifying. "You'd be with me. That's all I need."

Dawson looks at him with parted lips, still unsure. "I wouldn't know what to do."

Unable to stay away any longer, he makes his (very slow) way to Dawson. From this close, it's impossible to miss the alarmed look passing across Dawson's face. It doesn't sit right with Cal. Dawson shouldn't be looking at him like that. It reminds him of that time he tried to touch him and Dawson pulled away.

"Just stay with me and I'll be fine."

Dawson nods after a moment of hesitation. "Okay. Yeah, I can do that." He opens the door for Cal. "How far are we going?"

"I'll let you know when I need to turn around."

Dawson frowns. "But you'll still need to walk back."

Cal feels a smile pull at his lips, his skin tingling where his arm brushes against Dawson's. "It'll be fine, Dawson." He turns right, setting up a mental goal to walk all the way to the waiting area before having to turn around.

Dawson huffs, adjusting his step to match Cal's pace. "Like talking to a brick wall," he mutters, then snaps his wide eyes to Cal.

"Is that unusual for me?" Now he finally has a chance to learn more about himself. Dawson must know him the best, after all.

"Not really, no. You're pretty set in your ways."

Something about the way he says it rubs Cal the wrong way. Not knowing what to do with that, he says, "Thank you for coming. Ellis said you have a lot on your plate."

Dawson's cheeks darken, and he turns his gaze to the floor. "Sorry it took me so long to get here."

Cal feels a pang of guilt for putting that look on Dawson's face. He never meant to make him feel bad. "I'm sure you have other things to do. I'm not going anywhere for a while."

"Yeah, but with everything that's going on..." He glances at Cal. "I feel bad leaving you here."

"There's no need," Cal reassures him. "I'm a little bored—" Understatement. "But everyone is very nice. Except Eddie."

"Eddie?"

"My physiotherapist."

"Oh." Dawson laughs, the sound so sudden and refreshing Cal misses a step and has to brace himself against the wall.

Dawson's hands are on him in an instant, winding around his back and grabbing his waist.

"Shit. Are you okay?" He keeps his grip light, like he's afraid he might hurt him.

Oh, he's fine. Just embarrassed. "Wasn't looking."

Dawson heaves a sigh, looking a little shaken. "Almost gave me a heart attack."

"Good thing we're at the hospital, then," Cal says, finding his footing.

Letting out a small, breathy laugh, Dawson keeps a hand on Cal's arm as they move forward. "True."

Cal spends more time focusing on the sensation of Dawson's hands on him than where he's going. The place he touches him feels hotter than the rest of his body, like a brand. It feels right, so perfectly right, and he wants more of it. He's tempted to pretend to trip again just so Dawson will touch him more.

He doesn't realize how far he's walked until Dawson stops. "Are you okay? You're shaking."

Looking up, he can see he's walked all the way to the waiting area. There's no way he can go back without a short break.

"I'm fine. Just need to sit down for a bit." He finds the nearest chair and sits with Dawson's help. He doesn't really need it but he won't tell him that.

"Are you guys okay?" calls the lady behind the desk, watching them cautiously.

Dawson waves her off. "We're fine. Just taking a break." He takes the chair next to Cal, his expression disapproving. "Jesus, I told you."

"Yes, yes, I know." Smiling, Cal rolls his eyes. "We've already established I'm stubborn."

Dawson huffs, sounding both annoyed and amused. "What am I gonna do with you?"

Whatever you want, Cal's pining brain supplies unhelpfully. "I guess you'll have to keep an eye on me."

Dawson's reaction isn't what he'd expected. His smile disappears and his shoulders tense up. "Guess so."

The silence that follows is heavy and leaves Cal feeling cold and wrong. He wants to say something, but Dawson seems to be putting major effort into keeping his eyes averted.

Cal studies his profile, the slightly upturned slope of his nose and high, prominent cheekbones. His golden-brown hair curls at his temples, making Cal want to reach over and brush it to the side, just to see if it's as silky as it looks.

He wouldn't stop there. He'd touch Dawson everywhere, trace the contours of his face with his fingertips, memorizing it. Making sure he'd never forget again. Never again.

"Are you ready to go back?" Dawson asks, pulling him out of his daydream.

Calming his racing heart, Cal nods.

The walk back is even slower, and Dawson doesn't touch him this time. He stays close in case something happens, but to Cal the small distance between them is like a chasm. It only grows wider when they finally reach Cal's room, and Dawson doesn't waste time in putting more space between them.

But at least he doesn't leave. He watches as Cal wobbles to the bed and climbs into it like an old man.

Once settled in the least uncomfortable position he could find, Cal looks at Dawson. Despite wanting, so badly, to spend more time together, he's about to tell him he doesn't have to stay, that he's already done enough, but Dawson speaks first.

"You really don't remember, do you?"

The question catches him off guard. Has Dawson been hoping Cal would start remembering by now?

"You are...familiar," he says, choosing his words carefully. "I *know* I know you. It's all just...very hazy. I'm sorry."

For a split second, he thinks it's relief that passes across Dawson's face. But then he blinks, and it's gone. He must've imagined it.

Dawson hesitates before sitting down in the chair. "No, it's...it's okay. Just weird."

To put it mildly. Now that Dawson's here, Cal really wants to ask about his—about their life.

"How long have we been together?"

"Six years. Married for five," Dawson whispers.

Is that a long time? He's not sure. "How did we meet?"

Dawson inhales slowly, his fingers curling into his palms. "At an LGBT art expo. I was there with my sister but she had to leave, and then I bumped into you." He shrugs. "We started talking. You asked about my art and wanted me to show you pictures."

Cal wants to ask what LGBT means, but it's the last sentence that really catches his attention. "You're an artist?"

Dawson's eyes are hard and empty when he looks at him. "No."

Confused, Cal waits for him to say something else, but he doesn't. "I upset you. I'm sorry."

Dawson bites down on his lip and shakes his head. "Just feels strange thinking about it."

To him probably more than Cal. It's one thing not to remember anything and another to speak about it with someone you've spent years with and who should know this stuff.

Guilt crashes into him. "I hope I can remember about us one day." He really, really does. If the way he feels about Dawson now is any indication, they must've been wonderful together.

Dawson's eyes slide shut. His fingers curl into his palms. "I have to go." He stands up abruptly. "I—I'll see you later, okay?"

He's gone before Cal can say anything.

Chapter 9

"Have you been experiencing headaches?"

Cal sighs. They've been over this. So far, Carrie's asking the same questions she did two days ago. Even the memory tests they just finished were the same.

"No."

Carrie scribbles something in her notepad. She was surprised when Cal gave her the same answer the first time, somehow implying that tormenting headaches would be standard in his situation.

Cal's head was killing him when he first woke up and information was being rained on him from all directions. But he's been fine since.

"Dizziness, vertigo, nausea?"

"No, no, and no." He backtracks. "Actually, a bit of a stomach ache after they gave me solid food for the first time, but I'm fine now."

Carrie hums noncommittally, two small lines appearing between her brows.

"Is something wrong?"

"Not at all. It's just uncommon not to experience any side effects when the memory is impaired." She looks thoughtful.

"I thought my test results said there's no damage."

She gives him a smile that makes him feel like a child. "Scans don't always tell us everything. There's no physical injury to your brain, and yet..."

So basically, they don't know anything. Great. "How am I doing with this?"

She smiles for real. "A+. You're perfectly capable of creating and retaining new memories. Your analytic and problem-solving skills are unaffected, as is your communication." She pauses, studying him. "How are you emotionally? Have you been experiencing mood swings, or bouts of intense emotions, like anger, fear, or sadness?"

He shakes his head no for all of them, then remembers what happened in the bathroom the other day.

"There was a moment when I caught my reflection in the mirror, and I got...angry." The word doesn't quite fit. He'd compare it more to an uncontrollable rage.

She raises a curious eyebrow. "Oh, really? Was it just then, or has it happened since?"

He shifts on the bed, uncomfortable. "I've been careful not to look."

The second eyebrow joins the first. "You're avoiding your reflection?"

Cal shrugs, tension settling in his bones. He has a feeling he knows where this is going.

"You're going to make me look, aren't you?"

She lets out a small, breathless laugh. "I'm not very original, am I?" She stands up, putting her notepad and pen on the bedside table. "Nothing beats exposure therapy."

"Easy for you to say," he says, sliding his legs over the edge of the bed and rising to his feet with a wince. "I got it," he says when she lifts her hands as if to help him.

"Of course, you do," she says, amused, as though she finds his stubbornness endearing. She lets him take the lead, following him to the bathroom and standing next to him as they both face the mirror, though Cal keeps his gaze downcast.

"Alright, Cal. I need you to look. Take your time and tell me what you feel."

Taking the deepest breath his lungs allow him, he lifts his head.

His breath escapes him in a rush and his vision swims, making the sight of himself unfocused and misty. It's as though his own brain rebels against it.

He breathes through it, and his vision eventually sharpens.

"Tell me what you feel," Carrie nudges him gently.

"Anger," he presses out, gripping the counter. "Hatred. I want to—" *I want to hurt myself.* "I want to punch the mirror."

Carrie studies his face in the mirror. "Do you know why you feel that way? Is anything coming to you?"

Forcing himself to keep looking, he tries to think. Nothing comes up. These emotions are instinctual; like the feeling of excitement when he sees Dawson, or the deep-seated knowledge that he needs to take care of him. He can't explain it, it's just there.

"No. Sorry."

"That's okay. Chances are it's your brain's way of coping with information and facts that don't make sense to you."

"So what do I do?"

"Well, for one, you can stop avoiding your reflection." She grins at his scowl. "I'm not saying you should bulldoze through those emotions, but getting used to them and accepting them will eventually make them less intense and overwhelming."

Unlikely. But whatever.

"Okay."

They return to the room, and once Cal's settled in, Carrie is on him with more questions.

"You brother and husband have been to see you a few times now, correct? How did that go?"

His husband. "It was good." He thinks back on how heavy the air in the room was when Ellis visited him, and how Dawson left in a hurry. "But strange."

Carrie nods. "That's to be expected. Did you talk about the past?"

"Not much. I asked, but Dawson..." *Closed off the minute I asked.* "He seemed uncomfortable talking about it."

"Oh." Carrie's face falls. She probably feels bad for him. "I imagine he's going through a difficult time, seeing you here."

Ellis said something similar. "Ellis—my brother," he adds when it occurs to him, she might not recall the name, "Said Dawson was taking everything quite hard."

"Has anything reminded you of your time together?"

Dawson's face, tear-streaked and smeared with blood.

Dawson hugging himself as he lies on the floor, trembling.

Dawson—

"I've been having...dreams," he rolls the word over in his mouth.

"About Dawson?" She writes it down when he nods. "What kind of dreams?"

He doesn't really want to think about it, but Carrie should know, right? Maybe she can help him find out what it means.

"I keep seeing him hurt." He reluctantly elaborates when she gives him a confused look. "Blood on his face. Crying." An invisible vise closes inside his chest, making it hard to breathe. For a moment, he worries that something might be wrong with his lung again, but the feeling eases off as he focuses on evening out his breathing. "I want to save him. Protect him."

"It could be just dreams," Carrie says carefully. "It could be your brain projecting your accident onto someone else as an attempt at remembering." She taps her chin with the pen. "Or something might have happened in the past to Dawson and you're remembering. Maybe you could ask him next time he's here, so he can clarify for you."

The idea doesn't sit well with him. Dawson acts skittish when Cal asks him presumably normal questions, let alone something like this.

"Maybe."

"I have to admit, you're coping incredibly well," Carrie says, sounding awed. "Both mentally and physically. *And* emotionally."

It doesn't feel like it. "There's not much I can do. I mean, I'm stuck at the hospital, doing the same things every day. It's pretty straightforward. I'm more worried about the people who know me. Well, *knew* me."

"That's the thing about memory loss," she says ruefully. "It affects everyone around you."

So why is no one telling him what to do? Everyone talks about how recovery takes time, but what if—

"What if my memory never comes back?"

She sighs, as though she expected him to ask at some point. "I'll tell you what I tell all my patients who ask that same thing: If you can't remember the past, focus on building your future. This is a clean slate, Cal. It's scary and uncertain, but it's your chance to be the best version of yourself. So take it."

It sounds...nice. In theory. Starting anew might be easy—easier—for him, but what about Dawson and Ellis? They knew him before. What will they do if he's never the same person again?

It's a good half an hour before Carrie wraps the session up. By the time she leaves, Cal's tired and feels like he might actually have a headache. He thought that his sessions with Eddie were exhausting, but he's starting to reconsider.

Before he can settle down for a nap, there's a knock on the door.

He lets out an irritated groan. What now? There can't possibly be any more tests left to be done on him.

"Yes?"

All the irritation and annoyance disintegrate when Dawson appears in the doorway, timid as usual, and carrying a backpack.

"Hi." He summons a shaky smile. "Can I come in?"

Cal's heart gives a powerful thud. "Yes, of course."

He must be making a weird face, because Dawson asks, "What?"

"Nothing," Cal says quickly. "I just...I guess I didn't expect to see you today."

"Are you tired?" Dawson guesses, looking embarrassed. "I can go if you need rest."

"No!" Cal blurts out, short of catapulting himself from the bed to make sure Dawson doesn't leave. "No, that's not—I'm glad you're here. I just don't want to take up your time."

Dawson laughs, but his expression isn't amused. "All I have is time." He slings the backpack from his shoulder and makes his way over. Sitting down, he unzips it and pulls out two rectangular shaped items.

"I brought you something. This is your phone." He hands Cal the smaller of the two. Cal takes it awkwardly, turning it in his hand. "Sorry, I would've brought it sooner, but the screen was cracked from the crash, and I wanted to get it repaired first. And I brought your iPad." He puts the larger item on the bedside table. "They're both password protected but you can open it with your—"

Instinctively, Cal places his thumb over the small circle at the bottom of the phone. It vibrates and lights up, the screen revealing an image of a beach.

"Fingerprint," Dawson finishes with a small laugh. "I know you're not one for browsing the internet, you don't even do social media, but it should help you pass the time. You can download a reading app and get some books. Or something."

He hardly understands what Dawson's talking about, but he doesn't want to embarrass himself by asking. He doesn't care, anyway, his thoughts revolving around the man next to him who evidently put time and effort into making sure Cal has something to entertain himself with. He vaguely remembers mentioning how bored he gets here.

"Thank you." He hopes Dawson can hear the sincerity in his voice. "Really. I've been losing my mind a little."

Dawson shifts in the chair and rubs the back of his neck. "Yeah, I bet. I've only been to the hospital once, but God, it was torture."

Sensing a chance, Cal asks, "When were you in the hospital? Was it serious?"

Dawson chuckles. "My seven-year-old self would probably have something dramatic to say about it, but no. They just took out my tonsils. I went home the next day."

The answer is both relieving and disappointing. Of course, he's happy Dawson wasn't seriously injured, but it also gets Cal no closer to figuring out what his 'dreams' mean.

Turning his attention to the phone, Cal studies the colorful icons scattered over the screen. They don't seem familiar, but he instinctively knows what they mean—and they also have a description below. His eyes zero in on the one with four different-colored half-moons arranged into a shape that looks like a fan. The description says *Photos*, and his curiosity is peaked. There could be something to help him remember.

He taps the icon with his thumb, the action subconscious and familiar. The screen changes, showing countless little squares stacked in rows and columns. He swipes across the screen, rolling it down, searching for Dawson's face. He's not sure if he'll react as strongly to seeing his own face in the pictures as he did in the mirror, but hopefully Dawson's face will distract him.

He keeps swiping for a while, but there are no pictures of them—barely any people at all, actually. They all feature various sections of buildings, drawings, and numbers. Is this part of his job? Ellis said something about buildings.

"Are there any photos of us?"

Dawson seems taken aback. "Oh. I don't know." He pauses, chewing on his lip. "You've had several phones over the years. I'm not sure if you transferred all the media."

Cal looks at the phone. The pictures are divided by the month and year in which they were taken, the section he's at now showing pictures from March 2019. Clearly, he's been 'transferring the media'.

One picture in particular draws his attention. The person in it looks like Dawson, and is lying in the bed. He taps on it, and his mouth goes dry.

It *is* Dawson, with his silky-looking brown hair and long eyelashes casting shadows over his cheeks, lips red and slightly parted. He's on his stomach, one side of his face pressed into a pillow and his arms shoved under it. He's gorgeous.

And completely naked.

There are others, pictures of Dawson taken from different angles, while he's in this position.

Cal's heart rate goes rogue, heat spreading through his whole body. His insides feel hot, and his belly tingles as if someone tickled him from the inside.

He must make some kind of sound, because Dawson asks, "What?" and leans forward to see what Cal's looking at. He freezes.

"Oh my God," he gasps, his whole face red. "When did you—"

"I'm sorry," Cal blurts out, feeling ashamed. Dawson evidently didn't know Cal had taken those. "I didn't—I'll delete them." He taps the first picture with a shaky finger, trying to figure out how to get rid of it.

Before he can, Dawson says, "It's fine." He doesn't sound fine, avoiding Cal's gaze. "I was just...surprised." He gestures at the phone with a shaky hand. "I mean, obviously we'd just had sex, so... It's normal for people to have these..."

Cal frowns. That's...not right. Even if other people have them, there must be a reason why Dawson was shocked to see these. Shouldn't people ask each other before taking photos like this?

"But you're not comfortable with it." It's not a question. Dawson's shoulders curl inwards and he hugs himself. "And you didn't know I took them." Another not-a-question. Dawson's tiny headshake tells him everything he needs to know. He offers him the phone. "You should delete them."

Dawson's wide eyes snap up to him, and Cal hates the apprehension he sees in them. Dawson doesn't even protest. He takes the phone gingerly, like he's expecting Cal to change his mind.

"Thank you." His next exhale is full of relief. "Mind if I check the rest?"

"Go ahead."

For the next few minutes, the tension is so thick Cal almost chokes on it, his body tense. The heat he felt before has turned into ice, causing a whole new avalanche of emotions inside him.

"I...um," Dawson starts after what seems like an eternity. "I found a picture of us." His voice is small and empty, definitely not pleased by finding their picture. It makes Cal reluctant to look, but if Dawson is okay with him seeing it, then it can't be that bad.

"It's from a function I accompanied you to a few years back," he explains as Cal takes the photo in. Rage bubbles inside him when he sees himself, and he focuses on Dawson instead.

He's wearing a suit, similar to Ellis', just simpler, and his hair is longer and slicked back. He's beautiful as always, but something's not right. He doesn't look happy, even though they're there together, Cal's arm wound around his waist.

Slowly, Cal hazards another look at himself. Carrie wanted him to get used to seeing his face, so he might as well start now.

He hates it. There's a smile on his face, but it looks twisted. Cold. Just as his eyes.

"You look bored," Cal points out.

Dawson shrugs, licking his lips. "It's not my area. I didn't know how to act, and had no one to talk to."

"I was there. Why didn't you talk to me?"

Dawson scoffs. "You had better things to do than to hold my hand."

Cal would hold his hand any day, whenever Dawson asked.

"Then why did you come with me?"

Dawson looks at him. "Because you were my husband and I wanted to spend time with you."

So simple.

So why does it feel all wrong?

Swiping to the left, Cal finds another, similar photo. They're still at the function, just standing somewhere else. There are a couple more photos like that before another series of buildings comes up.

"That's all," Cal says, disappointed and relieved equally. He was curious and excited to see the pictures of them, or even just those of Dawson. But all the pictures he's seen have left an ugly, heavy feeling in his stomach.

"I might have some on my phone," Dawson says, pulling it out, his thumb flying over the screen with practiced ease. "Here. There are a few from our wedding."

Cal takes the phone from him, his mouth falling open at the sight of Dawson on their wedding day. He's so young and radiant—but, most importantly of all, he's smiling, wide and bright. His eyes sparkle with happiness and he looks at Cal like he's the most amazing thing in the world.

For once, Cal is smiling too. Not much, but enough to make his eyes crinkle and a dimple appear in his left cheek. And again, it all looks so...wrong.

"You look beautiful," Cal says, swiping through the photos. "Nothing more recent?" They've been together for six years. Surely, there must be more.

"You're a busy man."

"Who's this?" It must be from a hospital. There is a woman lying in a bed, her hair sweaty and plastered to her face, holding a baby. She looks exhausted, but happy. And so does Dawson, holding another baby and grinning ear to ear.

"That's Olivia, my sister." A soft smile grows on Dawson's lips. "That's when she just had twins. They're four now. Leia and Chloe."

Cal finds himself smiling at the photo. "They're very cute. Do we ever visit?"

Dawson's smile slips. "I do, sometimes. But like I said, you're busy and they live over two hours away."

Right. Busy.

There are a few more photos of Olivia and the twins, followed by a photo of Dawson with another man, both flushed and grinning, arms thrown over each other's shoulders.

Cal tilts his head, studying it. He's seen the man before. "Your friend?"

"Yeah. That's Kieran." Dawson's eyes flick to Cal's face. He looks nervous. "He's my best friend."

"I think I know him."

Dawson does a double-take. "Really? You've only seen him a couple of times."

Cal frowns. "Doesn't he come over if he's your best friend?"

"I usually go to his place, or we go somewhere else."

"You look happy."

"Yeah, we got a little drunk. It was ages ago." He runs a hand through his hair. "Well, he was more than a little. I don't drink anymore, not after—" He cuts himself off, looking away.

Cal has a feeling he knows what this is about. "After I started drinking?"

Dawson goes tense, fear flashing in his gaze. "You—You remember?"

"Ellis told me."

"What did he say?"

"That I crashed the car because I was drunk. And he implied it's not unusual for me," Cal adds testily.

"He shouldn't have said that," Dawson complains. "The doctors said we're supposed to try to trigger your memory by exposing you to familiar environments and patterns. Not by putting things in your head."

"But it was true."

"Still..."

"If it helps," Cal says, needing Dawson to know this, "I don't have any cravings now. Actually, I'm craving something sweet."

The food here is subpar at best, but Cal got a mini gingerbread muffin with his lunch yesterday. No matter how queasy his stomach has been since he's started eating normally, he swears he could have eaten a whole basket of those. He even asked one of the nurses who's always super nice to him if he could have some more, but she just laughed, as if he was a cute kid, and said they can't alter his diet. To say he's been thinking of today's lunch non-stop would be an understatement. Just two more hours...

"Really? You hate sweet stuff." He freezes, slapping his forehead. "Ugh, see? I shouldn't have said that."

Cal laughs, finding Dawson's frustration funny. "It's okay. What *do* I like?"

Dawson squints. "Not sweets."

Cal rolls his eyes. "Fine. Have it your way." It draws a chuckle from Dawson, the sound warm and beautiful, and God, he wants more of that. He wants to hear Dawson laugh, wants him to be happy and safe, always.

Some of the things that Carrie said this morning come back to him; how he seems to be coping well with his condition. It's...not exactly true. On the one hand, yes, he couldn't care less about his job, or his name, or what his hobbies are supposed to be. But on the other...

"I really wish I could remember you," he says, meaning every word. "I don't really care if I remember anything else, but you...I want to remember you."

Dawson looks stunned and on the verge of tears. Oh, crap. What did Cal say this time? Is Dawson going to bolt again? He really needs to learn to keep his mouth shut.

Wiping moisture from the corner of his eye, Dawson whispers, "It's alright. I'm not holding it against you."

This man...

If Cal can only do one thing in his life, it must be to protect Dawson. He *must* keep him safe.

"I'm holding it against myself. It's not fair to you. You come to see me and talk to me, and I don't even remember a single day of our life together." Anger bubbles up inside him again. He clenches his fists, trying to regain control. "I can feel it, you know?"

Dawson blinks. "Feel what?"

"How important you are to me. How much you mean to me." Dawson's speechless, his mouth agape and confusion written in his features. "I might not remember it here—" Cal touches his temple, then moves his finger to the center of his chest. "But I remember it here."

Whatever effect he'd expected his words to have, he hadn't thought they would make Dawson cry. "Dawson?" He pushes up on his hand, wincing at the pain that shoots through him when he turns, but he ignores it. "I'm sorry. I didn't mean to upset you."

Dawson laughs, sniffling. He wipes his face with his hands, shaking his head. "You know what? You don't need to remember me." He looks up, and the determination in his gaze effectively shuts down any protest Cal can come up with. "You don't need to remember anything. We can just make new memories."

Make new memories. That's what Carrie said. *If you can't remember your past, focus on building your future.* He's still unsure about it. Starting anew might be good for him, but not for the people around him.

But if Dawson wants to build something new with him...

"I'd like that," he says, his heart suddenly too big for his chest. Maybe they should've gotten rid of his lung after all, made more room. He's going to need it with Dawson in his life.

"Okay." A small, shaky smile appears on Dawson's lips, and in that moment, Cal swears he sees hope in his eyes.

"Okay," Cal echoes, matching Dawson's smile.

"Um, there's one more thing." Dawson reaches into his pocket. "The hospital gave it to me with the rest of your stuff." When he brings his hand up, he's holding a ring, not unlike the one he's wearing.

Cal looks at his bare hand. How come he didn't notice it was missing?

"I didn't realize," he admits.

"You probably had more important things to worry about."

Cal curls and uncurls his fingers and holds up his hand, looking up at Dawson in hope. "Would you mind?"

Dawson swallows, then nods. He gently takes Cal's hand and slides the ring onto his finger, sending a shiver through him.

Cal looks at it. It's such a small thing, but it causes a swarm of butterflies to fill his chest.

"Thank you."

Dawson smiles.

As far as new beginnings go, this isn't too bad.

Chapter 10

Five days and three hospital visits later, Dawson finds Cal the same way he did the last time—buried in a book. Well, in the iPad. It must be a good one, because it takes him a few seconds before he notices Dawson.

Dawson grins. "Am I interrupting?"

Cal puts the iPad aside, flashing him a smile. "Hi. Not at all. Come in."

Dawson takes his usual spot in the chair. "What are you reading? *Brisingr*?" Who knew Cal has a thing for dragons? Or fantasy?

Cal huffs. "I finished that series yesterday."

Dawson whistles. "You're on a roll."

"You mean bored?" Cal smirks. "This is another series. *The Twilight Saga*."

"Oh my God." Dawson covers his mouth, staring.

"What?"

"You're reading about vampires? You?"

Cal gives him an unimpressed look. "They're intriguing."

Taking a deep breath to compose himself, Dawson unzips his backpack. "Well, since you're such an avid reader now, you might appreciate these." He hands him a case containing his glasses.

Cal complained at their last visit that the letters get blurry if he reads for more than an hour. Dawson knows Cal is far-sighted, but he generally never used to bother wearing glasses unless he was reading something in bed before going to sleep—like financial reports or whatever. .

Pulling the glasses out, Cal studies them curiously before putting them on. He blinks a few times, probably trying to focus, and turns to Dawson.

Dawson smiles. "How's that?" Cal always hated wearing glasses, but in Dawson's opinion, they suit him. Thick, black, rectangular frames with a rounded bottom. They make the blue of his eyes pop. They also make him look like a nerd. Or a professor, especially with the short beard he's now sporting.

"Not very different."

"You likely won't notice the difference until you read. It should make your vision sharper."

"Oh. Thank you. That's very thoughtful."

So polite. Always so polite now. It messes with Dawson's head.

"If you like that, you'll like this even more." He pulls out his e-reader. "It's mine, but you need it more than me. It has a built-in light that's gentler on the eyes. The only thing is that it's registered under my account and you'll have to download the books again, so remember where you stopped before you switch."

Cal takes it carefully, cradling it like it's something fragile. "Thank you. I'll take good care of it, I promise."

Dawson's heart does something strange in that moment. Naturally, he ignores it.

"No problem," he mumbles. "So, tell me about *Twilight*."

On his way out, Dawson is approached by Doctor Lin. He's only met her once, when she was speaking with Cal and Dawson walked in. Cal seemed to like her.

"Let's talk somewhere private," she says, leading them through the maze of corridors until they reach a door with the number 3 on it. Inside, she gestures for Dawson to take a chair and sits opposite him.

Intertwining her fingers, she rests her forearms on the desk and smiles. "How are you, Dawson?"

"I'm good." It's a lie, and by the way she looks at him, he's not fooling anybody.

"I hope to speak to your brother-in-law at some point, but since Cal's going home with you, I wanted to talk to you first." She waits until he nods. "You've heard this from us before, but the brain is rather unique, and we can't certainly say what caused Cal's memory loss. I'm sure you're wondering about the possibility of his memories being restored."

Of course she's sure. Who wouldn't want their husband to remember, right?

"Yeah. And I guess you can't give me a definitive answer."

She chuckles briefly and leans back in the chair. "You're right, unfortunately. It's not uncommon to experience retrograde amnesia after a serious accident, but Cal's case is quite special." She shows her palms. "I can give you the same advice I've given to patients and families who were in a similar situation. You've probably been doing some of these already. The best thing to do is expose Cal to a familiar environment, engage him in activities that he used to do often. Talk about your history. It seems to be especially effective if there's a strong emotional connection to the memories." She gives him a meaningful look.

Dawson isn't an idiot. He knows what that look means.

"We'll have Cal come for a check-up in a month, to see if there's any change and also make sure he's healing nicely. Aside from the impaired memory, Cal is doing very well. If he sticks to the regime, he'll be fine to return to regular daily activities and more challenging exercise in four to six weeks. It's *crucial* to remain physically active, especially in the initial post-op stages. As for limitations—no strenuous activity in the first few weeks, no lifting heavy stuff." She raises an eyebrow but her lips twitch. "That includes engaging in intimate activities."

Dawson's stomach turns. He wills his expression to stay impassive. "That's not going to be an issue."

"I imagine things might be quite strained while he gets used to his life again. I know this will be hard on you as his husband but try not to take it personally if he's cold and withdrawn. You can expect frequent mood swings, anxiety, confusion." She pauses, leaning forward again. "In some cases, the patient can become aggressive when under pressure. Some people find therapy helpful."

Dawson almost laughs. She has no idea. Cal, cold and moody? Shocker. It's ironic how calm and pliant Cal has been since the surgery. Then again, who wouldn't be pliant after having their stomach sliced open and a garden hose sized tube rammed in their chest?

"I understand," he says at last.

The doc smiles. "If everything goes well, Cal will be ready to go home on Wednesday." Shit, that's in two days. "The discharge papers will contain all the information you need regarding what Cal can or cannot do, including how to care for the wounds as they heal. But remember—if unsure, you can always reach out to us."

Right.

Because he'll be the one to keep an eye on Cal's recovery. He'll be in charge of making sure he heals properly.

Right.

Dawson nods, wiping his sweaty palms on his jeans. He stands up on shaky legs. "Thank you." He leaves the office in a trance, trying to reconcile what all this means for him.

It means you're exactly where you started. Just worse.

He needs to go to Kieran's place, pack up his stuff. The holiday is over. It's time to come back to reality.

∽

"I can't believe you're going to do this," Kieran grinds out, gripping the steering wheel. Probably so he doesn't choke Dawson in a fit of indignation.

"And what would you do in my place? Please, I'm all ears," Dawson snaps, letting his frustration bleed into his voice. He's grateful for all of Kieran's help, for being there for Dawson and letting him stay even when it stirred shit up with his now ex-girlfriend, but he's tired of having to explain himself. Everyone thinks it's so easy to just let go and never look back.

"I sure as fuck wouldn't play house with my abusive asshole of a husband just because he knocked a screw loose. Dawson, you were going to ask for a *divorce.*"

Great. Just what he needs. Another reminder to set off the guilt trip all over again.

"Yeah, well, that was before he forgot everything about his life and himself."

"And you," Kieran reminds him, as if Dawson needs it. As if Cal's peculiar behavior and the way he acts with Dawson at the hospital isn't enough of a mindfuck.

Dawson is clueless when it comes to memory or the brain, but even he knows that Cal's abrupt personality change can't be normal. Even with his memory gone, there must be something of the old Cal left in him, right? People can change their opinions and beliefs, but they don't change their true nature. There must be plenty left in his subconscious, all his learned behaviors and traumas and addictions. Kind of like muscle memory.

Or maybe not. Maybe he's just making stuff up.

Because the way Cal treats him? The way he speaks to Dawson? Dawson's never seen him so calm and subdued. Granted, it could be Cal's pain meds that make him so, but meds don't explain why Cal looks at him like Dawson is the answer to everything. They don't explain the open curiosity in his gaze as he asked about the first time they met. Or, heavens above, his sudden affinity for teen fiction.

They certainly don't explain why underneath Dawson's apprehension and deep-seated fear, there's an element of intrigue, a little voice that demands to find out how much Cal has changed and what kind of man he is now.

Not that any of that matters. Cal might not remember who he was, but Dawson does. He remembers everything.

"You're right. He doesn't remember me. So you don't have to worry about me."

"Is that it?" Kieran demands. "You think it's fine because he doesn't remember you? What happens if he does?!"

Instinctual fear rises inside Dawson at the thought. "I'll cross that bridge if I ever get to it."

Kieran scoffs. "Yeah, I'm sure you will."

"What's that supposed to mean?"

Slapping his hand against the steering wheel, Kieran says, "This is what you do, Dawson. You always come up with an excuse, something to make you stay."

The words hit him, sharp and hot. Is this what Kieran thinks of him?

It's not like he's wrong, is it?

"I'm not making excuses for him." Kieran's eyeroll causes the next words to come out angrier than Dawson had intended. "I know what kind of person he is and I haven't forgotten the shit he's done. I'm just saying—" He stops, realizing how desperate he sounds. "Look, no one could see this coming. And everyone expects me to look after him."

"Screw what everyone expects," Kieran bites out. It almost makes Dawson smile. His friend has always been a little untamed. "Why can't you just hire a carer? It's not like you can't afford it."

It's crossed his mind, but it doesn't sit well with him. "And leave him with a stranger?"

"You're a stranger to him too! What's the difference?"

That... shouldn't sting as much as it does. He doesn't take Cal's amnesia personally, he's not that petty, but something about being seen as no different from an actual stranger creates a hollow sensation in his chest. Yeah, Cal can't remember, but Jesus, they've been together for half a decade. They have a history, as painful as it is.

"Don't you think he would wonder why his husband can't look after him?"

Kieran just shrugs, like it's not important. "Let him think whatever he wants. He's not your responsibility."

So why does it feel like he is? "I can't. I know what you're saying, and I get it," he plows on before Kieran can go off again. "But I just *can't*."

Watching him from the corner of his eye for a long moment, Kieran sighs. "Yeah, I know." In a more gentle voice, he adds, "You goddamn softie."

"Fuck off," Dawson says without malice.

"Did you tell Ellis?"

Dawson called him after he left the hospital. It went about as well he'd thought it would. "He thinks I'm making a mistake."

"Smart guy," Kieran comments. "Why can't he take care of him? You said he's relocating here anyway."

"Temporarily. And he'll have his hands full with the company and the lawyers and the police." Dawson still feels bad for dumping all that on him. Technically, Ellis chose to do it, but still. "I have to do this. I *need* to do this."

He needs to feel at least a little useful. He isn't good at anything, has one good friend and a sister who acts more like his mother and father combined. He's a nobody, so the least he can do is make a difference for someone who needs it. Even if that someone is the one person who's made his life miserable.

"Are you sure it's safe to be with him on your own?" Kieran asks.

"He just had a surgery. He's harmless."

"And after he heals? What will you do?"

What will he do?

He ponders it carefully. Even if Cal never remembers, the bottom line is that neither of them can change the past. It would hang over them like the Sword of Damocles, always there. Dawson would never feel safe. He hasn't in a long time, if ever. Maybe happiness isn't in the cards for him, but safety...yeah, he wants that.

"I'll finish what I started." He'll wait until Cal is better, until he doesn't need Dawson anymore.

Kieran gives him a long look, maybe gauging if Dawson means it or if he's just placating him.

"I really hope you will, Dee. I really do."

Yeah, Dawson thinks. *I hope so, too.*

Chapter 11

"YOU CAN'T BE SERIOUS, Dee!" Olivia shrieks, making Dawson pull the phone away from his ear. Dealing with Kieran was a walk in the park compared to breaking the news to her. "I thought you made up your mind about the divorce."

"I did," he says slowly, pacing around the living room. "But forgive me for not predicting that Cal would end up in a car crash and get his brain wiped like a memory stick."

"Not your problem," Olivia grunts.

"I made it my problem. I'll deal with it and move on." That's what he needs to keep reminding himself. Once this shitshow blows over and Cal is a little more self-sufficient, he can bid him farewell and go on his merry way.

"I'm coming down," Olivia says.

"What? No!" He loves his sister, but Jesus, she can be a controlling maniac.

"You clearly can't be trusted to act in your best interest."

Dawson bristles, short of hanging up on her right then. "Back off, Liv. I'm not a child you can boss around anymore."

"You certainly act like one!"

Shaking with indignation, Dawson closes his eyes and takes a deep breath. "You know what's funny?" He doesn't wait for a response. "For all your complaining about Cal controlling me, you sure like to do the same."

It's not the same thing, he knows, but he can see some of the same patterns there. It's always been like this with them. On a more logical level, he understands why Liv had to be in charge at all times, making sure all the bills were paid and that they didn't live off junk food. It was a necessity when he was growing up. But now he's an adult, and he doesn't need babying.

"I can't believe you just said that to me," Olivia says, her voice quivering.

"I'm sorry, but it's true. You don't have to take care of me anymore."

"Of course I do! You're my baby brother!"

Resigned, Dawson collapses on the sofa and rubs his forehead. The last thing he needs is a headache. "Your kids need you more than I do, Liv. I promise, I'll be fine."

Whether she's as tired of arguing as Dawson is, or she hears something in his voice, she finally lets it go. "You better be, or I'm going to whip your ass."

He snorts. "Duly noted."

"How was he?" she asks. "You've gone to see him, right?"

"Yeah. Physically, he's doing fine. He's still in some pain, obviously, but it's manageable."

"And otherwise?"

That's what he's been wondering, too. "It's...bizarre. He communicates fine and stuff, but there are times he's confused about things. I brought him his phone and iPad and he seemed really hesitant using them, like he didn't know what to do. I had to teach him how to download apps, so he could read ebooks." And that's another thing. "He likes fantasy, Liv. He binge-read the whole Eragon series."

"That's...interesting," she says after a moment of silence. He can practically see her frowning. "Anything else? How is he with you? I read a little on amnesia and most of the articles said those people tend to get aggressive and lash out when they're confused and scared."

"That's what the doctor said, but..."

The first couple of times Dawson visited him, he was on edge the whole time, waiting for the other shoe to drop. When he saw those photos of himself in Cal's phone, taken without his knowledge and in such a vulnerable and compromising state, he didn't know what to do. He was livid and ashamed and felt violated. Which was ridiculous because as he told Cal; they were husbands. There was no reason why he should be offended that Cal took, and kept, his naked pictures.

What surprised him was how embarrassed he felt that Cal saw them now, saw Dawson in such a state while knowing the bare minimum about him. He was just starting to get to know Dawson again, and one of the first things he finds is...that. Or maybe it was because Cal is so different now, and him seeing those photos felt like being exposed to an actual stranger.

And then the weirdest thing happened when Cal told him to delete the photos, because he could tell Dawson didn't like them. Because he didn't want Dawson to be upset.

Dawson was still cautious, but after that it became easier to be around Cal. He could breathe easier and stop walking on eggshells.

"But what?" Olivia asks when Dawson's been quiet for too long.

"He's fine. Confused and sometimes grumpy." Especially if Dawson comes in right after Cal's physio session. He's found out the best time to visit is after Cal's eaten. His grumpiness seems to have a direct link to his stomach and how well he slept. Dawson hates to admit it, can't *believe* he's even thinking it, but it's kind of...cute? Never in his life has he imagined he'd be associating that word with Cal. "He's about as aggressive as a goldfish."

"Those can get pretty vicious, you know," Olivia says, making him laugh.

"He's fine. Really."

"Well, just be careful. Things might change if he starts remembering."

His throat tightening, Dawson swallows. "I know." The doctors didn't say anything explicitly, but he could tell how skeptical they are of Cal recovering his memories.

It shouldn't please Dawson as much as it does.

Dawson is as ready as he'll ever be—meaning not at *all*—when Tuesday arrives and he's supposed to pick Cal up from the hospital. He spent the better part of yesterday making sure the apartment is spotless, more for his benefit than Cal's. Cleaning always helps him take his mind off things. He also poured out all the booze he could find, feeling immense satisfaction as he watched the amber liquid disappear down the drain. If Cal was truthful about not having any cravings for alcohol, it shouldn't make any difference to him.

Doubt overtakes him again when he gets in the car.

Can he really do this? He's supposed to help Cal remember, but is he actually going to do that if making him remember is the last thing he wants?

And Cal... He has no idea. He probably thinks they have a normal, fairly happy marriage. Of course he does. Because Dawson never gave any indication of the opposite. Sure, Cal was confused by the lack of photos of them together, and he knows about the drinking, but anything else? There's no way for him to know unless Dawson says something.

Which he won't. He can't. What would he say?

'*So, this is where we live. And by the way, if I'm ever withdrawn or quiet when talking about the past, it's because I've been your punching bag for years. But don't worry, I'll help you get back on your feet, so when you're all set, I can shove divorce papers in your face.*'

Yeah, unlikely.

He knows that Olivia and Kieran must think he's got self-sabotaging tendencies, but that's not true. He doesn't *want* to stay. He doesn't want to be part of this.

But he also knows that if he walks away now and leaves Cal to his own devices, it will always haunt him. He's not deluding himself; underneath all that confusion and cluelessness, Cal is the same son of a bitch he's always been. That hasn't changed. But this isn't about Cal. Well, not *only* about him. Dawson just isn't the kind of person who can walk out on someone because everyone is telling him he should.

God, he needs help. Professional help.

Actually...

Looking through his wallet, he finds the business card Gabe had given him.

Ashley Cleaver, a behavioral therapist, and she has an office just down south in Miami.

Dawson twirls the card between his fingers for a while before he finally makes the call.

When he arrives at the hospital, Cal is already waiting for him. It might be just his overactive brain imagining things, but he swears Cal's face lights up when Dawson walks in. He's been reading something on the e-reader Dawson had lent him, but he drops it in his lap and gives Dawson a wide smile.

"Hi."

To his surprise, Dawson finds himself smiling back, despite having been a ball of anxiety since yesterday.

"Hey. So, today's the big day." He takes a seat. "Ready to go home?"

"You have no idea," Cal says with a huff, kicking the blanket off and moving to sit on the edge of the bed. "I can't wait to get out of this bin bag." He pulls on his gown, and Dawson laughs.

"Speaking of, you'll be happy to wear some pants for a change." Unzipping his backpack, Dawson pulls out the clothes and the pair of shoes he packed for him. He tried to choose something that would be easy to put on and take off, so as to not aggravate Cal's wounds. "Hope these work for you."

Cal looks at them like they're a gift from heaven. "Yes. Definitely." Carefully, he slides off the bed and picks up each item one by one, inspecting it.

Dawson stands up. "So, I'll step out for a bit and let you—" He chokes on the rest of the sentence when Cal unceremoniously pulls the gown over his head one-handed, grunting a little as the movement pulls on his stitches. He drops it on the floor and reaches for a pair of simple, black boxer briefs, then bends over to put them on. He hisses in pain and holds himself up with a hand on the bed.

"Shit," Dawson yelps, jumping to Cal's side, holding him up around the waist. "Are you okay?"

"Yes, I just moved too quickly," he says through clenched teeth.

"Here, sit down and try it that way."

He averts his gaze when Cal sits on the bed and, instead of bending over, he brings his legs up one by one. Dawson's eyes are automatically drawn to the large square of gauze covering his abdomen and a smaller one placed over his ribs close to his underarm. Dawson's chest aches with sympathy pain and he looks lower, away from the wounds. Which reminds him that Cal is sitting there mostly naked.

"Um, I can wait outside," he mumbles, warmth rushing to his cheeks. Jesus, what's wrong with him? He's seen Cal naked countless times—the man's not exactly body-shy.

"Why?"

"T-to give you some privacy."

Cal looks down at himself, as though he didn't register his undressed state. "There's no need. I don't mind."

Good for you, Dawson thinks hysterically. Once he's fairly sure the underwear is securely in place, he turns his gaze back to see Cal fiddling with the T-shirt, then proceeding to put it on the wrong way.

"Wait." He takes it from him and turns it over. "Like this. The tag needs to be in the back."

Cal nods like he's filing the information away for some important future task, his expression serious. Lifting both arms up tears a noise of complaint from him, so Dawson helps him put the T-shirt on. He tries and fails to smother a smile when Cal's hair comes out in disarray. He looks different without any kind of product in it.

It makes Dawson want to run his fingers through it.

Which he doesn't do. Obviously.

"Is it comfortable?" he asks, desperate to fill the silence.

Cal tugs on the hem, pinching it between his fingers. "Yes, very. Thank you."

The heat in Dawson's face intensifies. "No problem."

Thankfully, Cal manages to put the pants on himself, after a little guidance from Dawson. The socks and shoes, Dawson has to help with. Holding the bent-over position for too long would only make the pain worse.

He sits cross-legged on the floor in front of Cal, tying up the shoelaces. He's aware of Cal's eyes on him. It makes his fingers uncoordinated, and it takes longer to get it done than usual.

"All done." Dawson looks up, taken aback by the way Cal is watching him. His eyes are soft and a little hooded, his lips slightly parted. His expression is nothing like Dawson's ever seen, but...he kind of likes it.

"Thank you," Cal says. *Again.*

"You're welcome," Dawson manages, standing up on shaky legs. "Come on. Let's get you out of here."

"Yes, please."

Dawson chuckles and they make their way to the front desk. After a bunch of paperwork is signed and even more is handed to them, they walk to Dawson's car. He wonders if Cal will recognize it, if it will stir anything up, but Cal gives no indication of his memory being jogged as Dawson helps him into the passenger seat and adjusts the seatbelt so it doesn't press on his wounds.

"Are you hungry? Have you had breakfast today?" Dawson asks, turning on the ignition.

"Yes. But I could eat." He licks his lips. "Do we have anything sweet at home?"

Dawson stares at him, then laughs. "You weren't kidding about the cravings."

Cal makes a miserable sound. "No. And they only ever gave me dessert with lunch."

Dawson grins at the petulant tone. "Nothing at home. But," he adds as Cal's expression falls, "I know just the place."

Chapter 12

"OH, SHIT," DAWSON SAYS as he takes another right turn.

"What's wrong?"

"The only decent parking is further down the road." He looks at Cal apologetically. "Are you okay to walk? I'm sorry, I didn't realize. I usually just walk here because we live so close."

"Oh, don't worry about it," Cal says. "I've been doing my exercises. I should be fine to walk for at least twenty minutes. Unless it's uphill."

Dawson is visibly relieved. "Okay, that's fine. It's, like, five minutes. Maybe longer if you need to go slowly. No hills."

"Then it's fine."

A few minutes later, Dawson's parking the car next to a line of others overlooking the beach.

"Where are we?" Cal asks, eyes glued to the golden shore and waves breaking against it.

Dawson turns off the engine and unbuckles his seatbelt. "Nobby Beach. It's small, but it's one of my favorites."

They exit the car, and Cal sucks in a lungful of fresh air, smelling salt and something else.

"It's beautiful. Do we live here?", he asks. Dawson said they're close-by.

"A little further north on Mermaid Beach. It's literally a fifteen-minute walk, that's why I don't bother driving. Plus, I love beach walks and running."

They live like this? At the beach, having access to this place whenever they want? What a paradise, especially after being shut away in a room without windows and the smell of antiseptic for almost two weeks.

"Come on, this way."

"Where are we going?" Cal asks as he falls into step with him. Or to be precise, as Dawson matches Cal's pace.

"It's a cafe. One of my favorite places on earth. The guys running it are wonderful. And they write little messages for you on the cups. Sometimes it's just a motivational quote, but they do personalized messages too. When I first found the place I thought they have, like, a bunch of them and they just rotate them between people. But in the three years I've been going there I've never got the same message twice."

"That sounds nice," Cal says, enchanted by the way Dawson's face transforms when he talks about something he loves. His face is so expressive and full of life. He's been smiling more lately, that demure aura that was around him in the first few days after Cal woke up almost gone.

A few minutes later, Dawson stops, pointing at the store in front of them. "We're here."

Craning his neck, Cal surveys the exterior of the place. As with most of the shops they've passed, the cafe has large windows with a clear view inside. Due to the sun reflecting on the glass he can't make out too much, but he can see tables lined along the windows, some of them occupied with people sipping their drinks.

"*Lost and Ground*?" he reads the banner, giving Dawson a confused look.

Dawson laughs, lifting a shoulder in a half-shrug. "Zeke's idea. He's a bit weird, and his sense of humor is a tad morbid. You'll love him. And Gabe." He pushes the door open. "Come on in."

Once Cal steps inside, a bitter scent hits his nose. He smelled something similar in the hospital when he wandered around during his walks, but this is way more pronounced. As they walk further into the shop, the scent changes, bitterness mingling with something sweet that has Cal taking in a greedy lungful. Whatever it is, it smells divine.

There's a queue of people all across the width of the shop. A rectangular machine sits on one end of the counter, a man standing behind it, his hands moving constantly. A younger man is jumping back and forth between the people waiting, chatting and laughing with them.

"Looks like we caught them during a rush." Dawson checks his watch. "Lunchtime. No wonder."

"Is this a bad time?"

"Not really. But I usually try to avoid the rush hour. Makes me feel bad to come here when they're swamped."

"Oh. Do you want to come back later?"

Before Dawson can reply, one of the men behind the counter calls out, "Dawson! Hey!" He waves, a big grin on his face. Then his gaze shifts to Cal, eyeing him curiously.

Waving back, Dawson chuckles. "Looks like we have to stay now. That's Gabe, by the way. He bakes all the stuff you see here."

They walk to the end of the line, waiting their turn. As it moves, they end up standing in front of a large glass display filled with all kinds of food. Cal's mouth waters even though he can't recall what any of it tastes like—or if he's ever had any of it in the first place.

"What would you like?"

What would he say if Cal told him he wants to try everything?

"I'm not sure. I can't really…" He stops himself. Maybe reminding Dawson how much he's forgotten isn't a great idea.

Dawson seems to get it anyway. His lips form an *o* shape, but he quickly plasters on a smile. "That's okay. Everything here is good, but I can pick some of my favorites, see if you like them."

Cal gives him a grateful smile. "Yes, please."

Dawson looks at him oddly, but starts pointing at various desserts, telling Cal what's in them and asking if he wants to try them. Cal just keeps nodding, trusting Dawson to take care of it.

When it's their turn, Gabe jumps in front of them with that huge grin of his. There's an energy about him that has Cal's skin prickling with awareness, but not the bad kind. He can't quite put his finger on it.

"Well, hello," Gabe says to Dawson, then looks at Cal. "And you brought a friend." His gaze is calculating. Not unkind, but not warm either.

Dawson seems uncomfortable. "This is Cal. Cal, Gabe."

Gabe's eyebrows flick up. "Ah. The husband," he says without inflection. It's hard to read his reaction.

Cal manages a terse nod, feeling tension descend around them.

"Cal was discharged today and he's craving something sweet after all the hospital food. So I brought him to the best place on the Coast."

Gabe's eyes flick between the two of them, settling on Dawson with a smile. "You flatterer. But you're not wrong." He winks and looks at Cal with an unreadable expression. "You were there for a while. How are you feeling?"

"A little out of sorts," he admits. "But Dawson's helping me to adjust. He visited a lot, so that helped."

Gabe cocks his head, and, for a split second, Cal swears that the outer ring of his irises glows gold. But then he blinks, and it's gone. Must have been Cal's imagination.

Surprise flashes across Gabe's face, his brows flicking up and his mouth parting on a silent *oh*. He leans forward to rest his forearms on the counter. "You must feel really lucky to have him."

He doesn't phrase it like a question, but Cal feels compelled to answer anyway. He shifts his gaze to Dawson, who seems shy all of sudden, his cheeks pink.

"Very lucky. I don't know what I'd do without him," Cal says honestly, watching in fascination as the flush spreads from Dawson's cheeks to his whole face and ears.

"Hmm," Gabe hums. "Lucky indeed." He pushes himself up. "So, what are you having?"

Taken aback by the abrupt change, Cal says, "Dawson will pick for me."

The corner of Gabe's mouth twitches. "Okay." He looks at Dawson expectantly.

"Let's go with a cinnamon roll, a donut, and an almond croissant."

Gabe whistles, turning around to grab a large plate and a pair of tongs. "Twenty bucks says you guys won't sleep tonight."

Doubtful. After sleeping in a hospital bed, Cal will sleep anywhere.

Gabe slides them the big plate and a smaller, empty one, then does something on the iPad set on top of the counter. "What are you drinking?"

"I might skip the chai this time," Dawson chuckles. "I'll have a kombucha."

"Wise choice," Gabe says, laughing. "Cal?"

"You usually get coffee," Dawson says when Cal turns to him for help.

Cal shrugs. "Sure."

"Okay. A long black for him."

Gabe raises an eyebrow, looking at Cal. "For a black coffee drinker, you sure have a sweet tooth."

"Yeah, it's a recent development," Dawson says.

"Interesting," Gabe says, tapping on the iPad. "That'll be $37.50."

Dawson does something on his watch and brings it to a small machine next to the iPad. It makes a beeping sound.

"Alrighty. You two take a seat, we'll bring the drinks over."

"Thanks." Dawson takes the plate with the pastries and the cutlery and they walk over to a table by the window. After sitting down, Dawson cuts everything in half and pushes the bigger plate towards Cal. "Go easy on this. Don't forget you had abdominal surgery."

Always so thoughtful, Cal thinks affectionately. He reaches for the croissant first and takes a bite, sweetness bursting on his tongue. A moan leaves his lips, his eyes falling shut.

When his eyes open, he sees Dawson looking at him with concern. "O-kay... Do you two need to be alone?"

"What? Why?" Cal says through a mouthful, taking another bite before he's finished the first.

"Just..." Dawson looks at him like he's lost his mind. "Never mind. The hospital food must have been pretty terrible." He takes a bite of the cinnamon roll.

Shoveling the last bit of the croissant in his mouth, Cal makes a grab for the cinnamon roll too. The glaze makes his fingers sticky, and he licks them before tearing into the dough, letting out a sigh of pleasure at the new, spicy taste.

Wondering which of the three is the best, he tears off a chunk of the donut before finishing with the cinnamon roll. Five seconds later, he has a winner.

"This is amazing," he moans, abandoning the cinnamon roll and devouring the donut.

"Okie dokie," comes a cheerful voice that doesn't belong to Gabe. "I've got a bottle of vinegar here and one long—" A man who must be Zeke stops at their table, holding a steaming mug of what must be coffee and a glass bottle with some other dark liquid. He stares at Cal with a slightly worried expression, then chuckles and slides the drinks to them. "Wow. I hope diabetes doesn't run in the fam."

Dawson lets out a breathless laugh. "No, but cardiovascular diseases do." To Cal, he says, "You, uh, might want to slow down."

Cal swallows the last bit of the donut. "But it's so good."

"A sucker for instant gratification. I approve," Zeke says, grinning. "I'm Zeke. I'd shake your hand, but they both seem to be occupied."

"Cal," he replies, tearing into the cinnamon roll again.

"Cal, seriously, slow down." Dawson pats his hand, his expression somewhere between amused and horrified.

Feeling thirsty, Cal grabs his coffee, careful not to burn his tongue as he takes a sip.

And instantly spits it back into the mug, gagging.

"That's... What's that?" He puts the mug down like it's filled with poison. Definitely tastes like it.

"Uh, coffee?" Dawson says, bewildered.

Cal makes a face and shudders.

"That bad?" Zeke asks, the corners of his mouth pulled down. "Huh. The extraction was spot on. I wonder if the machine is being a little shit again."

"Everything you make here is amazing," Dawson says. "Cal's taste buds have been going through quite a transformation."

Cal hums noncommittally, taking a bite of the cinnamon roll to chase away the bitter aftertaste of coffee.

"Interesting," Zeke says, his eyes sparkling. "Would you like something else instead? Hot chocolate. A milkshake?"

Cal perks up.

"Nuh-uh, no way." Dawson wiggles a finger at him. "I'm not taking you back to the hospital with a sugar overdose."

Cal's shoulders sag and he pouts.

"Damn, Dawson, you run a tight ship," Zeke comments, shaking his head. "Anyways, enjoy. I gotta go back to work. Gabe looks a little panicked."

Sure enough, when Cal glances over to the counter, there's another line with Gabe hurriedly taking orders.

"If I die from this, it'll have been worth it," Cal grumbles stubbornly as he polishes off whatever is left.

Rolling his eyes, Dawson sips his drink, but is interrupted when his phone rings.

"Hey, Aubrey," he says after he picks up. The person on the other end says something that makes him frown. "Well, I mean..." He glances at Cal, biting his lip. "Kind of. But I should probably stay at home." After a few seconds, he says, "Hold on." He presses the phone against his chest. "Cal? Would you be okay by yourself if I disappeared for a few hours tomorrow? They had a few people call in sick at the shelter and I already told them I can't come this week, so they're short-staffed."

Dawson mentioned the shelter when visiting at the hospital, showing Cal pictures of all the cute dogs he takes care of.

"Yes, of course."

Dawson hesitates. "Are you sure? If you'd rather I stayed—"

"I'm sure." An idea springs to his mind. "Do you think I could come with you?"

Dawson blinks at him. "You'd want to?"

"I'd like to see where you work." *And spend time with you.*

"Oh. Yeah, I think…" He waves the phone. "Let me ask. Hey, Aubrey? Yeah, tomorrow is fine. Yeah, really." He smiles, glancing up at Cal. "Could I bring someone with me? No, he doesn't. And he can't do any physically demanding jobs at the moment. Ah, okay. Yeah. That's great. Thank you. See you tomorrow."

Cal waits until Dawson's hung up. "Is it okay, then?"

Dawson nods, still smiling. "Yeah, it's okay. She got excited that they might get another pair of hands, but there isn't much that's safe for you to do right now. Cleaning the kennel, carrying bags of dog food, etcetera. You might get bored, mind you."

He's pretty sure he could do something anyway. Dawson worries too much. "I won't get bored. I just want to be part of your world again."

Dawson watches him with a strange expression.

"What?"

"Nothing. Just… I never thought you'd—" He cuts himself off, clearing his throat and turning his attention back to his drink. "Nevermind. I'm glad you're coming with me. Makes my conscience a little lighter."

That doesn't sit well with Cal.

"Dawson?" He waits until Dawson looks at him. "I know I'm going to be a lot of work since this is—" He gestures at his head. "A mess, but I promise you don't have to hold my hand at every step. I don't want you to put your life on hold just so you can babysit me."

Pressing his lips together, Dawson gives a curt nod. After a long moment of silence, he says, "If you're finished, we should probably take you home."

Cal looks down at his empty plate mournfully. "Could we come here tomorrow? Before we go to the shelter?"

Dawson stares at him in disbelief. "Cal!"

"I won't eat as much, I promise." That's probably a lie.

Snickering, Dawson shakes his head. "I created a monster." He finishes whatever is left of his drink. "Fine. But you only get to eat one thing, you savage." He stands up. "I need to pop to the loo. Be right back."

Once Dawson is gone, Gabe makes his way over. He looks at Cal's empty plate, a mischievous smile forming on his lips. "You liked these, huh?"

"They were amazing. Dawson said you made them?"

Gabe winks. "Sure did."

"You're very talented. I can't believe I haven't been here before." Then again, Dawson said he never liked sweets before, so maybe it's not that strange.

Gabe just continues to look at him. "From what I hear, you're into a little fancier establishments."

Cal looks around. "This isn't 'fancy'?" The cafe is very cute and welcoming. He can imagine spending a whole day here, stuffing himself with whatever is available that day and reading a book. He's halfway through *Breaking Dawn* and can't wait to finish it.

Gabe stares at him at first, unblinking, then starts giggling.

"What's so funny?"

Waving a hand in front of his face, Gabe manages between hiccups, "Nothing. Nothing at all. Let's just say you're not what I imagined." He cocks his head. "Fascinating how memories shape a person, huh?"

Indeed. The more he learns about himself—about who he used to be—the more alienated he feels.

"Yeah." Throwing a glance over his shoulder to check if Dawson is still gone, he says, "Honestly, I'm not sure I'll go back to being the person everyone talks about. It's been almost two weeks and I haven't... There hasn't been a single instance that I've heard something about myself or my past and thought, 'yes, that's me, that sounds familiar'." He runs a hand through his hair. "I don't think Dawson is ever getting his husband back. But...I don't know how to tell him. He's doing so much for me, and I don't—I don't want to crush his hopes."

That's way more than he'd been prepared to share, but once he opened his mouth, the truth just poured out. He doesn't know who else to tell. The doctors would tell him not to give up hope, that anything can happen. And he can't talk to Dawson or Ellis, because they're too involved. And something about Gabe, despite having just met him, makes it easy to open up.

He looks up when Gabe doesn't say anything for a while, wondering if he should've kept his mouth shut. No one needs to hear him whine. They *just* met.

But Gabe doesn't seem bothered by Cal's emotional unloading. There's intensity in his eyes that wasn't there before. The way he looks at Cal makes him feel like he's staring right into his very soul. It should probably make him uncomfortable, but it's...it's fine. He doesn't mind.

"I think..." Gabe says slowly. "I think you shouldn't be so hard on yourself. Even if you don't remember, you can still have a relationship with Dawson, or any other person you were once close to. In fact—" His next smile is different, like it's carrying a secret, something only he knows. "Maybe you could create something even better. Something amazing."

That...sounds really good. It reminds him again of Carrie's words about building a future from scratch. It's daunting because he'll have to go and find new pieces to build with, since the old ones aren't there anymore. And what if Dawson loses his patience while Cal is looking for those pieces? What if he doesn't want to wait around until Cal has finished putting it all together?

"What if he doesn't want to build something new with me? What if he only wants the old me back?"

Gabe lets out a breathless chuckle and slowly, as if to give Cal a chance to move away, he lifts his hand and puts it on top of Cal's.

A strange sensation spreads from the point of contact up his arm. Almost like an electric current, but not quite. It doesn't hurt; it tingles, buzzing under his skin.

Confused by the sensation, he looks up, finding Gabe's expression frozen in shock.

Before he can ask what happened, Gabe shakes himself.

"I promise you, Cal," he says, enunciating each word with care. "That's not something you have to worry about." He gives Cal's hand a gentle squeeze and pulls away.

A few seconds later, Dawson appears next to Gabe. "Ready to go?"

"Yeah. Ready." Cal looks at Gabe, who gives him a wink.

"See you later, guys."

"We'll be here tomorrow morning." Dawson nods his head towards Cal. "Someone hasn't had enough."

Gabe grins. "I take it as a compliment."

"You should. Your stuff is amazing. Right, Cal?"

"Yeah," Cal says, still reeling from what happened. "Amazing."

They wave Gabe and Zeke goodbye and head back to the car.

"I probably don't have to ask, but what did you think?" Dawson asks.

"I liked it. The cafe, and Gabe and Zeke."

"Saw you and Gabe talking when I was leaving the loo."

"Yeah, he's...easy to talk to."

"I know, right? Makes you want to reveal your soul."

That's literally what it felt like. "You two talk a lot?"

"Not *a lot,* but we always chat when I stop by. I always feel better after spending some time there." He chuckles. "I swear, the place is magical. Or at least that's what Gabe and Zeke say, but there really is something to it."

Cal smiles, Dawson's affection for the place emanating from him. "It's lovely."

"Yeah. That place and the beach are my favorite spots."

They've already left the streets and are back on the gravel path. Looking over at the ocean, Cal asks, "Do you want to stay for a bit?"

"You want to?" Dawson says, surprised. "Well, I guess you could use some sun after being a vampire for two weeks."

Instead of continuing on the path, they take the stairs to the beach.

"You might want to take off your shoes," Dawson says, tugging at his own shoelaces.

Holding onto the railing, Cal manages to take off his shoes one-handed, though it takes him twice as long. Dawson offers to help, but Cal declines, wanting to be more independent. He can't have Dawson hold his hand for every little task, as nice as it sounds.

They walk along the beach for a few minutes before Cal's breath starts getting a little labored and Dawson decides to take a spot in the shade and sit down.

"If I knew we'd be doing this I'd have brought a blanket or something," he comments, but Cal doesn't mind. The feeling of the sand under his body and slipping through his toes and fingers is strangely comforting.

"Next time."

Dawson nods, looking pleased. "Next time." They sit in silence for a while, overlooking the ocean and watching the waves rise and fall, changing size and speed. It looks dangerous, but a reckless part of Cal wants to jump in and find out what it feels like to be swept in one.

"I can't believe you hated the coffee," Dawson says, shaking his head with a smile. "You're usually unbearable without at least a cup a day."

"But it's disgusting!" Cal protests, making Dawson laugh. "You like it?"

"I did when I could still drink it."

"Why can't you?"

"Because it's one of the triggers for my migraines."

"What's a migraine?"

Startled, Dawson turns to him. "Oh. Well, it's like a really bad headache. It can last for days, make you want to throw yourself off a bridge." His face contorts in a grimace, as though the mere thought invokes the painful sensation. "Everything irritates you; sounds, light, smells."

"That sounds horrible." Cal had a headache the day he woke up and it left him grumpy and snappy. He was tempted to gouge his eyes out. He can't imagine how much worse it can get. "I'm sorry you have to go through that. Is there anything that helps?"

"Avoiding triggers, for one. Stress is a big trigger too. I have pills for it, but I use them only when it gets really bad." At Cal's confused expression, he explains. "I don't want to become resistant to them. There was a guy back in uni who'd swear by holistic treatments, like acupuncture. Never worked for me."

That catches Cal's attention. "What did you study?" Dawson hasn't mentioned it before.

A shadow passes over Dawson's face. "Art."

"But you don't do it now?"

"I was never very good." Dawson's voice is strangely hollow. "And anyway, I dropped out halfway through my second year."

"Why?"

He takes a long breath, hitching his knees up and hugging them to his chest. "I just couldn't handle it. Too much pressure, I guess."

"I'm sorry to hear that." Hoping he's not overstepping, he adds, "It sounds like you miss it."

Dawson sniffles, running a hand over his face. He hasn't looked at Cal the whole time. "Doesn't matter. It's not in my stars." Not giving Cal a chance to respond, he stands up, brushing sand from his pants. "We should go back. You need to rest."

He's been resting since they sat down, but he doesn't say that, sensing Dawson's reached the pinnacle of his patience for today.

"Okay."

They walk to the car in silence and stay like that all the way home.

Chapter 13

"So..." Dawson opens the door wide, stepping aside. "This is it." He toes off his shoes, so Cal does the same before continuing deeper into the apartment.

His first thought is how bright everything is. Not just because of the huge windows and sliding doors taking up the full length of the wall, but because apart from black and white—and gray—no other color exists in the apartment.

"We live here?" Somehow, he didn't think this would be his style. Or Dawson's.

"I take it it doesn't ring a bell?"

Dawson's been watching him with an air of anxiety since they walked through the door, probably hoping it'd stir his memory.

Cal sweeps his gaze around the apartment again, paying attention to details. "A little. But that could be because there are some pictures in my phone that must've been taken here, or a place similar," he adds begrudgingly. He has stupid pictures of buildings and apartments but none of him and Dawson.

Dawson releases a breath, his shoulders relaxing. "Right. That makes sense. And otherwise? What do you think?"

The place is fine. Nice, even. Cal just doesn't like it for himself. For *them*. "It's...big. Why do we need so much space?"

"I don't know. It must be a rich people thing." Dawson snickers. He beckons for Cal to follow him as he steps closer to the sliding doors.

"Oh. Okay," Cal says, a little breathless, when Dawson slides the doors open and they step out on the balcony. "I understand now." The view is otherworldly. They are high enough to get the full panorama of the beaches and of the horizon touching the ocean.

"That's level thirty-six for you. Pretty nice, huh?"

"Beautiful. Everything looks so small."

"That's because it's about four hundred feet down."

After he's got his fill, Cal looks around the rest of the apartment.

"Why is everything so white?" The walls, the carpet, the counters. Just the sofa is black.

Dawson gives him a curious look. He's been giving him lots of those lately. "You prefer neutral colors." When Cal scrunches his nose at the statement, he laughs. "Now you remind me of Ellis."

"How come?"

"The first thing he said when he came here was: This place is a dump."

"It's not a dump. Just very..." He searches for the word.

"Sterile?"

"Yes! Like the hospital, but with windows." Cal studies the sofa, then rounds it and sits down. Bouncing a little, he makes a face. "This is very uncomfortable." Even his hospital bed was more comfortable.

Dawson presses his lips together, his eyes sparkling. "You picked that."

Cal gives the piece of furniture a loathsome look. "I have horrible taste."

Instead of disagreeing, Dawson smiles, making it clear he doesn't like the set up either.

"Is there anything *you* picked?"

Dawson shakes his head. "You'd already lived here for a while when I moved in, so it was furnished by then. Here, I'll show you around. It's not as big as it looks—four bedrooms and two bathrooms."

"What do we need four bedrooms for? Do we get a lot of guests?" Cal asks as he trails behind him.

Dawson snorts. "Yeah, no. We do have a guest room, though. One of the remaining rooms is used for storage and you set up an office in the other."

"Probably won't need that one anymore."

Dawson gives him an odd look. "You never know."

True. He doesn't know anything, to be honest. Which is why he dutifully follows Dawson around and tries to re-familiarize himself with their home.

The rest of the apartment looks pretty much the same—mostly white and bare, safe for impractical-looking furniture and strange decorations. Like the pictures on the walls, for instance.

"Why don't we have any of your art here?"

The way Dawson looks at him, Cal might've as well just hit him. "My art wouldn't fit here."

"Why not?" Surely it's better than the meaningless lines and shapes that are hanging there now.

Dawson shrugs, not saying anything. It's a clear dismissal, so Cal doesn't push.

The tour is swift—as Dawson said, the place isn't that big. After he shows Cal their bedroom with an adjoining bathroom, they return to the living room. Since it's an open space, it transits directly to the kitchen. The counters are spotlessly clean. It hardly seems used at all.

"What's this?" Cal points at the machine sitting in the corner of the counter.

Dawson's lips twitch. "It's a coffee machine."

Cal instinctively takes a step back, making a disgusted face. "I don't think we'll need this anymore."

Dawson seems to be trying very hard not to laugh. "We should keep it. You could change your mind. Coffee is an acquired taste, anyway."

"Not going to happen." Of that, he's absolutely sure. On the contrary, the reminder of the coffee makes him crave something sweet.

Curious, he goes over to the fridge. Opening it, he stares at its illuminated, empty interior—unless he counts the bottle of milk and some hot sauce. Closing it, he goes to check the cabinets, finding them equally vacant, save for a box of cereal.

"Why don't we have any food here?" He turns around, wondering why Dawson has that spooked animal kind of look again.

Flicking his gaze between the cabinets and Cal, he says, "Oh. Well, we usually eat out or order in."

"All the time?" Cal looks around the large kitchen space. "The kitchen is so big. Why don't we cook?"

At that, Dawson barks out a laugh. "You don't cook. The extent of your skill in the kitchen is boiling water. Which you never needed to do anyway because..." He nods pointedly at the offending swill-making machine. "And you're not here much. Usually eat at work."

It's been several times now that Dawson has mentioned him working a lot. It makes him wonder why Dawson's been putting up with him for so long. They don't spend time together, they don't have any pictures. Do they just sleep next to each other or does Cal spend the night at work too? It wouldn't surprise him at this point.

"What about you?"

"Me?" Dawson touches his chest, uncertain. "Uh, I can cook. Had to when I was younger when it was just me and Olivia. It's been a while, though."

Cal's heart aches for him, same as it did when Dawson told him how his parents died in a car crash when he was fifteen. How he was lucky that his sister was twenty and they didn't have to be separated. How they sold the house because they couldn't afford to pay the mortgage and Olivia's student loan at the same time, and got a one-bedroom apartment instead.

Hearing about Cal's car accident must've been really hard for him.

"So why don't you cook now? You don't enjoy it?"

Dawson fixes him with a look. "*I* do. But *you* don't like my cooking."

"Really?" That's hard to believe. Even if Dawson isn't the best cook in the world, Cal would never tell him to stop because he doesn't like it. Surely, he wouldn't...

"I tried to cook for you a few times," Dawson goes on when Cal remains skeptical. "That was back when we'd just met. Wanted to impress you or something." He shrugs, letting his gaze wander. "But you're used to something else and I'm pretty much an omelet or pasta kind of guy."

Cal doesn't see a problem with that. He'd eat anything Dawson made. "I'd like to try something you cooked."

Dawson's mouth opens and closes a few times. "You do?"

"Only if you want to." Dawson's already done too much for him, practically being at his beck and call this whole time. The last thing he needs is to feed Cal like a child.

Before he can overthink it and tell Dawson not to worry about it, Dawson speaks. "Well..." He rubs the back of his neck, looking around the kitchen. "We have nothing better to do, so...might as well go shopping and fill up the fridge and the pantry."

"That sounds good," Cal agrees quickly, not even trying to hide his excitement.

"When would you like to go?"

"Now is good."

Dawson's brows pinch together. "Aren't you tired? We did quite a bit of walking."

"We rested on the beach. I'm fine."

Dawson seems dubious, but eventually relents. "Alright. Guess you might as well burn all that energy after you just ate your weight in sugar."

And now Cal's thinking about sweet stuff again. He licks his lips reflexively, and Dawson laughs, throwing his head back.

"God, you're unbelievable." Walking over to the massive TV embedded in the wall, he searches through the drawers underneath. As he stands, he waves a paper and a pen in front of him. "Fine, you junkie. Let me make a list first, then we can go."

It takes Dawson a good few minutes before he's done with the list, but that's not surprising, considering that their kitchen is a desolate wasteland.

"That should do it," Dawson says, reading back through the list. Sliding the piece of paper in the back pocket of his jeans, he grabs his car keys and goes to the front door.

"Could we walk instead?" Cal asks. He wants to get back in shape as soon as possible. He's been doing pretty well already, and now that he gets to have some fresh air, he's even more eager to get on with it. "How far is it?"

"Didn't you have enough?" Dawson rolls his eyes, smiling. "It's a 45 minute walk. Fine for me, but not for you." He holds up a finger when Cal goes to protest. "And I'm not carrying all the shopping bags back here."

Cal pouts but must concede Dawson has a point. "Fine."

Rolling his eyes again, Dawson mutters something under his breath. Cal thinks he hears 'grumpy' and 'demanding'. While Dawson doesn't seem upset, Cal decides to tone it down a little with the demands. After all, Dawson would know better, seeing as he's the one with his memory intact.

He dutifully follows him to the car, listening carefully as Dawson points out things and places on the way to the store.

"That way is Sea World" and "That's the exhibition center" and "That's the Greek place you like to order from".

"Kieran and I went there the other day." He points at what looks like a cafe. "It's vegan, so he was skeptical, but it was really good. They make acai bowls and all that healthy stuff." He gives Cal a conspiratorial smile. "You'd like it. They have a plethora of vegan desserts."

"So we can go sometime?" Cal asks hopefully.

Dawson grins. "Sure, we can go. But don't tell Gabe and Zeke we cheated on them."

"I thought it would be further," Cal comments when they park in front of Woolworths less than ten minutes later.

"On foot, yeah. We'd need to go around. This is the highway."

Inside the store is too cool for Cal's tastes. He shivers, and Dawson must notice.

"Yeah, I know. They blast the aircon all year long like crazy. But you'll appreciate it in the midst of summer with the temps flying up to forty." He pulls out the list he'd made, and, after a short consideration, tears it in half. "Here." He hands Cal one of the halves. "You can get stuff from the shelves, and I'll go produce. If you can't find something, just look up at the signs for each aisle."

"Okay," Cal says, scanning his half with apprehension. It'll be fine. Dawson said there are signs for everything. How hard can it be?

Taking two trolleys, Dawson hands one to Cal and takes the other. "Meet you at the registers." He waves as he strolls away, presumably to the produce section.

Cal scans the list again. Flour, sugar, bread, pasta, rice... That should be easy enough. No need to panic.

A little more confident, he pushes his trolley in the direction Dawson showed him. Keeping his gaze up, he passes three aisles before coming across the sign that mentions both flour and sugar. Great. At least he doesn't have to look for each single item scattered all over the supermarket. Better even, flour is right at the beginning of the aisle. Happy with his discovery, he reaches for a bag with blue packaging—and panics again.

Oh no.

His eyes jump erratically between countless types of packaging, with different colors and different names. *Plain flour, self-raising flour, spelt flour, gluten free self-raising flour—*

He reads the list again, which is absolutely unhelpful. Dawson didn't specify which one. Maybe it doesn't matter?

If it didn't matter, there wouldn't be so many options.

Oh God. How is he supposed to do this? If he grabs the wrong one, Dawson will be disappointed with him, but if he doesn't take any, Dawson will have to do it himself. Again. And Cal will look like a useless idiot.

"Are you okay, dear? You seem to be having a crisis," someone speaks next to him. He turns towards the voice, finding an elderly woman watching him with a combination of concern and amusement.

"I...I'm supposed to get flour, but there are so many choices." He looks at the list again, part of him hoping it has changed since he last looked.

The woman hums thoughtfully. "Are you making anything specific?"

"No, we're just restocking."

She taps a finger on the bag in blue packaging Cal was looking at earlier. "Can't go wrong with plain, as the name suggests."

He nods, grabbing the bag and putting it in the trolley. "Alright. Thank you. I was worried I'd mess up."

She chuckles knowingly. "Let me guess. Missus would rip you a new one?"

Cal blinks at her. He didn't understand a word she just said. "Missus?"

"Your wife?"

"I have a husband."

Before he can ask why Dawson should be 'ripping him a new one', she says, "Oh." Her surprise is quickly replaced by a smile. "A man who knows his way around the kitchen. I like that." She nods at Cal's hand still gripping the list. "Anything else on the list you need help with?"

Does he? What are the chances that there is more than one type of sugar? Or bread?

"Everything," he says, just to be safe.

"Oh, boy," she murmurs, her eyes sparkling as she runs them over Cal. "You're like Bambi. Come on, love." She wraps her slim fingers around his wrist. "Let's get this done so your husband doesn't lose his mind. I'm Margaret, by the way. You can call me Maggie."

Ten minutes later, it's clear Cal made the right call asking Maggie for help with the rest of the list. Turns out that there are more types of bread than there are flour. He's not going to comment on sugar. Also, why is it so important what shape the pasta comes in? Doesn't it all taste the same?

When he asked Maggie, she just patted his cheek, smiled, and said she wished she'd had a child like him instead of the 'fussy-pants boy' she'd brought into the world.

Does that mean the shape matters? Probably. Just to be safe, Maggie made him buy three different types: spaghetti, fettuccine, and penne. He didn't dare object.

When they finally get to the end of the list and make their way to the registers, Dawson is already there, a frown on his face and his phone pressed to his ear. His trolley is almost full. How on earth did he manage to get all that while Cal struggled to find the few items on the list?

Dawson notices them approaching, and his shoulders droop as he expels a huge breath and pockets his phone.

"Thank God, I was about to start looking for you." He fixes Cal with a glare. "Where have you been for so long?"

Panicking. Not that he's about to admit that.

Maggie pats his shoulder and says to Dawson, "Go easy on him. He was a tad confused with all the different names of the products, but we managed."

Dawson must only now notice Cal's not alone, because he looks at Maggie confusedly.

Maggie isn't deterred. If anything, her smile grows. "You must be the husband. Such a handsome lad." She turns to Cal. "You're lucky."

Cal just stands there, not knowing how to react. Dawson is beautiful, of course, but what does it have to do with Cal being lucky?

When he looks at Dawson, he finds him blushing furiously and fidgeting. "Um..."

Sensing his discomfort, Cal takes Maggie's hand. "Thank you, Maggie. I don't know what I'd have done without your help."

She waves the thanks away. "Not at all. It was fun. But I need to do my own shopping now. Take care, boys." She waves at them and steers her trolley away.

"Making friends in the supermarket?" Dawson asks, amused.

"I didn't know what flour to pick. She helped."

Dawson seems to be trying very hard not to laugh at him. "Okay, no letting you wander off on your own next time." Cal wants to object—he should learn to do this stuff. "I tried calling you. You didn't pick up."

"My phone is in the backpack." He didn't even think to take it with him. For the past week, he's used it solely for 'googling stuff'.

Dawson huffs. "Right. Well, all is good now." He turns with the trolley and Cal follows him.

"This is a lot of stuff," he says, watching Dawson scan and bag up his items.

"Yeah, you don't wanna carry all that." He gives him a pointed look, probably because Cal wanted to walk. As the sixth bag is filled with their shopping, Cal is really glad he's not the one making decisions.

They put everything in one trolley and head back to the car. Dawson opens the trunk and starts loading the bags. Cal reaches for the last two bags, but Dawson jumps in front of him.

"Nonono, don't do that. It's too heavy."

Cal tries the weight. "No, it's not."

Dawson gives him a stern look. "Do you want to go back to the hospital? Four white walls and no windows?"

Cal lets go of the bags. "Here you go."

Dawson smirks. "That's what I thought."

Cal's resolution to do everything in his power to not have to go back to the hospital lasts until Dawson parks in their apartment building and attempts to carry all the bags to the elevator himself.

"Cal..." he warns when Cal tries to steal a bag from him.

"I don't want you to carry it all yourself."

"I'm fine."

"So am I." At Dawson's raised eyebrow, he says, "Just give me a lighter one. I need to start regaining my strength at some point anyway."

Pursing his lips, Dawson seems to think it over. He looks at the bags, then reluctantly hands one to Cal. "Brick wall," he grumbles, making him smile.

"Get used to it." His smile grows when Dawson rolls his eyes, clearly enjoying the banter.

But Cal meant it. He needs to get stronger and he won't manage that solely by walking. The doctor said no strenuous exercise and lifting heavy stuff for at least a month, but it's been nearly two weeks since they opened and patched Cal up. Surely, carrying some shopping bags won't kill him.

I might've spoken too soon, he concedes as he and Dawson unpack and put everything in its respective place in the kitchen, which requires lots of bending over and reaching up. By the time they're finished, he's actually more tired than he'd be from a half-an-hour walk.

Dawson, unsurprisingly, notices. "Jesus Christ. I told you, Cal!"

"I know, I know," he mumbles, allowing Dawson to steer him towards the sofa and sit him down on it.

"Just sit down and rest, will you?"

"I've been resting for two weeks. I hate just sitting on my ass."

Dawson chuckles. "Funny, because that's what your job requires most of the time. Sitting on your ass and running numbers and whatnot."

"That sounds horrible."

Dawson gives a small huff, then holds up a finger. "Gimme a sec." He disappears in the room he previously said was Cal's office and comes back with something flat and rectangular, kind of like the iPad.

"This is your laptop." He waves it in front of Cal's face. "It's password protected, so how about you make yourself busy trying different combinations?"

Cal takes it with a frown. "Can't I just use my fingerprint?"

"Not on this one, I'm afraid. But you have an unlimited number of tries, so go for it."

"You don't know it?" He takes the laptop and opens it carefully. It is like the iPad, but with a keyboard. He presses what he thinks is the power button and it starts.

Dawson frowns. "You're not supposed to share passwords, you know?"

"But we're married," Cal argues. When Dawson only stares at him, he turns to the screen asking him for a password. He types the first thing that pops into his mind.

Incorrect password. Hm. So it's not *Dawson*.

"When's your birthday?"

Dawson's brows shoot to his hairline. "I assure you; the password is not my birthday."

"When?"

Dawson sighs, shaking his head. "May 15th."

He types *1505*. "Year?"

"1997."

Cal adds the numbers to the password, grunting when it doesn't work.

"Told you," Dawson says, unsurprised. "We can have someone have a look at it later."

"Okay." He doesn't care much either way. "Does it do anything I can't do on my phone or the iPad?"

Dawson thinks. "I mean, the screen is bigger, duh. But you mostly use it for work. Pretty sure all your projects and documents are on there. And probably backed up on a drive or something."

"Well, I can't work now." He sets the laptop aside. "Is it going to be a problem? For us, I mean?"

"Money-wise? You own the company, Cal. Well, you and Ellis."

"Oh. I thought I just run it or something."

Dawson snorts. "*Just* run it." He sits down on the other end of the sofa. "You're the eldest and your dad wanted you to be in charge. But you're not obligated to run it." It looks like he's going to say something else but changes his mind.

"What?"

Dawson hesitates, chuckling uneasily. "Nothing."

"It's something."

"It doesn't matter. You don't need to hear all my rubbish thoughts. And I'm not supposed to put things in your head."

"How else am I going to learn?"

"It's just..." He sighs. "Look, this is my opinion only."

"I want to hear it."

Dawson shoots him an incredulous look. "Well, if you must know...I always thought you hated the job." He seems to be holding his breath, waiting for Cal's reaction.

"You said I worked all the time," Cal reminds him. "Wouldn't that mean I enjoy it?"

Dawson pulls his bottom lip between his teeth, hesitating. Cal zeroes in on his mouth, strangely transfixed. He kind of wants to...

"You're good at what you do," Dawson says carefully. "You worked hard for it. But I'm not sure you actually like it. You're always so stressed, and I know it comes with the territory but..." He looks up. "I don't think you're happy."

"Then why do I do it?"

Dawson shrugs. "I don't know. Maybe you're trying to prove something to yourself?"

"Well, that sounds silly."

Dawson laughs. "Can't argue with that."

Thinking of his job reminds him Dawson doesn't have one and that their apartment doesn't exactly look cheap. It's the first time the concept of money crosses his mind—maybe because Dawson never mentioned it to be a potential problem—but now he has to ask.

"What happens if I can't get back to work?"

Dawson seems surprised by the question, which confuses Cal. Didn't he just say Cal probably hates his job? The idea of him not going back shouldn't be that astounding.

"I guess Ellis would take over. But maybe if he shows you the ropes, you'll pick it up again."

"But I hate it."

"You wouldn't have to go back to being the CEO. You could do something else. Whatever you want, really."

Whatever he wants. That doesn't exactly narrow it down. The things he knows he wants have nothing to do with work. Unless he can get paid for spending all his time with Dawson and eating candy.

"I want to get to know you. Again, I mean."

It's not what Dawson asked, but Cal felt compelled to say it. It might simply be his imagination—after all, he doesn't have a reliable point of reference—but Dawson's been kind of...withdrawn. Yes, he's become a little more approachable as days went by, but Cal had naively hoped that coming home would bring them closer, make everything feel more normal. At least for Dawson, who must be as confused as Cal, even if it's in a different way.

Dawson doesn't seem to know what to do with Cal's confession. He looks at him like Cal lost his mind, not like he's excited about the prospect of rekindling everything Cal's forgotten. And that's another thing...

During his visits, Dawson was content to talk about anything and everything, from books to food to letting Cal complain about all the exercise he has to do. He had no issue giving Cal a rundown on his childhood and accomplishments. He was gentle as he explained that Cal's mom left when he and Ellis were little, and their dad passed away shortly after he met Dawson. He told him that Cal loved motorcycles but hadn't touched one since his accident four years ago that nearly cost him his arm.

He talked about everything.

Everything *but* them.

And when Cal asked something that involved their marriage? Dawson closed off, gave a vague answer, and changed the topic.

Cal understands that it's not easy for him—for Dawson to look at him and not see the man he loved and married. But if Dawson gives him a chance, Cal will do anything to make it work again. He just wants Dawson, in any way he can have him in his life.

It's strange how his conscious mind doesn't remember a single thing, but something inside him remembers, with startling urgency, how important Dawson is to him. How much he feels for him. And he knows, without a shade of doubt, that it's his job to make sure Dawson is happy. That he's safe.

If only Dawson would let him in.

Dawson chews on his bottom lip, reluctance oozing out of him. "What would you like to know?"

Excitement flutters in Cal's chest. "Everything. I know this has been hard on you, even though you like to pretend otherwise. I just want you to feel like you have your husband back. Not like you're living with a stranger."

Dawson squeezes his eyes shut, a flash of pain passing across his face. Cal was right—Dawson is taking it hard.

But Dawson shakes his head, taking a deep breath as he opens his eyes and scoots closer to Cal. "Cal, I meant what I said at the hospital. We don't have to force this. It's okay to start with a clean slate."

"But it's not fair to you. If there's a chance that we can revive even a little of what we used to—"

"Stop!" Dawson yells. "Please, just...just *stop*." The last word comes out like a sob. He hides his face in his palms, breath coming out in harsh pants.

Everything inside Cal screams at him to reach for Dawson and comfort him, hide him from anything that might hurt him. But it was Cal who had hurt him this time, and the rush of guilt that hits him is like a paralytic. He can't do anything.

When Dawson uncovers his face, his expression is blank. Tired. He looks Cal in the eyes. "I don't want to *revive* anything. I want to leave the past in the past and start from here. Can we please do that?"

If that's what he wants... "We can do that."

"Thank you," Dawson says. His shoulders drop like a weight has been lifted off them. "Do you, uh..." He gestures at the large TV in front of them. "Wanna watch a movie?"

Taken aback by the abrupt change in conversation, Cal takes a moment to reply. "I'd like that."

He watched some Netflix after Dawson showed it to him on the iPad. It was either that or the books to pass the time at the hospital and while he enjoyed some of the Disney movies, he prefers reading. But if watching movies means he gets to spend time with Dawson? Sign him up!

"What are you in the mood for?"

"You choose." He wants to know what Dawson likes.

Dawson's fingers play with the remote, then he starts going through the movies. "Well, you always liked John Wick."

Cal looks at the TV. There's a man in a dark suit and gun in his hand, chaos unraveling around him. "What's it about?"

"It's several movies. I think the fourth one came out recently, but it all starts when the protagonist's—John Wick's—wife dies and leaves him a letter and a puppy. The thing is, he's a retired assassin who left that life behind, but it finds him again. Some guys attack him and kill the puppy, and then he gets angry and starts killing—"

"No," Cal says decisively. "No dead puppies."

"Okay." Dawson flicks through more movies. "You also liked—"

"What do you like?"

Dawson shrugs. "Most stuff."

"Dead puppies?"

"No!" Dawson shouts, a look of horror on his face. "I work at a shelter. Come on."

"So what do you like?"

Dawson stalls, tapping his fingers against the remote. "Rom-coms. True stories, as long as they aren't too sad." He pauses. "Disney."

"Really?"

Dawson nods.

"Okay. I'm happy with any of those."

Dawson's still unsure as he skips through the movies and genres, but when he hears no protest, he offers, "How about *Tangled*?"

"Sounds ominous," Cal teases, earning an eye roll.

"It's a take on *Rapunzel*."

Cal doesn't know what that is. "Sounds good."

Dawson lights up and presses play. "Oh, I forgot—there's singing." He says it like he expects an objection.

"Singing is good," Cal says, and that seems to do it. Dawson relaxes. Kind of. He taps his fingers nervously on his knee as the movie runs, and fidgets as Rapunzel sings the first song. It's a good song—about how bored she is, and Cal can definitely relate to that—and she has a nice voice. It's energetic and hopeful, and it has Cal bouncing his foot in sync.

Dawson notices and laughs. "Catchy?"

"It is."

"Okay." He can hear the smile in Dawson's voice. "I'm glad you like it."

"You should be in charge of picking movies. Clearly, I can't be trusted."

Cal does like the movie. Loves it, to be precise. It's funny in that silly way that most fairy tales are, making him laugh hard enough that it pulls on his stitches.

Dawson loves it too, he can tell. His eyes are glued to the TV screen, his cheeks pulled taut in a big smile, and his eyes crinkling at the corners.

Cal would give anything to have Dawson look at him like that. To make him laugh like that. The smiles and small laughs he's drawn out of Dawson have been like the sun breaking through the clouds, spreading a rush of warmth through his chest every time. He craves more of it.

He can't hide his disappointment when the movie comes to an end. It's only partially because of the movie itself and mostly because of how much he's enjoying Dawson's proximity. Just sitting here with him, nearly shoulder to shoulder after they've gradually gravitated towards each other is amazing.

Dawson notices his reaction, smiling knowingly. "Another one?"

"Is that okay?" Hopefully, he doesn't sound too eager.

"Yeah, of course. Damn, if I'd known we'd binge movies, I'd have bought popcorn."

"I don't think I could eat now, anyway." He's still quite full from the pastries.

"Snacks are not for when you're hungry. It's more of a ritual."

Interesting. "Next time, then."

A strange look passes over Dawson's face, but he smiles. "Next time. So, what are we watching?"

"You pick. I enjoyed your choice."

"Okay." Dawson purses his lips. "You wanna give a comedy a go?"

"Sure." As he waits for Dawson to pick, his thoughts wander back to *Tangled*. "There's one thing I don't understand."

"About what? The movie?"

Cal nods. "Rapunzel wasn't happy with her life. So why did she want to go back to the tower?"

"She was worried it would break her mother's heart. That she would disappoint her."

"But her mother wasn't a good person. She was using her."

He can feel Dawson freeze next to him, his body growing tight. He keeps his gaze averted as he replies, "She didn't know that. She thought her mother loved her."

Cal frowns. "But she kept her locked up her whole life. She controlled everything Rapunzel did."

Dawson sighs. It's a sound that feels like it's coming from deep within his soul, tired and resigned. "Sometimes it's hard to let go of the only thing you know, even if that thing hurts you or doesn't make you happy. You don't know any better, so you don't even bother trying."

That sounds...incredibly painful. He can't even imagine. "That must be horrible."

Dawson takes a deep breath and releases it slowly. "Yeah. It is." He looks at Cal with a forced smile. "But she got out."

"She did," Cal agrees. "And she knows better now, because she has Eugene."

"Yeah." Dawson points at the TV. "How about this one?"

"*Jumanji*?" Cal reads the title, which means absolutely nothing to him.

"It's a classic. Well, a remake of one. A bunch of teenagers are sucked into a video-game and forced to play and win, or they die."

"That doesn't sound funny," Cal says apprehensively.

Dawson gives a small, frustrated huff. "I'm not good at describing stuff. I promise, it's hilarious, but it has this deep life lesson to it too."

Not wanting to make Dawson feel like he's criticizing him, Cal nods. "I'm curious. Let's watch it."

Turns out Dawson was right—it is hilarious, in an over-the-top way, and Cal loves it. He loves Dawson's incessant laugh and giggling even more, and makes a mental note to always pick comedies from now on if it gets him to see Dawson like this every time.

By the time the credits roll, Cal's stomach gives a loud rumble. He looks at it with betrayal.

"Are you hungry?" Dawson asks with a laugh.

"Yes."

Dawson checks his watch, his eyebrows shooting up. "Damn, no wonder. It's almost seven." His eyes go wide. "Jesus, we haven't eaten in six hours. Are you okay? I'm sorry, I should've checked—"

"Dawson," Cal says calmly, and Dawson goes quiet. "I'm fine. I told you before we watched the last movie that I wasn't hungry."

"Yeah, okay." He looks over to the kitchen, then back at Cal. "So, do you still want me to cook or just order in?"

What kind of question is that? "I'd love it if you cooked."

"Alright," Dawson says, cheeks flushing. "Any requests? I can't promise I'll be able to make it, but at least it will give me an idea."

"Well—"

"And don't say something sweet!"

Cal seals his mouth shut, disappointed, and Dawson laughs. "Don't give me that kicked puppy look."

He's not giving him—

Whatever. Crossing his arms on his chest, Cal shrugs. "You decide."

Dawson rolls his eyes at the petulant tone. "Fine." He makes his way to the kitchen and starts looking through the cupboards, as though they didn't just fill them up a few hours ago. At last, he pulls out a bag of pasta.

Curious what he's going to create, Cal walks over, pulling out one of the stools behind the island and sits down.

Dawson startles when he notices him. "You're going to watch?"

Cal, who's been planning to do exactly that, shrugs. "If you don't mind. I'd like to learn." Plus, there's also something relaxing about watching Dawson do...anything, really.

It earns him another of those odd looks. "Well, just remember it's been years since I cooked," Dawson warns, then proceeds to utterly blow Cal's mind. Dawson's hands are a blur as he chops up garlic, cuts up chicken breast, slices mushrooms. In a matter of minutes, the apartment is filled with a mouthwatering aroma while ingredients continue to sizzle in the pan where Dawson is constantly pushing them around, a saucepan filled with pasta boiling on the other burner.

Cal is so fascinated by the whole process that when Dawson announces, "That should do it," he can't quite form words as a plate is put in front of him. He inhales the scent as Dawson fills up a plate for himself. He hands Cal a set of cutlery before diving into his own plate. His expression is thoughtful as he brings the first bite to his mouth and chews.

"Looks like I still got it," he says after he swallows.

"You do. It smells wonderful."

"Thanks." He gives Cal a smile that's adorably shy. "Hopefully it tastes like it too. I went easy on the cream. The doctors said to avoid anything heavy for the first few days."

"I'm sure it's amazing." Taking his fork, Cal stabs it into the pasta and eagerly shoves it in his mouth. He instantly regrets it, sputtering and coughing.

"Oh my god, are you okay?" Dawson gasps, grabbing a glass and filling it up with water.

Cal mutters something unintelligible as he fights to swallow, his eyes watering. He downs the whole glass Dawson slides towards him. His mouth burns and his face must be bright red, but he manages to say, "I was wrong." At Dawson's crestfallen expression, he quickly adds, "It tastes even better."

"Really?"

"Really," he says, already scooping up more food. He remembers to blow on it this time.

Dawson's gaze drops to his plate, his cheeks turning pink. "I'm, um, glad you like it." He pushes the pasta around, a small smile on his face.

"What kind of dish is it?"

"Dawson Special," he says with a laugh. "Uh, I don't know. Kind of like stroganoff? It's mushroom and chicken. Like a super basic version."

"Well, I really like the Dawson Special," Cal says, just to see that blush darken. It fascinates him to see Dawson react so strongly to a simple—and well-deserved—compliment.

They finish their food in comfortable silence. He can feel Dawson's eyes flick to him here and there, but whenever he looks up, trying to catch him, Dawson quickly looks away, pretending to be engrossed in his food. It's kind of...cute. He's been rather bashful since they'd left the hospital, even though he has no reason to. It's Cal who's out of his element, feeling like a stranger in his own home and not knowing which way to turn.

Too busy ogling Dawson—he can't seem to stop—Cal manages to drop the last piece of pasta on his t-shirt. His white t-shirt.

"Crap."

Dawson looks up, then cracks a laugh. "Guess it was bound to happen, since you eat like someone's going to steal it away from you."

Heat crawls up Cal's neck. He thinks back on how he demolished the pastries at the coffee shop. Dawson must've been so embarrassed to be there with him.

"I'm sorry."

"Don't worry about it. I'm used to it from Kieran." He takes their empty plates and puts them in the sink. "I was about to do laundry today, anyway. Just leave it in the hamper when you shower."

"Can I see?"

"What?"

"How you do laundry. I can do it next time." Just another of those things his brain has decided to send into oblivion.

And there it is again. That look that makes Cal feel like some alien creature.

"I mean, if you want? But you don't have to. I've always done it."

That pulls Cal up short. "I must have done it too at some point."

Dawson shrugs. "You were busy. I was at home most of the time."

You were busy. You're a busy man. He can't count the number of times he's heard that line from Dawson.

"I'm not busy now," he says, irritation spiking in his veins. Is he good for anything but his job? The job he apparently doesn't even like?

"Okay. Yeah, sure. I'll show you."

He follows Dawson to the second bathroom. There's a basket of light-colored clothing on top of the washing machine. Dawson pops it down on the floor, opens the round door of the machine and loads it with the clothes. "So, I already washed colors this week. These are whites, grays...anything that won't run and ruin other stuff."

Dawson stands up and pulls open a little drawer in the top left corner of the machine. "So, this is normally for the detergent and the fabric softener, but lucky for you—" He grins, reaching for a square paper box in the back. "There are these magic things that already contain all you need and you can just pop one in with the clothes."

As he throws it into the machine, he notices Cal's confused look and chuckles. "Looks weird, I know. But they're super eco-friendly and you need just one thing for everything." His gaze drops to Cal's shirt. "If you...uh, if you wanna take that off, we can just pop it in now."

Right. The shirt he ruined.

He starts pulling it up, sucking in a breath. A sharp sting reminds him why he needed Dawson's help this morning.

"Are you okay?"

"Yes. Forgot to move slowly."

Dawson looks conflicted, his eyes roaming over Cal. "Let me." He steps into Cal's space, reaching down to grab the hem of his shirt. "Just raise your arms as far as it's comfortable."

Cal raises his arms to shoulder height before the stitches make themselves known. Jaw tight and gaze locked on Cal's chest, Dawson pulls the shirt up, slowly, carefully. His knuckles graze Cal's sides and chest, making his breath hitch. The soft touch makes him shiver, and it's not from pain. It's like nothing he's ever felt before. Probably. Who knows with his memory wiped.

"Thank you."

"No problem," Dawson mumbles, averting his gaze. He throws the shirt in with the rest of the clothes before shutting the door with an audible click. "Ready to continue?"

"Sorry?" Continue with what? Doesn't he just press a button now? He recognizes the play/pause icon. That must be the one.

Dawson laughs like he can read his mind and pats a weird-looking silver knob. "It's not that hard. Yeah, there are a few settings that can turn your head, but if in doubt, you can use the standard one. This—" He points at the setting called *daily wash*, "Is your go-to if you're not sure. Everything is already set. You can use it pretty much on anything, and, unless something is super dirty, it will do the job. And if you press this button, it will preserve water too."

Okay. That's not too bad. Feeling brave, he asks, "And if I want to do it the hard way?"

Dawson flashes him a proud grin. "Well, all the settings have a name. And if that's not always clear, this little bar will tell you how hot the water will be and how long the cycle will run for. I generally use hot water for towels and sheets."

"So, which one will you use now?"

"Most of the clothes in there are mine. Some of it I wore to the shelter or for a run, so I'll just do the daily wash." He turns the knob. "Makes sense?"

Cal nods, even though it all looks a little dreadful. "Yes." He looks at the machine. "Is it on now?"

"Ah." Dawson presses the big button Cal was eyeing earlier. "Don't forget to press that one." The machine whirrs to life, hissing and rumbling. "But you really don't need to know this. I can take care of it."

"I want to," Cal says firmly. "It's not fair that you do all this."

"I don't mind."

"I do."

Dawson's lips part, then twitch. "Yeah, okay. Gosh, you're stubborn."

"Yes," Cal says, utterly unapologetic. "Shall I shower now?"

"Yeah, if you want to. But not here. All our stuff is in the en-suite bathroom. You go ahead. I'll bring you some clothes for the night.

Cal almost protests that he can do it, but he's forced to admit that he does enjoy Dawson taking care of him. Not exactly something he's proud of, but he can't deny it. He hopes Dawson will allow him to do the same.

The bathroom is smaller but nicer than the other one, the counter and sink littered with various products, and there's a huge mirror above it. It's impossible to avoid his reflection, but Cal's been practicing as Carrie asked him. And while the sight of himself doesn't bring any fond feelings to the surface, he no longer has an inclination to punch himself. Much.

Dawson appears in the mirror next to him.

"Hey." He puts the clothes he picked on the counter next to the sink. "You, um...don't usually wear a shirt to bed but I figured...the extra layer will be better for you."

Makes sense. "Thank you. I appreciate it."

Dawson turns to leave and stops. "When you're done, I can...I mean, if you want me to, I can help. With the wounds. Redressing. Yeah."

Cal's done that himself plenty of time at the hospital, but he's not about to say no to a chance to feel Dawson's hands on him.

"I'd like that."

Dawson gives a curt nod, then excuses himself as he backs out of the bathroom, closing the door.

After taking off the rest of his clothes, Cal gingerly peels off the dressing covering his abdomen, then the smaller one from his ribcage where the tube was inserted into his lung. That one is almost healed, and, compared to the huge gash running down his belly, it's nothing.

He steps into the shower and turns it on, squealing when he's instantly blasted with a jet of cold water.

"Dammit." He tries to angle the showerhead, so it doesn't aim at him while the water heats, shivering in the meantime. Once it's warmed up, he focuses on cleaning the wound first, grimacing as he does it. He hates this part, no matter how many times he's done it.

He decides against washing his hair, which would require him to lift both arms at once, and that...he doesn't fancy doing. Maybe Dawson could help next time—

Stop asking him for every single thing. You're a grown man, an annoyed voice in his head growls at him. Yeah, he really needs to stop acting so helpless and taking advantage of Dawson's good intentions and kindness. He gets the feeling that Dawson does this a lot, ignoring his own comfort and helping others while refusing any himself. *Well, that's about to change.* Dawson wants a clean slate—he'll get one. Squeaky clean.

The idea of taking care of Dawson causes a tingle to run down his spine, making him shiver. It makes a home low in his belly, heat spreading through the area and...

His soapy hand slides between his legs where, for some reason, his penis started doing...something. He looks down at it quizzically, wondering why it's suddenly bigger and stiffer. And why it's so sensitive. Not knowing what to do with the sensation of his hand running over his length—it didn't feel like this when he cleaned himself before—he quickly finishes showering and slowly steps out.

He snatches a towel from the rack. It's folded and clearly unused, so he doesn't have to worry about accidentally using Dawson's. He carefully dabs it over the wounds, patting them dry before running it over the rest of him. Hanging up the towel, he picks up the pants Dawson brought him. They're soft and light, and he smiles at the thoughtfulness Dawson must have put in choosing this particular piece. It takes some maneuvering, but he manages to put them on.

As he pulls himself up, his gaze moves to the mirror, snatching on his reflection again. He stares at it unwaveringly, determined to eradicate the uncomfortable sensations his face invokes as soon as he can. Is that even possible? Carrie was certain he just needs to get used to it and that, in time, he'll come to recognize himself and those feelings will disappear. But what if not? What if—

Something happens. For a fraction of a second, everything goes dark, like someone just flipped the switch and turned off the light. He blinks and when his eyes open, he sways on his feet. It's no longer him who stares back from the mirror. It's Dawson, his cheeks tear-streaked and blood dripping from his lip. His eyes are red-rimmed and swelling rapidly. He's gripping the edge of the counter, shaking, pain and disgust written on his face as he stares in the mirror.

Sharp pain slices through Cal's temples, like a shard of glass embedding itself in his skull. He clenches his eyes shut, his hands shooting forward to brace himself against something. There's a loud noise as something breaks, shattering on the floor.

The next thing he knows, Dawson's there, repeating his name, his voice panicked. He recognizes the feel of Dawson's hands on him as they grab his arms and lead him somewhere. As the pain subsides, Cal opens his eyes. Dawson is leading him around what looks like shards of the soap dispenser and sits him down on the toilet.

"Cal? Cal, hey. Are you okay? What happened?"

Even through the throbbing in his head, Dawson's panic gets to him, and he forces himself to say, "I'm fine. Just dizzy. Everything went black for a moment."

Dawson studies him, brows pulled together as he decides whether he believes him or not.

"Does this happen a lot?"

Cal goes to shake his head, then decides against it. "No."

Dawson's frown deepens. "You're okay, though?"

"Yeah."

"Alright. Stay here, I'm gonna get rid of the shards."

While Dawson cleans the mess, the images keep flashing through Cal's mind. He's had dreams about Dawson being hurt, but they were just...dreams. *This* felt real. It can't be, because it doesn't make sense that Cal would see Dawson's reflection in the mirror. But the way his stomach twists and clenches, nausea climbing up his throat... Something tells him that whatever it means, it's very, very bad.

"Okay, that's done," Dawson announces some time later. He gestures at Cal's abdomen. "Let's take care of that now." He disappears again for a moment and comes back with a small bag that reveals medical supplies. He drops to his knees between Cal's legs, studying the forming scar. "I'm not an expert, but it looks good. Healing nicely."

Cal shrugs, not really caring at the moment. He remembers to look out for inflammation, swelling, and weird smell, and hasn't noticed any of it. So he's probably fine. But Dawson...

"The doctor said to put a little bit of the—" He swallows the words when Cal reaches for him, cupping his face with one hand and stroking his cheek like he's trying to wipe away the tears he remembers seeing there. But Dawson's face is dry, his eyes bright and wide, and his lips are intact, full and pink, parted as he gazes up at Cal in shock. He's beautiful and, right now, he's okay. He's safe.

"Cal?"

"I keep seeing your face," he blurts out. "There's blood and...you're crying." He slides his hand down, stroking the edge of Dawson's jaw. "I thought they were just dreams, but..."

A trembling breath tumbles out of Dawson. Slowly, he reaches for Cal's wrist, his hold gentle and unsure as he pulls it away from his face.

"It's okay, Cal. I'm okay." He waits until Cal nods. It's the only thing he can do, because he knows he's not making sense. He's probably just freaking Dawson out, too. "Let's have a look at your injuries, yeah?"

Cal closes his eyes and leans his head back against the wall. It's a relief when those dreadful images don't flash in front of him as he'd feared, and he aims his focus on what Dawson's doing. He's gentle, so incredibly gentle as he applies some ointment to the wounds, apologizing when Cal shifts ever so slightly when it stings a little. He can feel him covering the wound and smoothing down the edges before moving onto the one on Cal's ribcage.

"There. All done," he says after some time, sounding strange.

Reluctantly, Cal opens his eyes. Dawson watches him expectantly, as if trying to gauge his mood. It takes all of Cal's willpower not to reach for him again, take his face between his palms and—

"Thank you," he breathes out, pushing up to his feet.

Putting everything back into the small bag, Dawson rises, running his gaze quickly over Cal. "Are you sure you're okay?"

No. "I'm fine."

Dawson looks dubious, but doesn't argue. "Okay. Are you done here?"

"I need to brush my teeth."

"Oh, yeah." He nods towards the sink. "Yours is the black one. I've got the blue one." He opens the cabinet above the counter. "Everything you need is here. Floss, mouthwash, shaver." He throws a look at Cal's face. "If you want to shave."

Cal scratches his beard self-consciously. In the few pictures of himself he's seen, he has no facial hair.

He reaches for the shaver, studying the settings. At least it looks less complicated than the washing machine. "What setting should I pick?"

"You usually do clean-shaven but..." Dawson shrugs. "Up to you."

"Do you have a preference?"

Dawson laughs, pointing at himself. "I do clean-shaven too."

"I meant for me."

Dawson looks at him like Cal just spoke a different language. "Uh... No. Do whatever feels good."

Well, that's not helpful at all.

Dawson excuses himself. Cal brushes his teeth, then picks up the shaver again. Whatever feels good, huh? Maybe it's time to try something different. Keeping himself clean-shaven must be a lot of work, but also, the beard is kind of itchy and annoying.

He chooses setting number five first and leans over the sink as he runs the shaver over his jaw, chin and cheeks. Afterwards he looks at himself in the mirror for the longest time, running a hand over his face as he speculates if he looks good. Deciding it's still a little long for his liking, he moves the setting to three and repeats the process.

Better, he decides after he's done. He needs to ask Dawson what he thinks.

He finds him in the living room, frowning at the phone in his hand. He looks up when he hears Cal approach, doing a small doubletake.

"Uh..."

That doesn't sound promising.

"What do you think?"

Blinking several times, Dawson swallows. "Um...looks good." He gives a breathless laugh. "Stubble, huh?"

"I was just trying it. Maybe I should just stick with what I usually do and—"

"It looks good," Dawson repeats, sounding flustered. He must be annoyed with all of Cal's questions. "Really. It suits you."

"Alright," Cal says, unconvinced. If he ends up hating it, he can always get rid of it.

"Gonna turn in?"

"In a bit. I haven't done my exercises yet," Cal says with disdain, making Dawson laugh.

"Go easy on yourself. We've done quite a bit of walking today."

"Right." Cal throws a glance over his shoulder at the bedroom, then looks at Dawson. Is it weird that he doesn't want to say goodnight yet? He's going to see Dawson in the morning. So why is he reluctant to call it a night? "I guess I'll see you in the morning."

Dawson nods. "I'll be up for a little longer. There's some stuff I need to sort out." He waves the phone at him. "You sleep on the right, by the way."

"Right. Got it." Feeling like he needs to tell Dawson how much his help means to him, he says, "Thank you. I know I've been saying it a lot, but I mean it. I don't know how I'd manage without you."

Color rises to Dawson's cheeks, and he stutters. "Y-yeah, of course. Anytime."

"So...goodnight?"

"Goodnight."

He just stands there for a moment, waiting for God knows what. Probably for lightning to strike or something. Realizing he's making Dawson uncomfortable, if the nervous shifting is anything to go by, he mumbles goodnight again and turns to leave. Hopefully, the exercise will help him focus on something other than the obsessive need to have Dawson by his side at all times.

It's not likely, but he can still hope.

Chapter 14

WHAT. ON. EARTH. WAS that? Did he land in an alternate universe? Has he been abducted by aliens? No, wait. Maybe *he* was in an accident and now he's lying in the hospital, hooked to a bunch of machines and being pumped full of painkillers and whatever chemical cocktail causes scarily real hallucinations.

Because there's no way this is his life now. There's no way that this...*this man* is his husband. He thought that his visits at the hospital had prepared him for what it was going to be like from now on. Ever since he woke up, Cal's been nothing like the man Dawson remembers, but he assumed that would change once he brought Cal home. He'd expected some confusion and frustration. Maybe some of that anger and moodiness the doctors talked about—that would be a blast from the past, anyway.

What he hadn't expected was...this. This guy who is probably huffing and puffing from exertion in the other room before going to bed. This person who wants to learn to do laundry, who enjoys Disney movies, who likes to watch Dawson cook—and likes the food he makes!

Maybe it was Cal who got abducted by aliens. Maybe they experimented on him, swapped his brain. That's possible, right? Or he could be a changeling. Weirder stuff has happened. Someone could've swapped Cal for his good twin while nobody was looking.

Dawson collapses onto the sofa, pressing the heels of his hands against his eyes. Yeah, it's more likely he's hallucinating. Or maybe he died and is in hell. Not that there's anything particularly hellish about this. Stressful and confusing, yes, but compared to what his life has been, it's not too bad.

Sighing, he opens his phone, going through the messages from the day. Kieran's been bombarding him the whole arvo and left several voice messages. Dawson was so mired in the bizarreness of it all he hasn't even thought to check his phone. There's also a missed call and a message from Olivia. Well, better get it out of the way.

He dials Kieran first.

"Dude!" Kieran shrieks. "I was legit about to summon the cavalry. Where the hell have you been?!"

A tentative smile pulls on Dawson's lips. That protective little shit. "Sorry. It's been a day."

"That bad?"

"No." It's true, it wasn't. It was a *good* day. Confusing as fuck, but good. He doesn't remember the last time he and Cal watched a movie together. And the few times they did, it was never something up Dawson's alley. "It wasn't bad. But my god, you'd have to be here to believe this."

"What happened?"

"I'm like Alice in Wonderland, I swear. You know how I said Cal was really mellow and chill at the hospital." When Kieran makes a gruff sound of agreement, he continues. "Well, that was just the tip of the iceberg."

"You gotta be more specific, man. I really don't know what the fuck you're talking about."

Dawson rolls his eyes. "Look, I know that forgetting everything about yourself is bound to change your personality, but I swear if I didn't know better, I'd say I brought home the wrong person." Realizing he's still being pretty vague, he rushes to continue. "We watched *Tangled*, Kieran. *Tangled.* He let me pick the movie, twice. Then we watched *Jumanji.* And he *liked* it."

"Get out," Kieran says after a pause.

Dawson nods frantically as if Kieran can see him. "And that's not all. He hates coffee, Kieran. We stopped at *Lost and Ground*—"

"You took him to *Lost and Ground*?!" Kieran yelps, appalled.

That's fair. Dawson can't blame him. The café is their safe haven, the one place Dawson would go to get away from Cal.

"He was craving something sweet."

"O-kay?"

Right. Context. "Cal hates sweet stuff. And he lives on caffeine." *With a dash of whiskey to give it a kick.* "He all but spit it back into the mug when he tasted it."

"Hm, yeah, that's a bit weird," Kieran concedes. "But he's probably still out of it because of the meds. They mess with your hormones and shit. Maybe he has like...pregnancy cravings."

"Pregnancy cravings."

"You know what I mean. It's hormones, man!"

"Right," Dawson says, dubious. "I suppose hormones made him like Disney movies?"

"Isn't his brain all fucked up after the crash? Maybe he just needed something chill."

Dawson's not sure what it is that's begging him to argue. Kieran's skepticism isn't exactly misplaced and the explanations he's offering are perfectly plausible. So why does Dawson find them irritating instead of helpful?

"He wanted to learn how to do laundry. You can't explain that away with hormonal changes."

"Huh?"

"I went to do laundry, and he asked if he could watch, because he wanted to do it next time."

"Cal. Doing laundry," Kieran says, then bursts out laughing. "I'd pay good money to see that."

Dawson grins. He'd like to see that too. See him do any house chores, really. "How about I call you when the day comes?"

"Deal. Anything else bizarre?"

He could write a book. "Well, he was shocked to find out we don't cook, so I suggested we go shopping. And then...I cooked."

"You cooked?" Kieran repeats. "I thought he hates your cooking." The way he says it makes it clear what he thinks of Cal's opinion.

"Me too. But he said he liked it."

Kieran hums. "Alien abduction, maybe?"

"That's what I was thinking!"

"Where's he now?"

"In the bedroom, doing his rehab exercises."

"Cute," Kieran snarks. "Enough about the asshole. How are you handling this?"

"I'm...handling it."

"Dee..."

"Don't *Dee* me. I'm handling it, okay? It's a lot. It's weird, but..." He huffs. "Honestly? I expected worse." And he'd been worried as heck that all the memories would come rushing back to Cal once he set foot in the apartment—an environment that was the most familiar, apart from his office.

"I just worry about you."

"I know," Dawson says, defensiveness draining out of him. "And I hate and love you for it equally."

"The feeling is mutual," Kieran grumbles. Dawson can tell he's smiling. "Promise me you'll keep an eye on him. Don't let him fuck with your head again."

Dawson frowns. "Kieran, he has no idea who he is. Or who I am, for that matter."

"Yeah, maybe. But he could still remember."

"Unlikely. If he doesn't start remembering within the next two weeks, the chances become pretty much zero." The doctors said so.

"It almost sounds like you're hoping he won't remember." Kieran says.

Dawson bristles at the accusation in his tone. "So what if I do? I'll take weird, oblivious Cal over the—"

"Asshole Cal?"

"—any day," Dawson finishes.

"Sure, makes sense," Kieran agrees easily. Too easily. "I just hope you're not gonna slide on your rose-colored glasses and pretend the last six years never happened."

"What's that supposed to mean?"

"It means that I don't want you to forget what kind of person he is just because he seems like a harmless puppy now. I don't care if he's all clueless, helpless, or oblivious, or whatever you wanna call it. He's a dick, and you promised to finish what you started."

Tension settles in Dawson's body. He thinks back on the day a couple weeks ago, when he was sitting right on this sofa, Kieran next to him, determined to cut himself loose from the shackles.

"Yeah, I remember," Dawson murmurs, thinking of the divorce papers sitting in his nightstand. "And if it gets you off my case, I'll have you know that I made an appointment with a therapist."

"That Ashley chick?" Kieran asks, sounding surprised.

"Yeah. I have an appointment next week."

"Okay. Wow. Yeah, that actually makes me feel better." Which is saying a lot, considering Kieran's narrow-minded opinions on mental health professionals. He could use one too, in fact. Maybe then he could stop dating all those...ehm...interesting people he gravitates towards.

"Great. I'm happy for you," Dawson says, very dryly.

"Fuck off."

"You fuck off."

"Fine."

"Fine."

Kieran snickers. "Love you, man. Check your phone, will you?"

"Yeah, yeah. Love you, too."

Dawson hangs up, a smile on his face that lasts all of five seconds before it percolates that he needs to call Olivia as well. With a bit of luck, he won't have to go through all the details again.

"Oh, thank god," she says in lieu of a greeting. "I was worried sick!"

"You're always worried."

"For good reason."

"How are the girls?"

"Dead to the world. How are *you*?"

"I'm okay. Cal's settled in...kinda."

"I don't care about the shithead," she bites out. "How's he coping with the brain thing?"

Dawson stifles a laugh. "Exceptionally well." *So far.* "He asks the weirdest questions, but he's fine. Healing nicely, too."

"Weird how?"

Dawson shrugs. "I don't know. Like...stuff that wouldn't be my priority if I forgot the last 38 years of my life." He still doesn't know what to make of Cal's obsession with their pictures. Or the lack thereof.

Olivia harrumphs. "But *you're* okay?"

"I am."

"And the divorce? Have you talked to him about it?"

"I just got him home, Liv." Can't he get a goddamn break?

"I don't see how that's relevant. This is actually perfect. You don't have to explain anything. You can just tell him you were about to divorce anyway. That you already talked about it. "

Dawson takes a slow, deep breath before replying. "Liv, he lost his memory, not his IQ. And you can't seriously be asking me to do that." And frankly, the idea of packing his bags and leaving Cal to his devices leaves a bad taste in his mouth.

Olivia huffs irritably. "Fine. Then tell him the truth. You were about to ask for divorce when the accident happened."

"Right. And when he asks why?"

"Tell him the *truth*, duh. That he's an asshole."

Sensing an incoming headache, Dawson pinches the bridge of his nose. "Yeah, sure. Let's say that works. Then what? I leave him on his own?"

"Um, yeah?" Olivia says like he's the one being unreasonable. "You said it yourself; his IQ is intact, so he can take care of himself. He's not an invalid. And doesn't he have a brother?"

"Yeah. One that's currently ironing shit out at the company."

"Well, there you go."

"Liv..."

"I swear to god, Dee. You're gonna give me gray hair."

"You already have gray hair."

"I do not!"

"I saw a few last time."

"Fuck you too." Letting out a deep sigh, she says, "Seriously, Dee. Don't be an idiot about this."

He swallows, throat dry. "I have it under control."

She scoffs.

"Liv," he warns. "I know what I'm doing." *Lies, lies, lies!* "I have to go."

"I'll call you soon. You better pick up or I'm coming down there."

"I'm shaking in my boots." He really is. He'd rather deal with Cal than his sister, that's how bad she gets.

"Goodnight, you little shit."

"Night."

His whole body goes limp once he hangs up. Thank fuck that's done.

The phone goes off again. He groans. If it's Olivia again—

Dawson bites back a curse when Ellis' name flashes on the screen. He'd promised he'd update him on Cal since he was getting released today and Ellis is back in Sydney. It completely slipped his mind, but in his defense, Ellis hasn't tried to get a hold of him.

"Hey, Ellis." He doesn't wait for a response. "I'm sorry I forgot to call. Obviously. It's been full-on."

Ellis doesn't sound irritated as Dawson would've expected. "It's fine. I almost forgot what day today was, too."

"Busy?"

"Fucking crazy," Ellis corrects. "Driving home now. I need to finish packing."

Dawson grimaces in sympathy. Although he's felt uprooted ever since he'd received the call from Ellis that Cal was in an accident, at least he's not the one who has to leave everything behind and move states.

"So you've found a place?"

Ellis grunts an affirmation. "Yeah. Just a rental for now."

"Have you found a buyer for your apartment? That was quick."

A pause. "I haven't put it up yet."

"Why not?"

"Cal can still get his marbles together and return to work."

"Yeah, I don't think that's going to happen," he says carefully.

"Why?" Ellis asks, suspicious.

How to put this... "Let's say the marbles have scattered in all directions."

"Is he okay?"

Dawson looks towards the bedroom. He doesn't hear anything now, so Cal must've gone to bed. "I don't think there's anything *left* of him. And I don't mean just his memories. I mean...*him*. I don't really know how to act around him."

Ellis sucks in a breath. "Dawson, if you feel unsafe—"

"No," Dawson tells him. "Not like that." He's been tiptoeing around Cal for most of the time they've been together. This isn't like that. Yes, he's on edge, but it's different. "I'm just afraid I'm going to mess up. Say something that will confuse him. I don't know."

"Dawson, he's been in a car-crash, had a collapsed lung, and a ruptured spleen. He almost died *twice*." Technically, he did die once. "You're fine. You won't kill him by saying something to him, although I wouldn't blame you if you were tempted."

Dawson laughs. "That's pretty morbid."

"If the shoe fits."

"Yeah, okay, I get it. When are you flying in?"

"Tomorrow."

"I thought it'd be some time next week. Is it falling apart without you here?"

"Something like that."

Geez. Dawson doesn't envy him. "We could have dinner if you'd like."

Ellis makes a sound, something between a snort and a chuckle. "Hate to break it to you, but I don't bat for your team."

Dawson sputters, his cheeks flaming. He scowls when he can hear Ellis suppressing a laugh. "Ha ha. I meant you, me, and Cal, you dick."

Ellis gives a rumbling laugh. "Sure. Family dinner. How could I miss that?"

"Is that a yes?"

"Sure. Just text me the place and time."

"I thought you could just come over. I'll cook."

"You'll cook?" Ellis says incredulously.

"You don't have to sound so excited," Dawson grumbles, offended.

"No, that's not…" He goes quiet for a moment. "I just haven't had a home-cooked meal in…Christ, almost ten years."

"What?" Dawson squeaks.

"I don't cook. Couldn't even if I had time."

"What about your girlfriends?"

Ellis makes a choking sound. "Yeah, definitely not."

Dawson feels bad for him. It only makes him more determined to get him over for dinner.

"It's settled, then. I'll cook for us when you get back."

"I'm a terrible person to cook for. Dairy doesn't agree with me."

"That's an easy fix. There are so many alternatives these days."

"You really don't have to—"

"Ellis, just shut up and come for dinner. Please?"

Ellis heaves a sigh. "Alright."

"That wasn't so hard, was it?" He hears Ellis' answering grunt and smiles. "Say Friday, six o'clock? If you're not too tired."

"Sounds good."

"Great. See you then!"

"See you."

Once he hangs up, the fatigue that's accumulated throughout the day descends on him, making his eyelids heavy. He rubs his eyes, willing himself to stay awake long enough to take a shower. And then...

Then he'll go to sleep. Next to Cal. Like he's done for years. So why does the idea of getting into bed with Cal make him queasy? Is it because he'll essentially be sleeping next to a stranger? If that's the case, he has nothing to fret about, because that 'stranger' seems safer than Cal ever was.

Kieran's words ring in his ears. *'I don't want you to forget what kind of person he is just because he seems like a harmless puppy now.'*

Right. He'd better not forget that.

The bizarreness carries over to the next day. For one, Cal is up before Dawson which happens...never. Second, it's weird not to see him inhaling a cup of coffee like his life depends on it.

"Well, aren't you chirpy first thing in the morning," Dawson comments saltily while trying to drag his ass out of bed.

"The mattress is so comfortable. It was like sleeping on a cloud," Cal says dreamily. After sleeping in a hospital bed for weeks, it's no wonder. "Did you sleep well?"

He didn't sleep for shit, tossing and turning while his thoughts wreaked havoc in his mind. It wasn't until three or four that he finally started to drift.

"I slept fine."

He takes a quick, cold shower to wake himself up, brushes his teeth, and slides into a pair of well-worn joggers and an old t-shirt with a small hole around the collar.

"Should I change?" Cal questions when he sees what Dawson is wearing. Cal put on a pair of jeans and a nice dark blue t-shirt

"Nah, you're fine. You're not going to get your hands dirty like me."

Two small lines appear between Cal's brows. "It sounds like hard work."

Dawson still remembers how achy he was after the first couple of shifts when he started two years ago. His back was so sore he couldn't find a comfortable sleeping position and didn't even feel like going for a run. These days, he doesn't even notice the soreness.

"You get used to it."

"You like doing it for free?" Cal asks, but not in that incredulous kind of way that people usually do, and which annoys Dawson to no end. But Cal asks like he's genuinely curious.

"Yeah. I love dogs. All animals, really, but especially dogs," he admits, feeling a smile forming on his lips. A pang of sadness passes through him. He'd love to have a dog, something to cuddle and take care of, something that would be happy to see him when he comes home. "You might get bored there. Are you sure you wanna come with?"

Cal makes a point of looking around the living room and shrugs. "I'd be bored here too."

"You could watch something. Read a book."

By the face he makes, Cal doesn't find the idea appealing. "I'd rather be with you," he says, so freaking casual. "And this is obviously important to you. I want to be a part of it." He acts like he doesn't know he just threw Dawson for a huge fucking loop.

Then again, Cal's been saying things like that since Dawson began visiting him at the hospital. Just a small thing here and there that no one would think about twice—except for Dawson. At first, he kind of suspected Cal was taking the piss, enjoying making Dawson flustered and confused. It wouldn't be the first time.

But no, that's not it. Dawson knows what Cal is like when he's in a manipulative mood. He knows the signs; the dark glint in his eye and the authoritative power oozing from him.

There's none of that here. Cal's expression is open and so earnest it's fucking with Dawson's head.

Who is this man? This man who likes Dawson's cooking and hates coffee. Who watches animated movies and enjoys walks on the beach. Who has an obsession with donuts and insists on going to the shelter with Dawson just so he can be with him.

What. The. Actual. Fuck?

"If you're sure," Dawson says when he finally finds words. After yet another confirmation from Cal that yes, he's indeed sure, they make their way to the garage and head to the cafe.

Since it's not rush hour, there are only two people waiting at the counter and they're served quickly.

Gabe's ever-present smile widens when he spots them.

"Hey! Two days in a row. You weren't kidding."

Dawson points an accusatory finger at Cal. "That's on him."

Cal ignores him, his nose practically plastered to the glass of the pastry cabinet.

"Hey, no complaints here." Gabe holds up his hands. "It's good for business."

"Right." Dawson looks around. "Where's Zeke?"

"He texted me last night, saying he's not feeling well. I told him to sleep it off."

"You look rather perky for someone who'll be flying solo during rush hour."

Gabe waves his hand at that. "Been there, done that. Plus, I'm charming, and even if there's a long wait, the customers always forgive me."

"Is that part of your superpowers?" Dawson teases. Gabe does indeed have a penchant for making people love him, though Dawson contributes it to his bubbly personality rather than supernatural forces.

Gabe sends him a conspiratorial wink, and his gaze moves behind Dawson.

"Well, hello, stranger!"

"Hi, Gabe!" comes a familiar voice that makes Dawson whirl around.

The initial happiness he feels at seeing his best friend is promptly replaced by suspicion. "What are you doing here?"

Strolling over, Kieran throws his arms around Dawson and says, "Checking on you." He slaps his back and lets him go, his eyes wandering towards Cal.

"That's unnecessary," Dawson scowls.

"I'll be the judge of that," Kieran says with a pinched smile, glaring daggers at Cal, who finally got distracted enough to look away from the display.

"Hello."

"Hey. Guess you don't recognize me," Kieran says, plastering on a fake smile.

"Kieran, yes? Dawson's best friend," Cal says, unsure. When Kieran's brows flick up in surprise, he adds, "I saw your pictures. It's nice to meet you. Again." He hesitates, then offers his hand reluctantly.

At first, it looks like Kieran's not going to take it. Dawson really doesn't feel like explaining his behavior to Cal. He considers poking Kieran in the ribs but it's unnecessary. Kieran reaches out, taking Cal's hand and giving it what looks like a very firm handshake. To his credit, Cal doesn't even blink.

Dawson turns his attention to Gabe who's watching everything with an uncomfortable expression. He claps his hands together, making the tension dissipate a little. "So, Cal, what's it gonna be today?"

"Don't go crazy, Cal," Dawson warns as Cal opens his mouth.

Judging by Cal's crestfallen expression, he was planning to do just that.

"Can I have some for later, too?" he tries.

Dawson levels him with a stare. "You can't eat pastry for the whole day, Cal."

"Why not?"

"Because you just had a major abdominal surgery, that's why."

Like a damn kid, seriously.

Letting out a disappointed sigh, Cal turns to Gabe. "I'll have the pumpkin spiced donut, please."

Gabe puts the donut in a paper bag, handing it to him. "Drink?"

"Not coffee," Cal says with disgust.

Gabe chuckles. "Right. How about hot chocolate?"

Cal turns to Dawson pleadingly.

Not having the strength to argue again, Dawson relents. "Fine."

"Dude, what the fuck?" Kieran asks in a whisper, staring at Cal like he's watching an alien.

"Don't ask me. I don't know."

"He's been like that the whole time?"

"Yup."

"Damn. You weren't kidding." He snickers. "It's kind of funny."

"I guess," Dawson admits begrudgingly. While this whole thing is messing with him, he does find amusement in Cal's antics.

"I still don't like him."

Dawson rolls his eyes. "Will you stop stalking me, at least?"

Kieran ponders it for a moment, sharp eyes glued to Cal who's just being handed his finished drink and looking like an overgrown puppy that just got a treat. "Yeah, seems like you're safe."

"Like I've been telling you repeatedly?"

"Shut up and place your order. It's your turn."

Dawson gets his usual chai and an almond croissant, then nods at Kieran. "Having your usual?" Not that he deserves anything for this stunt, but they always treat each other when they're somewhere together. It's hard to break a habit.

"Yup."

Dawson adds an order of a medium cup with two sugars and goes to pay. He hasn't even turned on the app on his watch when Cal pushes up next to him.

"I'll do it," he announces, pulling out his phone. After a few quick swipes, he places it on top of the card terminal to pay.

Dawson smiles. He had to remind Cal how to use the digital wallet, but he only had to show him once before he picked it up again.

"Did he just buy me coffee?" Kieran asks, appalled.

Dawson gives him a blank look. "You do realize whenever I paid for something it was his money, right?"

Kieran clearly never thought about it like that, because his nose scrunches with distaste. "Yeah but...weird."

"Well, get over it."

A loud moan snatches both their attention. They look at Cal to see him sipping his hot chocolate with a blissed out little smile.

"This is amazing," Cal says to Gabe, making him preen. Then he starts on the donut, his cheeks bulging like a chipmunk.

Dawson sighs. "Great. Now it's official. He's addicted to sugar."

"Beats alcohol addiction, in my opinion," Kieran mutters. It's a tasteless joke, but Dawson lets out a small chuckle, because the situation is rather ridiculous.

"When you put it like that..."

"Where do you want to sit?"

"Actually, we need to head out."

Kieran eyes him critically. "You gonna eat and drink while you drive?"

Cal jumps in before Dawson can answer. "We're going for a walk."

Kieran looks at Cal as if he speaks a foreign language. "For a walk."

Cal nods, smiling as he sips his chocolate. "On the beach."

"On the beach." Kieran looks at Dawson. "You're going for a walk on the beach."

"Yes," Dawson says irritably. "A walk on the beach. It helps build up Cal's lung capacity."

"Right," Kieran says in that way that makes it clear how much he thinks this is bullshit. He takes Dawson's elbow. "A word, Dee?"

"How about no?"

"Don't make me drag you away."

Dawson sighs. "Fine."

Once they are out of earshot, Kieran spins him around, fixing him with a stern look. "Explain."

Dawson sips his chai. "Explain what?"

Kieran gives him an unimpressed look. "Remember our little talk about playing house with your abusive husband?"

Dawson grinds his teeth until they ache. "I remember. Do you remember what I said?"

"We should focus more on what you didn't say. You didn't say you'd pretend to be a lovey-dovey couple who goes for romantic walks on the beach—"

"I told you; Cal needs the exercise."

"—not to mention you're taking him to our cafe—"

"It's a public place and he wanted donuts."

"—or to the shelter. Didn't you say he hates dogs?"

"He doesn't hate dogs. He just never wanted one."

"What's next, Dee? A romantic, candlelit dinner? Gonna listen to some Celine Dion. Stargaze? I bet you've got a great view from your place."

"Kieran," Dawson says slowly. "Enough."

"No!" Dawson shushes him but it has no effect. "Not enough, Dee! What the fuck are you doing?"

Dawson swallows back angry words. He knows Kieran means well, even if he wants to deck him right here, right now. "Just drop it, okay? I'm not pretending to be anything." He glares at him when Kieran scoffs. "I'm gonna help him get adjusted, help him familiarize himself with stuff again. He doesn't remember being a jerk, so I'm not gonna treat him like one."

"A jerk," Kieran mumbles. "Jesus Christ. I swear when they were giving out self-preservation instincts, you must have been taking a nap."

"I don't think you have a leg to stand on when it comes to self-preservation. Or common sense for that matter."

"Hey!"

"Kieran," Dawson tries again. "I'll be okay. I promise. You're catastrophizing."

"It's called contingency planning."

"Again. No leg to stand on."

"Jesus. Fine!" He throws his hands up, then points at Dawson. "But if I get a bad feeling about this—"

"You mean more than you already do?"

"If I get a worse feeling about this, I'm calling your sister."

Dawson gasps. "You wouldn't dare."

Kieran smiles smugly. "Try me, bitch."

"I hate you."

Kieran sends him a kiss and lifts his coffee cup in cheers. "Later, shithead." He waves at Gabe before leaving. Dawson watches him walk down the street. Before he disappears, Kieran points two fingers at his eyes, then at Dawson and mouths what seems to be *I'm watching you.*

Dawson flips him off and nearly spills his drink when Cal manifests next to him.

"Everything okay?" he asks with a frown.

"Jesus, you gave me a scare," Dawson laughs breathlessly.

"I'm sorry," Cal says. "You looked upset."

"Kieran is just being a shit," he explains, but Cal looks confused. "He was worried about how we're handling the...situation."

"Oh. That's nice of him."

"Uh-huh." If only Cal knew. "Ready to go?"

"Yeah."

"Wait, what's that?" Dawson points at the paper bag in Cal's hand. Panic flashes across Cal's face.

"The donut."

"If that's the donut, why is there chocolate on your lips?"

Cal wipes his mouth, but it's no use. Dawson snatches the bag, opening it. "Cal!" He dangles the chocolate donut in front of him like evidence of crime.

Cal sputters. "Gabe made me take it!"

"Hey!" Gabe calls out indignantly. "You weren't supposed to tell!"

"I'm sorry! I panicked!"

Dawson is seriously starting to rethink his choices. "Gabe, stop enabling him."

"But he looked so sad."

"Gabe..."

"Gosh, you're such a slavedriver!"

"I wasn't going to eat it now," Cal says guiltily.

"Good. Then you won't mind if I keep it and give it to you later."

Cal pouts all the way to the beach, but at least he looks a little happy about his hot chocolate. Because Cal now loves hot chocolate, of course he does.

"Hot chocolate, huh?" Dawson asks with a chuckle.

Cal hums happily, extending the cup to Dawson. "Want to try?"

Smiling, Dawson shakes his head. "I've had it. I know it's good." He raises his own cup. "I prefer chai, though. Try it."

Cal takes the cup, his expression intrigued. He seems thoughtful as he takes a small sip, then a bigger one. "It's...strong. But good." He gives an approving nod.

"Yeah, lots of spices. This is Zeke's recipe. He doesn't go easy on the cardamon."

"Gabe wrote you a message," Cal says, turning the cup in his hand.

"He did?" Dawson reaches for it. How did he miss it? Probably because he was too preoccupied with getting Kieran off his back and making sure Cal doesn't eat himself into a sugar coma.

Now that Cal pointed it out, the words jump straight out at him. *Not everything has to make sense.* Well, that's...cryptic. Then again, Gabe's messages generally are.

"Did he write you one?" he asks Cal.

Cal shakes his head. "Do you know what yours means?"

"Nope. But Gabe loves mystery. You'll see when he writes something for you."

Cal smiles. "Looking forward to it."

They walk slowly, having taken off their shoes. They talk about Gabe and the cafe. Cal asks if they could bake some stuff at home. Dawson says no. Cal pouts again.

They eventually find some shade under the trees and sit down in the sand.

"That looks like fun," Cal says.

Dawson follows the direction of his gaze to a group of people surfing further down the beach.

"You can surf too." It's been a while since Cal had found the time for it, but he used to do it a lot when they first met.

"Really?" Cal asks with disbelief. His expression turns rueful as he watches the surfers. "I doubt I could now."

Dawson thinks back on what Doctor Connelly told him. "The doctors said that muscle memory relates to a different part of the brain from the one that stores your memories. Your body probably still knows how to do this stuff."

Cal mulls it over, then gives a decisive nod. "I'd like to try."

"Yeah, sure." Dawson laughs. "In a few months when you're not all stitched up and won't be attracting sharks with bleeding all over yourself."

Aaand there goes the pouting again. "Do you surf?"

Dawson nearly snorts out his chai. "Really badly. I have two left feet and zero body coordination."

"Did I ever try to teach you?"

"Yeah," Dawson admits quietly. He still remembers the excitement of that first time Cal got a training board for him and spent hours trying to teach him basic stuff. He also remembers how stupid and embarrassed he felt when the one time he actually managed to stand up, he ended up going down in two seconds flat.

He remembers how annoyed Cal was with him, although he didn't say anything. Not until Dawson asked him a few weeks later if they could try again. Cal had given him a patronizing look that spoke volumes, then made it abundantly clear that he had no such intention, because he had better things to do than waste time teaching him stuff that a kid could do. Needless to say, Dawson never asked again.

"But I was really bad so you gave up."

Cal frowns. As though he hadn't heard a word Dawson just said, he says, "Maybe we could go together next time. When I'm not stitched up."

Dawson should say *no, thank you*. He has no interest in having a repeat of that humiliating experience. Evidently, not all of him is on board, because his stupid heart flutters at the idea, at the thought of being able to rewrite the experience. Not that there would be any rewriting, because time might change many things but ridding Dawson of his status as a major klutz isn't one of them.

Despite that knowledge, he finds himself saying, "That would be nice." And when Cal gives him a brilliant smile, his blue irises turning turquoise in the sunlight, he can't bring himself to take it back. "But you'll have to promise me not to leave me out there when you lose your patience." It's meant as a joke, a distraction. He feels too open and vulnerable, Kieran's warning ringing in his ears.

"I wouldn't do that." Cal's expression is positively horrified. "Did I ever do that?"

"No," Dawson assures him quickly. "But I wouldn't blame you. I *am* pretty bad."

Cal makes a displeased sound. "Maybe I just wasn't a good teacher."

Having no idea what to say to that, Dawson throws back whatever is left in his cup and changes the topic.

"Oh, I meant to tell you. I spoke to Ellis last night. He's flying in today. I invited him over for dinner tomorrow. Is that okay?"

"Yes, of course. I haven't spoken to him in a few days. Is he moving here permanently?"

"He rented a place. He doesn't want to go all in if there's a chance your memories might come back."

"I'm not sure I should go back to the job, anyway. If what you said about me hating it is true, then it wouldn't be a wise choice."

Rendered speechless once again, Dawson says diplomatically, "You might feel differently if you remember. You dedicated most of your life to it after all."

"I don't know if that's a good thing," Cal says with a frown. "We're married, but I never made time for you. All the pictures we have are from some social event that means nothing to me."

There they go again with the pictures. "It really bothers you, doesn't it? That we don't have pictures."

"It's...confusing." Cal gives a frustrated sigh. "I have all these...emotions swirling inside me and no point of reference for them. Aside from you."

"What do you mean?"

"I don't know who I am, Dawson," he points out the obvious. "Maybe it's not such a bad thing, because honestly? After all you've told me? I sound like an ass." His expression becomes pinched. "But even though I don't know who I am, I know my feelings for you."

"Your feelings for me?" Dawson repeats dumbly, blushing at how squeaky his voice has become.

Cal nods, looking Dawson in the eye. "I can feel it. How much you mean to me. And it's just so wrong that I don't have anything to show for it. Nothing at all. I even went through our text messages. There's only one from you, apologizing for not being able to make it home on time. That's it."

The world around him sways for a second. The text. Cal read the text. The one that Dawson sent on Olivia's birthday when the migraine hit. The one he knew he would regret later. The one that made Cal mad and...

Dawson clenches his eyes shut, shaking his head as if that could erase what happened.

"Dawson? What's wrong?"

He takes a deep breath, opening his eyes slowly. He's afraid to look at Cal, unsure how he'll react when he sees his face after he was just thrown into that particular memory. When he finally opens them, it's slow and cautious, and he holds his breath the whole time.

Despite his fear, his flight or fight instinct stays dormant. It doesn't awaken even when he notices how close Cal is, concern etched into his features. And yet, Dawson doesn't feel an overwhelming need to move, to hide.

A thought comes to him out of nowhere. "Let's take one now."

"What?"

"A picture." Dawson fishes his phone out of his pocket, suddenly eager about the idea. "Let's take one."

"Oh." Cal's face lights up. "I'd like that."

After a moment of hesitation, Dawson shuffles closer to Cal until they're almost hip to hip. He turns the camera on and stretches out his arm, trying to get a good angle, but their faces are too far apart to fit properly in the frame.

"I'm really bad at taking selfies. I, uh, think we need to be closer."

Entirely oblivious to Dawson's internal struggle, Cal leans slightly back and puts a hand on the ground behind Dawson, so his body is angled towards him and their faces only inches apart.

"Better?"

Dawson swallows around the rock that's suddenly in his throat. Trying to steady his trembling hand, he says, "Better. Alright, smile." He's not sure who he's telling it to. It feels like a major effort to summon a smile that doesn't look completely deranged. It gets easier when he focuses on Cal instead. Cal's trying to smile, but his brows are furrowed like the concept of smiling for a picture is foreign to him. It makes Dawson grin, and he presses the shutter, the automated function taking five pictures in a quick succession.

"How does it look?" Cal asks when Dawson swipes through the photos, shaking with how much he wants to laugh.

"Like we have no idea what's going on." He positions the phone so Cal can see.

Cal cocks his head, studying the picture intently. "I like it."

"What?" Dawson snorts in disbelief.

Cal smiles—now that's a smile worthy of the camera—then lifts his gaze to Dawson. "You're very beautiful."

"Uh, thanks." Dawson's face feels like it's sunburned. He fumbles with the phone, not used to Cal looking at him like that. "Do you want me to send it to you?" He'd rather delete it—they look like idiots—but that would probably upset Cal.

"Please."

Cal's phone pings with a notification a few seconds later. He pulls it out, that soft smile in a full bloom now.

Beginning to feel antsy and restless, Dawson stands up, brushing sand off his clothes. "We should go."

It's a small relief when Cal doesn't protest.

"Are you sure there's nothing I can do?" Cal asks for the fifth time since arriving at the shelter.

Before Dawson can repeat, for the fifth time, that it's too early for Cal to do anything strenuous, Aubrey cuts in.

"You could play with the dogs. We take them to the playground when it's time to clean the kennels."

Cal turns hopeful eyes to Dawson, making him feel like an ass for shaking his head.

"They get excited. I don't want them to jump on you or anything."

"Maybe take them for a walk?" Aubrey suggests. She's purposefully choosing activities that don't really require prior training.

"He can't walk too much just yet."

"I can walk almost half an hour. And I can take breaks," Cal tries to argue, looking like one of the dogs when they're begging for a treat. Realizing he's outnumbered, Dawson admits defeat.

"Okay, let me introduce you," Aubrey announces excitedly. "Or do you want to do it?"

Dawson might as well. No reason to pull Aubrey away from the pile of work she has to do. "Sure."

They make their way around the kennels, a few already vacated. There are labels with the dogs' names and a brief description on each kennel, but Dawson introduces everyone to Cal, telling him a little something about each dog. While he loves all of them, he can't deny he has his favorites.

He grins when Donut is already waiting for him, his tail wagging and one of his paws stuck outside the door.

"I want you to meet someone." He kneels in front of the kennel and reaches inside with two fingers to scratch his head. "This is Donut."

"Donut?" Cal says with amusement.

"I know, right?" He knew Cal would like it. "But please don't eat him."

"I'll try very hard not to," Cal retorts, very dryly.

Donut's been here longer than the other dogs, so it's only natural Dawson became attached. While he loves coming here to see Donut, it breaks his heart that no one wants to adopt him. People normally go crazy for Frenchies—Dawson has opinions on that—but clearly having a pet who requires a little extra care due to a mild health issue is way too inconvenient. Fucking figures.

A few more scratches, and then they move onto the last kennel containing a feisty Pomeranian.

"Cal, meet Lola." Lola growls, shaking on her skinny legs. "Unlike the others, she's a bit of a bitch, so if she snaps at you, it's not personal." Her eyes are sharp and aimed at Dawson, as if she can tell he's badmouthing her. "Wanna walk her?"

"What?" Cal takes a big step back when Lola lets out a high-pitched bark. "She doesn't seem to like me."

"She doesn't like anybody." Taking a leash from the compartment attached to the kennel, Dawson unlocks the cage. He opens it a crack, using his body as a barrier so Lola doesn't escape. "Come on, you little shit," he says affectionately. "Walk time."

At the word 'walk', Lola's tiny ears twitch. She cocks her fluffy head, then walks into Dawson's arms. He rewards her by rubbing her back, chuckling when she licks his hand. Standing up, he hands the leash to Cal who looks at it like it's a snake.

"Don't look so spooked. I promise she has more bark than bite." When Cal doesn't move, Dawson takes his hand, loops the leash around it. "Scream if you need rescuing."

Judging by Cal's expression, he's considering screaming right now.

Biting back a smile, Dawson shoos him away, reminding him to take breaks and to call if he starts feeling even a little off.

As Cal takes off with a growling Lola in tow, Dawson gets to work, hosing down the empty kennels and making sure everything is clean for the fur babies. For the time being, he forgets about the hospital, and Cal's amnesia, and even the conversation with Kieran, the familiar physical activity soothing his whirling thoughts. He loves doing this, and, strangely enough, he's glad that he can do this for free. He knows the only reason he can afford to do this unpaid is thanks to Cal's assets, but for once he's glad for it.

He wishes he could contribute to the shelter more, especially financially, but he can't just go around spending Cal's money. But maybe if he asked him now...

Shit, he doesn't want to take advantage. He really doesn't. But Cal's been pretty laid back about, well, everything since he woke up, so if Dawson brought it up...

He shuts the idea down before it gets out of control.

"So, that's your hubby, huh?" Aubrey says from behind him, opening Donut's kennel to take him outside. "Shame you never brought him here before."

Dawson thinks what to say. Aubrey's nice; she's great, actually, but the two of them aren't close. She knows about the crash and the surgery, but Dawson doesn't feel like sharing anything else with her.

"Yeah, well. He's busy with work and stuff. He needs to take it slow now after the surgery, but he gets bored at home." He shrugs. "It was his idea to come with me."

"Hmm. He sure is nice to look at."

Dawson snorts. "He's gay."

Aubrey rolls her eyes. "And married, yes. But I'm only human."

Huffing out a laugh, Dawson focuses on cleaning.

Cal's always been a head-turner, and not even Dawson was immune, duh. But that was a long time ago. He knows better now.

"What kind of surgery was it?"

"I can't remember the medical term. He had a collapsed lung, which was quite easy to treat, but then he started bleeding inside and they had to open him up. It's...going to take a while before he's back to normal." He doesn't say anything about the memories.

"Shit," Aubrey breathes. "You must have been scared for him."

Dawson's hands still, his stomach hollowing out. For a second, he's back at the hospital, standing outside Cal's room while the doctors and nurses are rushing in, the machines going off. "Yeah," he says. "Scared."

Aubrey lets him be after that. By the time Cal returns, Dawson has composed himself. Cal, on the other hand, looks a little worse for wear and is watching Lola like he's expecting her to attack any second.

Dawson brushes dirt off his knees and goes to take Lola from him. "You survived!"

Cal visibly relaxes once the leash is in Dawson's hand. "She's planning my murder, I'm sure of it."

Dawson giggles, crouching down to ruffle Lola's fur. "You're not planning Cal's murder, are you? Tell him you're not." When Lola just pants happily, lifting her head so Dawson can scratch the juncture of her neck, Dawson laughs. "See? No homicidal thoughts."

Cal's skeptical. "I'll stay away, just in case."

Dawson laughs. "Before you do that, could you take her to the playground? I haven't done her kennel yet."

Cal reluctantly takes the leash back. "What should I do next?"

"Rest."

"But—"

"Take a break. A long one. And then you can walk another dog, how's that sound?"

Pursing his lips in thought, Cal nods at last.

"It's settled then." Dawson grabs the hose, pausing when Cal keeps standing there. "Yes?"

"Do you need help?"

Dawson manages not to groan. "No, I don't need help. But you need to sit down. Now, Cal," he says firmly when Cal wants to argue.

Putting on that ridiculous pout, Cal finally wanders off.

When Dawson goes to check on him twenty minutes later, Cal's nowhere to be seen. He asks Aubrey, who happily tells him Cal's taken another dog for a walk.

Dawson has to close his eyes and take a few very long, very deep breaths to keep himself in check. Fucking Cal will give him gray hair. He needs to start doing yoga. Meditation. Anything to be able to deal with him in the long run.

He goes back to work. That counts as meditation, right? Whether it does or not, it helps. He's mostly calmed down when Aubrey sticks her head through the door some time later.

"Hey, Dawson?"

"Yeah?"

"Don't panic, but Cal was a little dizzy when he came back, so I made him sit down. He insisted he's fine and not to call you, but I figured you'd want to know."

The bottom of Dawson's stomach drops. He tells himself to keep calm, it's just some dizziness, like she said. He grabs a few paper towels and dries his hands.

"Thanks. I'm finished for today, so I'll just take him home."

Aubrey smiles, holding the door open for him. "Good idea."

Dawson marches out of there with the sole intention of giving Cal a piece of his mind, but the indignation drains out of him when he finds him. He's sitting on a bench near the yard and leaning against the wall behind him with his eyes closed. His features are taut with concentration—he looks like he's doing his breathing exercise.

"Cal? You okay?"

Cal's eyes drift open and land on Dawson. He grumbles under his breath, looking annoyed. "I'm fine."

Dawson grunts. "From now on, you're not allowed to use that word. You clearly have no idea what it means."

Cal grumbles something again.

"What's that?"

"I said you're bossy."

"That's right," Dawson says, rushing forward when Cal starts to stand up. "So you better listen when I tell you to take it easy."

"I did take it easy. I took breaks."

"Not easy enough. Come on, let's go home."

"Are you finished?"

"Yeah."

"Oh." Cal licks his lips. "Can we go to the beach, now?"

"No. We're going home."

"But I'm f—" He halts when Dawson glares at him. "I'm okay."

"That one is banned too."

"Please?"

"Jesus." Dawson resists the urge to slam his head against the wall. "We'll go later, how about that? When you're rested."

"Okay!"

The ride home is quiet but quick. They stop for takeout on the way because Dawson can't be bothered to cook, but Cal doesn't complain. Dawson can feel him looking at him, and he seems like he wants to say something. Cal lasts until they get home and digs into their styrofoam-wrapped lunch before he speaks.

"I'm sorry about today. I didn't mean to upset you."

Guilt slams into Dawson. Has he been giving Cal the cold shoulder or something? That wasn't his intention. He's just tired.

"I'm not upset, Cal. I was worried. You just got out of the hospital."

"But I feel okay." He chuckles when the word leaves his lips. "Honestly, I feel okay. A little sore, but I'm recovering much quicker than the doctors told me I would."

"They did say it's different for everybody, but I prefer to err on the side of caution."

"I understand." His smile has Dawson's breath catching. "I won't worry you anymore. But you can't baby me all the time."

"I'm not babying you," Dawson mumbles, shoveling food into his mouth.

"Yes, you are."

"Fine. Then you can change your bandages yourself."

Predictably, Cal pouts, frowning at his food. "I can. The nurses taught me how to do it."

"Okay, then."

"Okay."

"Okay."

Dawson bites the inside of his cheek. "Stop saying okay."

"You said it first."

"You repeated it."

"So did you!"

"Okay." Dawson holds his hands in the air, laughing. Then he reaches one arm across the table. "Truce?"

Cal eyes his hand for a second, then shakes it. "Truce."

Dawson smiles. "Okay."

"Hey!"

"I'm sorry! It's a reflex."

Cal huffs, but doesn't say anything.

"So, apart from you almost fainting—"

"I did not—"

"—did you like it today?"

Cal nods enthusiastically. "Lots. Thank you for taking me with you." He presses his lips together, pushing his food around. "I'd like to volunteer with you when I get better."

That brings Dawson up short. "Really?" Cal nods, and Dawson needs a moment to come up with a response. He definitely didn't see this coming. "Well, we'd have to give you proper training first, but...yeah. If you're sure."

Cal gives him a brilliant smile. "I am."

Dawson mumbles something incoherent. He's struggling to imagine what working with Cal at the shelter would be like. It's just so...strange. But what's stranger is how much he likes the idea.

Dawson keeps his promise and takes Cal to the beach later that afternoon. Thankfully, Cal's more than happy to just sit in the shade and watch the ocean, so Dawson doesn't have to worry about pushing his limits.

In the end, it's Dawson who feels like he's being pushed to his limits. He's not sure if it's Kieran's words from this morning, or Cal's insistent questions about the past, or if it's the whole fucked up situation Dawson so stupidly put himself in, but he suddenly feels an overwhelming urge to run. From Cal, from all of this. Not because he's afraid, but because he's...not. Because he can feel himself relaxing around Cal, relaxing into this fragile little bubble they started building around them. He's only known this Cal for a couple of weeks, has been home with him for two days, but it's like he's known him longer. Like taking walks on the beach and watching movies on the sofa is something they've always done.

It's not. It's not real and it's dangerous. And Dawson keeps forgetting that.

He forgets it again when they get back home and sit down to watch *How to Train Your Dragon.* All three movies, because Cal gets hooked.

He forgets it again when he helps Cal with changing his bandages, even though he said he wouldn't.

He forgets it when they stand next to each other as they brush their teeth, the scene so domestic and normal that it makes Dawson wish for things he had given up on a long time ago.

He desperately tries to remember it when they turn in for the night and instead of being on high alert, the only thing Dawson can think of is what a good day it's been and how he wants more of them.

Chapter 15

THERE'S A CRASHING SOUND as something shatters. He ignores it. It's not important. There's only one thing that matters.

A pained cry reaches his ears. He looks for the source, something inside him tearing open when he finds it. Dawson is on the floor, his body twisted to the side and his arm raised like a shield. There's a hand-shaped bruise blooming on his forearm. He's shaking terribly.

Someone is standing over him, a man. His fists are clenched tight, his knuckles smeared with blood. There are a few specks of red on his pristine white shirt, his face shrouded in darkness. He says something, the words sounding like static. There's a threat in his voice, and it draws a sob out of Dawson. The man speaks again, getting a small nod in response.

Dawson scrambles to his feet and hurries away on unsteady legs. Now that his arm is out of the way, his face is on display. Tear-streaked and bloodied, one of his eyes swelling shut, his split lip dripping blood.

The man has moved, revealing the shards of glass littering the carpet where a table must've been before. In the kitchen, he turns the tap on, shoving his hand under it as if that could erase the violence and pain he caused. The water stops running, and he grabs a bottle of something amber in color, taking a swig and swaying on his feet. When he turns around, his face isn't hidden anymore. His features are twisted into something ugly, a deranged smile on his lips.

That's not the worst, though.

He knows that face.

It's the same face he sees in the mirror.

Cal wakes with a start, a silent scream lodged in his throat. His heart is beating erratically, and his breath is coming out in stuttered gasps. If he didn't know better, he'd think there's something wrong with his lung again. He almost wishes there was. He could do something about an injured lung. These dreams, on the other hand...

The dream. He lifts his hands, checking them over frantically. No blood. Of course there isn't. It was just a dream.

He turns to look at Dawson and finds him sleeping peacefully. Relief loosens his chest. Dawson is here, safe and sound, but his back is facing Cal, making it impossible to see his face. He needs to see Dawson's face. He needs...

Cal reaches out, his hand spreading over Dawson's back.

Dawson stirs, his back growing rigid under the touch. He flips over, scrambling away, looking like a spooked animal.

"What...what are you doing?" He's clutching the duvet to his chest and watching Cal carefully.

Cal swallows, curling his fingers into his palm so as to avoid temptation and reach for Dawson again. "I'm sorry. I didn't mean to scare you. I had a bad dream."

Dawson is silent at first, watching him. He relaxes somewhat, propping himself up on his forearm. "What about?"

"You." Dawson's brows furrow. "But you weren't—" Cal hesitates. He can't tell him exactly what happened in the dream. He can't tell him the man hurting him was wearing Cal's face. "You were hurt. And scared. There was blood on your face." Just describing it out loud makes him want to wrap Dawson in his arms and never let go.

"Oh," Dawson breathes, gaze raking over Cal's face. "It was just a dream. I'm fine."

Cal forces a smile. "I thought we're not allowed to use that word."

Dawson huffs, lips twitching. "That was just you."

"That's not very fair," Cal teases, the humor not quite hitting the mark.

He collapses onto his back, hands curled into fists on his chest. He stares up at the ceiling, the images flashing in front of him like it's a large projector screen. He squeezes his eyes shut. "Just a dream," he whispers to himself.

After a moment, he feels Dawson move, probably settling in for sleep after Cal woke him up so abruptly. He's not sure he can get back to sleep himself, or if he even wants to.

His eyes fly open when he feels something touch his arm, tentative and barely there.

"It's okay, Cal," Dawson whispers, so quiet that Cal might've missed it if he wasn't holding his breath.

His hands uncurl.Slowly, so as to make his intention clear and not startle him again, Cal's larger hand slips over Dawson's, covering it fully. The contact soothes him, tension leaving his body until he begins to sink into the mattress. Wanting—*needing* Dawson closer, he brings their joined hands to the center of his chest, over his racing heart.

Dawson doesn't try to pull away. They stay like this until Cal's eyelids start to grow heavy again. He's still reluctant to let himself fall asleep, but with the comforting weight of Dawson's hand on his chest, it's a little easier. Dawson's probably already asleep, not haunted by nightmares like Cal.

It's not until sleep has pulled Cal almost completely under that he hears Dawson speak, voice quiet and shaky.

"Who *are* you?"

He doesn't understand the question. He wants to ask, but he's too far gone, too detached from his body. Maybe he's not awake at all and simply dreaming of his husband again. Whichever it is, the words reach deep inside him, settling heavily in his heart. They feel important, but he can't put his finger on why.

He doesn't know who he is, but he'll be whoever Dawson needs him to be.

Cal is still out of sorts the next morning, the visions of the dream—the nightmare haunting him. He sneaks a peek at Dawson whenever he's not looking, needing a constant reminder that everything is okay. He's aware he's acting like a creep, but Dawson got annoyed when he noticed Cal looking, so it's probably better to hide it.

Cal's spirits are lifted when Dawson announces he's making pancakes. He tries to pay attention to what Dawson is doing but keeps getting distracted—both by the dream and by Dawson's lovely face. Then there's a moment when their eyes meet and Cal almost looks away, pretending he wasn't staring, but Dawson doesn't seem bothered this time. He gives him a big, gentle smile that transforms his whole face, and Cal wants to...he wants to...

He doesn't even know, and before he can figure it out, the pancakes are ready.

Cal doesn't hold back, piling several of them on his plate as they sit down at the table. He feels a little bad for not waiting for Dawson who put all this effort into making breakfast, but he's starving, the vanilla scent taunting him and making his mouth water.

"Why do I even try?" Dawson says with a dramatic sigh. His expression is disapproving as he watches Cal pour a quarter of the bottle of maple syrup over his pancakes.

Cal shrugs sheepishly. At least he's not asking for donuts. Dawson should take it as a win.

After they've finished, Cal offers to do the dishes which Dawson shuts down.

"Ellis is coming over tonight, so we might as well just load the dishwasher and deal with it afterwards. Speaking of, I need to make a short run to get some stuff for dinner. You wanna come with?"

"More shopping? Didn't we get enough?"

Dawson snorts. "Yeah, we're all stocked up, but Ellis has some dietary restrictions. There's this organic shop a couple blocks down. I literally just need to grab a thing or two."

"Oh. Yeah, sure. I'll come with you. When do you want to go?"

"Now's good."

"Can we stop at the cafe on our way?"

Dawson gives him a chastising look. "It's the other way, and no. No more sugar for you. I'm surprised your pancreas is still working."

"My pancreas works just fine," Cal grumbles.

It's a short walk to the store, as Dawson said. He finds what he's looking for quickly, except his shopping basket definitely contains more than 'a thing or two'.

"I got carried away," he mumbles, blushing, when Cal looks at him in question.

"Uh-huh."

Dawson scowls. "Hey! You're the one who gets to eat whatever I cook with this, so shush."

He makes a good point. Cal keeps his mouth shut.

On their way back, they pass by what looks like an art studio. He stops, looking inside through the glass. There's no one in, but the place is littered with paintings, bottles of paint, brushes, paint-streaked aprons and easels. The banner says *Pinot & Piccaso*.

"Are these painting lessons?"

Dawson snorts. "Depends on who you ask. Not really lessons. More like an excuse for girls to get together and pop open a few bottles of wine. It's called Paint 'n' Sip. Or Sip 'n' Paint. Take your pick."

"Oh. So it's not for men?"

Dawson laughs. "It's for anybody. As long as they're over eighteen, I think. But it's mostly popular among women."

Well, Cal might not be a woman, but he's intrigued. "We could go some day."

Dawson does a double take. "You want to paint?"

Cal shrugs. "It looks like it could be fun."

"It's overpriced for what it is," Dawson says, voice tight.

"Can't we afford that?" Cal asks, confused.

"We can. It's the principle."

"Oh." Cal's shoulders droop. "I see."

"You really want to try this?" Dawson asks, sounding dubious.

Cal gives him a reluctant nod. "Only if you come with me." Maybe it's not fair to put that pressure on Dawson, but what's the point of doing this without him?

"Fine," Dawson finally relents, though he doesn't seem happy about it. "But I'm not drinking."

Cal shrugs again. "Neither am I." He's made it clear several times that he has no interest in picking up his old habit, and that hasn't changed.

"Alright. I'll book us a session if there's anything good," Dawson promises, steering Cal away from the studio.

"I'm looking forward to it," Cal says. "What art did you do?"

"I dabbled in pretty much everything. My favorites were acrylics and watercolor. The more color, the better. I tried digital art but it's not the same."

"That would fit nicely in our sterile apartment."

Dawson's eyes narrow. Oh yes, he knows very well where Cal is going with this. "Or it would clash."

"I don't believe that. Maybe after we paint something, we can hang it up?"

"I haven't painted anything in a long time. As for you, your art is limited to the pencil, ruler, and compass."

"That doesn't sound like fun." Cal makes a face, pulling a chuckle out of Dawson. "Do you still have some of your old paintings?"

A muscle in Dawson's cheek jumps. "There might be some in the storage room."

"If there are, can we hang them up?"

Dawson takes a deep breath, stopping to look at Cal. "Cal, I told you—"

"That it doesn't fit the apartment, yes." Cal rolls his eyes. "It would seem that anything that's not bleak and has personality wouldn't."

Stunned by the mini outburst, Dawson stares at him, then laughs. "Tell me how you really feel." He shakes his head. "You are pretty insistent."

"And stubborn, yes. We've established that."

"And now he sasses me too."

"I'll stop if you want. But you're smiling."

"Well, you're being funny."

"I like seeing you smile. Hearing your laugh," Cal says. "You always look so sad when you think I'm not looking."

Dawson's gaze snaps to him, a little shocked. "I'm not sad. Why would I be sad?"

Cal doesn't miss how his pace quickens, but the long walks have paid off. Cal catches up to him without much struggle, speaking again once they enter the lobby of their building.

"Maybe because you miss your husband?" He wants to take the words back once they've left his mouth. "Sorry, I know you don't want to talk about it. And I know I'm not like him."

Dawson calls for the lift, the silence between them heavy as they wait for it to arrive. "No, you're not," he agrees. Before Cal can apologize again, he says, "And I don't want you to be. I like you, just the way you are. And I'm not sad, just...overwhelmed."

"Overwhelmed," Cal repeats. "Because of me."

"Partially," Dawson admits.

The lift arrives and they step in.

Dawson waits until the doors are closed before speaking again. "Look, I'm not gonna stand here and tell you that this whole situation is not at all messed up. But just because it's messed up doesn't mean it's all bad. We simply need to learn how to navigate stuff from here. Probably start doing things differently."

He's right. It's not bad. Difficult, yes, but not bad.

"And we can start with decorating our place," Cal challenges, giving Dawson a pointed look.

Dawson lets out a groan. "I swear to God..." Then, "Fine. Have it your way."

Cal couldn't wipe the stupidly excited grin from his face if he tried. He hovers around Dawson when they're back at the apartment.

"What?" Dawson asks suspiciously.

"Can I see the paintings?"

Chapter 16

SO FUCKING STUBBORN. DAWSON bites back a smile, despite feeling a little irritated now. And also nervous because Cal saw these paintings before and...well, he didn't love them.

"Just...give me a second." He disappears into the storage room, eyes zeroing in on one of the boxes in the corner

It was a lie when Dawson said there might be some paintings in the storage room. He knows they're there. All of them. Despite giving up on art, he never had the heart to get rid of them completely.

He drags the box into the living room, brushing off dust, before flipping open the top. His heart starts to pound when he sees the edges of several paintings sitting inside.

"So, um...I painted these a long time ago..."

Cal is oblivious to his internal panic. He steps forward, looking into the box, lighting up when he sees how many there are. "Let me see." Before Dawson can do anything, he reaches for one.

Dawson holds his breath, his anxiety spiking when Cal doesn't make a sound, just looks at the painting, his eyes wide as he takes it in.

"Dawson, this is..."

"...ludicrous. You can't seriously want to sell these."

"I thought... You said you liked my art."

"Jesus. Yeah, sure, your...art is fine if you want to hang it up in your room or give it to your beloved sister. It's not something to present to the public. And it definitely isn't something people will pay for."

"Why are you paying my tuition then? If you've been thinking this the whole time, why bother?"

"What, like you can do something else? You want to study business? Law? Why don't you go straight for med school, Dawson? And don't give me that look. Without me, you'd still be flipping burgers at Macca's. Be my guest if that's what you want to do."

"Incredible. You are so good at this," Cal says with wonder, putting the painting down and pulling out the rest, one by one. Dawson's a little stuck on the gentle, careful way Cal is handling the canvases. "Can we hang them all up?"

Blinking back tears, Dawson snaps back to the present. He must look like an anime character with the way his eyes threaten to pop out of their sockets. "All? No way."

"Why?""Just..." He looks around the walls, like an answer will be written on them. "How about we just replace the pieces that are already there?" At least that way the apartment won't look like a bad art gallery.

Cal looks around the walls too, and Dawson thinks he might be counting how many paintings there are.

"Can I pick?"

"Yeah, sure."

As Cal starts going through them all and setting aside the ones he likes the most, Dawson notices he seems to have an affinity for landscapes, mainly the beach or the ocean. It doesn't exactly narrow it down, because living on the Gold Coast did result in Dawson painting a lot of the beach. It shouldn't surprise him that Cal likes them, given how much he likes to go for walks there.

"Have you been to all those places?"

"Most of them, but that's because you can find them along the Coast." He points at the painting which Cal seems to be the most enamored with. "This is a spot in Burleigh Heads. It's a little further south. A bit of a climb to get there and...uh...trespassing?" In his defense, Kieran made him do it. "But the view from the Cock Rock is great."

Cal's gaze snaps up, a slightly horrified expression in his face. "A...cock rock?

"Yeah, it's a...uh, just a rock, sticking out towards the ocean," Dawson explains with a nervous laugh. For some reason, saying cock to Cal's face makes him feel embarrassed. "It kind of looks like a cock. Hence the name."

Cal doesn't look convinced that Dawson's not some kind of lunatic. "So, you painted this while you were...sitting on the Cock Rock."

Oh, Jesus. Can the ground swallow him now?

"It sounds really obscene when you say it like that. And no, I didn't bring my supplies with me. I have a picture, though."

"Can I see?"

"The Cock?" Dawson smirks. "Or the view?"

"The view," Cal deadpans.

Chuckling, Dawson pulls up his phone and swipes way, way down. He doesn't remember the exact date, but he's pretty sure about the year. That should narrow it down.

He finds the picture in the pile from October 2017. Wow. Time really flies.

"The resemblance is remarkable," Cal says when Dawson shows him. He looks between the picture and the painting, taken aback.

Dawson tries his absolute best not to blush. He already has a hard time acting normal when Cal compliments his cooking. When did he become such a sucker for validation and praise?

"Thanks," he says lamely.

"Could we go together sometime?"

"You wanna see the Cock?" Dawson jokes to cover up his emotional turmoil.

"Yes, Dawson, I want to see the famous Cock," Cal says dryly.

Dawson would laugh, but hearing Cal say cock makes him flush even harder than saying it to his face did. He has to clear his throat twice before attempting to speak.

"Sure, we can do that. When you're not—"

"When I'm not stitched up. Yes, I know," Cal finishes for him. He's trying to sound irritated but looks more amused than anything.

"Still sassy," Dawson comments, surprised at how affectionate he sounds.

There are currently three pictures hanging in the living room and one in each of the rooms apart from the storage room. Dawson lets Cal pick six of his paintings and they swap them for the existing ones.

Dawson's stomach clenches as he peruses his art. It will take a while before he gets used to seeing it around. But Cal looks so happy that he can't even say anything.

They watch a movie after that. Dawson's first idea is *Interstellar*. He could watch it over and over, but...maybe not today. He's feeling way too raw already, and the emotions in that movie would just finish him off.

He ends up picking *Heartbreakers*, because *hello?* Sigourney Weaver. His plan to unwind and stop thinking for a while doesn't pan out. Cal gets all confused by the whole premise, so Dawson has to explain that some people, for religious or personal reasons, don't want to have sex before marriage (even if in the movie, that's just an excuse for another agenda).

It doesn't end there. Cal comes up with more questions, then puts a cherry on top when he asks, completely serious, "Did we wait until marriage to have sex?"

It's a small mercy Dawson isn't drinking or eating anything, because he would be in acute need of a Heimlich maneuver.

"Uh...no, Cal, we didn't," he says with a nervous laugh and flushed face. The irony is strong, considering that they had sex when—

"When did we first have sex?"

No matter that Dawson isn't ingesting anything. He manages to choke on his saliva. This was a bad idea. He'd rather have Cal pester him about the paintings. Lesser of two evils.

"We...well," he struggles to get the words out. "On the first date. Don't judge me," he adds defensively when a wave of shame overtakes him at the memory.

"Why would I judge you?" Cal asks, sounding so genuinely confused Dawson instantly feels bad for lashing out for no reason.

He shrugs uncomfortably. "It's just...putting out on the first date is kinda frowned upon."

"Why?"

Jesus. Cal's killing him. "I don't know, Cal. It's just one of those things that society deems inappropriate."

"Well, that's stupid," Cal says after a moment of silence. It's said in such a matter-of-fact tone Dawson can't help but laugh.

"I won't disagree with you there."

He's a bit of a hypocrite, to be honest. He used to be one of *those* people. That's why he felt so ashamed after he went to Cal's place when Cal invited him when their date was over. Sure, he could blame it on the two glasses of champagne he'd downed at the fancy restaurant Cal had taken him to. He could even blame it on Cal's natural charm and the smooth way he had with words. He could put it up to feeling pressured because what guy wants to be a virgin at the fresh age of twenty? Not to mention that after the fancy date and all the money Cal had spent on him, Dawson felt obligated to give him something in return. He understands in retrospect how toxic that kind of thinking was, but he was young and lonely.

But no matter the excuse, it doesn't change the fact that he said yes when Cal asked.

"You look sad," Cal says. "Did you—was it a bad experience?" He looks absolutely shattered at the idea.

Dawson quickly schools his expression. "No, it was...it was good." He mustn't sound very convincing because Cal seems worried, frown lines settling between his brows. "Really, it was fine."

"Fine," Cal repeats mechanically.

"It was good, Cal. I was just...a little nervous, okay? And clumsy. I had no idea what I was doing. I doubt anyone does the first time."

It really wasn't bad. Cal was experienced at least, but that also meant he had no qualms about asking for what he wanted. He wasn't rough, but he wasn't gentle either. If Dawson got a do-over, he'd have asked him to go slower, be a little more patient when Dawson started to panic. Or maybe not grip the back of Dawson's neck and press his face into the mattress as he drove into him.

It was overwhelming but it wasn't...bad. It was good. It *was*. Cal even managed to make him come, and Dawson knows that not everyone does their first time. And even though he was a little (a lot) sore in the morning, it was quickly forgotten when Cal flipped him onto his back and went down on him before Dawson was fully awake. That was a nice wake-up call.

"I was your first?" Cal asks, reminding Dawson he's not alone and he should fucking stop going down memory lane.

"You were my first everything. First date, first kiss—with a man, first...time." He almost said first love, but something stopped him. It wouldn't be a lie but...it wouldn't be quite true.

That doesn't even make sense, you weirdo.

"Oh." Cal licks his lips, a thoughtful expression on his face. "I suppose the same is true for me as well."

"What do you mean?"

"Maybe it's silly, but I feel...because of the memory thing..." He points vaguely at his head, as if Dawson could've forgotten about 'the memory thing'. "I get to experience everything for the first time. So in a way, you are my first everything too."

It is silly, though he doesn't tell Cal that. Which is why Dawson can't logically explain his own reaction.

He can't logically explain why the idea makes him feel warm and fuzzy, and why he's suddenly thinking of crossing the distance between them and putting his lips on Cal's, wondering if he kisses differently now too. Or why he wonders what kind of date they would go on now that Cal seems to have aversion to fancy stuff. *We'd probably go to Lost and Ground. Anywhere with donuts,* Dawson thinks. He almost wonders about other things too, things he hasn't thought about in a very long time, things he didn't even think he'd want anymore.

He shakes himself before his mind can wander off any further and make him even more confused than he already is.

"Didn't know you were such a romantic," he says, just to break the silence.

Cal shrugs. "Are you?"

"What?"

"Romantic."

He used to be. He used to be the King of Sap, dreaming of a Prince Charming who'd sweep him off his feet.

He got a reality check pretty fast.

"Not really. But that doesn't mean I'm not a sucker for rom-coms," he adds. Hopefully Cal gets the point that Dawson is trying to make him watch the movie.

Cal doesn't say anything to that, but Dawson feels his gaze on him throughout the movie. He pretends not to notice.

"Hey. Thanks for coming," Dawson says as he lets Ellis inside. He gives him a quick once-over. Under all that meticulous style and neat clothes, it's obvious Ellis is bone tired.

"Thanks for the invite."

Ellis walks in, hesitating when he sees the row of shoes lined up and takes in Dawson's bare feet. "Shoes off?"

"Don't be a barbarian. Of course, shoes off," Dawson says, trying to sound stern. It doesn't work.

Ellis chuckles, kicking his shoes off. "You let me keep them last time I was here."

"That doesn't count. I was distressed."

Something passes across Ellis' face. It looks like concern, and Dawson thinks he might be about to ask something, but Cal chooses that moment to join them. Ellis' attention is instantly on him.

"Hi."

"Hello," Cal says, a little awkwardly. "It's nice to see you again."

"Yeah, you too. Sorry I've been MIA."

"Why are you sorry? You've been busy with work because of me."

Ellis looks taken aback, probably not used to such treatment from Cal. Dawson feels a deep sense of kinship.

"How's it going, by the way?" Dawson asks, his guilt for not being of much help making a comeback.

Ellis does a so-so gesture with his hand. "It's settling down, finally. Also, I talked to the lawyer."

"Lawyer?" Cal asks. "For what?"

Ellis looks like he's not sure if Cal is serious. "To deal with the charges against you and get the police off your back."

If anything, Cal looks even more confused when he turns to Dawson with a helpless expression.

"The police get involved when there's an accident. And you had alcohol in your blood while driving, so..."

Cal visibly tenses. "Am I in trouble?"

"Not nearly as much as you could be," Ellis says sternly. "The lawyer thinks you will get away with a fine and won't even have to go to court. But they'll suspend your license for at least 27 months and you should have a few thousand at the ready."

"Thank you," Cal says with a huge sigh of relief. "I didn't know. I'm sorry."

Ellis' eyes find Dawson for a moment. Dawson can hear the unspoken question: Why haven't you talked about this?

"Just stay away from the bottle and we're golden," Ellis says, a dark undertone to the words. Cal must hear it too because he has trouble looking Ellis in the face.

"I...have no need to be close to the bottle."

Ellis raises a skeptical eyebrow, then turns to Dawson.

"It's true," Dawson confirms, still quite disbelieving himself.

Before the following silence can get any worse, Ellis speaks. "So, what's for dinner? I'm starving." As far as transitions go, this wasn't smooth at all, but at least they got the most uncomfortable part out of the way.

"Parmesan mushroom risotto." Dawson beckons them both to the table, shooing Cal away when he tries to help with plating up. "I managed to get my hands on dairy-free parmesan and cream, so you should be fine.

"You didn't have to go through the trouble," Ellis says, sounding surprised.

"Oh, yes, running a shopping errand that took twenty minutes was such trouble."

Ellis rolls his eyes, the beginnings of a smile settling in the corner of his lips. "Fine, I'll shut up. It smells amazing, by the way."

"He's great in the kitchen," Cal says proudly. The combined compliment from him and Ellis makes him blush. He busies himself with plating up so nobody notices.

"I'm decent," he mumbles.

"And a liar," Cal says with a snort.

"Hey!"

Yeah, Cal liking his food does strange things to Dawson, he can admit that. But then again, Cal's only point of reference is hospital food. Anything's better than that.

He listens to Cal and Ellis' conversation while he works. Ellis is mostly asking about how Cal is healing, pointedly avoiding any questions about his memory.

"A dog-shelter?" he hears Ellis ask.

"Dawson works there. He agreed to show me around, then got all bossy when I wanted to help."

"Oh, shut up, you!" Dawson spins around, pointing a wooden spoon at Cal in warning. "You were sliced open a couple weeks ago and you expect me to let you do whatever?"

"I'm fine."

"Nuh-uh. That word is banned from your vocabulary, remember?"

"But it's true!"

"You fainted."

"I didn't faint!"

"You got dizzy."

"But I didn't faint."

"You almost fainted."

"I—"

"O-kay," Ellis sing-songs, watching them with a very concerned expression. "I get it. Dawson is bossy, and you're pushing your limits."

"I'm not bossy!" Dawson yells at the same time that Cal yells, "I'm not pushing my limits!"

"Yeah, sounds totally convincing." Ellis snickers. "Can we eat, now?"

Ellis lets out a moan as he swallows the first spoonful. "Damn. You are a liar, Dawson."

"I told you," Cal says.

"Shut up," Dawson mumbles, embarrassed. He should've known that his reaction would only serve as ammunition to both of them, though, as they continue teasing him. His face is never going to be a normal color again.

By some miracle, they start talking about something other than Dawson's cooking skills, giving him the much-needed reprieve. Then the topic moves onto Ellis and how he's settling in.

"Where's the apartment again?" Dawson asks.

"Surfers Paradise. It's not what I'm used to, but that's fine. It's only temporary, anyway."

"How long are you staying?"

"As long as I need to." Ellis' eyes shift to Cal.

"Dawson said you don't want to make permanent changes in case my memory comes back."

"It's a possibility."

"Maybe, but..." Cal pauses, rolling a napkin between his fingers. "I'm not sure I'd want to go back to it even if I remember."

Ellis drops the spoon onto the plate. "What?"

"I know it's not fair to you, but—"

"That's not what I meant," Ellis cuts him off, leaning forward. "Cal, you lived and breathed that job. It annoyed the fuck out of me, but that's the way it was. So why the sudden change of mind?"

Dawson can feel Cal's gaze on him, then Ellis' as well. He just hopes Ellis doesn't take it to mean that it was his idea.

"As you just said," Cal starts. "It came to my attention that I had no life outside of work and didn't care about much else. That's...not okay." He shakes his head. "I don't want to be that guy anymore."

"You're serious," Ellis says, stunned. He doesn't sound angry, which is a relief, but definitely out of sorts.

"I am. And I'm sorry for putting even more pressure on you."

Ellis waves his hand. "No, that's... Look, I was ready to step in either way. I just never expected to hear something like this from you. Do you... What are you planning to do instead?"

"For work, you mean? I... Dawson said that we own the company, and we'll profit whether we're actively engaged or not."

Ellis frowns. "Sure, yeah. But... Man, you'll be bored out of your mind if you don't do something."

"There's no rush," Dawson says, sensing Cal could use a back-up. "Cal's still recovering. I'm sure something will pop up that will catch his interest." He gives Cal an encouraging smile

"Fair enough, I guess," Ellis says. He picks up the spoon again, scooping up the rice. "Any ideas? A new hobby, perhaps?"

"I like books," Cal says after taking a moment to ponder it.

"He's been reading a lot since he woke up," Dawson explains when Ellis looks at him questioningly.

"Ah, yeah. I suppose, given the extent of your...condition, you can read all the books you liked for the first time again." Ellis chuckles, reaching for his water. "What are you reading? Dan Brown? Daniel Silva?"

"At the moment? I recently started *Vampire Diaries.*"

Ellis inhales at the same time he takes a drink and ends up coughing up a storm.

"Oh, Jesus." Dawson is out of his chair instantly, suppressing a laugh as he hits Ellis' back. "Guess I should've warned you."

"Y-you," Ellis sputters. "You knew?"

"Last I checked, he was halfway through *Twilight.*"

"I finished that ages ago."

"Oh, god," Ellis groans, still gasping for breath. "What's next? *Fifty Shades of Gray*?"

"I haven't read that." Cal says. "Is it good?"

"Christ."

"I'd skip that one if I were you," Dawson says. To Ellis, he explains, "He prefers fantasy."

Ellis holds his thumb and forefinger half an inch apart. "I'm this close to checking for hidden cameras."

"Oh, don't bother, I've checked already." Dawson pats his shoulder and sits down.

The rest of the dinner is an experience. Ellis interrogates Cal on his new hobbies, probably wanting to avoid any future surprises. Dawson is content to listen to them talk. The disbelieving looks Ellis keeps giving Cal are both relatable and comforting. It's nice to know he's not the only one who struggles with all the changes.

"Seconds?" Dawson asks when they've all finished eating.

Ellis shakes his head. "It was amazing, but I'm full."

"I'll have some more, please," Cal says.

Dawson chuckles. "Your stomach is a bottomless pit."

"It's just too good."

Blushing, Dawson takes their empty plates and carries them to the kitchen. Ellis follows him with the glasses, standing close to him as he whispers, "This has been going on for how long?"

"By *this* you mean..."

"You know what I mean."

"Is this about the vampire fiction?" Dawson snorts.

"It's not the vampire fiction." A pause. "Not *just* the vampire fiction. My brother, a former alcoholic and workaholic, no longer has an interest in alcohol nor his job, reads teen fiction, volunteers with you at a dog shelter and..." He raises an eyebrow. "Any more surprises I should know about?"

So many. "Watches Disney movies and rom-coms, hates coffee, is addicted to sugar. Oh, and he hates this apartment."

"Well, finally something I can relate to. Wait, watches Disney?"

"Oh, like you wouldn't believe. You should see the top recommendations on our Netflix."

"Maybe we should... Do you think we should get him checked? Like..." Ellis points at his head.

Dawson tenses, a wave of irritation slamming into him out of nowhere. "He's got a check-up scheduled in two weeks."

"But that's just because of his wounds and his memory. What if there's something else wrong?"

"You think something's wrong because he suddenly likes different things?" Dawson says in a tight voice.

Ellis must notice the sudden change, because he looks at Dawson in surprise. "It's not just because he suddenly likes different things. He's a whole different person."

"And that's bad, why?"

Ellis looks at him for a moment, his eyes widening. "Jesus Christ. Don't tell me you're enjoying this."

"Enjoying what?" Dawson snaps. "Babysitting? Keeping an eye on him at all times in case he hurts himself? Being confused out of my fucking mind because I don't know how to act around him?"

Ellis sighs, and his shoulders slump. "Dawson, if it's too much for you, I told you I can—"

"No."

"Dawson—"

"You worry about the company. I'll worry about Cal. Not like I have anything better to do." He didn't mean to say the last part out loud. Ellis' intense stare is highly unnerving. "What's your problem, anyway? Are you upset that your brother isn't an asshole for once?"

Ellis grabs Dawson's arm. His hold isn't painful, but it reminds Dawson of things he'd rather forget. "My problem is that I worry."

"You don't have to worry. I'm keeping an eye on Cal." When he tries to pull away, Ellis grips him tighter, panic starting to rise in his body.

"Not Cal," he says. "I worry about you. I didn't like it in the first place when you wanted to do this on your own."

"Yes, I remember. You didn't want me to be alone with Cal because of all the possible...side effects that come with memory loss. As you can see, he's harmless."

"You've let your guard down, haven't you?"

"What's that supposed to mean?"

"What are you doing?"

They both startle, neither of them having noticed that Cal has moved. Standing behind Dawson, he frowns at Ellis' hand and says in a low, dark voice, "Let go of him. Now."

Ellis slowly removes his hand, watching Cal warily as he takes a step back.

Later, when he's alone and not as overwhelmed, Dawson will go back to this moment and try to dissect why feeling Cal's presence behind him made him relax. Or why hearing that growly voice ordering Ellis to let go sent a shiver through him, making him want to press himself against Cal for protection. There's something different about his voice. Dawson's never heard it like this. It sounds almost...familiar but also not. At least it's not how Cal normally sounds.

But he can pick that apart later.

"We were just talking," Ellis says.

"Dawson was upset."

While that's not wrong, Dawson should do something. He should step in before the situation escalates. "It's fine. We had to discuss some stuff. Boring stuff."

Cal doesn't look like he quite believes him, but at least he's not making things worse.

"I think I should go," Ellis says. "I still have some unpacking to do."

Dawson is still annoyed with him, but now he feels bad.

"Stay. You just got here. You can unpack anytime."

Ellis opens his mouth, then stills as something behind Dawson catches his eye. "Was that there before?"

Dawson turns around to see Ellis is pointing at one of his paintings. Oh man. "Um..."

"We hung it up today. Dawson painted that," Cal says, sounding so damn proud Dawson doesn't know what to do with himself.

Ellis' brows shoot up. "You painted that?" He looks around, noticing there are more, then goes to have a closer look. "Blimey. Those are great. I knew you were an artist, but..." He turns to look at Dawson. "Are you selling your art?"

Dawson swallows, starting to feel claustrophobic. "No. Never got to do that."

"You totally could," Ellis goes on. "Do you have enough pieces for an exhibition? I know a guy who could set you up—"

"No, thank you," Dawson says, reminding himself to take deep breaths. "I haven't painted in years. I have nothing new to offer."

Something in his voice must've alerted Ellis, because he backs off.

"Okay. Sorry for being nosey."

"It's fine," Dawson says. "Are you staying? There's dessert. Lava cake."

Ellis does stay. The rest of the evening carries out in a more subdued spirit, some of the tension from before remaining, but not suffocating them.

"Do you have Cal's office now?" Dawson asks.

"For the time being, yes. Actually," Ellis points a blueberry sauce covered fork at Cal. "If you wanted, you could come to work? Just to look around, see if anything clicks."

A ball of anxiety settles in Dawson's belly. He must be the worst person on the planet for thinking this, but Jesus, he doesn't want stuff to click for Cal. He really doesn't.

"I don't know..." Cal says, frowning.

"I'm not forcing you or anything. Also, some of the employees think that the whole amnesia thing is a joke. Apparently it sounds like a movie script."

"That's so rude," Dawson says. Cal has been coping exceptionally well with being thrown into the unknown, but those people can't know that. It'd be really disrespectful if it happened to someone who struggled hard to adjust to their new reality.

"There are movies about this?" Cal asks with curiosity, oblivious to Dawson's chagrin.

"Oh, yeah," Ellis says. "*50 First Dates* comes to mind. But that's a comedy, a little over the top."

"That's such a good one," Dawson grins. There's no going wrong when Adam and Drew play together. "And also *The Vow*."

"Which one is that?"

"The one with Channing Tatum." When Ellis just looks at him blankly, Dawson says, "Rachel McAdams."

"Ah." Ellis' eyes light up with recognition. "Yeah, I know."

Dawson snorts. "Typical."

Ellis lets out a gasp of mock offense. "You're drooling over Tatum, and I'm typical?"

"Who's Tatum?" asks Cal.

"Every woman's—and non-hetero man's—wet dream." Ellis rolls his eyes.

"He's cute," Dawson says with a pout. Ellis isn't wrong, though.

"Cute, huh? Built like a tank, you mean."

"Stop it," Dawson orders, not really wanting to discuss other men in front of his amnesiac husband and his annoying brother.

By the time Ellis stands up to leave and thanks Dawson for dinner, the air is mostly clear, although Ellis does give him a pointed look when he says goodnight, and that they can let him know if they need anything. Dawson acknowledges it with a nod, and then it's just him and Cal again. Well, the two of them and a pile of dishes.

Cal practically elbows Dawson out of the way when he tries to prewash them before putting them in the dishwasher.

"You cooked, I'll clean."

Dawson, who's not used to eating this much and feels like he's pregnant with a baby elephant, doesn't argue for once and goes to collapse on the sofa.

"What setting should I use?" Cal asks when the dishwasher is loaded.

"Sixty-five should do it."

After the machine comes to life, Cal dries his hands and joins Dawson on the sofa.

"I want to watch the movie," he blurts out before Dawson can ask like he'd planned to.

Dawson laughs. "Which one?"

"With Tatum."

Oh dear god. "Cal," Dawson says with a patient smile. "Ellis was just taking the piss."

Cal makes a grunting noise. "It's about amnesia."

"We can watch *50 First Dates,* then," Dawson suggests innocently.

"Next time. I want to watch this first."

Well, it was worth a try. Dawson finds the movie on Netflix and presses play, hoping Cal will let Ellis' teasing go.

Two minutes in, it's clear no such thing will happen.

"You think he's cute?" Cal asks, glaring at the TV.

Dawson's gonna kill Ellis and he'll make it hurt. "Yes, Cal, I think he's cute," he says tiredly. "That's it. That's all there's to it. Okay?"

Cal doesn't talk for a long time. He's probably sulking, but Dawson would rather take that than the insistent questions. The peace lasts until Tatum's character takes off his shirt.

"Do you think I should exercise more?" Cal asks, looking down at himself critically.

"With twenty plus stitches in you? No, I don't think so," Dawson says, nearly groaning out loud when Cal continues to sulk. Time to pull out the big guns. He can't take this much longer. He's never had to deal with a self-conscious Cal. "You're fine, Cal. And you're an attractive guy, okay? You don't have to be ripped like that."

Cal's always kept himself in shape, mostly through cardio and bodyweight training instead of heavy lifting. He's one of those lucky fuckers who have to do very little to stay fit, and that's why, after weeks of minimal to zero physical activity, he doesn't look that different to his pre-accident shape. Whatever weight he lost at the hospital, he's probably gained back in the last three days he has spent with Dawson, eating his food.

"Does it have a happy ending?" Cal asks during the third-act drama when it looks like the characters will never find their way back to each other.

"Yeah, it does."

When the credits roll, Cal turns to Dawson with a look of betrayal. "You said it had a happy ending."

"It did."

"But she never remembered him."

Oh.

Is that the ending Cal was hoping for? To be honest, Dawson didn't even think of that. To him, the movie has a happy ending, but he should've known that for Cal, who's literally living the story, it would be different.

"She didn't have to. She just fell in love with him all over again. And they were happy."

"Like...a clean slate?"

Dawson smiles. "Yeah, like that."

"Oh."

Cal's expression softens. His gaze travels over Dawson's face, searching for something. His lips part, as if he's about to speak. Dawson finds himself breathing quietly, wanting to hear whatever Cal's about to say, but it never happens. Instead, Cal moves, leaning ever so slightly into Dawson's space, close enough that Dawson can smell chocolate on his breath. For a moment, he almost wants to...

As if someone yanks him by the collar of his shirt, Dawson draws back, making Cal jump with the sudden movement.

He scrambles to his feet, swaying a little as he tries to shake off the strange haze that just came over him. God, he almost... He wanted to... "I'm gonna go to bed. I—I'm pretty beat."

Cal's face falls, disappointment written all over it. "Oh. Sorry for keeping you up." He peers up at Dawson through his eyelashes, smiling a little. "But thank you for keeping me company."

"Anytime." Dawson hovers, feeling like he should say something else. Deciding to let his gut feeling guide him, he says, "I like this.

Hanging out and watching movies with you. When you're not obsessing about some guy's abs."

"I wasn't—" Cal stops, narrowing his eyes. "What about his abs?"

Dawson throws his hands in the air in despair. "Oh, for Christ's sake. Nothing! Nothing about his abs, or anyone's abs. You worry about your abs, because they're sliced in the middle."

Cal sinks back into the sofa. "I can get abs like that."

Dawson nearly sobs. "I can't do this. I'm going to bed. Forget about Tatum, okay?"

If Cal's face is anything to go by, that's not gonna happen.

Ellis is so, so dead.

Chapter 17

A LITTLE OVER A week later, Dawson has almost gotten used to this being his life now. 'Almost' being the keyword.

Which is why he's currently on his way to the psych appointment, his left foot drumming nervously against the floor next to the brake. It's not that he's having second thoughts about therapy, per se. He's well aware he desperately needs it, and if Cal hadn't been in charge of their finances and controlled where Dawson spent the money, he'd have gone way sooner. It's just when he made the appointment, he had a specific goal in mind. He made it meaning to talk about Cal. The old Cal. Now, he needs to talk about the man who wears his husband's face but is nothing like him.

As if it hadn't been complicated enough.

He arrives at the location shortly, sitting in the car for a few minutes to gather his bearings.

He takes the stairs to the third floor where Ashley's office is supposed to be and comes to a stop, looking around curiously. No reception desk, just an unassuming leather bench pushed against the wall opposite the door with Ashley's name plate. Huh. Okay, so he probably doesn't need to announce himself. Ashley will come out once she's done and call him in. Probably.

A jittery sensation pooling in his lower back, Dawson sits down, wringing his fingers together. He checks the time—he's six minutes early. Six minutes of torture while he waits. His left leg starts bouncing again.

Trying to focus on anything other than his racing thoughts, he attempts to listen in on what might be going on inside. Yeah, not the most polite thing to do, but he's not trying to eavesdrop, just distract himself. And maybe gauge what's awaiting him. Not that it matters because he can't hear a thing. Maybe Ashley's not there? Dawson could be her first client today. Sure, it's already three o'clock, but what does he know about therapists' working hours?

He startles when the door swings open, a man in his mid-thirties standing on the other side. Must be the client Ashley just finished with. His gaze falls on Dawson, and his lips quirk up in a half-smile.

"You must be Dawson."

"Yes?" Dawson says, not quite understanding why the man wants to know.

The half-smile grows into a full one, and the man steps to the side, casually leaning against the door-frame. "I believe we have an appointment. Ashley Cleaver—" He flicks an imaginary hat. "But call me Ash."

Dawson continues to sit there, staring with his mouth slightly ajar. "You're a man."

One of the man's—Ash's—brows flicks up, his lips pursing like he's fighting a smile. "Yes, and believe me, there are days I wish it weren't so, but..." He gives a slow shrug. "We have to work with what we've got."

It occurs to Dawson that Ash is waiting for him to say or do something, anything that probably doesn't involve staring like a moron. He jumps to his feet, his face on fire. "I'm so sorry. I sound like a douche. I just...your name and..." He tries to remember if Gabe has mentioned at any point that Ash is not a chick, but he vaguely recalls only hearing him refer to Ash by his name or calling him 'cousin'.

Ash waves it off. "It's fine. Not the first time it's happened, and won't be the last. My parents have a lot to answer for. But if I remember correctly, you booked an appointment via a phone call." He says like a question, clearly for the sake of Dawson disputing him.

That's right. Dawson did call and spoke to someone who had a decidedly male voice. "I thought I was speaking to the receptionist." Which he realizes in retrospect was a stupid assumption. Don't most therapists have a private practice and handle everything on their own? At least that's what it says in the movies and books.

"Ah. That explains it," Ash says easily, not even bothering to point out how inaccurate that assumption was. "Are you comfortable with a male therapist?"

And that's the bottom of it, isn't it? Dawson subconsciously expected Ash to be a woman because he'd be more comfortable with one. "Depends. Do you have anything against gay men?" he asks without thinking it through. It's a legitimate question, but surely Gabe wouldn't hook him up with a homophobic ass, right?

If Ash is taken aback by the question, he doesn't show it. He snickers, then flashes Dawson a toothy grin. "Yeah. Usually myself." Dawson must make some comical face, because Ash presses his lips together, like he knows he said something he shouldn't have. Oh, how Dawson can relate. "Probably too much to share from the get go. Anyways—" He sweeps one arm in the direction of the office. "Come on in."

Dawson does so reluctantly, feeling strangely on display. It's apt, they're going to be dissecting him after all. Maybe it's not too late to turn back—

"Have a seat," Ash says, gesturing towards the sofa that has some pillows and a Pusheen the Cat plushie sitting there. Dawson makes a grab for it as he sits down, finding himself smiling. The cat is holding a pink donut in its tiny paws, munching on it, and it reminds him of Cal's newfound obsession with the pastry.

"Would you like anything to drink?" Ash asks.

"Water would be nice, thanks," he decides, his throat already drying up.

Ash pulls out a bottle of water from the mini fridge behind his desk and pours two glasses. He offers one to Dawson, who takes it with a quiet 'thanks'. He sits in the armchair opposite Dawson, the only thing between them a low-lying table made of dark timber.

Gripping the glass in a shaky hand, Dawson brings it up to take a small sip, then puts it down on the table. He sinks back into the sofa, the plushie in his lap while he plays with its ears.

Ash nurses his water, watching Dawson over the rim of the glass before setting it down as well. He folds his hands comfortably on his thigh, one ankle crossed over the other leg. It's an open posture, Dawson notes, and to his surprise, Ash isn't holding a notepad or a pen.

He smiles again, soft and knowing, and a gust of breath rushes out of Dawson's lungs. "How can I help you, Dawson?"

Dawson doesn't have one solid answer for that. He doesn't even know where to start.

"You could help me figure out what's wrong with me. And why I'm such a mess." He instantly regrets it. If he learned anything from the self-help books he's read over the years, it's that words like 'wrong' or 'normal' are all but banned at a therapist's office, because there's no such thing as normal and thus you can't be wrong yadayadaya.

If that were true, he wouldn't be feeling like this.

He braces himself for being chastised in a way that pretends to be gentle but is patronizing in nature. But Ash stays quiet, and when Dawson looks up, he finds Ash watching him with that ever-present smile.

"I can do that," he simply says, making Dawson's jaw drop. He cocks his head. "Is everything alright?" By the glint in his eye, he fucking well knows. He just wants Dawson to engage with him.

"I... I guess I've been reading way too many self-help books, because I've been kind of expecting you to jump in and argue that there's nothing wrong with me and that I'm normal."

Ash nods, like Dawson's rambling makes sense. "Would you believe me?" When Dawson frowns, he says, "I'm happy to tell you all that, if it helps. But I'm going to wager a guess and say that it would do fuck-all. Just like those self-help books you've been reading."

Processing everything that just came out of Ash's mouth—his therapist's mouth—Dawson fumbles for his glass, chugging down what remains in it. "Gabe wasn't kidding." He says it mostly to himself, but Ash catches it.

"What's that?"

"Gabe. Your cousin? He gave me your number. Said that if I don't want to be treated with kid gloves, I'm supposed to call you."

"I see," Ash says, a kind of realization settling in his gaze. "Are you two friends?"

Dawson's first impulse is to say yes. He does consider Gabe a friend, but is that who they are? Just because Dawson tends to pour his heart out to the freaking baristas doesn't make it friendship.

"I guess? I mean, I'm a customer at *Lost and Ground*. But we chat quite a bit."

"Right. Well, in case Gabe hasn't told you, my methods are rather...unconventional." The prideful tone in Ash's voice is unmistakable. He holds up his hands. "Nothing illegal. I think," he adds absentmindedly, probably for a dramatic effect. "To be honest, people usually reach out to me when they've tried almost everything and everyone, but nothing worked. You will likely find yourself overwhelmed at some point."

You don't say.

"Mission accomplished," Dawson says without heat, making Ash laugh. "But don't most people get overwhelmed in therapy?"

"Yes. But it's also the therapist's job to ground them again."

Dawson arches an eyebrow and gives Ash a scrutinizing once-over. "Do *you* do that?" He doubts this man has any intention to calm people down. More like rile them up so they spill all their secrets.

Ash grins like a feral cat. "I prefer to kick the heat up a notch." He's been leaning forward a little, but now he falls back into the armchair, propping his elbows up on the armrests. So freaking relaxed. "Well, Dawson. I can go on and talk your ear off about myself and my

methods, or we can try them out. Figure out what's wrong with you."
He winks and Dawson is helpless to stop the laugh bubbling in his
chest. At the same time, something inside him unclenches, making his
breathing easier.

"Yeah, okay."

Ash nods. "Whenever you're ready." He means it too. It takes
Dawson a few solid minutes to gather himself together, the poor cat's
ears now properly abused. The whole time, Ash doesn't say a word,
not a flicker of annoyance or impatience in his expression as he watches
Dawson with soft eyes.

"Okay, so...I'm married."

Ash glances at Dawson's left hand, then back at him. "Yes."

Dawson rolls his eyes, a grin pulling at his lips. It falls when he starts
talking. "We've been together for about six years and...most of them
have been...challenging," he chooses the words carefully.

"In what way?"

Right. No getting off easy.

"In the way that my husband is a control freak and a narcissist with
alcohol addiction and used to take his frustration out on me."

Ash doesn't so much as blink, and that...that feels pretty damn
good. Dawson's shoulders have been tense with the expectation of
pitying looks and sad eyes, but there's none of that. Ash just...listens.

"You say 'used to'. Has something changed?"

Listens and pokes around. Ugh.

"Everything." Looking down at the plushie, Dawson hooks his
finger in the hole in the donut, pulling on it playfully. "He was in a car
accident a few weeks ago. He was in an induced coma for a few days
and when he woke up, he didn't remember anything."

"Retrograde amnesia?"

"*Full* retrograde amnesia," Dawson corrects, not missing the first
flicker of surprise in Ash's face. "He doesn't remember *anything*.
Didn't know his name, where he was..." He shrugs. "Or who I was."

"That's a very unusual situation."

"So I've been told." Dawson chews on his lip, turning his attention back to the plushie. "The night of his accident, I had finally decided to ask for a divorce. I had the papers ready, packed my shit. I was going to leave. After all this time." He shakes his head, letting out a derisive chuckle. "It clearly wasn't meant to be. Guess some higher power really has it out for me."

"Does it?" Ash asks. "From where I'm sitting, it sounds like the perfect opportunity to leave."

A bubble of irritation begins to form in Dawson's gut. "That's what everybody says."

"What do you say?"

Dawson fidgets, truly uncomfortable for the first time since he sat down. He should've known it wouldn't be as easy as Ash was making it seem. "I couldn't live with myself if I just left now. He was... He wasn't a good person, but he doesn't remember any of it."

He was never under any illusion that Cal was a good guy. He knows the typical MO for victims of abuse, and while he definitely ticks plenty of boxes, making excuses for the person who abused him isn't one of them. And yet, he never got brave enough to leave.

Because he's messed up.

"His memory could come back," Ash points out. It's obvious he's trying to get a rise out of Dawson.

"The doctors say it's unlikely if it doesn't start happening within the first couple of weeks. And the chances are almost zero if it doesn't within the first month," Dawson recites like an encyclopedia.

"But you didn't know about that back then."

Dawson's fingers dig into the plushie. "There was no one to help him."

"No family?"

"A younger brother. He flew over from Sydney, but... They're in the same business and he's drowning in work. I couldn't throw that on him. He's a good person."

Ash hums thoughtfully. Dawson knows that whatever comes out of his mouth next, he's not gonna like it.

He's right.

"And you aren't?"

Dawson clears his throat and eyes the empty glass mournfully. "I'd like to think I am. A good person helps other people."

"Even those who hurt them?"

Dawson shoots Ash a glare. "Shouldn't we all try to be better people than those who hurt us?"

Ash laughs, though Dawson doesn't see anything funny. "Is that what they teach kids these days? That you're good only if you put everyone else first?"

The plushie abandoned next to him, Dawson curls his fingers into his palms. "What's your *problem*?" Who does this man think he is?

Ash holds up his hands but doesn't look apologetic in the slightest. "I don't have a problem, Dawson. Well, I have many, but none of them involve you." He gives him a pointed look. "But you do. That's why you're here right? To find out what's wrong with you."

The fucker is taunting him, Dawson's sure of that. What he's not sure of is whether he can sit through the rest of the fucking session.

"You're really starting to piss me off," he grits out, uncaring if he comes across as threatening.

Ash, the fucker, looks awfully pleased, as if Dawson passed a test. "Good." He fumbles for something behind him, bringing up a small ball. "Need stress relief?" Without waiting for a response, he pitches it to Dawson.

Dawson catches it on reflex, squeezing it. That definitely feels good. "I'll probably end up flicking it in your face," he says when he sees Ash's self-satisfied grin. Does this man actually have a license?

"I'm used to it. Plus, it's very soft," Ash admits, grinning. "You keep talking about your husband in the past tense, but you still live together."

The sudden change in topic has Dawson fumbling for words. "We do, but honestly, it's like living with a complete stranger."

"Is that good or bad?"

"In my circumstances?" He only gives it a briefest thought. "Good. Definitely good." He sighs, shame coursing through his veins. He squeezes the ball until he hears his knuckles crack. "And that's the problem."

"How so?"

Fuck. How does he admit this to someone else when he only recently admitted it to himself? He thought he was messed up before when he wished his husband didn't survive his accident, but this? This is a whole new kind of fucked up.

He looks at Ash, trying to gauge his reaction. He's a therapist. A fucking weird one, possibly a bit mental himself, but still a therapist. He must've seen and heard all kinds of shit, right? If Dawson admits it to anyone, it should logically be him.

"I was determined to go through with it, you know? The divorce," he starts, having reached for the plushie again, stroking it with his free hand. "I promised my sister and my best friend that once Cal was on his feet, figuratively speaking, I'd drop the bomb. I meant it too." He did. That wasn't a lie. "I knew it'd make me feel guilty as hell for springing it on him out of nowhere, but my mind was made up. I knew he'd probably be okay." He hesitates, wanting to make something clear. "I should mention, he does well for himself. He and his brother own a building company, so it's not like he'd end up on the streets because he can't go back to his job. And I knew that Ellis, that's his brother, would take care of him if needed." He reminded himself of all those points on repeat, needing to back up and explain his decision.

Ash nods, watching him patiently. "But?"

Dawson strokes the donut again, a smile that's almost painful forming on his lips. "I'm not sure I can do it anymore. He's different. *Cal* is different. And before you say anything, I've thought about it. I was thinking that maybe I was just falling into some misguided sense of security and safety, because he's pretty much harmless. But...it's not that. It's worse. Much worse." He lets out a shuddering breath, and some of the last restraints he has on the truth come loose with it. "I like him."

Silence. Then, "You like him."

He lets out a watery laugh. "Messed up, huh?"

Ash hums. "Pretty messed up, yeah." There it is again. That teasing tone. It makes Dawson breathe a little easier. "So, you've known this new Cal for a few weeks now?"

"Almost three weeks, I think. It took some time before he came out of the coma, and I visited him during that following week at the hospital. So...yeah, we've been living together since he was released."

"How's that been?"

"Surreal. Absolutely bizarre. It's like I was dropped in an alternate universe, or like there are hidden cameras everywhere I go and someone is having a good laugh about all this." He sees Ash smile and it makes talking about it a little easier. "But it hasn't been...bad. It's so fucked up because—because there's nothing left of the man I knew and—and I kinda like this one. And that scares the hell out of me. I knew how to act around him when he was..."

"An abusive asshole?" Ash supplies helpfully, earning another laugh. He's good at that, Dawson notes.

"Yeah."

"And now you don't?"

That's not an easy one to answer. Technically, there's no reason to have to figure out how to act around Cal now. There's no need to act, because Dawson feels sa— He doesn't feel *unsafe* with him. But then there's this part of him that doesn't know how to relax, how to not act, how to just let things be instead of being on alert for any little sign, any change in Cal's mood.

"You know, I made this appointment before Cal came home. I needed someone to help me stop feeling like absolute crap for wanting to walk out on a guy who needed my help. And yeah, obviously, I need help processing some of the shit that happened before." Easy times. What he wouldn't give to be back at that dilemma. "Now, I... Fuck, I just don't know what to do. It's a shame you're not allowed to give advice because I could really use one."

He doesn't expect an answer but is surprised again.

Ash makes a thoughtful sound, opening his arms. "I can give you advice," he says like it's no big deal. "I can tell you to pack your bags and get the hell away from that fucker as fast as you can and never look back because people like that don't change and losing memories doesn't change who we truly are deep inside. But it wouldn't make any difference because you're not ready to make that choice."

Clearly taking enjoyment in Dawson's struck expression, he leans forward. "I'll let you in on a secret, Dawson." Funnily, Dawson finds himself leaning forward too. "People don't come to therapy for advice. You can go on Reddit for that. People come here to stop feeling the way they feel. Because on a subconscious level, you know that if you just had an off-switch for your emotions, you could easily make that choice. Imagine it—you're not weighed down by guilt, you're not afraid of the consequences and you don't care if someone thinks you're selfish or a bad person, or if you're hurting anybody else." He pauses to give Dawson space to imagine it. "Now it's pretty easy to make a choice, huh?"

Holy shit. "That's an interesting way to look at it." Dawson never thought about it like that. He always wished if only there was someone to make decisions for him, but not like Cal used to make them. He means decisions that would be in his best interest. But now that Ash said it...yeah, having someone to make those decisions wouldn't help him stop feeling the way he feels. "Wish there was an actual off-switch."

"Oh, there is," Ash says jovially. "It's called drugs. Your husband discovered one. Then proceeded to make your life a living hell. And it was easy to do, because he didn't feel any remorse. Not that alcohol is the only thing to blame. It mostly just exacerbates the shit that's already hiding underneath. But yeah, no, can't say I recommend using an off-switch."

"What do you recommend?"

Ash smiles like he's been waiting for him to ask that the whole time. "Getting it off your chest and trusting me to make sense of all that mess."

And fuck, Dawson has no idea what Ash has done to him in the short time they've been talking, but that sounds really, really good at the moment.

"I like the sound of that."

"Good," Ash says, proud and pleased. He leans back into the armchair, making himself comfortable. "Now tell me about your childhood."

"You did great today, Dawson," Ash says after what must be a few centuries.

"That was horrible," Dawson whines, not a single spark of energy left in his body. Stupid childhood dissection. And yeah, fine, maybe the dissecting brought a few things into perspective—like Dawson's pushover tendencies—but it doesn't mean he has to like it.

Ash snickers. "Thanks, I strive to deliver on my promises." He pulls out his phone. "When do you want to do this again?"

Dawson huffs, folding his arms across his chest. "Bold of you to assume I'll want to do this shit again."

Ash hums, completely unbothered. He swipes through his phone, pursing his lips.

"How about Tuesday the week after next? Two o'clock."

Dawson glares at him, expelling a breath through his nose. "That works."

"Excellent." Dawson would give his left leg to wipe the self-satisfied smirk off Ash's face. "Well, Dawson, it was a pleasure meeting you." He stands and Dawson does too.

Dawson grunts. "Wish I could say the same."

Ash's grin is so wide it nearly doesn't fit on his face. "You'll be alright, Dawson," he says with an uncharacteristic solemnity. What's stranger is how easy Dawson believes him.

Dawson waves at the couch. "Thanks, I guess…"

"Any time. Are you feeling okay?"

Dawson does a quick scan of his body. "Tired but...a little lighter? Does that make sense?"

"It makes perfect sense," Ash assures him. "Don't be mistaken, though. Next time, I won't go so easy on you."

Dawson gapes at him. "This was *easy*?!"

Ash throws his head back, laughing, and walks him to the door. "Guess you'll have to turn up and see for yourself."

"Yeah, don't bet on it," Dawson grumbles, loud enough for Ash to hear.

"Take care, Dawson," he says, opening the door.

"Yeah, you too." When he steps into the hallway there's a middle-aged woman sitting on the bench where Dawson had sat earlier. She looks up at the sound of the door opening, her gaze catching somewhere behind Dawson, probably where Ash is standing. Her face lights up when she sees him.

"Hi, Stella," Ash says, and she hurries to stand up. "How are you?"

"Oh gosh, don't get me fucking started," she groans, making Dawson do a double take.

Ash just laughs. "That's what I'm here for, though. Come on in."

She hurries inside, and Dawson turns around in time to see Ash give him a wave before he goes in after her.

Well, Dawson's definitely having words with Gabe.

Stepping back into the apartment after his session with Ash is strange. It was strange just leaving Ash's office, like coming back to reality after spending an hour in a different world.

"I'm home!" he calls out as he toes off his shoes and hangs the keys on the hook on the door. There's no answer. "Cal?"

Silence for a moment, then, "Uh, yeah?"

Dawson looks around, wondering where it came from, then notices the light in the laundry room.

"Are you okay? You sound weird." He makes a slow approach.

"I'm fine! Don't come in here!" Cal blurts in a way that's decidedly not fine.

Feeling his growing panic—what if Cal hurt himself?—Dawson stalks into the laundry room. "Cal, what—" He comes to a halt in the doorway, taking in the scene in front of him. "What's going on?"

"Nothing," Cal says quickly, standing up from his crouch in front of the washing machine and holding something behind his back. His eyes are wide, his expression guilty.

Nothing, my ass. Dawson looks at the machine, then at Cal, then at the machine. The door is open and there are some pink towels hanging over the rim and—

Wait. They don't have pink towels.

Realization dawning, Dawson places a hand over his mouth to stop himself from breaking out into hysterical laughter.

Cal must take it for something else, because his already alert expression blooms into full panic. "Don't be mad," he says miserably.

Dawson shakes his head, snickering into his hand. "I'm not," he mumbles into his palm.

Cal starts rambling, showing Dawson his hands, where he's holding a small—and pink—towel. "I wanted to make myself useful and do laundry. Like you showed me."

"Okay?" Dawson manages to keep his voice neutral.

"I screwed up," Cal says, his voice so tragic you'd think someone died. "I'm sorry."

Swallowing down a laugh, Dawson walks inside. "It's fine, Cal."

Cal blinks at him owlishly. "You're not mad?"

Dawson shakes his head, a coil of affection burning bright in his chest. "I'm not mad."

Cal lets out a harsh breath. "Still, sorry."

"I appreciate the thought," Dawson assures him. He takes the towel from Cal, studying it. "I like this. It's cute."

Cal's nose twitches. "It's pink."

"Hey! Pink is badass," Dawson argues, chuckling. "But if it bothers you, we can give them away. They're always looking for towels and blankets at the shelter."

Cal lights up. "Really?"

"Yeah."

"Oh. Yes, I like that idea," he nods enthusiastically. "We could get them some more. Go shopping."

Jesus, who is this man who gets so excited about the prospect of helping animals and doing something just because he can? "Sure. That would be great."

"Now?" Cal asks, backtracking before Dawson can reply. "Oh, wait. You just got here. You must be tired. How was your appointment?"

Dawson was honest with Cal about the nature of the appointment and answered all the questions he had. Cal was mostly worried he was doing something wrong and that's why Dawson needed to see a therapist. It was a tricky situation, explaining things truthfully without revealing too much.

"Well, it was a lot." He busies himself by pulling more towels out of the machine. His red t-shirt falls out, revealing the culprit of the pink disaster. "For one, Ashley—Ash—is a man. But it was good. Made me really think about some things. I have another one in two weeks."

"Did you talk about me?"

Not wanting to lie—plus, Cal isn't stupid, he must've figured it out—Dawson admits, "Yeah, we did."

Cal nods, as if filing that information away. "Next time you see him, please don't tell him your husband turned our towels pink."

Dawson laughs at the thought of describing the incident to Ash. "I can't promise anything."

"Dawson!" Cal gasps, grabbing the other end of the towel Dawson's holding and giving it a pull. "Promise you won't."

"Nope." He tugs at the towel, then Cal does the same. Soon, they're both pulling at it, laughing and yelling. Cal somehow manages to win and get the towel, so Dawson reaches into the machine and pulls out another one, throwing it on Cal's head.

Cal lets out a muffled yelp, fighting the towel off. His hair is in disarray when he pulls it off, and he glowers at Dawson, which only makes him laugh. Cal throws the towel at him, and while Dawson is busy catching it, Cal reaches into the machine and starts pulling out whatever is there, throwing the whole pile at Dawson.

Dawson squeaks as he gets buried under the pile of wet, cold towels. He doesn't know how it happens, but the towels end up on the floor, and so do the two of them, laughing and roughhousing. Somehow, Dawson ends up on top, and Cal lets out a grunt. It snaps him out of the playful mood straight away, and Dawson scrambles off him.

"Shit. Sorry. Are you hurt?" He starts pulling up Cal's shirt to check, but Cal's hands stop him.

He lets out a choked laugh. "I'm fine." Taking advantage of the distraction, he grabs a towel and throws it over Dawson's head, making him squeal.

"You cheater!"

"You weren't paying attention!"

Dawson fights the towel off, glaring down at Cal, prepared to fight back, when his next words lodge in his throat.

Cal is laughing, his shoulders shaking with it. There's a dimple in his left cheek Dawson's never seen before, and his crow's feet are incredibly prominent with the force of his smile.

He notices Dawson watching him, and his laugh slowly dies off, replaced by something serious, more intense. They stay like that for a moment, Dawson hovering above him, making sure not to press on any injuries but unable to move further away. His heart hits his sternum with enough force to make his breath catch and he wants to...he wants to...

"Are you hungry?" he asks, his voice sounding strange to his own ears, like he's hearing it through a veil.

On cue, Cal's stomach growls. It makes them both chuckle.

"I could eat."

Nodding, Dawson pushes himself off Cal and stands up. "Let me whip something up." He reaches down to help Cal stand, trying to ignore the way their joined hands send a trickle of...something up his arm. He lets go, hurrying to the kitchen and pulling from the fridge whatever he gets his hands on.

Cal trails after him, leaning his elbows on the island and watching him work.

"Can I help?" he asks after a while.

"Uh, yeah. Sure," Dawson says with surprise. Even though he probably should've expected it. Lately, Cal has been nothing but a ball of curiosity. "How about you drizzle a bit of oil in the pan and let it heat. Then chuck these in." He hands him the chopping board with the onions.

Nodding, Cal does just that, watching the pan with intense gaze. "How do I know it's hot enough?"

"You can put a drop of water in there. If it sizzles and hisses, it's ready." To demonstrate, Dawson wets his hand, then flicks his fingers at the pan, a few droplets flying inside it. The oil starts spitting, making Cal jump.

"I take it it's ready?" he says dryly.

"Yup," Dawson says with a chuckle.

Cal puts the onions in, taking a wooden spoon and pushing them around.

They work together like that and it's nice; domestic. It brings back memories from the time Dawson's parents were still alive and he'd assist his mom in the kitchen, asking so many questions.

This time, it's Cal who asks questions, but Dawson doesn't mind, smiling at his curiosity and how intently he focuses on completing the tasks like he's going to be graded on them later.

"Do you mind if I take a picture?" he asks after a while as Dawson is chopping up spring onions.

"Go for it."

The sound of the shutter goes off, and Dawson blinks when he sees Cal's phone pointed at him instead of the food. "Oh. I thought you were talking about..." He points at the ingredients sizzling in the pan.

Cal's smiling at the picture, but it's replaced by worry when Dawson's words register. "Oh, sorry! I'll delete it."

Jesus, he looks absolutely devastated. What's with him and his obsession with pictures? "No, no. Don't. It's fine. I was just taken aback. My candids are atrocious."

Cal studies the picture with pursed lips. "You look lovely." He looks at Dawson uncertainly. "Can I take more?"

"You don't have to ask each time," Dawson says gently, shooting him a smile. "I'm giving you blanket permission."

"Sorry, just after last time..." He looks uncomfortable, and Dawson doesn't have to guess what the last time is that he's referring to.

Dawson clears his throat, his mind flashing back to those pictures and the deep humiliation and betrayal he felt at seeing them. "Yeah, maybe no nudes for now."

"No nudes," Cal says solemnly. "Got it."

He tries to act naturally and not focus on Cal as he takes more pictures. Hopefully, he'll only keep the good ones. After a while, it seems that Cal is done, looking at the phone with a soft smile on his lips. It makes something inside Dawson ache, but he's not brave enough to examine it too closely. He's done way too much examining today already.

Once the sauce is done, he switches the burner off, wipes his hands on a tea towel, and pulls out his phone.

"My turn," he announces, not giving Cal a chance as he clicks the shutter, taking several pictures in quick succession. He checks them, a laugh bursting out of him. "You look like a deer caught in the headlights!"

Cal's cheeks turn pink, and he glares at Dawson. "You took me by surprise."

Dawson snaps a pic of his annoyed face, making it deepen. "Revenge." Giggling at the picture, he doesn't notice Cal taking a picture as well.

"Ha," Cal says smugly.

Dawson props his hands on his hips. "Oh, so that's how it's gonna be?"

Cal straightens his back, lifting his chin. "That is how it's gonna be."

"This means war. You know that, right?"

Cal smirks. "Bring it on."

Dawson narrows his eyes. "I'm gonna take a picture when you least expect it. It will be sooo baaad."

"I'll take a worse one of you."

Dawson narrows his eyes in challenge. "We'll see."

The war will have to wait, though, if Dawson doesn't want to burn their dinner.

Spooning up a bit of the sauce, Dawson brings it to his lips, tasting it. It's okay, but...not quite what he was going for. He dips the spoon in, scooping up more sauce and holding it out to Cal. "Can you try this for me? I think it's missing something. Not sure if it's just salt—" The words get stuck in his throat when Cal's fingers circle gently around his wrist, maneuvering it a little as he leans forward and takes the spoon in his mouth.

Some inhuman noise comes out of Dawson, but it must be quiet because Cal doesn't comment on it. He hums as he savors the sauce.

"It's perfect. Don't think it needs more salt."

"Okay." Dawson winces when it comes out as a squeal. He clears his throat for the hundredth time. "Good."

Making a grab for the wooden spoon, he continues stirring the sauce, even though it doesn't need it anymore. His heart hammers in his chest like a wild beast and his wrist tingles where Cal touched him.

Jesus, what's happening to him?

A thought-annihilating high-pitched noise jerks Dawson awake, his heart pounding. He lifts his eyes to the ceiling, seeing the smoke alarm flashing red. What on earth? They test the alarm the first Thursday of each month. Today is Wednesday, and—Dawson checks his phone—it's way too early anyway. Which means...

The smell of burned toast reaches his nose, and he kicks the duvet off. "Shit!" He flings the door open, the burned scent intensifying. "Cal? Cal!"

He finds Cal—unsurprisingly—in the kitchen, standing on a chair and ruthlessly waving a chopping board in front of the smoke detector.

He looks at Dawson, panic flashing across his face. "I'm sorry, I didn't mean to."

Dawson relaxes when there's no actual fire in sight. The beeping of the alarm becomes irregular, signaling it will turn off soon.

"It's fine. See? It's already stopping." He goes to open the windows while Cal continues waving the chopping board. They always keep the windows open a crack to let fresh air in, but the burned smell makes Dawson's eyes sting. Talk about a brutal wake-up call.

The alarm finally stops, and Cal steps off the chair with a relieved sigh and a guilty expression.

"Are you cooking?" Dawson asks with amusement.

Cal's shoulders slump. "I wanted to surprise you. I watched you make pancakes last time and thought I could replicate the recipe. But they were cooking too quickly, and I couldn't get them off, and then the smoke started coming from them—"

"Hey, hey. It's fine, Cal, really," Dawson reassures him before Cal starts hyperventilating. "No harm done. You have no idea how many things I've burned over the years. It's a learning curve." His mind is still stuck on *I wanted to surprise you*. Harsh wake-up call or not, that's unfairly sweet.

"I just wanted to do something nice for you," Cal murmurs, dejected. "You do everything and I...I wanted to be useful. But I screwed up like I did with the laundry."

Dawson's insides go all gooey.

He's not used to this, to people giving a shit, let alone doing something for him. He's always done everything by himself. Losing his parents meant he had to pull his weight. Olivia was working herself into an early grave juggling multiple jobs and her studies. And Dawson was old enough to take care of himself. There was no room for being coddled.

He was already stunned when Ellis didn't miss a beat and offered to take care of the legal stuff—but Dawson could at least contribute that to the fact that Ellis is Cal's brother and Cal getting in trouble could lead to the company being in trouble.

But Cal making breakfast for Dawson just *because*... Yeah, he has no idea how to process that.

Cal's expression is crestfallen, and fuck, Dawson hates seeing him like this. He notices Cal managed to get some of the batter on his face—and his t-shirt. He looks so...normal, so human. His hair is still bed-tousled, and he's wearing the flannel pants he slept in and—

"What?" Cal asks. It occurs to Dawson he must be staring.

He clears his throat. "You have a smudge on your cheek."

"Oh." Cal runs the back of his hand over the wrong cheek. "Did I get it?"

Dawson chuckles. "Let me..." The batter has already started to dry, so he wets the corner of a tea towel under the tap, steps into Cal's space, and runs the fabric over his cheek.

Cal holds still like a statue—and not just with his body. He seems to be suspending his breath, his gaze fixed on Dawson's face. They're close enough that Dawson can smell his breath, fresh and minty, and feel the heat radiating from his skin.

Later, Dawson will blame this on his brain not being properly awake and on Cal being unreasonably sweet and endearing, but somehow, he ends up pressed up against him, chest to chest, and their lips connected.

It's a simple kiss, almost innocent, close-mouthed and so light it might as well not be there at all. But it's there. Dawson knows because he feels it all the way to the tips of his fingers.

Then Cal makes the softest sound, like a whimper but not quite, and it's enough to snap Dawson back to reality.

He falls back on his feet from where he's been rising on his tiptoes, his eyes as wide as Cal's, expression just as surprised. God, what's gotten into him?

"Thank you," he croaks out when the silence becomes too long, too heavy. "For wanting to make me breakfast."

Cal's tongue darts out, almost as if he's trying to taste Dawson on his lips. He lets out a breath. "But I screwed up."

"Let's see if it's salvageable."

Hesitant, Cal pushes the mixing bowl with the batter towards him.

Dawson scoops some with a ladle and lets it pour back into the bowl. "Well, it's a tad runnier than it should be, that's why you couldn't get it off the pan. The consistency should be like... Pass me the flour?"

Cal passes him the container. Dawson goes to add more flour to the batter but gets a better idea. He pushes the container back towards Cal. "Actually, you have a go. Go on," he prompts, smiling encouragingly when Cal doesn't make a move. Finally, he takes the container and the spoon, looking at Dawson expectantly.

"Okay, add a few spoons, then mix it in like before. You want the whisk to leave a bit of an imprint for a second or two, that's how you know it's right. A little more flour. Now, see?"

Cal studies the batter intently. "Oh. Yeah. I didn't notice last time."

"I didn't point it out." Maybe he should start explaining what he's doing and why when he's cooking. In his defense, he hadn't expected Cal to have any culinary interests. "What else did you put in?"

"Um...eggs. Baking powder, milk, a little oil."

"How many eggs?"

"Two."

That should be fine. The ingredient ratio will be a little off since he doesn't know how much batter there was initially, but they'll make it work. If the first pancake is crap, they'll simply add more of the other ingredients.

"Perfect. Wanna try again?" He offers Cal the mixing bowl.

Cal looks at it warily.

"I'm kind of hungry," Dawson tries to sway him. It works.

"Okay." Cal takes the bowl. "But I ruined the pan."

Dawson gives the pan a quick glance. "It should scrub off. In the meantime, you can use the ceramic one."

He lets Cal do everything, pointing out a thing or two when Cal struggles with something. He takes pancake making so seriously Dawson has to capture the moment.

Cal shoots him a dirty look when he hears the shutter of the camera. "That was low."

"It's a good picture!" It really is, which means Dawson can't use it for their game, but he doesn't care. Cal holding a spatula and glaring at the pan, willing it to cook faster, is priceless. Hell, he might set it as his wallpaper.

Ten minutes later, they have a plate full of warm, perfect-looking pancakes, not a single one burned.

Dawson takes a picture, then makes Cal hold the plate in front of him and snaps another one. He tries not to laugh at Cal's poker face.

"Great job, Cal." He means it. He's never taught anybody anything, and seeing Cal so proud of his accomplishment, blushing at the compliment, makes Dawson all warm and fuzzy. He wants to remember this feeling, this moment, the simple domesticity of it all.

"Let's take a picture together."

Cal looks surprised but is eager to agree. Dawson goes to stand beside him, but with Cal being a good head taller, he can't get a good angle.

"You'll have to take it. My arms aren't long enough."

Cal takes the phone, extending his arm. "Is this good?"

Dawson checks—it's not bad, they're just a little too far apart. Hesitating for a second, Dawson winds an arm around Cal's waist, plastering himself to his side. Cal does the same, his hand coming to rest on Dawson's ribs.

"Like this?"

"Yeah," Dawson says, his throat feeling raw. "Say cheese."

Cal frowns at the camera. "Why would I say cheese?"

"Oh, Jesus," Dawson groans. "Just smile, will you?"

"Oh." His lips twitch. "Okay."

Dawson doesn't smile; he bursts out laughing, Cal's attempt at a smile setting him off. His confusion makes Dawson only laugh harder, and soon Cal joins in too. They're still laughing, their faces red and eyes watering, when Cal snaps a picture.

"Oh my god." Dawson covers his face. "That's horrible."

Cal grins. "It is." He runs his thumb over the screen reverently. "Can we print it out and frame it?"

And damn, he looks so hopeful Dawson doesn't have it in his heart to say 'no fucking way'.

"Yeah, we can do that."

Frame shopping it is.

Chapter 18

THE NEXT TIME THEY go to the shelter, they bring along the pink towels. Cal was skeptical when Dawson told him they'll make use of them at the shelter, thinking Dawson was just trying to make him feel better, but one look at Aubrey's face when they drop the bag with the towels in front of her changes his mind.

It also plants an idea in his head.

He waits until they finish at the shelter and Dawson is driving them home before he asks.

"Is there another way to help? If not, I'm more than happy to ruin as many towels as needed."

Dawson laughs. It's a beautiful sound, his whole face transforming with it. Cal loves making him laugh.

"Several. Of course, money donations are always welcome."

"Don't we already do that?" Cal's confused. He was under the impression they were already donating money, since Dawson's volunteered there for so many years.

Dawson glances at him sideways. "Um, no?"

"We should do that."

"Really?"

"We have a lot of money, no?"

"Technically, you do."

"You're my husband. It's your money too."

"I mean, yeah but…" Dawson shrugs. "I didn't earn any of it."

"I haven't worked in weeks, so, technically, I haven't earned any of it in that time either."

"You own the company, Cal. It will bring you profit whether you actively work or not."

Dawson has said that before, but it doesn't change the fact that Cal's been a couch potato for several weeks now.

"Marriage is the same. In that analogy, I'm like a company."

Dawson gives him a mildly horrified look. "That's a horrible analogy. You're not a cash-cow, Cal."

Cal doesn't understand that term, but the tightness in Dawson's voice is unmistakable.

"I upset you."

Dawson sighs. "I just don't want you to think I married you for your money."

That thought had never even crossed his mind. "I'd never think that. You're too kind and selfless to take advantage of people." He's been taking care of Cal this whole time, even though he didn't have to.

Dawson doesn't say anything to that, so Cal stays silent, not wanting to say something else that could upset him.

He waits until they're home to bring it back up. "So, about the donation. Could we do that?"

Dawson gives a reluctant nod and pulls out his phone.

"Yeah, I can do it now if you want." Cal nods. "Do you...um...want to do a one-off or a recurring donation?"

"Which is better?"

Dawson studies him and he hesitates with his answer. "We could set up a recurring donation for every month. That would probably work the best."

"Alright. Sounds good." He has no idea how this works. Better to leave it up to Dawson.

"How much do you want to donate?"

"What amount will actually make a difference?"

"Whatever amount is helpful."

"Dawson." Why is he so sketchy when it comes to money?

"Okay, uh...five hundred?"

That's not what Cal had expected. "Can we afford it?"

"Yeah, easily."

"Then double it."

Dawson sputters. "W-what?"

"Double it. If we can easily afford five hundred, then a thousand should be fine too."

"If you're sure..." Dawson says, but he doesn't move his hands, like he's expecting Cal to change his mind.

"I trust your judgment."

Dawson lets out a small, incredulous huff. "Okay. Yeah, okay, that's...that's really generous." His fingers hover over the phone, still unsure. Finally, he presses his thumb to something on the screen. "Done."

"Wonderful."

Dawson pockets his phone, still looking a little dumbstruck. "So, um, what do you want to eat?"

"Are donuts an option?"

That earns him a hard glare. "No."

Yeah, he didn't think so. Worth a try, though. "I'll leave it up to you."

Dawson rolls his eyes, muttering 'typical' under his breath. "I was thinking we could make pizzas today. From scratch."

"Is it hard?"

"Super easy, actually. But it takes a while, because we need to wait for the dough to rise."

"We can watch something in the meantime."

Dawson grins, likely thinking the same. "Good idea. Any preference?"

"Maybe the other amnesia movie?"

"*50 First Dates*? I love that one! It's a classic."

Finding Dawson's excitement suspicious, he's compelled to check, "Does it have Tatum in it?"

Dawson gives him an exasperated look. "No, you weirdo."

Thank god.

"Come on, let's start on the pizzas."

Dawson wasn't lying—it seems to be rather easy. The only tricky part is the yeast—Cal would just dump it in the bowl with the rest of the ingredients and expect it to work anyway. He had no idea that yeast needs to *activate.* Once it does, and Dawson adds the rest of the ingredients, he asks Cal to take over.

Using his hands, Cal pushes the mixture around until it starts to stick together—and to his skin. It's uncomfortable, and the slimy dough sliding between his fingers feels icky, but Dawson reassures him he's doing it right.

"It's in the wrist. I'll show you." Dawson gets one of his hands in the bowl, demonstrating the right technique. Cal struggles to pay attention to what he's doing instead of relishing how Dawson's hand touches his during the process. "Got it?"

"Got it," Cal lies, disappointed when Dawson removes his hand and lets Cal take over. Dawson moves away to wash his hands, and a few seconds later, Cal hears a familiar clicking sound.

Sure enough, when he looks up, Dawson has his phone aimed at him and is grinning from ear to ear.

Heat crawls up Cal's neck. He must look so awkward doing this. "That's not fair."

Dawson sticks his tongue out. "Everything's fair in lo—uh, war."

"I have no way to defend myself," Cal complains.

"I know." Dawson looks way too pleased with himself. He looks at the picture he just took, his wide grin morphs into something softer. "Do you want another picture together?"

Cal looks down at his messy hands and flour-covered shirt. He wouldn't be surprised if there was some on his face too. "I look a mess."

Dawson shrugs, then reaches into the container with flour and smears his fingers across his shirt and cheek. "Now I do too."

God, Cal wants to kiss him so bad.

He gets the next best thing. Dawson steps towards him, side to side, and leans into Cal as he raises his phone, arranging it so it fits both their faces.

Yup, Cal was right. There's flour on his nose and in his hair. He doesn't even care. His eyes are glued to Dawson and his gorgeous smile. Cal finds himself unable to contain his own smile, his heart doing a wild little dance.

Dawson takes a picture.

He laughs when he checks it. "This is horrible. I love it." He shows Cal, who laughs too. It is horrible, and also perfect.

"We're framing that one."

"And putting it up here." Dawson pats the island.

"Yes."

After Dawson deems Cal's kneading satisfactory, he throws a tea towel over the bowl and leaves it on the counter. "It needs to keep warm and undisturbed for a couple of hours."

Cal nods, filing the information away. He washes his hands and face, and wipes his shirt. It takes ages before the dough bits come off. He's not sure he wants to do it again, even if he really enjoys it when Dawson teaches him new things.

They settle on the sofa, sitting almost shoulder to shoulder, and Dawson browses Netflix until he finds the movie.

"Is this based on a true story?" Cal wonders.

"Nah. It's trashy, in the best way. Just roll with it."

Cal just 'rolls with it'. And enjoys it very much. The movie is different from the other one they watched, and Cal finds he likes it even better. There's no Tatum, for one.

"Could this actually happen?" he asks when the credits roll.

Dawson takes a moment before replying. "Anterograde amnesia is real, but, realistically, I don't think they could keep her in the dark that long. Even though it's a small community."

That's what Cal was thinking too.

"And obviously, lots of stuff in there is questionable. The lying, the fact that he's basically stalking her..."

Dawson is right. It was funny and romantic in the movie, but in reality, it would be creepy.

"I'm surprised how much effort he puts in, knowing she will forget him tomorrow," Cal says.

Dawson's lips purse as he thinks. "Sometimes you meet people who are worth fighting for, no matter how hard it is."

Something about the words hits close to home. Is Dawson talking about him? About them? Or is Cal just projecting what he wants to hear?

"You think so?"

Dawson looks at him, smiling softly. "I do. The world is a shitty place. I'd like to hold onto hope that there are things that will always be worth fighting for."

Cal likes that. He likes that a lot.

"So..." Dawson clears his throat. "Did you like it?"

"I did. Even more than the first one." Even though neither of the two had a typical happy ending. Maybe there's no proper happy ending after a person loses their memory.

"Who do you think had it worse?" Dawson asks. "Him, because she never remembered him and never will, or her because she would have to fight hard every day to be able to adjust to her new life?"

"Him, I think," Cal says after a moment. "She still remembered him, in a way. Her memories were gone, but not her feelings. I kind of get that."

"Get how?" Dawson asks, perplexed.

Cal's not good at this. Explaining stuff. Most of the time, he doesn't even understand his feelings. But for Dawson, he tries to put it into words.

"I don't remember you, but... I remember loving you. I've felt it since I laid my eyes on you at the hospital. I wanted to hold your hand." He was so confused back then. All those people, all the things and information they kept shoving down his throat, and none of them made sense to him. And then, he opened his eyes and there Dawson was. And everything became clear.

Dawson's gone awfully quiet, and when Cal looks at him, he sees unshed tears in his eyes. His stomach clenches with alarm.

"Dawson?"

Dawson's lips part, a small, barely audible sound escaping. His glistening eyes drop to Cal's mouth for a split second before he lurches backwards and stumbles to his feet.

"The...the dough is ready," he presses out, slowly backing away. "We should...uh, finish with the...yeah."

Shocked by Dawson's reaction, Cal doesn't immediately follow him. He knows it would be better to give him some space to process...whatever just happened to him. Cal has an ugly inkling it's his fault. It's usually his fault when Dawson goes quiet and distant all of a sudden.

He manages to stay put for several minutes before joining him in the kitchen. Dawson's already lined up the stuff for the pizza on the counter. And there's a lot.

"Are we putting all that on top?" Cal asks. Talking about food will hopefully put Dawson at ease.

"Whatever you want," Dawson says without looking at him. "We made enough dough for about four small pizzas. We can each have one, then freeze the rest." He takes out some mushrooms and starts chopping them up.

"I'm sorry for upsetting you," Cal says, regretting it when Dawson stiffens.

"It's fine. Don't worry about it." He lets out a sharp hiss and drops the knife. "Ah, shit." He brings up his left hand, blood trailing down his pointer finger.

"Are you okay?" Cal steps into his space.

"Yeah. It's just a small cut."

It doesn't seem small. The blood is still running.

Stepping over to the sink, Dawson turns on the tap and puts his finger under the thin stream.

"Let me see," Cal demands, reaching for his hand.

"It's fine, Cal." He tries to pull away, but Cal holds on tighter.

"Let me see. Please." That seems to get through to Dawson.

Once he has permission, Cal inspects the cut, wincing in sympathy when he can see how deep it is and that a bit of blood is still oozing from it. This is his fault. He made Dawson upset, then he distracted him while he had a knife in his hand.

Air gets stuck in his lungs when the world around him tilts and images flash in front of his eyes, too quick to catch any details. But as always, Dawson's there, hurt or crying, or both. There's blood on his lip, and a bruise on his cheek and—

"Cal?"

Dawson's voice snaps him back. He blinks, the world coming into focus once again. The first thing he sees is Dawson's concerned expression, his hand cradled between Cal's.

Cal swallows, trying to make his vocal cords cooperate. "I'll get a band-aid." He rushes to the bathroom where they keep the first aid kit. Once he has a box of band-aids in his hand, he makes his way back. "This one should fit." Dawson obligingly offers his finger while watching Cal with a strange expression.

"Role reversal, huh?"

"What?"

"You bandaging me for a change."

"Yeah, well, it's time I return the favor. Although I'd prefer it to be under different circumstances. I hate seeing you hurt."

"It's just a cut," Dawson says in a small voice.

"It doesn't matter."

Trying to be as gentle as possible, Cal peels away the small, plastic strips and covers the cut, making sure the sticky parts adhere properly to his skin.

"What's the diagnosis, doctor?" Dawson asks with a smirk. "Will I live?"

"You'll be okay. I'll just have to keep an eye on you. Starting now."

"Huh?"

He takes Dawson's elbow and leads him to a stool behind the island. "You sit down. I'll finish this."

"I can cook, Cal." He tries to wriggle away. "I can just wrap a piece of glove around it."

"You'd make it bleed. Sit." He pulls a stool out and applies pressure on Dawson's shoulders until he sits. "I'll finish this."

Miraculously, Dawson listens.

Under his husband's instruction, Cal cuts up the dough into four pieces, keeping two and freezing the rest. Dawson guides him through the process and it's not as hard as Cal feared. The pizzas are far from round, but Dawson insists it doesn't matter because it's going to taste the same as long as the thickness is consistent. Then he tells Cal to spread the tomato sauce on top and put it in the oven for a few minutes.

In the meantime, Cal chops the mushrooms. At first, he worries he's going to end up in a similar predicament as Dawson, except he'll probably cut his whole finger off, but he gets the hang of it quickly. He finishes with the mushrooms and moves on to the other things Dawson has laid out, and by the time he's done, the oven timer goes off.

Dawson tells him which toppings he wants and laughs at Cal's reaction when he asks for pineapples, insisting it tastes good.

Whatever. Cal will play it safe with olives instead.

"Is this okay?" Cal asks before putting both pizzas back in the oven.

Dawson smiles. "Perfect."

When the pizzas are done and they both have their own plates, Dawson cuts off a piece and offers it to Cal. Cal takes it, doing the same for Dawson. He takes a bite, and nearly gags, having to force himself to swallow instead of just spitting it back on the plate.

"This is awful!"

Dawson lets out an offended gasp. "How dare you!"

Cal shakes his head, washing the horrendous taste down with water. "It's fruit. On a pizza!"

"Clearly, you don't know what's good."

"Clearly, my husband has no shame."

In revenge, Dawson picks a piece of pineapple and flicks it at Cal. It bounces off his—thankfully black—shirt. He picks it up with barely concealed disgust and throws it back at Dawson. Dawson catches it, laughs, and pops it in his mouth.

"Oh my God," Cal cries, which only makes Dawson laugh harder.

"Five second rule."

"What?"

"You can eat something you dropped—"

"You threw it at me!"

"—if you pick it up in less than five seconds."

"That was longer than five seconds."

"No, it wasn't."

"It was."

"It was not."

"It was!"

They continue back and forth, until Dawson threatens pineapple war on Cal, so he surrenders. He still keeps an eye on Dawson and his excuse for a pizza, just in case. He'll never get over watching him eat something Cal made—for the most part—and enjoy it.

"I'll need to extend my running time after this," Dawson comments as he licks tomato sauce from his fingers.

"I wish I could go with you. Do you think I could finally start swimming?"

Dawson pauses with a finger in his mouth. The sight does something to Cal, making his belly tingle.

"I think it's worth a try. It has been about a month since the surgery, after all."

Cal nods, thinking the same. "Yeah. And I feel good, just a little rusty. I want to move properly."

"Can't blame you. But yeah, I say give it a go. Treat it like you did walking in the beginning. Build it up slowly."

"I will."

And he's starting tomorrow.

Chapter 19

CAL'S TAKEN TO SWIMMING like, well, like a fish to water. Almost every day, Dawson wakes up alone. Cal usually wanders back before breakfast, his hair wet and the scent of chlorine clinging to his skin. He's looked more energized since he's started and usually ends up going for one more round in the evening. A little more and the man will grow gills.

Dawson was worried about him over-exerting himself at first, but Cal got a green light from the doctors when he went in for a check-up, so it's all good. Naturally, he still needs to take it easy with resistance training, but he's happy to stick to his bodyweight exercises instead. Thankfully, he seems to have dropped his obsession with Channing Tatum and his washboard abs. Small mercies.

As for Cal's memory, the test results didn't show any changes. That wasn't surprising, given that nothing so far has triggered a single memory, but Dawson was still worried about how Cal would react to the official news. Cal took it in stride, though, and when Dawson asked about it, he replied that he doesn't care about his lost memories because he's already made new ones with Dawson.

Cal can be damn smooth, Dawson will give him that.

He can also be restless as hell.

Similarly to yesterday and the day before that, Dawson wakes up to cold, rumpled sheets and an empty apartment. When Cal doesn't come down in the next twenty minutes, he goes to look for him. He wouldn't bother him normally, but they have the shelter today and if they don't want to leave without having breakfast first, Cal will have to drag his ass back.

There's no one else in the pool apart from Cal. That's not surprising, since those people who actually go for a morning swim do so in the pool on one of the lower levels, not the rooftop where there's no protection against the sun. Not that Cal cares about that.

"Still haven't had enough?" Dawson calls out when Cal finishes a lap.

Cal turns towards him, rubbing water from his eyes. He smiles when he sees Dawson.

"It just feels so good to be able to do something."

"I know." Dawson would go crazy without his running. It helps him clear his mind. "You might want to wrap it up, though, or we'll be late."

"Oh, sorry." He swims towards the steps. "I'm coming out."

Dawson's throat goes dry when Cal climbs out, water streaming down his body in rivulets. He runs his fingers through his hair, squeezing the water out. Dawson must be staring like a moron, but Cal just smiles and says, "Can you hand me the towel, please?"

Dawson nods, then takes at least five full seconds before he actually makes a move to get it.

"Thank you," Cal says when he takes the towel from him and starts running it over his chest.

Dawson averts his eyes. What's wrong with him? He's seen Cal shirtless before. Only about a million times.

"I'm making scrambled eggs. That good with you?"

"Yes."

"Okay. I'll see you downstairs."

Dawson does *not* run, he just adds a little spring to his step to get everything ready before Cal comes down. And they really need to hurry if they want to make it to the shelter on time.

He's already transferring the eggs from the pan to the plates when he hears the front door open.

"Right on time!" he calls.

"Smells good," Cal says, walking into the kitchen.

Dawson rolls his eyes. "It's eggs. And toast."

"Well, it smells good."

Dawson doesn't even have the strength to argue, too busy hiding a smile. Cal liking his food has turned him into a good little housewife. It'd worry him if he didn't actually enjoy it.

They polish off their breakfast quickly, with plenty of time to spare.

Now that he's better, Cal's started to take on more tasks at the shelter. On Monday, he even cleaned and dried the kennels, but Dawson is still apprehensive about letting him carry heavier stuff. He likes working with Cal, though. Not that they always work together, but it's nice seeing him around, making friends with the dogs and other volunteers. The dogs have finally started warming up to him, with a few exceptions. Lola hates everybody, so that's no surprise, but Donut seems to have some personal vendetta against Cal. Dawson attributes it to being jealous, because he's so fond of Dawson and doesn't like sharing him.

Aubrey greets them the second they walk in, but there's something about her today that sets off Dawson's alarm bells.

"Hey, Aubrey."

"Hi, boys." She smiles at them tersely. "Could I talk to you a sec?"

The alarm bells ring louder. Something's definitely going on.

"Yeah, sure."

They follow her to the staff room, anxiety churning in Dawson's stomach. Once the door is closed, she turns to them, but keeps her eyes predominantly on Dawson.

"I didn't want to say anything until it was confirmed, but..." She sighs. "We're moving Donut to a different shelter. I know you two connected, so I wanted to let you know personally."

Dawson swears he can feel the blood freeze in his veins. There's more to it, he's sure. Aubrey wouldn't look so crestfallen if Donut was just changing locations.

"What shelter?"

Her lips form a thin line. "Nancy and Friends Rescue."

Dawson takes a step back, as if he can somehow distance himself from this moment. "No."

"Dawson..."

"Please don't do that," he begs, voice quivering. His vision begins to blur, his chest tight. "Give it some more time. Someone will—"

"Donut's been here far longer than we normally allow," she cuts in, her tone taking on a sharper edge. "We knew there was a good chance he wouldn't get picked up due to his eye condition and his behavior around other dogs, but we hoped that his breed would make him appealing to potential owners."

Yes, Dawson knows. He understands. Aubrey's not wrong. But he doesn't want to understand, doesn't want to hear it. It makes him hate people in that moment, makes him hate how, unless the pet is young and cute and perfectly behaved, they aren't interested. Donut is amazing. And he *is* cute. So what if he gets cranky around other dogs? Plenty of dogs are like that. And his condition is nothing too difficult to deal with. He just needs to have his eyes cleaned and moisturized regularly, no biggie.

A large, gentle hand lands on his shoulder. "Dawson, it's okay," Cal says, squeezing lightly. "Wherever that shelter is, we can visit him there."

"No, that's not..." Fuck, of course Cal doesn't understand. "The other place isn't a no-kill shelter like this one."

Cal's brows furrow. "What do you mean?"

"The animals are put down within a week if nobody picks them up," he explains, swallowing the bile he can taste on the back of his tongue.

Cal's expression is one of sheer shock, and for some fucked up reason, it makes Dawson feel a little better. It's good to know he's not the only one who finds this practice utterly abhorrent. He doesn't understand how some people just accept it.

"I'm sorry, Dawson," Aubrey speaks again. "He's been here for six weeks. There's nothing else we can do. We have more dogs coming here every day."

"I know," Dawson says miserably. He presses the heels of his hands to his eyes. "Fuck, I know."

For the first few moments, everything is so quiet Dawson is convinced that everyone can hear his heart thumping against his ribcage. God, he knew it. He knew something bad was about to happen. Granted, he didn't think it would involve poor Donut, but he knew. Things can never go well for him for too long. He had a suspicion something would go down when he started to feel happy. But it's always like this with him. There's always a shoe waiting to drop and smack him in the face.

"Why don't we take him?"

Dawson's head snaps up. He couldn't have heard right.

"What?"

"We can take him," Cal says, then looks at Aubrey, unsure. "Right? We have no other animals, so we wouldn't have to worry about him acting out."

While Dawson is only capable of opening and closing his mouth like a fish, Aubrey speaks.

"Oh my god, that would be *absolutely amazing* if you could do that. But you'd have to be prepared for the expenses. His condition isn't life-threatening, but it's incurable. You'd need to keep on top of his care at all times. You'll also need to learn about his breed-specific diet."

Cal shrugs. "Someone is always home. Usually me. Money isn't an issue. And I can learn about the rest." To Dawson, he says, "You can teach me."

His soft smile reaches to the deepest parts of Dawson's soul, putting all the broken pieces back together. There's no way he can hold the tears back anymore. They spill down his cheeks with an ugly sob that's wrenched out of him, and then he's throwing himself at Cal.

"Thank you!" he sobs into Cal's neck, clinging to his shoulders in case his knees give out. "Thankyouthankyouthankyou."

Cal's arms come around him, steady and strong, and it only makes him cry harder.

"Well, this was an unexpected turn of events, and I'm here for it. You guys made my day," Aubrey says after an unidentifiable amount of time.

It's been long enough that Dawson's sobbing has subsided and now he's just holding onto Cal and soaking his shirt with tears and snot.

He hears Aubrey move around. "I'm gonna go, give you some space, but I'll steal you for a bit before you leave to get the paperwork sorted."

"No problem," Cal says, the words starting out as a rumble in his chest. It's nice and comforting, and Dawson burrows deeper into him. Cal, for his part, doesn't say anything after Aubrey leaves, seemingly content to just hold Dawson and let him cling on like a koala. One of his hands comes up to stroke Dawson's hair, and he presses a kiss into it.

Dawson shivers and forces himself to let go. He wipes away the mess on his face, embarrassed to look Cal in the eye. Cal lets him pull away, but keeps his hands on Dawson's waist.

"I can't believe you just did that."

"Why not?" Cal cocks his head.

"You never wanted any animals."

Irritation flashes across Cal's features. "Yeah, well, I was a dick before, so..."

Dawson wants to laugh, but it comes out as a tragic wheeze. Before he knows it, he's hugging Cal again.

"Thank you. So much."

"Of course. Hopefully, Donut doesn't kill me in my sleep."

Dawson manages a chuckle. "Don't be dramatic. He's not that bad." He panics when he realizes all the things they need to sort out before they bring a dog home. "We'll need to get stuff for him. A bed, toys, food. And we'll have to—"

"Dawson, calm down." Cal's smile is eternally patient as he rubs Dawson's arms. "We'll do all that. So take it easy."

Dawson relaxes under Cal's touch, the tightness in his chest finally letting off. It's gonna be fine. They've got this. They're in this together now.

And they're about to have a dog.

"Yeah, okay. And just so you know, I'll buy you as many donuts as you want for this."

"Deal."

So, it's possible Dawson went a little crazy shopping for dog toys and whatnot, their trolley hardly able to contain everything. But Cal hasn't said a word, dutifully following Dawson around and simply nodding when Dawson suggested they buy something. Well, then. No need to try and control his impulses. Plus, they don't have much time. Aubrey said they can pick Donut up tomorrow, because the sooner the better. The whole process of adoption would be more complicated if she didn't know both Dawson and Cal and thus was able to pull a few strings.

More than an hour later, Dawson wheels the trolley towards the parking garage. He comes to a halt when he passes one of the claw machines. The shopping center swaps the prizes every few weeks, but this is the first time Dawson's seen Pusheen the Cat in it. If he's lucky, there will be at least one that he's looking for. And if he's super ultra lucky, it won't be buried on the very bottom.

He scans the contents quickly, letting out a victorious shout when he spots a plushie identical to the one in Ash's office.

"More toys?" Cal asks with amusement, having noticed what caught Dawson's attention.

"Damn right." Leaving the trolley on the side, Dawson steps towards the machine and fiddles with his watch to pay for the game. The claw comes to life, moving around with a whirring sound.

"What are you doing?" Cal asks, regarding the machine distrustfully and pressing himself against Dawson's side, as if he's ready to jump in and protect him from the evil machine if needed.

"You've never played claw machine?" He mentally slaps himself once the question is out. "Nevermind. I'm too excited to think straight."

"About?"

Dawson grins at him. "Watch." With that, he moves the claw above the cat holding a donut, then presses the drop button, smashing it again once it's down. The claw grabs the plushie, but the grip is too loose, and it falls out as the claw moves towards the dispatch door. "Oh, you fucker," Dawson growls, ignoring Cal's wide-eyed look.

He analyzes the situation. The cat is now closer to the door, so the second try should do it. Once again, he positions the claw above the plushie, making sure it's perfectly aligned and ready to grab the cat without letting it go. Once he's satisfied, he brings the claw down, pushing the button again. This time, the plushie goes straight to the dispatch door.

"Yes!" He fist-pumps the air. Bending down to retrieve the plushie, he presents it to Cal with a proud smile.

Cal's eyes cross as he blinks at it, tilting his head. "Is that...a cat?"

"Pusheen the Cat. It's quite famous. And look, it's holding a donut!" He wiggles the plushie, shoving it against Cal's chest. "It's for you."

Cal points a finger at the center of his chest. "Me?" He looks so adorably confused, Dawson wants to pat his cheek.

"Yeah!" His enthusiasm diminishes as it occurs to him that he might be the only man-child excited about plushies. "But if you don't want it—"

The cat is snatched out of his hands.

"I want it," Cal blurts out, clutching it to himself like he's afraid Dawson is going to take it from him. He gazes down at the plushie, running a reverent hand over its head. When he brings his gaze up, his face is incredibly soft. "Thank you."

Heat spreading across his face, Dawson shrugs lamely. "You're welcome. It reminded me of you, because of...uh..."

"Donuts," Cal finishes with a smile. He traces the shape of the donut. "I love it." He eyes the machine with a thoughtful expression. "I want you to have one too."

"So yours doesn't get lonely?" Dawson jokes, already getting a payment on his watch ready. He pays for the next two games and moves to handle the stick, but Cal pushes him gently aside.

"Let me," he says with a determined expression.

"You want to play?"

"I want to win one for you." He looks around the inside of the machine. "What are the rules?"

Dawson laughs. "There are no rules, but arcade games set you up to fail There's a trick, though. Once it's down, you smash the button again. You need to be quick. It will grab the plushie and drop it over here. Also, you want to pick one on top. The claw won't be able to grab it otherwise."

Cal's focused expression turns even more serious. He gives a curt nod, like he's making a battle plan. "I can do it."

"Go for it," Dawson says with a chuckle, Cal's seriousness making his chest fill with warmth.

"I'll get you the one with the pineapple."

"Why pineapple?"

"Because you put it on the pizza," Cal says with obvious disgust.

"Because it tastes good!" Dawson argues as usual, but Cal is too focused on playing to join him.

He watches as Cal positions the claw, his other hand hovering over the button. Dawson surveys the position of the claw and places a hand on Cal's shoulder.

"You might want to move it a little..."

He hopes Cal won't be mad at him for interfering, but he needn't worry. Cal leans to the side to make room for him, letting Dawson wrap his hand around Cal's and shift the claw a few degrees. The warmth of his body seeps into Dawson from where they're pressed together arm to hip, and his scent fills Dawson's nose, making him want to press closer. He smells like their fabric softener and ocean air.

"Yeah, like that," Dawson mumbles once the claw is in place, then steps aside to let Cal do the rest.

Cal punches the button. The claw descends, but he pushes the button the second time a tad too late, so the claw never closes around the plushie properly. His expression is absolutely devastated as he watches the claw come up empty.

"Hey, that's fine," Dawson jumps in to reassure him. "You get two tries. You have another shot. Remember: you need to be quick. It descends quite fast."

Cal's jaw works, his eyes narrowing like he's assessing a target. "I'll get it this time."

Dawson can't help but smile at the dedication. He doesn't need to correct Cal this time—the claw is positioned perfectly. Then Cal punches the button, doing it again once the claw surrounds the plushie. It wraps around it, moving back to the dispatch door and dropping the plushie.

Cal steps back from the machine, looking stunned that it worked.

"Hey, look at you! Nicely done."

After a few seconds, Cal reaches inside for the plushie, gazing down at it with a huge smile. He offers it to Dawson, and Dawson takes it, giving Cal his plushie in return.

"Now they won't be lonely," Cal says, absolutely precious.

Dawson can't stop the huge smile that stretches his lips just as he can't stop his legs from moving him forward until they're chest to chest, the plushies squashed between them. He's grateful for the make-shift barrier, so Cal can't feel his frantically beating heart. With a shaky hand, he cups the back of Cal's neck, his fingertips grazing the soft hair on Cal's nape.

It's longer than Cal ever let it grow, religiously getting a haircut every month. He hasn't had one in almost two, and the difference shouldn't be so stark, but, for some reason, it is. Or maybe it's because his hair isn't gelled and slicked back in an immaculate style which had always pronounced his facial features and the cut of his jaw.

Dawson never knew that Cal's hair has a slight curl to it in its natural state, a few strands falling over his forehead and curling at his temples. It makes him look softer, younger, as does the short scruff on his face. Dawson always thought that facial hair makes men look older and more mature, but on Cal it has the opposite effect.

It also has the effect of making Dawson want to pull Cal down and find out if what he felt in the kitchen the other day was just a fluke, just a moment of weakness and confusion.

So he does.

He rises on his tiptoes, putting the slightest pressure on Cal's neck. Cal gives into it, meeting Dawson halfway this time, not standing stock still like he did the first time, as if he was too shocked to reciprocate.

Cal's eyelids flutter, his mouth parting on a sharp inhale, and he lets out a small, desperate sound as their lips slot together.

One thing becomes abundantly clear: it wasn't a fluke.

Dawson sighs into the kiss, only now realizing how much he's been wanting to do this the whole day. Now that he's here, he doesn't want it to stop, never wants to forget the feeling of weightlessness that envelopes him with each press of Cal's lips against his, or the way his head empties of any worries and fears.

Jesus Christ, it was not a fluke.

A whimper lands Dawson on his feet, grounding him in the moment. When he opens his eyes and finds Cal already looking at him with worry, it occurs to him that the whimper came from him. It sends blood rushing to his face, but at the same time, he can still feel the ghost of the kiss clinging to his mouth. Suddenly, his bloodflow changes direction, causing warmth to pool elsewhere than his face.

It's been so long since he'd felt like this that he takes a stuttering step back, staring at Cal like he was the one to spring the kiss on him out of nowhere. He doesn't get far, because Cal has his arm wound around Dawson's waist.

Cal licks his lips, the blue of his irises clouded over. He tears his gaze away from Dawson, looking down at their plushies. Dawson does the same, watching as Cal brings his plushie closer to Dawson's until their faces are touching. With a shy smile, he says, "There. I figured they deserve a kiss, too."

Laughter bubbles up in Dawson's chest, sounding on the verge of hysterical and kind of incredulous, but mostly really, really happy.

I'm happy. I'm actually happy. The realization makes the ground under his feet quake, shaking up his very foundation.

Fuck. When did this happen? *How* did this happen?

Most importantly, what does he do about it?

Fuck. His appointment with Ash can't come soon enough.

Chapter 20

Dawson considers asking Kieran to drive them to the shelter in the morning, because he '*doesn't trust himself not to drive into a ditch on their way there, he's that excited*'. Cal insists they're going to be fine and to '*just drive slow*'."

They don't drive into a ditch, but Dawson does run through a red light.

Aubrey and Donut are already waiting for them when they arrive. Donut's tail swishes through the air like he understands he's going home with Dawson. Dawson drops into a crouch to greet him, and Donut practically leaps into his arms, licking all over his face. Naturally, he ignores Cal.

There's a bit more paperwork to be signed, but less than half an hour later, Dawson is driving them home with their new family member strapped in the backseat, his tongue out and lolling as he pants (and probably drools over the seats).

Last night, Dawson gave Cal a rundown on taking care of a dog. It wasn't as overwhelming as Cal feared. His main worry remains that Donut will never like him. Dawson assured him it would change, that Donut just needs time to get to know him and trust him.

"Look," Dawson says as they step into the apartment and unclips Donut's leash. "This is your new home."

Donut's little flat nose twitches as he sniffs the air, then bends his neck to inspect the floor, wandering further into the apartment. He stops, lets out a small huff, and takes off like a bullet.

"I think he's going to like it here," Cal says, snickering.

"Yeah?" Dawson sounds uncertain, which is ridiculous. Of course, Donut's going to love his new home. He loves Dawson, for one, and he doesn't have to be around other dogs. Win-win.

"Definitely."

The day passes in a flash. Cal doesn't remember ever seeing Dawson so happy. He doesn't even care if Donut doesn't like him, as long as he makes Dawson beam like this. And Cal was right; Donut loves it here, which he demonstrates by rubbing his butt over all available surfaces. At least he doesn't pee anywhere.

He also loves the beach, letting the crashing waves wash over his paws and chasing seagulls when they go for a walk together.

They make a stop at *Lost and Ground,* since Dawson is certain they allow dogs. Gabe is, of course, beside himself when he sees Donut, cuddling him and letting him lick his face. Zeke has to ask him to come back and wash his hands several times. Dawson looks guilty for disturbing their workflow, but Gabe waves him off, saying they can bring their new pup any time.

As promised, Dawson buys Cal a bag of donuts, begging him not to eat them all at once. Cal promises he won't. Dawson doesn't look like he believes him.

Later, Donut lounges on the sofa with them while they watch a movie. The little devil strategically uses his body as a barrier between Dawson and Cal, and he growls menacingly every time Cal tries to move closer to Dawson. Cal ends up banished to the end of the sofa. Dawson mouths 'sorry', but doesn't do anything to remedy the situation, so Cal just makes peace with his fate. He will no longer have the luxury of having all of Dawson for himself.

After the movie, he watches Dawson clean Donut's eyes and put the treatment in it for the first time. It looks uncomfortable, especially when Dawson runs a Q-tip around Donut's eyelids, but Donut holds perfectly still. If it was Cal doing this to him, he'd lose a finger or two.

That evening, when Dawson goes for a run (which he didn't manage that morning) he takes Donut with him. 'To tire him out', as he put it. It turns out that Donut likes exercise and running, which, according to Dawson, is usually hit or miss with dogs of his breed. At least now Dawson has a running partner, since Cal isn't quite ready for that yet. He would only slow Dawson down.

When they go to turn in for the night, they find Donut spread out on their bed. They exchange a look, Dawson silently asking him if it's okay. Cal rolls his eyes and nods. The bed is huge, it will fit a smallish dog easily.

"So much for the dog bed," Dawson says with a grin as they climb under the covers. Instantly, Donut gets up and walks up to Dawson, snuggling into him.

"It's okay," Cal says. "He just wants to be close to you."

How relatable.

"Stay," Dawson orders when Donut continues to squirm. He doesn't quite manage to pull off that stern voice, but Donut looks up to him with worship and drops down on his hunches, then lies down. "Good boy." He gets a scratch for that.

"Thank you," Dawson says after a while. "I know I've said it a million times already but thank you." He has an arm thrown over Donut and inches his hand towards Cal.

Cal takes it, squeezing it gently. "I just want you to be happy. Donut makes you happy. It's quite simple."

"And donuts make *you* happy."

Cal chuckles. "They do."

"Oh, I forgot to tell you. I booked a Paint 'n' Sip session for us. It's on Monday."

"You did?" It's been in the back of Cal's mind since they passed by the studio, but since Dawson has never brought it up, Cal hasn't either. "What are we painting?"

Detaching his phone from the charger, Dawson browses through it, the light from the screen illuminating his face. Once he's found what he's looking for, he offers it to Cal.

"It looks simple, but there's a reason why the sessions are three hours long."

"Believe me, simple is good. But you might get bored."

Dawson's definition of simple is vastly different from Cal's. The painting is one of a desert with dunes of different shapes and sizes. The setting sun paints the sky different colors and casts shadows over the sand. There's also a camel and some cacti.

Simple, his ass.

"Nah," Dawson says. "It will be...interesting to hold a brush again."

Cal gives him the phone back. "I'm looking forward to it." Even if his painting will be unrecognizable from the original.

Dawson reaches for his hand once more. "Me too."

Cal's bladder wakes him up in the middle of the night. He pulls the covers back and climbs out of bed, careful not to wake Dawson. Donut is pressed up against him as he was when they fell asleep, snoring lightly. Cal's heart does a little flutter at the sight, even though he wishes it was him pressed against Dawson like that.

After relieving himself and washing his hands, he returns to bed. Or attempts to.

"Um...hello?" Donut must have seen an opportunity and rolled over to Cal's side of bed, giving him a look of utter loathing. "Sorry, can I have my spot back?" he whispers, trying to nudge Donut gently out of the way and nearly losing his hand in the process. "No? That's fine. Can I have my pillow at least?" If he lies down the other way around, keeping close to the foot of the bed, he might fit in.

Donut lets out a hellish growl when Cal touches the pillow.

"Okay. Alright. All yours." He holds his hands up, backtracking slowly.

Admitting defeat, he goes to sleep in the guest room instead, leaving the door open wide in case Dawson starts looking for him. The mattress feels pretty much the same, but it will be strange not to sleep next to Dawson. What if he'll have to sleep here from now on? What if he's not allowed in his own bed anymore?

In the morning, he wakes to someone gently calling his name. He blinks his eyes open to see Dawson's concerned face.

"Cal? Did you sleep here?"

He heaves himself up into a seated position and rubs his eyes. "I got up in the night to use the bathroom. When I came back, Donut took over my spot."

Dawson laughs, then stops when he sees Cal is serious. "You could've just moved him."

Cal gives him a flat look. "He was going to *kill* me, Dawson."

"Oh my god." Dawson covers his mouth, his shoulders shaking. Cal's not sure how he feels about Dawson laughing at his misfortune. This is serious! "Please don't go sleep in a different room. Just wake me up and I'll move him for you." His smile drops and his eyes widen. "You're not having second thoughts, are you? I promise, once he gets used to you—"

"I'm not having second thoughts," Cal tells him. "Not a chance. This is Donut's home now and we're his family. Whether he likes it or not," he adds with an eye roll. "He's not going back."

Dawson releases a breath and nods. "I need to walk him first but then I'll make breakfast."

Cal moves back the covers and stands up. "I can walk him. Spend some *quality time* together."

Dawson barks out a laugh. "Oh, he'll love that."

Chapter 21

"YOU'RE NERVOUS," ASH POINTS out—quite unnecessarily—when Dawson finds himself in the therapist's office three days later. His assumption that, after practically cutting himself open last time, it would be smooth—well, smooth*er*—sailing was wrong. He thought that things were complicated two weeks ago, but that's nothing compared to the mayhem that his life is now.

"Excellent deduction skills, Sherlock," he snarks without any real bite. Ash's cool composure simply annoys him. And he's not totally oblivious—he knows that Ash gets some weird kick out of making him squirm. He wonders if all therapists are like that or if Ash is just a dick.

"Hmm," Ash hums, wearing that all-knowing, infuriating smile. "Using snark as a defense mechanism. You must be *very* nervous." He leans forward in his chair, opening his hands before clasping them together. "Why? It's our second appointment."

"There's a lot on my mind."

"Care to share?"

"Not really, no."

There's a familiar glint in Ash's eye, telling Dawson he's enjoying the back and forth all too much. The fucker. As Dawson stares back at him, something catches his attention. He's not one for ogling people. In fact, he's terrible with faces, let alone other details, but he'd swear that Ash's irises were an unusual steel-blue color. Now they look more green?

He shakes the thought away. It must just be a trick of the light. His eyes change color too, depending on the lighting.

"How are things with Cal?"

Okay, then. "Straight for the jugular, huh?"

"Would you prefer we talk about the weather?"

"It's been getting warmer, ey?"

Ash's shoulders shake as he laughs, and it takes him a few seconds to calm down so he can talk, his tone more serious again. "Why are you nervous?"

"You want it alphabetically or chronologically?"

Ash flashes him a grin. "Dawson."

"I'm afraid of what you'll have to say."

"About?"

Dawson looks away, his gaze catching on the plushie he'd used for emotional support during his first visit. It only makes him think back on the day at the mall, the claw machine and Cal winning a plushie for him, looking so proud and happy that Dawson couldn't possibly stand it and had to—

"I think you know."

Ash's silence is a resounding yes.

"I take it things have been going well, then."

Dawson looks at Ash to stop his mind from wandering, because when it wanders, it keeps going back to Cal and that kiss, making Dawson's body tingle.

"We kissed. Twice," he adds after a short pause.

Maybe that first kiss should have been more ground-breaking because it was...well, first, but it's the other way around. When he kissed Cal in the kitchen, it was impulsive. He'd just woken up and Cal took him by surprise, making pancakes for him, and it felt so natural to rise on his tiptoes and press his lips to Cal's.

But the kiss at the mall, that was all him. Not just an impulse, not something he hadn't thought through. All him.

Ash's expression is unreadable when he asks, "Who initiated it?"

Dawson has a feeling Ash already knows—because why else would Dawson act so cagey about it?—but he answers anyway. "Me."

"Both times?"

"Yeah."

"Did you want to?"

Dawson gives him an annoyed look. "Isn't it obvious?"

"Not at all. People don't always do things because they want to. In fact, they rarely do."

That's...depressingly accurate. Dawson can attest to that.

"I wanted to," he murmurs, a wave of shame rising inside him. "He... He made me pancakes." He chuckles wryly. It sounds so pathetic when he says it out loud, yet the memory feels like a warm blanket settling over him. "Well, he tried. Ended up setting off the smoke alarm, but I love that he tried."

"Has he done that before?"

"Made pancakes?"

"Cooked for you."

Dawson laughs. "God, no. Our kitchen used to consist of a bottle of tomato sauce and a carton of milk." And whiskey, but he doesn't say that. They've been over this.

Ash's expression is so empathetic it nearly brings tears to Dawson's eyes. How pathetic is it that he gets emotional about stupid stuff like pancakes?

"Must have been nice, having him try like that."

"Yeah." He swallows. "Nice."

"That was the first time? That you kissed him." When Dawson nods, he asks, "And the second? What did he do?"

"Nothing. Nothing at all." Yeah, he won him a plushie, but even Dawson has enough self-awareness to understand that that didn't really have anything to do with him wanting to kiss Cal. "He was just being..."

"He was being?"

"Sweet. Thoughtful." The memory of Cal pressing the two plushies together in an imitation of a kiss springs to mind, making him smile like a love-struck teen. "We went shopping and there was a claw machine with these." He picks up the plushie. "I won him one and he won one for me and...I don't know. We just...had a moment."

Ash hums again, watching him calmly. "What are you afraid I'm going to say about that?"

"That I'm fooling myself. That I'm being reckless. That I'm playing happy family and ignoring the big fucking elephant in the room."

"That's very specific," Ash says. "Doesn't really sound like something I'd say. In fact, it doesn't sound like something you'd say." He lets that hang in the air for a while. "Where's this coming from?"

Damn. Dawson really is transparent. "Kieran, my best friend, had some things to say about the whole arrangement. And so did Cal's brother. And my sister."

"Does it bother you because they might be right?"

Dawson closes his eyes, fighting the bout of nausea he feels building up. "It bothers me because I know they're right, but I don't care because I'm happy. I mean, I do care, just...not enough, I guess. I probably should." He looks at Ash for help. "Right?"

Ash, of course, doesn't answer that. "Do you feel unsafe around Cal? When it's just the two of you?"

"He's not exactly in a position to do anything to me." Yesterday, Cal was so sore after implementing a few new exercises that he didn't even feel like going for a walk.

"I didn't mean just physically unsafe."

Startled by the question, Dawson takes a moment to carefully ponder it. "At first, yeah," he admits. "The doctors kept talking about the aftermath of memory loss, the mood swings, anxiety, aggression. Cal was difficult to be around as it was, so I braced myself for the worst but...it never happened."

Something occurs to him right then, causing his heart rate to go haywire. His epiphany must manifest on his face because Ash gives him a curious look and asks, "What is it?"

He considers lying. He's admitted plenty of embarrassing, stupid things to Ash, but this can't even compare. It's one thing to admit he likes Cal, actually likes to be around him, but this...

"Can I tell you something really messed up?" he asks in a quiet voice.

Ash, in his true fashion, lights up like a fucking Christmas tree, grinning devilishly. "Oh, please do."

Dawson knows what Ash is doing, trying to make him loosen up. It actually works, startling a laugh out of Dawson and helping him lose some of the tension. It doesn't make confessing the truth much easier, but at least he doesn't feel so judged.

"He makes me feel safe. I don't remember ever feeling safe before. Not just with him, with anyone. Ever. My sister, my best friend, and before that my parents... They all expected me to act a certain way, to make certain decisions, and if I didn't, they were disappointed and, boy, would they let me have it."

Ash nods. He probably guessed as much from the long conversations they'd had about Dawson's childhood and his marriage. "And what does Cal expect?"

"He doesn't expect anything. Not a single thing. I didn't even know what kind of person I could be until..."

"Until people stopped telling you who to be?"

"Yes. That."

"So who are you?"

Someone who has no idea what he's doing. "I'm still figuring that out."

Ash's smile is understanding. "Are you Cal's husband?"

There are certain emotions and feelings he associates with the title, things like obligation, compromise, expectation. They don't quite fit now.

"Honestly? It feels like we're...dating. Very badly, may I say." Things between them are definitely awkward. Kind of like dating your highschool crush. Not that Dawson has any experience with that, but he assumes that's what it's like.

"Can you imagine a life with him?" Ash asks, his voice uncharacteristically gentle, like he's afraid he might spook Dawson. Oh, Dawson is spooked alright.

"I've already had a life with him for six years," he retorts, knowing that's not what Ash is asking.

"That was before, though. Can you imagine a life with him where the past doesn't keep haunting you?"

"I...haven't thought it through in the long term." He's tried, and it always scared him enough to shove all those thoughts in a box and shut the lid. "But, I mean...we already live together, do pretty much everything together, so..."

Ash taps his fingers against his thigh, watching Dawson intently. Whatever he's thinking, Dawson isn't going to like it.

"There's something I'd like to talk about, and I noticed you didn't mention it the last time we talked about what Cal used to be like."

Apprehension settles heavily in Dawson's gut, but he knows that if he doesn't answer, Ash will keep going back to it until Dawson cracks. Better to get it over with.

"Do your worst."

Ash looks almost proud. "Would you like me to be blunt or sugarcoat it?"

"Can you be blunt, but like...sprinkle it with sugar just a little?"

Ash snickers. "Sure. What would you say about your intimate life?"

Every single muscle in Dawson's body tenses up. "You mean sex?"

"Yeah, I mean sex," Ash says, smothering a smile. Dick.

"Fine." Dawson shrugs. "I could take it or leave it."

Ash isn't happy with the answer. "And if you had to choose, would you take it or leave it?"

"Leave it, probably." No point lying about it. It makes Dawson feel like a disgruntled housewife who couldn't care less, but he just never cared much. Sure, he went through a horny phase as a teen, but that was just hormones. And sex with Cal was...fine, Dawson just never got what all that hype was about. Orgasms were great, but he could get the same result using his hand and his vivid imagination. Plus, flying solo has the perk of doing it only when he feels like it. So yeah, sex is definitely overrated. He has no idea why people lose their minds over it.

"Were there times you were just being agreeable if Cal wanted to have sex?"

Dawson snorts. "Duh. Isn't that the status quo for married couples?"

Judging by the look Ash gives him, Dawson has managed to put his foot in his mouth.

"Look, it wasn't a big deal," Dawson says, feeling defensive. "We're married and this is what married couples do."

"Do they, now?"

"Yes." He's starting to get pissed off. It's one thing to have his behavior picked apart and shoved under a microscope, but sexual urges or the lack thereof are very individual. Ash has no right to tell him what is normal or not.

You just said all married couples are like this, the annoying part of Dawson's brain that likes to call him out on shit reminds him. He tells it to shut up.

"It wasn't terrible or anything," he says, feeling pressured to explain even though Ash didn't ask. "I was just rarely in the mood. And Cal, he was... He had certain expectations. Plus, with all the pressure from work and stuff, it was kind of a stress relief for him."

"People exercise to relieve stress."

"He did that too."

"Was he ever cruel?"

"No." *Except* that *time, right?* "He was... He got off on control. Not just in the bedroom. And I...wasn't a fan."

'*You don't make the rules here, sweetheart. You follow them. And if you don't? I'll make sure to remind you of your place.*'

Dawson lets out a shaky exhale. "There was one time when he... I made him mad, didn't do what he asked, so...he decided to teach me a lesson." He feels nauseous just talking about it, and of course Ash notices and decides to twist the knife.

"Can you say it for me?"

It feels like an eternity but is probably only seconds before Dawson finds his voice. "He...forced me. It was just the one time," he adds quickly.

Ash's gaze is cool and calm when Dawson looks at him. There's no pity or discomfort in his expression, and Dawson is so fucking grateful he could cry.

"When was this?"

"Not long ago. A couple of weeks before the accident. It—Actually, it was why I finally decided to go through with the divorce. Until then, I'd thought there were lines he wouldn't cross. I was wrong."

"After all this, can you imagine ever being intimate with him again? And I mean wanting it, not just enduring?"

"I don't know," he says honestly. His mind hasn't even wandered in that direction since the accident. He suspects part of it is because Cal hasn't given a single indication of expecting to get...physical. It's likely due to the meds and the ongoing soreness after the surgery.

He tries to imagine it, imagine touching Cal. Or Cal touching him. Undressing him. Raking his gaze over Dawson's naked body before pushing him into the mattress, settling between his spread legs and—

Dawson snaps back to the present. His skin feels hot, and his throat is dry.

"Maybe if I had more control of the situation. What's that look for?" he quips when Ash looks at him funny.

"I asked because I wanted to know if the idea appeals to you at all. But I'm starting to sense that's not the issue," Ash says, and Dawson feels his face warm up like he was just caught red-handed committing some serious crime. "It's not about whether you want Cal that way, it's about whether you feel safe to want him that way."

"I..."

"Let me change my question," Ash interrupts. "You said he makes you feel safe. Does he make you feel safe enough to be with him that way?"

Dawson doesn't answer. He can't. There is nothing under the sun, not one reason why the answer shouldn't be a resounding *no*.

So he stays quiet, because there's nothing that could explain why his heart keeps whispering yes.

There is a pressure behind his forehead when he leaves Ash's office, but by the time Dawson arrives home, it's developed into a full-blown headache. He has a nasty feeling it's not going to stay like that for long. He takes two Panadol before leaving the car. Hopefully, they'll kick in. Unless he absolutely has to, he'd rather not take the migraine pills.

When he stands in front of the apartment, hovering with the keys over the keyhole, he's not sure he's not hallucinating already. He strains his ears, listening to the sounds coming from inside. It sounds like the vacuum cleaner and pop music.

He opens the door. Donut immediately comes running to greet him, his tail wagging and desperate noises leaving his open mouth. Nothing unusual about that.

What's unusual is Cal vacuuming the living room while blasting what seems to be—

"Is that Lady Gaga?"

Cal lets out a shriek, the vacuum stick slipping from his hand. He presses a hand to his chest when he sees Dawson. "I didn't hear you come in."

"I wonder why," Dawson says with a chuckle, then cringes when the music makes his head pound. "Could you turn the volume down?"

"Yes, sorry!" He grabs the remote, turning the music off completely.

"Thank you. And don't apologize. My head just decided to kill me today."

"A migraine?" Cal asks, worry etched into his features.

"Not yet. Hopefully it won't develop into one."

Cal's worried expression fills with disapproval. "You drove like this?"

Not smart, he knows. "I couldn't leave the car there."

"Why not? It's just a car." He doesn't give Dawson a chance to contradict him. "I don't care about the car, Dawson. I care about you."

Dawson's insides all but turn into mush. He blames it on the headache. "I'm sorry. I won't do it again."

"Thank you," Cal says, visibly relieved. "What can I do?"

"I just need some dark and quiet. Lots of water. I already popped a couple of Panadol."

Cal is an absolute godsend. He all but manhandles Dawson into bed, ordering him to stay put. He draws the blinds shut and goes to fetch him some water. Dawson doesn't have to lift a finger. Donut follows him to bed, keeping him company. He could get used to this kind of treatment.

Cal brings him a tall glass of water, and Dawson gratefully downs half of it before collapsing back into bed.

"Thank you. So, Lady Gaga, huh?"

Cal shrugs. "It's catchy."

"And so gay."

"Is it?"

"Uh-huh. But since we are both gay, it's alright."

"You like it?"

"Lady Gaga or being gay?"

Cal huffs a small laugh. "Lady Gaga."

"Oh, yeah. She's the best. I just can't listen to anything when I'm like this."

Cal's expression turns thoughtful. "I'd like to try something, if you allow me. I did a bit of reading on headaches and migraines after you told me you suffer from them. Some people said that a massage helps to alleviate the pain."

It takes a minute to process the words. "You read up on migraines? For me?"

"I wanted to help."

Dawson doesn't know what to say. No one's ever done something like this for him. Hell, sometimes even *he* can't be bothered to do any more research.

"Can I try?"

"What?"

"To give you a massage."

"Oh. Um. Yeah, sure. If you want."

"I do." Cal slowly climbs onto the bed. "There are a few ways to do it, but the instructions said it's best if I sit behind you and you rest your head in my lap."

Glad that Cal can't see his blush in the dark, he shifts around until Cal can easily slot behind him. He waits until Cal settles into position, his legs crossed and a pillow in his lap.

Dawson lies back, head on the pillow and heart pounding.

"I've never done this. Obviously. So if you don't like something, just tell me."

"I will."

Then Cal's hands are on him, touching his neck and nape. There's no way he can see properly, so he has to go by touch alone. His thumbs press into the two spots on either side of Dawson's spine that are always tight, and a long, drawn-out moan escapes him. He freezes, embarrassed by his reaction.

"Is this okay?" Cal asks.

Dawson gulps. "It's good."

That seems to be all the permission Cal needs. He spends some time on Dawson's shoulders, which is *divine,* then slowly makes his way up his neck, finding sore spots in places Dawson didn't know he had. He doesn't care if it helps his headache or not. The massage itself is perfect.

He starts to drift off when Cal reaches his head, massaging his scalp in a circular motion. His temples, in particular, are super achy, and the pressure Cal applies is just right. It might not cure his headache, but Dawson can feel some of the tension bleeding out, making the pain less intense.

"How's that?"

"So good," Dawson mumbles, already halfway to dreamland. "I think you found your calling."

"My calling?"

"Professional massage therapist."

Cal lets out a low chuckle, the sound sending a thrill through Dawson's spine. "Thank you. But I don't think I'd enjoy touching random people. I enjoy doing it for you, though."

Cal really should be banned from saying shit like that.

"Good. I might get you to do it more often."

"I'd be happy to."

Dawson drifts off with a smile on his face, Donut stretched across his thighs and a coil of warmth in his chest.

It's evening when Dawson wakes up, his headache nothing more than a mild throbbing in his temples. Cal's hands totally worked some magic on him. When he can't find him or Donut anywhere, he assumes they've gone for a walk.

He uses the time to take a shower and change into his pjs. By the time he emerges from the bathroom, Cal and Donut have come back. Donut makes a beeline for him once he's off the leash.

"Hello, you. Yes, yes, I'm up."

"How are you feeling?" Cal asks, looking him over.

Dawson gives him a tired smile. "Much better. The massage definitely helped."

"That's good. I wasn't sure if you'd sleep through the night, so I didn't order anything. And I didn't trust myself to cook dinner." He rubs the back of his neck. "Are you hungry?"

"A little. I'll just have an avo toast or something. That's usually my go-to migraine food."

"Oh, I can make that," Cal says eagerly. "You rest. I'll get it ready."

Dawson shakes his head fondly. It's not bad to be fussed over, once he's gotten used to it.

He obediently takes a seat on the sofa, Donut joining him after slurping down half of his water bowl.

"Do you want to watch something?"

"Is that okay for your head?" Cal checks.

"Yeah, that's all good. Maybe no explosions or singing, but anything else is fine."

"Sure, why not."

They eat their toasts on the sofa for a change, while watching *Shark Tale*. Dawson's seen it several times, so it doesn't matter that he's not really paying attention, too drowsy to be fully awake. It only gets worse after he finishes the food, all the blood rushing to his stomach, and he starts to doze off again.

Cal notices, of course, and keeps bugging him until Dawson relents and returns to the bedroom. He manages to stay awake long enough to brush his teeth, but goes straight to bed afterwards, Donut on his heels.

"Are you coming to bed?" he asks Cal.

"Not yet. I'm not tired."

"Okay." He yawns. "Goodnight." He burrows under the covers, letting his eyes drift shut. He feels Cal's lips brush his forehead, murmuring 'goodnight'.

He sleeps like a baby.

The aroma of something sweet and spicy gently pulls Dawson back to reality. He sits up with a grin, his stomach rumbling. God, he's craving carbs.

He's surprised to find Donut gone. Hopefully, Cal's not feeding him whatever he's making. Dawson refuses to deal with a dog in the throes of indigestion.

Before he can gather the strength to get up and see what's going on in the kitchen, the door opens and Cal steps in with Donut in tow. Donut barks and jumps on the bed when he sees Dawson is up. Dawson gives him obligatory cuddles, then looks at Cal, who's smiling as he watches them, a plate of something that isn't pancakes in his hand.

"Good morning. How are you feeling?"

"Good. But I'll be better after I eat whatever *that* is." He can feel his mouth watering. Is that cinnamon? "Breakfast in bed. That's new."

Cal gives him a bashful smile, color rising to his cheeks. He hesitates before coming to sit on the edge of the bed, and Dawson finally gets a proper look at the plate.

His stomach swoops, causing him to pull in a breath.

"Is that…"

"I can't guarantee how it's going to taste, but I scoured every French toast recipe on Pinterest and this one had the best reviews. It probably won't be the same as your mom used to make, but hopefully it's edible."

Dawson's eyes begin to burn, his throat closing up. Cal remembered. Dawson mentioned it during one of their cooking sessions—about his mom making the best French toast when he and Olivia were little. So…Cal just went and made him some.

"Where…where did you get the brioche bread?" He's sure they didn't buy it during their last grocery run.

"I woke up early, so I took Donut for a walk and we stopped at a bakery on the way." He tenses when he sees Dawson's about to cry. "Dawson? I'm sorry, I didn't—I shouldn't have assumed—"

"Come here."

"What?"

Dawson takes the plate from him and sets it aside on the nightstand. He reaches for Cal's wrist, giving it a tug. "Come here."

Confused, Cal listens. He climbs on the bed, and once he's close enough, Dawson takes him by the neck and pulls him into a needy kiss. Cal's noise of surprise is muffled against his lips.

Dawson falls back, taking Cal with him. They collapse against the pillows, the kiss breaking. Cal looks down at him, eyes blown wide and pupils expanded. His lips are parted, glistening. Dawson wants to feel them again. He fists the front of Cal's shirt, pulling him down. Cal goes willingly, accepting Dawson's kiss with delighted little sounds that send a zing through Dawson.

He wraps his arms around Cal, deepening the kiss. He tastes like sugar and home and all things good, and fuck, Dawson wants more of him. And he would have gotten more, if Donut hadn't decided to bulldoze his way between them, grunting and licking their faces.

They pull apart, staring at each other for a long moment, then bursting into giggles.

"I believe someone doesn't like not being the center of your attention," Cal remarks with humor.

"He's a little attention whore," Dawson says, patting Donut's back and turning his head away when Donut tries to slobber all over his face.

Chuckling, Cal pushes up and moves away. Dawson instantly feels cold.

"Is it okay that I made you French toast?"

"Yeah, Cal. It's okay. More than." He leans forward for another kiss. Cal obliges, taking Dawson's mouth with a gentleness that threatens to completely destroy him. "Now, bring me a fork and a knife, will you? I want to dig in."

Cal grins, kissing him one more time. "Yes, sir."

Chapter 22

"THAT'S QUITE A COMMOTION," Cal comments when they arrive at the Paint 'n' Sip studio. He'd expected a peaceful, harmonious setting, so he's a little startled by the noise a group of women can make.

"I did warn you," Dawson reminds him. "And it will get worse. Look at all that wine."

"We're better off. We have kombucha and crackers."

"That we do."

"Hey, guys!" A young, blonde woman skips towards them, holding a notepad. "Welcome! Have you been here before?"

Dawson shakes his head. "First time. We have a booking under Dawson Reeves."

"Lovely." She ticks their names off and smiles. "I'm Jo. I'll be guiding you through the painting process today. Take a seat." She points at two empty seats at the end of the long table. "We're waiting for a couple more people, but we'll start soon."

"That's a lot of brushes," Cal says as he peruses the set up. A canvas, a jar of water, a palette with several colors and four—four!—brushes.

"Relax, Cal," Dawson says with a chuckle. He unzips his backpack and pulls out their drinks and the crackers. "It's supposed to be fun. And don't forget it was your idea."

"Yeah, yeah."

Another two girls arrive in the next few minutes, and when everyone finds their seats, Jo begins the instruction.

They paint a faint line through the middle of the canvas and start mixing the colors for the sky first. That part *is* quite fun, and Cal's intrigued by all the color combinations he can create. He runs into a problem when his sky turns out patchy, with areas of white seeping through. He turns to Dawson for advice, but stills when he sees a look on his face.

Dawson's jaw is tight, and he's gripping the brush too hard, hovering it over the canvas like he's never done this before.

"Dawson?"

Dawson jolts at the sound of his name. "Yeah?"

"Is everything okay?"

"Uh-huh, just thinking." He gives Cal a tense smile. "How are you doing?"

"This doesn't look right." Cal points at the patches.

Dawson gives them a sweeping glance. "Don't mix too much water in, or it will be see-through. Go over it again, but let it dry first."

Dawson is so smart. No wonder his paintings are so beautiful.

Cal listens to his advice, and it works. He's relieved when he sees Dawson's started to paint as well, his brush flying over the canvas effortlessly. He's a natural.

Once the sky is finished, they move on to the sand. That part isn't as much fun, and the colors are boring. It gets harder when they have to outline the dunes. Dawson tells him it will all come together in the end, but Cal doesn't see that happening.

After that comes shading, which is the worst so far. When it's time to add the camel and the cacti, Cal just gives up and makes peace with the fact he's painting a blob.

When they're adding some finishing touches to the paintings, Jo stops by their seats and goes wide-eyed when she sees Dawson's work.

"Look at you, that's amazing!"

"Thanks," Dawson mumbles, a shy smile appearing on his lips. "It's been a while."

"Well, you still got it, let me tell you."

She's right. His painting even surpasses the original, so vibrant and precise.

"Oh. Wow," Jo says when she moves onto Cal. "That's...interesting."

Cal lets out a frustrated huff. Yeah, he knows it's terrible. But it *is* his first time and—

"Oh my god," Dawson cries, sputtering a laugh. "Is that a dick?"

"What? No. Where?"

"This!" He points at one of the cacti. "That's a cactus dick, Cal."

"No, it isn't," Cal defends, studying the cactus. "It's just a cactus."

"It's a dick," Dawson insists, giggling like one of the girls a few seats over. "It's a green dick with spikes. You even gave it balls, look!" He points at the two protrusions on each side. Cal just painted what he saw in the original! "What were you thinking about, huh?"

"Not dick!"

The rest of the session, though short, is painful. Dawson continues teasing him, and Cal tries his best to ignore him while blushing beet red. He might as well spread the red paint over his face; no one would be able to tell the difference.

"This was fun," Dawson announces after the paintings have dried and they've added their initials. He packs up what remains of their snacks and throws the backpack over his shoulder.

"No, it wasn't," Cal grunts.

"Aww, don't be like that." Dawson pokes him in the ribs. "I like your dick. We're so hanging this up."

"Absolutely not!"

Dawson gives him a haughty look, crossing his arms on his chest. "Fine. But if we don't hang up yours, we won't hang up mine either."

Cal scowls. He wants Dawson's painting in their apartment. "You're playing dirty."

Dawson pretends to study his nails. "It's your call."

Cal begrudgingly relents. Maybe if the painting goes mysteriously missing...

"Thanks for coming, guys!" Jo waves at them as they collect their paintings.

"Thank you," Cal says. "Can I use your bathroom?"

She hooks her thumb over her shoulder. "Through there and to the left."

"Thanks."

"I'll wait outside," Dawson tells him, taking Cal's painting from him. "Your dick will be safe with me."

"Stop saying dick. It's not a dick."

"Member? Manhood?" He waggles his brows. "Mighty tool?"

Cal looks at him with mild horror. "Was there any alcohol in that kombucha?"

"God, it's so easy to wind you up." Dawson strides off, cackling the whole time. Well, at least he's having fun. That's all Cal wanted, after all.

It can't have taken him more than two minutes to use the bathroom, but when Cal goes to look for Dawson outside, there's a man with him. He's standing way too close to him, saying something Cal can't hear.

And Dawson looks scared.

"Not interested," Cal hears him say. Dawson shows the guy his left hand. "And I'm married."

"That's not a disease, you know?" the guy says in a suggestive, slimy voice, and grabs Dawson's elbow.

Cal's vision tunnels.

"The answer is no."

"Oh, come on! Don't be such a p—What the fuck, man!" the guy yelps when Cal grabs him by the collar, spins him around and slams him against the wall. He grips the lapels of his jacket, pinning him in place.

Words arise from the deepest part of his body. "Do. Not. Touch him."

"Jesus, chill, will you? We were just having a nice chat."

"That's not what it looked like."

"Not my fault he's an uptight little bitch."

Cal's lips curl over his teeth, and he pulls his hand back, making a fist.

"Cal, no!" Dawson grabs his arm, not allowing him to punch the disgusting excuse of a human in the face. To make up for it, he lets go of the guy's jacket and wraps a hand around his throat.

His eyes nearly bulge out of his skull, and he rasps out, "Are you fucking crazy?!"

Leaning in until Cal's face is the only thing in the guy's line of vision, he growls, "Leave. Him. Alone." He tightens his grip ever so slightly for a second, and lets go.

The guy pulls in a gasping breath, nearly tripping in his haste to get away. "Jesus. Fine! Not worth it, anyway. Fucking psycho." Then he takes off.

Cal spins around, cupping Dawson's face and checking for harm. "Are you alright? Did he hurt you?"

Dawson gently claps his wrists, looking at him in shock. "I'm fine. God, Cal, you gave me a fright. You could've got hurt."

"I can handle myself."

"You're still healing."

Cal strokes a hand through Dawson's hair. "Are you sure you're okay?" If something happened to him...

"Positive." He smiles. "Your dick is safe, by the way."

Scowling, Cal lets him go and takes his awful painting. "I don't think we'll be coming back."

Dawson snorts. "Quitter."

"This is mortifying," Cal complains, his face on fire when they finish hanging up their paintings. Even without the teasing, his painting looks horrible compared to Dawson's. And now they'll be next to each other.

"I like it. It has—"

"Don't say dick."

"—character." Dawson is having way too much fun on Cal's account.

Cal pretends to sulk, but when Dawson steps in front of him and circles his arms around Cal's waist, he all but melts.

"I really enjoyed it today," Dawson says in a soft voice. "I was scared, at first. But it was good. Really good."

"You're just trying to make me go back," Cal grumbles. But for Dawson? He'd go back in a heartbeat, dick or no dick.

Dawson giggles. "I'll pick a better painting next time. Something not too phallic looking."

Cal smacks his lips, pretending to think it over. "I'll consider it."

Dawson hums, then rises as Cal bends down. They meet in a kiss that's heartrendingly sweet. Except it doesn't stay so. It turns heated, a little frantic, and Dawson is making all these desperate little noises that threaten to eviscerate Cal's self-control.

With a single step forward, he crowds Dawson against the wall, tilting his chin up so he can deepen the kiss. Dawson lets out a moan like it's coming from deep within his soul. The sound etches itself to Cal's brain like a branding, annihilating every thought that doesn't belong to Dawson.

He presses himself against Dawson until there's not a hair's breadth of space between them, until he can feel him everywhere, taste him deep in his mouth and—

A low, growling noise makes them pull away. They're both breathless as they look down to see Donut glaring at them with betrayal.

"Yes?" Dawson asks, catching his breath. "May we help you?" Donut just wags his tail and continues growling. "Attention whore," he mutters affectionately, then looks at Cal. Dawson's face is flushed, his eyes glazed over, and he keeps licking his lips, which are red and swollen from Cal's kisses and scruff.

"You hungry?"

Starving.

"I could eat," he says diplomatically. He couldn't care less about food right now, but Dawson might be hungry. "Something light?" The snacks were quite filling.

"Caprese salad?"

"Perfect."

While Dawson prepares the salad, Cal uses the time to check in with his body. He's never reacted like that before. Sure, they haven't kissed that many times, but when they did, it was amazing. Made Cal tingle all over. But he never felt like he was about to lose control and do...

He doesn't know what would have happened if Donut hadn't interrupted.

Cal manages to sneak him a piece or two of mozzarella when Dawson isn't looking. So what if he's using food as bribery to make Donut hate him less? He's desperate, okay?

Dawson's phone pings with a message when they sit down at the table. A small frown appears between his brows as he reads it, and his eyes flick up to Cal.

"Something wrong?"

"No." He bites his lip. "Kieran's asking if I want to go to the movies on Saturday."

"Do you?"

"Yeah. It's been a while." He taps his fingers on the tabletop. "Do you want to come?"

"Is he inviting us both?" That doesn't sound like Kieran. Cal doesn't think Kieran likes him.

Dawson fidgets. "Not explicitly..."

"Dawson," Cal says with fondness. He gets what Dawson's trying to do. "You can do things without me, you know that, right? In fact, you should. You've been stuck with me this whole time."

"I haven't been stuck," Dawson argues. "I like spending time with you."

Cal stretches out his hand for Dawson to take, smiling when he does. "And I with you. But you're allowed to go see a movie with your best friend. Okay?"

"Okay."

He squeezes Dawson's fingers before releasing them. "What are you going to see?"

"The new *Guardians of the Galaxy*." A hint of excitement fills his voice. When Cal gives him a curious look, he explains, "It's part of the *Marvel* Universe. We'll need to start you on that."

"Sounds good. You want to start now?"

"Now?"

Cal shrugs. "We were about to watch a movie anyway, no?"

"I mean, yeah... But be warned, you're about to go down a very deep rabbit hole. There's no turning back."

"I'm fine with that."

They sit next to each other on the sofa with Donut between them, as usual. It *is* unusual when Donut props his head on Cal's thigh.

Dawson gives Cal a wide grin. "See? I told you he'd warm up to you."

Cal makes a non-committal noise, pretending he has no idea how this happened.

Dawson says the first movie in the Universe is *Iron Man*. Cal likes it. It will never cease to amaze him how some people's minds are so creative that they give rise to whole universes, completely from scratch.

"I've been thinking," Cal murmurs, purposefully picking a scene with no talking. "Maybe I could write a story."

"Like a book?" Dawson gapes at him. "You're serious?"

Cal instantly deflates. He knew it was silly. But all the book-reading and movie-watching he's done in the past two months kind of...woke up his creative streak, and he started wondering what it would be like to create something of his own. Write his own story.

"It was just an idea."

"I love it," Dawson says quickly. "You should give it a go."

Cal chances a look at him, finding nothing but honesty and affection on Dawson's face.

"Yeah?"

"Yeah." He reaches for Cal's hand and interlaces their fingers, careful not to disturb Donut. "What would you write? Fantasy? Action?" He lets his voice grow husky. "Erotica?"

Cal smiles, then admits, "Romance. Fantasy romance, maybe?"

Surprise lights Dawson's eyes. "Like *Twilight*?"

"Something like that." He hasn't thought it through that much yet.

"Nice." He licks his lips, his head lolling back against the sofa. "You'll let me read it, right?"

"You'll be the first," Cal promises.

Dawson gives him a wide smile, all teeth and dimples, and starts to lean in.

Cal's heart rate picks up, and he does the same, inching his face closer to Dawson.

And then Donut lets out a loud fart.

They both freeze, staring at each other.

Dawson's eyes narrow. "Did you feed him something?"

Crap. "No?"

"Cal."

"A couple pieces of mozzarella," he admits with shame. "But they were tiny!"

Dawson throws up his arms. "Cal! We talked about this!"

"I know! But he likes me more when I secretly give him treats."

Dawson isn't impressed, especially when the smell reaches their noses. "Buying affection, huh? I'm disappointed."

"But it's working. Look!" He points at Donut who's still resting his head on Cal's thigh, like he didn't just release a biological weapon.

Dawson groans. "I can't even be mad at you, dammit."

Cal tries and fails to smother a victorious smile. "I'm sorry?"

"No, you're not."

It almost seems Dawson has forgiven him, but Donut farts again, even louder than before.

Dawson just looks at Cal, his expression stony.

"I'll take him for a walk," Cal says, resigned.

"You do that."

Cal's in the middle of a plot-twist in the latest book he's picked up, which is why he nearly jumps out of his skin, and off the sofa, when the intercom rings. Donut, who's been lounging next to him, runs to the door, barking his head off.

Did Dawson forget his keys?

Setting his e-reader aside with a mournful sigh, Cal gets up to answer the door. He must be slow because the person rings again before he gets there. Donut's barking gets louder, and Cal shushes him. "Sit. Good boy." He presses the intercom button. "Hello?"

"Dawson, you ass," an angry, high-pitched voice that's decidedly not Dawson's answers him. "Pick up your damn phone."

Cal frowns. He doesn't like this lady, who's addressing his husband as an ass. "I'm sorry. Dawson's not here."

A long stretch of silence follows, followed by a stern, "Let me in. Now."

Irritation bubbles in Cal's gut. His previously calm voice takes on a rough edge. "I don't know who you are. And you called Dawson an ass. That's not nice."

"Are you fucking—" A sharp inhale, and then, "I'm his sister."

Cal deflates, irritation replaced by confusion. "Olivia?"

"No, the other one," probably-Olivia snaps. "Jesus."

She's clearly not happy, and Cal doesn't really feel like inviting her in, especially since Dawson isn't here, but he can't possibly let her wait outside. "I'm opening the door for you."

"Fucking finally," he hears, accompanied by the sound of the door buzzing. It can't be more than a minute before there's a sharp knock on the door. Cal, who's been rooted to the spot since he opened the main entrance, reaches for the doorknob, bracing himself.

He's seen Olivia in the pictures, but seeing her in person makes it clear that she and Dawson are siblings. The same hair-color, same facial features—though Dawson's cheekbones are a little more pronounced and his lips just a tad fuller. Even their eye color is the same, but where Dawson's eyes are soft and kind, Olivia's have daggers in them. And they're pointing at Cal.

Cal opens his mouth for a proper greeting—and an introduction, despite Olivia knowing who he is, but he doesn't get far. Olivia shoulders her way past him, looking around the apartment frantically. It reminds Cal of one of the movies he and Dawson watched, where the main character stormed into her boyfriend's apartment, certain he was having an affair.

Olivia whirls around, eyeing Cal like she's about to obliterate him. It takes all of Cal's willpower to ignore his self-preservation instinct and not take a step back.

Then her gaze falls on Donut sitting quietly at Cal's side. Her jaw slackens. "What's *that*?"

Donut whines, and Cal bends down to pet him. "That's Donut. He's a rescue."

Olivia gapes at him. "You have a dog?"

"...Yes?"

Olivia's confused expression transforms into a hard mask. "Where is Dawson? Why is he not picking up?"

"He went out to the movies with Kieran." Figuring he should make nice with his sister-in-law, he forces a strained smile and offers a hand for a shake. "Hi. Nice to meet you."

Olivia's eyes narrow dangerously, then stare at the offered hand like it's a weapon. When she lifts her gaze, it's not as venomous anymore, but not kind either.

"You really got everything knocked out of you, huh." It sounds like a statement rather than a question, but he doesn't want to stay uncomfortable in silence.

"I guess so?"

Olivia watches him, her gaze never wavering. "When's Dawson gonna be back?"

"I don't know for sure. He didn't mention if he has plans after the movie. Would you like to wait for him?" Dawson won't mind, right? This is his sister after all, and Cal knows he misses her.

"Do I have a choice?" Olivia complains, like it's Cal's fault Dawson's not here, or picking up her calls.

"Well..." Cal starts, wanting to point out she's welcome to leave, but a sharp look from her changes his mind. "Would you like anything to drink?"

Olivia lets out a derisive snort. "Like the whiskey from your stash? No, thanks."

Cal winces. It's so strange to hear people talk about his addiction when he hasn't felt the urge to pick up a drink since the accident. But he also knows he can't argue with them. After all, it was the reason why he ended up in the car crash and with his memory wiped clean in the first place.

"I don't drink alcohol," he says simply, keeping his voice even. He walks over to the fridge, opening it. "I have water, orange juice... Dawson's kombucha." Dawson is very protective of it, but Cal'd rather receive a stink eye from him than experience any more of Olivia's wrath. "But I don't think he'd mind if you had some."

Olivia's silent at first, then she sighs. "Juice." When Cal reaches for the bottle and goes to pour her a glass, she stalks forward and all but rips it from his hands. "I can get it myself."

Cal holds his hands up in peace. "Glasses are—" Olivia's already pulling open the cabinets. "Over there." He stays silent, watching Olivia fill the glass and leave the opened bottle of juice on the counter. She leans against it, watching Cal over the rim as she drinks.

Cal's palms sweat, an uneasy feeling spreading in his stomach. "You don't like me, do you?"

She raises an eyebrow. "Whatever gave you that idea?"

Cal doesn't react to the jab, though it stings a little. He doesn't know Olivia, but she's Dawson's family. He hoped they could be friends, just like he wanted to be friends with Kieran, because he's important to Dawson. He wonders what he did to warrant such disdain from so many people Dawson cares about. Is the drinking the main reason? Part of him doesn't want to know, but...he'd just like an opportunity to make it better.

Olivia's eyes roam around the kitchen, judgment clear in her gaze. Cal didn't like it either when he first came here from the hospital, but he and Dawson have made so many beautiful memories here since then. It's different now.

Olivia pauses with her glass halfway to her lips, her gaze setting on something in front of her. She stalks towards the island and grabs the framed photo of Cal and Dawson from the day they were making pizzas, flour in their hair and on their faces, both of them grinning at the camera.

She looks at the photo, then at Cal. "When was this taken?"

Cal racks his mind. "A few weeks ago. We don't have many pictures from...before and it didn't feel right." A small chuckle makes it past his lips. "We are competing."

Olivia frowns. "At what?"

"Who can take a worse picture of the other."

She studies him like he's some peculiar critter. He's surprised when she puts the photo down and asks, "Who's leading?"

"Dawson," he says with a fond laugh. "I look like a moron when I'm not ready to pose. Actually, even when I am ready."

Is it his imagination or does Oliva smile? Or maybe it's just a tick.

"Sounds like something my spawns would like to do."

"Chloe and Leia?" Cal asks, hoping he didn't mess up the names. Olivia gives him a struck look. "Dawson talks about you a lot. All of you. I was thinking we could visit when you're not busy."

Yeah, right. This woman won't be inviting you to her home anytime soon.

Her eyes never leave Cal as she approaches him with slow, almost soundless steps. She tilts her head as she scrutinizes his face. Cal tries not to fidget.

"That must have been some blow you took," she murmurs, like she's talking to herself. Figuring it doesn't warrant a response, he doesn't say anything. After a few seconds of staring into his soul, Olivia goes to roam the living room, her focus mostly on the walls. Cal holds himself back from asking her to remove her shoes because he and Dawson always do before leaving the foyer.

She stops in front of some of Dawson's older paintings. "What are these?"

"Paintings Dawson kept in the storage room." Cal goes to join her, keeping a safe distance. "He fought me on it, but I convinced him to hang them up." He can't help the smitten smile that always appears when he looks at Dawson's work. "They're amazing, aren't they?"

"Yeah," Olivia says, her voice distant and...sad. Cal wants to ask her if she's okay, but she speaks first. "So, they're not new? He still hasn't picked it back up."

"Not quite but..." He points at the other wall, regretting it instantly when he realizes his 'art' hangs there too. "We did a Paint 'n' Sip session earlier this week."

He follows Olivia when she makes a beeline for the paintings. "Is that a dick?"

Cheeks aflame, Cal forces out, "Um... That's mine. Not my dick. Jesus," he rushes to correct when she snaps her head up to look at him with horror. He rubs a hand over his face. "My painting. I painted that. I didn't want it up, but Dawson forced me."

This time, it's definitely a smile on Olivia's lips. "Oh boy," is what she says. Before she can make Cal even more miserable and make him wish the ground would swallow him up, he's saved.

"I'm home!" his salvation calls out. Donut runs to greet him, making excited little noises. "Cal, guess who we bumped into. Ash and Gabe! And you should've seen Kieran when—" Dawson's voice cuts off, as do his footsteps. "Liv?!"

"Hey, bro." She waves at him.

Dawson's eyes flick between the two of them, his brows furrowing. "What are you doing here?" He's decidedly not happy being surprised like this, and Cal questions his decision to let Olivia in.

"Visiting. Which you'd know if you'd picked up your phone."

"I was busy."

"Spending time with your friend for once. Good on you."

Cal tries to summon his best apologetic face, feeling guilty for making Dawson so uncomfortable.

"What are you doing?" Dawson questions.

Olivia shrugs. "I was just admiring Cal's dick."

"The painting!" Cal blurts out when Dawson looks like he might pass out. "She means the painting." Jesus, this family is going to kill him. Not alcohol or car crashes—this family.

"You're painting again," Olivia says matter-of-factly, ignoring Cal's mortification.

Dawson ducks his head. "Just a little. It's a social thing."

"Sure, sure." She huffs a laugh. "God forbid you fully commit to something for once."

Dawson's eyes flash. "What do you want, Liv?"

"I wanted to see you," she replies, actually sounding earnest. "Check on you."

"I'm fine."

"Yeah, I can see that."

"You clearly have a lot to talk about," Cal says, itching to make himself scarce before the tension chokes him. "I'll take Donut for a walk."

"That's not necessary," Dawson says at the same time that Olivia chimes, "That'd be great. Thanks."

While Cal grabs Donut's leash and clips it to his collar, Dawson sends him a betrayed look, mouthing "Traitor."

It makes Cal feel a little bad, but he honestly believes that his presence would make the already unbearable tension escalate. Better to just let them talk it out.

He's never been so grateful to have a dog.

Chapter 23

OLIVIA'S WHOLE DEMEANOR CHANGES once it's just the two of them. Her expression turns stormy. She's preparing for a strike, and Dawson is in the impact zone.

"What *the hell* are you doing?!"

Aaand there it is.

His phone was blowing up throughout the whole movie, so of course he ignored it. And he did plan on calling Olivia back...later. He figured there was no rush, since she's been spamming his inbox the whole week and Dawson made sure he always replied.

He did not expect her to come all the way here.

"What are you talking about?" Dawson feigns innocence. He knows that look. It's the same one Kieran's been giving him, that Ellis has been giving him. Hell, he's seen it in passing on Ash's face too.

And it's really getting on his nerves.

"I'm talking about this!" Liv flings her arms out, encompassing the whole living room. "And this!" She points at Donut's food and water bowls and the dog bed he never sleeps in.

Dawson wonders what she'd say if she saw the photo collage they blue-tacked to the wall above their bed.

"What the fuck, Dawson?! Are you playing house with the guy who used to manipulate the shit out of you? The one who wouldn't let you see your family?" A vein in her temple pulses dangerously.

He understands where she's coming from, but she's not seeing the whole picture, she never has. That's mostly on Dawson who's never let her see, will never let her see the extent of what he's been through. But he gets it.

"Things are different now."

"You're kidding, right? That's what people in your situation always say, don't you see?! He broke you, Dawson. He completely fucked with your head."

He physically recoils, the words like a blow to the solar plexus. He knows his brain is kind of fucked up—not even Ash tried to argue with him about it. No one gets out of an abusive relationship and miraculously has their shit together. He knows he has a long way to go before he can trust himself.

But he's never thought of himself as broken. And hearing the words from his own sister hurts in ways he'd never expect.

The therapy must finally be rubbing off on him, because instead of spiraling into self-hate and doubt, he gets angry. Angry is good. It means he's drawing boundaries. Ash would be proud of him.

"I'm not playing house," he presses out through gritted teeth. God, he wishes Cal was here, holding his hand. Dawson will have some words with him for bailing like that. "And I'm not broken," he spits the word out like poison.

Olivia scoffs and gestures at his painting. "He made you think so low of yourself that you gave all this up. You loved it and you gave it up because *he* didn't like it."

Dawson doesn't flinch, doesn't even waver. He's talked about this over and over with Ash, trying to understand his growing feelings for the man who'd turned his life upside down.

He has no idea how he arrived here, to this place where the mere thought of Cal invokes feelings of affection and happiness, where having Cal by his side makes him feel safe. But he's realized that the road that brought him here isn't important. Instead of fixating on the 'how' and the 'why', he wants to focus on the now. Instead of having his life happen to him, he wants to start *living* it.

And he wants it with Cal.

"You're right. I did give it up for him. But that was before. He's not that person anymore."

Olivia looks at him like she doesn't recognize him. He doesn't blame her. He's changed a lot—over the years with Cal, and in the past couple of months. For the first time in forever, he feels like himself. Like the kind of person he always wanted to be.

"You think that having a few screws knocked loose suddenly changes a person?"

Suppressing the urge to defend Cal—there are no screws loose, he just doesn't remember things—he focuses on the obvious. "Look around you. How much clearer can it be that he's nothing like the man I married?"

Olivia's hands fly to her hair, tugging at it. "Oh my god. Are you listening to yourself?! At least before, you didn't jump to his defense. You knew what kind of person he was."

"Was, yes."

"What are you going to do when you drop the D-bomb, huh? How do you think he'll take it after all this?"

Dawson has always worn his heart on his sleeve, his emotions out there for everyone to see. Evidently, it's still true, because one look at him and Olivia's furious expression is replaced by one of horror.

"Oh my god. Oh my god. Don't fucking tell me..." She starts pacing, shaking her head as though that could get rid of the thought that's just planted itself in there. Her back is to Dawson when she speaks next. "You were never going to do it, were you?"

Dawson's gaze steers to Cal's cactus dick painting, reminding him how Cal grew flustered at Dawson's teasing. How he protected him from the guy who wouldn't take no for an answer. How, when they got home, Cal pressed him against the wall and kissed him until nothing existed but the two of them. And Donut.

"I was. But things have changed. *He* has changed. And I've changed with him."

Slowly, Olivia turns. The fight has drained out of her. She just looks resigned now. Resigned and devastated. "You love him."

The words strike like lightning, stealing Dawson's voice.

There's nothing to say anyway. Olivia didn't ask a question, and Dawson can't even deny it.

Because it's true.

"I love him," he repeats, more for his own benefit. It's the first time he's said the words out loud, though not the first he's thought them. They scare him to death, but he can't bring himself to take them back. "I love him," he says again, just to see how they taste. He imagines what it would be like saying them to Cal. Would Cal say them back?

"I thought you were going to therapy," Olivia says, voice heavy with disappointment.

"I am. It's put a lot of things into perspective. Helped me make some decisions." His stomach clenches when he notices a single tear sliding down Olivia's cheek. "Liv..."

"Don't," she sobs out, rubbing at her eyes. "Fuck. I knew it. I knew I should've come here after it all went down. I should've taken you away from him."

"Take me away?" he says incredulously. He's not a thing to be taken. "Like Cal took me from you?"

It's Olivia's turn to recoil, hurt clear in her gaze. She stalks towards Dawson, pushing at his chest, not very hard, but enough to make him stumble back. Then she stabs his chest with her finger. "Don't you dare fucking compare us. Everything I've ever done was for you."

Trying to remember everything he's been working on with Ash, he takes a steadying breath, willing himself not to lash out and say things he would regret later.

"I know. But I'm a big boy and I can take care of myself. Everything you see here? That's because of him." He spreads his arms, letting them fall back against his sides. "I can't tell you how it happened. It took me a long time to stop expecting the other shoe to drop. Then I realized I just...need to let the past go. If I want a future, I need to let it go."

"And you want a future with *him*?" she asks in that same incredulous tone.

"I do." He really does. He wants everything with Cal. All the things he's never done, and all the things he has but that felt wrong. He's done hiding from the past, but no one said he can't try and rewrite the future. Like...a second edition. Cal would like that metaphor, he's sure.

"I don't want you to be another statistic, Dee," she whispers, her eyes red-rimmed. "Before, you at least knew that what he was doing was wrong, but now?" She shakes her head. "You actually trust him, don't you?"

"I do. And..." He laughs, barely believing it himself. "He makes me feel safe. He makes me happy. Really, truly happy." Another laugh he can't suppress. "We got a dog, Liv."

Olivia's face softens for a split second. "The girls would go crazy for him." Then the stern mask is back. "I'd ask you if you really are happy, but I can see it in your eyes. And that scares the shit out of me." She sighs, pulling her shoulders back. "If he so much as touches a hair on your head, there's nowhere in the world where he will be able to hide from me. And I'll make him regret the day his mother pushed him out of her vagina."

Dawson makes a disgusted face. "Eww."

"I mean it. I'm talking full-on Hannibal Lecter shit. I'll rip his fucking lungs out."

"And eat them?"

"Don't test me."

"You need to stop watching that show."

"No chance in hell. Mads is fucking hot."

Dawson raises a challenging eyebrow. "You're giving me shit but you find a psychopath hot."

"That's a completely different situation, so don't change the subject."

They both chuckle. It feels like a throwback to Dawson's teens, when he and Olivia would drive each other crazy and argue about the most ridiculous things. He misses it.

"Guess I'll get going," Olivia says, casting a helpless glance around. Then she grabs Dawson and pulls him into a fierce hug, releasing him just as quickly without giving him a chance to reciprocate. She slaps the back of his head. "Pick up your fucking phone next time."

Dawson rubs his head, even though it barely stung. "I will."

He walks her to the door, ready to say goodbye.

"He said you wanted to visit," Olivia says.

"Cal? Uh, yeah. Been thinking about it."

He hesitated when Cal brought it up because he didn't know how Olivia would react at seeing them back together. But now that it's finally done and over with, maybe...

"Well, stop thinking and fucking do it," she grits out, not quite meeting his eyes.

Dawson has to bite his lip to hide a shit-eating grin. "Yes, ma'am."

She narrows her eyes, and he takes a step back in case she's about to smack him again.

Olivia huffs irritably, then pulls him into another hug. "Love you, you insufferable little shit."

Dawson wraps his arms around her waist, hiding a smile and teary eyes in her nape. "Love you too, you controlling bitch."

She pulls back and delivers that dreaded smack. "Watch your language."

Dawson sticks his tongue out, watching her go with a mixture of sadness and relief. Olivia's acceptance feels more like resignation, but Dawson will have to work with what he has. At least Olivia is willing to try for him, which is more than he could've hoped for.

Their whole interaction, while resulting in a positive outcome, has left him drained and emotional. It's true what they say about family bringing out the worst in you sometimes. As a cherry on top, he can feel pressure starting to build behind his eyes.

Great. Another fucking headache incoming.

Chapter 24

WHEN CAL COMES BACK from the walk with Donut, he mentally braces for another confrontation with Olivia and an earful from Dawson for leaving him like that. He takes his shoes off and unleashes Donut, managing to get one stroke of Donut's spine in before the little terrorist is growling at him. Typical. Donut was snuggling up to him before, and now he's back to hating Cal's guts.

"Okay, okay. Hands to myself."

With a derisive snort, Donut takes off, nails clapping across the floor, probably in search of Dawson. After a few seconds, Cal hears, "Hello, buddy. How was the walk? Were you a good boy?"

Chuckling, Cal follows the sound of Dawson's voice to the kitchen.

"If by a good boy you mean—" Concern wipes the smile from his face. "What's wrong?"

Dawson is leaning against the counter and sipping what seems to be a glass of ice water, the space between his brows pinched in pain. Olivia's nowhere to be seen.

"Just a headache," Dawson says miserably, pressing the cool glass against his forehead.

Cal moves towards him, cupping his face with both hands. "How bad?"

"Not too bad. Annoying, mostly." Which in Dawson's language means: *I'm dying but I'm not about to admit that.*

Cal takes Dawson's hand and tugs him across the living room. "Let's get you in bed."

Dawson doesn't argue, adjusting his grip so their fingers thread together. Cal squeezes his hand, stroking his thumb over Dawson's. When Dawson is crawling into bed, Cal goes to roll down the blinds. The sun will set soon, but the sooner he gets Dawson in a dark room the better. Once that's done, Cal climbs onto the bed next to him and strokes his hair. Dawson hums, eyes closed and the faintest smile on his lips.

"Would you like a massage? It helped last time."

"Okay," Dawson whispers, blinking one eye open and smiling up at Cal. "How do you want me?"

In my arms, ideally forever. "Here," he rasps out and moves to sit up against the headboard, Dawson's head in his lap. "Like last time. This good?"

Dawson hums, eyes closed.

With a kiss to Dawson's forehead, Cal begins rubbing small circles into his temples, then moves across the scalp slowly, taking his time.

After several minutes, Dawson is so relaxed Cal thinks he's fallen asleep, but then Dawson says, "I'm sorry about Olivia ambushing you like that. She's a force of nature. Was she mean to you?"

Cal presses his lips together, not wanting to upset Dawson. "She wasn't happy you weren't here and that she couldn't reach you," he says evasively. "But I think we bonded a little over my dick."

Dawson laughs so hard he chokes a little, then grimaces like he just bit into a lemon. "Please, stop. I find the thought of your dick and my sister very disturbing."

"Me too."

They both laugh.

"I'm sorry if she was mean. She's protective," Dawson says, making Cal sigh. He had hoped he'd distracted Dawson with the silly joke.

"I know. Don't worry about it, Dawson."

"But I—"

"Shh, rest. Don't stress over silly stuff."

"S'not silly," Dawson pouts. "I want you to get along. You're both so important to me."

Cal smiles, his heart overflowing with all the love he has for this man. He bends down to brush his lips against Dawson. "Don't worry. I'll win her over. I promise."

"Oh, yeah? What, you'll paint her a picture?"

Cal smirks. "Maybe. Or I can cook for her."

"Cal, please, don't poison my sister. That would be a hard one to explain to the police. I'm not sure even Ellis could help."

"That was uncalled for."

"Hmm."

"What were you about to say? When you got home. You mentioned running into Gabe and Ash."

"Hm? Oh, yeah." Dawson giggles. "We got the seats next to them, can you believe it? Kieran was being a smartass and kept making jabs at Ash when he found out he's my therapist."

"What did Ash say?"

"That Kieran sounds like someone who could use his services."

Cal snorts. "Ouch."

"Yup. God, you should've seen Kieran's face. I thought I was about to have to pay bail for him."

"But everyone survived?"

"Close call, but yeah. Kieran's never living this down, though." Dawson yawns. "I should probably pop a painkiller before I fall asleep."

"You haven't taken one yet?"

"I got distracted by the massage."

Cal sighs. "Dawson..."

"I know, I know. But I'm fine. The massage helped." He smiles at Cal upside down and Jesus, Cal can't be mad at him. He gives him another forehead kiss.

"Stay. I'll get them for you." Carefully moving Dawson off him, Cal shuffles across the bed. "Are they in the bathroom?"

"Nightstand."

Throwing his legs over the edge, Cal flicks the lamp on and pulls out the first drawer, searching through the contents. The pills aren't there, just a heap of chargers tangled together.

Closing the drawer, he moves onto the second one. There's a large manila envelope lying on top, and he takes it out to get a look underneath. The envelope must've been open, because the content spills out, falling to the floor. Thankfully, the papers inside seem to be stapled together so they don't end up scattering everywhere. As he bends to pick them up, his gaze catches onto the big bold letters on top of the first page.

And the whole world shifts on its axis.

The bed shifts, and Dawson's hand touches his leg, startling him.

"Cal? Did you find them?"

Found them? Found what? What was he looking—

Right. Dawson's pills.

"Sorry," he manages. A dark void fills his chest as he shoves the papers in the envelope and puts them back in the drawer. He shuts it with force, as though it could turn back time and erase the last sixty seconds.

He scours the last drawer until he finds the pills and hands them to Dawson. "Here."

"Thank you."

The obvious pain in his voice as he presses up on his elbows to swallow the pill is enough to snap Cal from his mind-numbed state. He puts a hand on Dawson's back, holding him up as he pops the pill in his mouth and washes it down with the rest of his water.

"I..." He swallows, his throat feeling as though it's collapsing on itself. "I'll get you more water." He takes the glass from Dawson and hurries away. In the kitchen, he turns the tap on, holding the glass underneath it with a shaky hand. He stalls before returning to the bedroom, trying and failing to process what he just learned.

This can't be happening. This can't be—

"Cal?"

He shakes himself. "Coming!"

Dawson smiles at him when Cal steps back into the bedroom, holding the water out for him. It damn near breaks his heart in half.

He wants to—no, *needs to* ask questions, demand what it all means, and why Dawson...why he would want that. But Dawson needs to rest, and Cal needs time to pull himself together. He needs to talk to someone.

"Is there anything you need?" he asks, voice rough and scratching the inside of his throat.

Any hope of having a chance to remove himself for a minute and be by himself disappears when Dawson buries himself under the covers and pats the empty space next to him.

"Can you stay and hold me until I fall asleep?"

Cal closes his eyes. He doesn't understand. How can Dawson want him here when...

His legs carry him forward of their own will. There's no point in trying to resist, to stay away. He could never stay away from Dawson.

Not until he asks me to, a bitter voice inside his head says.

He switches the lamp off and lies on his back, slightly propped against the headboard, hopelessly trying to put some distance between them. It's no use. Dawson lets out an amused huff, shuffling closer and draping himself over Cal, head on his chest and one of his legs thrown over one of Cal's. A small sigh of satisfaction escapes his lips as he snuggles against Cal's chest.

Instinctively, Cal pulls him closer, fingers threading through Dawson's hair and pressing against his scalp. Dawson hums contentedly and burrows further into Cal's chest.

"You make a good pillow," Dawson mumbles sleepily. He's probably not even aware of what he's saying, but that doesn't make it any easier to hear. Then it gets worse. "Wish I could stay like this forever. Sans the headache," he chuckles softly, unaware that every word out of his mouth is like a knife slicing through Cal.

Cal's vision blurs. When he blinks, a single tear escapes from the corner of his eye. He holds Dawson closer to him. He doesn't say anything. Doesn't trust his voice.

He always thought that when people in books describe heartache like someone reaching into their chest and crushing it with their fist, they are being overly dramatic. He doesn't anymore.

Because that's exactly what he feels like right now.

He waits until Dawson's breaths even out and his hold on Cal relaxes enough that he can slip away.

He must have a masochistic streak he never knew about, because there's no other reason for him to open that drawer again and take out the envelope.

Making sure Dawson is fast asleep, he leaves the room, shutting the door as quietly as possible. In the living room, he stares at the envelope in his hand for a long time before finding courage to open it again.

He slides the papers out slowly, naively hoping that his eyes were just playing tricks on him. Maybe when he looks at them now, they'll be something else, and he can laugh about being so silly.

It doesn't happen like that. The papers fall into his waiting palm, the dreadful words printed black on white, irrefutable.

Divorce agreement

How is this real? Why would Dawson want a divorce? They're happy, aren't they? Dawson seems happy. He was timid and withdrawn after Cal's accident, but who wouldn't be after finding out their husband forgot everything about them?

Could it be the drinking? Or because Cal worked so much? Dawson mentioned repeatedly that Cal used to spend all his time in the office, his life revolving around work. Maybe Dawson got fed up with it? But if that's the case, why didn't he tell him when Cal left the hospital? Why did he stick around?

Because he's an amazing person and he didn't want to leave you on your own.

Is that it? Did Dawson stay because he felt sorry for him?

Cal has to know. He won't like the answer, but he can't shove this under the rug and pretend he doesn't know about it. He can't live like that, always wondering if Dawson's staying because he feels obligated to do so.

It will be a while before Dawson wakes, but Cal can't wait that long. He needs...something. There's only one person he can think of who could give him some answers.

Picking up his phone, he dials Ellis' number.

Ellis picks up on the third ring. "Cal, hey."

"Can I talk to you for a minute?"

"Is it urgent?" Ellis asks, sounding distracted. "I'm quite busy."

"Did you know Dawson wanted to apply for a divorce?"

There's a long silence on the other side, followed by the sound of rustling papers and a chair moving across the floor.

"He told you," Ellis says, surprise clear in his voice.

Cal stomach bottoms out. "You did know."

"I found out by accident."

"So did I."

A pause. "How?"

"I found the divorce papers in his nightstand. I wasn't going through his stuff," he adds when he realizes how it must've sounded. He throws the papers on the coffee table and drops down on the sofa. "I don't understand, Ellis. I thought... He seems happy with me. And just now, he..." He takes a deep breath, his eyes stinging. "He asked me to hold him. He was in pain and needed sleep, and he asked me to hold him."

"Cal," Ellis says, sounding pained. "I don't know what to tell you. I'm sorry."

"You knew," Cal reminds him, anger and betrayal simmering under his skin. "So you must know the reason."

"I do," he admits. "But it's not mine to tell. You need to talk to Dawson."

Cal grinds his teeth. "Thanks." He's about to hang up, but Ellis stops him. "What?"

"Just... Whatever he tells you, keep an open mind. You're a different person than you were before, but Dawson remembers both of you. It might be hard for you, but it's harder for him."

If that was supposed to help him, it didn't. It just made him feel worse. What kind of person *had* he been?

And why will no one tell him?

Hoping to find answers in the papers, Cal goes through the pages one by one. He doesn't understand all the legal talk, but everything is there, already prefilled, his and Dawson's personal details, employment and income information, the date of their marriage, their address.

And then there's a page called *financial settlement.* A page stating that everything they have belongs to Cal, and Dawson doesn't have a right to any of it.

He contemplates burning the papers, but that would achieve nothing. It wouldn't change the fact that Dawson wanted to get away from him—maybe he still does.

Cal's eyes roam around the apartment, the space that used to feel cold and uninviting but which they've turned into a home. It's filled with beautiful memories, moments Cal will cherish forever. It's filled with Dawson's paintings and their photos. Finally, they have photos.

Has it all been a lie? A fantasy? And why has Dawson been playing along?

An unidentifiable time later, the bedroom door opens and a disheveled-looking Dawson steps out. His eyes are barely open, adjusting to the light, and Cal takes the opportunity to grab the papers and shove them between himself and the back of the sofa.

"Hey, you," Dawson says when he sees him. "I was wondering where you'd gone off to."

"Sorry. I needed to…" He has no idea how to finish that sentence. "How are you feeling?"

"Like a million bucks," Dawson exaggerates, crossing the living room towards Cal and sitting down next to him. "I'm fine, actually.

The pills and the massage worked like a charm." He gives Cal a soft smile and starts to lean in.

A swell of panic rises inside Cal, freezing his body in place, no matter how much he wants to feel Dawson's lips on his. Thankfully, Dawson's stomach chooses that moment to grumble loud enough to be heard on another floor.

He chuckles sheepishly. "I might be a little hungry."

They should talk. Cal knows that. It's easier said than done, though.

"Go back to bed. I'll make you something. What would you like?"

Dawson gives him a sunny smile that nearly splits Cal's heart in half. "A smoothie."

Cal nods. "Smoothie it is." That's easy enough that he won't mess it up even in his current state.

"Thank you," Dawson says, surging forward to kiss Cal's cheek. Then he disappears back into the bedroom, completely oblivious.

Cal makes the smoothie on autopilot, wondering if it's the last time he's making something for Dawson. Is everything going to change after they talk? Will Dawson want him to leave?

The papers in one hand and a glass in the other, Cal has to concentrate not to spill the smoothie as he carries it to the bedroom. He pushes the door open, the room bright again because Dawson opened the blinds, but he's not there. Cal can hear the shower running, then switch off. He sits on the bed, the papers hidden behind him.

Dawson emerges shortly, dressed in low-slung gray joggers and a red t-shirt, his hair wet and tousled. A big smile appears on his face when he notices Cal.

"Sorry, I was all sweaty and really wanted a shower." He crawls back into bed, perking up at the sight of the smoothie. "Is that a raspberry one?"

"Yes. With almond butter." Just as Dawson likes it. He hands him the glass when Dawson reaches for it.

Dawson takes a long drink, his eyelids fluttering and a happy sigh leaving his lips as he swallows. "Yeah, that hits the spot ." He props himself up against the headboard, is head lolling to the side to peer up at Cal with a soft smile. "Thank you."

His throat refusing to cooperate, Cal nods, tearing his gaze away. It's always nearly impossible to stop looking at Dawson once he starts. But the papers tucked behind his back get heavier with each passing second, and he knows he can't stall much longer. He waits until Dawson puts the glass down, but it seems he can't find his voice again.

Dawson notices something is amiss, his brows furrowing. "Are you okay?"

After countless attempts, Cal finally manages, "There's something I need to talk to you about."

Dawson heaves a sigh and sags back. His expression is apologetic when he looks at Cal.

"I know. I'm sorry, Cal."

Cal freezes, waiting for Dawson to speak.

"Listen, whatever Olivia told you, just ignore it. I knocked some sense into her before she left, so please don't dwell on anything she said."

Cal wants to tell him that's not it, that he meant it when he said not to worry about it, but something dawns on him in that moment.

"There's a reason she can't stand me," Cal says. "What is it?"

Dawson cracks a nervous smile. "She's an older sister. Older sisters do that. Plus, she was never happy with our age difference. But I'm not a kid anymore, so…"

No. That's not it. Cal can feel it. That's not something you get divorced over.

"Are you sure there isn't something else?"

If Cal weren't looking for the signs, he might've missed the way Dawson's shoulders grow tense, or the wariness in his gaze. But knowing what he knows, it's evident Dawson is hiding something from him.

"Nothing comes to mind," Dawson lies. Why is he lying?

Silently, Cal reaches back and sets the papers down in the space between them.

Dawson's confused at first, but it only takes him one look to realize what he's looking at. Color drains from his face, making him look like a ghost. His wide eyes snap to Cal's, filling with fear.

Dawson is afraid.

"Cal..." His name comes out broken. Shaky.

"I found these when I was looking for the pills," he says, though Dawson didn't ask. "Do you—" The words catch in his throat. He forces them out anyway "Is this what you want?"

Dawson is shaking his head before Cal even finishes speaking. It should make Cal feel good, but it doesn't.

"But you wanted it once. Why? What did I do, Dawson?"

Dawson's mouth opens and closes, his chest rising and falling rapidly. Cal hates doing this to him, but he can't let this go.

"I spoke to Ellis. I needed to know if he knew and...if he knew why. He told me to ask you."

Dawson's eyes close and he inhales shakily. When he opens them again, they're filled with tears. "There's... A lot happened before. Before your accident."

"Tell me," Cal prompts, trying to keep his voice calm.

Dawson shakes his head.

"Dawson," he tries. "Please. Whatever it is, I need to know." Another headshake. "I thought we were happy. Thought *you* were happy."

Dawson's throat works, his lips trembling. "I am. I *am* happy, Cal."

"Now?" Dawson nods. "And before?" Dawson looks away. "Tell me."

"You were...different," Dawson starts. It's too vague to give Cal any clues, but he doesn't want to interrupt now that Dawson finally started talking. "You had a temper and when you'd get stressed, you'd drink." He picks on a loose thread of his joggers, his hands unsteady. "And when you'd drink, you'd get..."

Pinpricks of ice spread through Cal's veins. "I'd get what, Dawson?"

Dawson's eyes flick up and he speaks quietly. "Mean."

Cal swallows. "Verbally?"

A pause. "Yes."

"Just verbally?" Another headshake, so miniscule Cal would miss it if he wasn't so hyper aware of Dawson. His stomach turns with what he's about to ask next. "Did I hit you?"

After a small eternity, Dawson lets out a shaky "Yes."

Closing his eyes, Cal asks, "More than once?"

Dawson doesn't say anything. He doesn't have to. The rigid line of his shoulders and the way he's curling in on himself tells Cal everything he needs to know.

He stands up, his back to Dawson. His fists clenching and unclenching, and he fights the urge to punch something, preferably himself.

Something snaps inside him, a realization filling him with dread.

"Cal?" Dawson calls out. The fear in his voice makes Cal want to turn around and take Dawson into his arms where nothing could hurt him.

You hurt him.

"They're not dreams, are they?"

"What?" Dawson says, confused.

Cal turns around, hating the fear in Dawson's face. Hating himself for putting it there.

"All those times when I saw you hurt. Crying. They were never dreams." He looks at Dawson and sees the truth. An overwhelming feeling of powerlessness slams into him, choking him. "Why didn't you tell me? Why did you stay, after everything?"

Dawson could've left. He *should've* left. Forget all about Cal and go live his life. He wasn't supposed to get saddled with him, pretend that he wasn't breaking inside while Cal lived in blissful oblivion.

"You needed me." Dawson says it like the question confuses him. Like even thinking about leaving Cal to his own devices is unthinkable.

And it occurs to Cal...it probably is. For Dawson, it is. Because that's who he is. This wonderful, selfless, most amazing person with a heart of gold who wouldn't leave anyone behind even if it meant being miserable for the rest of his life.

Not on Cal's watch.

"Where are you going?" Dawson asks, panicked, when Cal goes to the door. How he can still want Cal near him is beyond him.

"I just need to think." Not that there's much to think about. He knows what he needs to do. "You should rest."

He leaves the bedroom before his resolve breaks. The first thing he does is pull out his phone and call Ellis again.

"Cal?"

"How could you not tell me?" Cal hisses, anger bubbling inside him.

"I didn't know until recently. He told me the night of your accident—"

"Two months?! You've known for two months, and you let him stay with me?!"

"Hey!" Ellis snaps, and there's a sound of something hitting the floor. "I told him not to do it. I told him I'd take care of it. Of you. But he was adamant."

"So you just backed off?"

"I'm not his mother to order him around," Ellis grits out. "He had enough of that from you."

Once the words are out, silence hangs heavy between them. Maybe Ellis didn't mean to say it, but he doesn't take it back. As he shouldn't.

"You should've fought him on this," Cal stands his ground, but he's turned the anger back at himself.

"You didn't remember, Cal."

Cal shakes his head even though Ellis can't see him. "I could've still hurt him." What if his memories came back? The doctors said it can happen any time. If he suddenly remembered when Dawson was with him...

"Have you?"

"Of course not!" Cal yells, furious.

"Then let it go," Ellis says, like it's so simple. "Go talk to him. Ask him what he wants. For once, let him decide for himself."

Cal grips the phone hard, slamming the red button. The temptation to throw it against the wall is strong, but he holds himself back. He wants Dawson to be free, but Dawson doesn't seem to know what that means. And how could he, if this whole time he hasn't been allowed to want things for himself?

Dawson is too good—for anyone, but especially for Cal. Too good to make decisions that are in his best interest.

So someone will have to do it for him.

Chapter 25

DAWSON DOESN'T MOVE FOR a long time, his body feeling as though it's filled with lead. It all happened so fast that he's struggling to wrap his head around everything. It doesn't *make sense.*

Everything was good; they were good. One moment, Cal was being sweet with him, chasing his pain away and kissing his face. The next, he was holding up a memento of Dawson's past and asking him to relive it.

It's been so long since the idea of leaving Cal had crossed Dawson's mind that he forgot the papers even existed. How could he forget? For years he hadn't thought of anything but leaving and never found a way out. And now that he finally has something worth staying for, it's ripped away from him in the blink of an eye.

Donut must sense his distress, whining and demanding access to Dawson's lap. Dawson makes space for him, pulling him close and burying his face in Donut's short fur. Cal must have taken him to the beach when Olivia was here because he smells like the ocean. He was probably chasing seagulls again.

"What do I do, Donut?"

Donut answers him with a lick to his chin, pulling out a weak laugh out of him.

"Give Cal a kiss? That's what you think I should do?" He gets a lick to his nose. "Maybe you should kiss him. He thinks you don't like him. You should show him it's not true. You like Cal, don't you? Don't you?" A lick to his chin again. "Yeah. Me too. Like him a lot. Crazy amount." He swallows, tears burning his eyes. "I love him, Donut."

Donut lets out an encouraging little growl, his tongue flicking out to lick his chops. He gazes up at Dawson with expectation.

"I should do something about that, huh?" Donut answers him with a bark, shooting out of Dawson's lap and doing a circle. "You're right. Let's go."

He doesn't get far. His foot has barely touched the floor when the door opens and Cal walks in. It takes monumental effort not to jump straight into his arms and kiss him until he doesn't remember the last few hours. Dawson wouldn't say no to another bout of amnesia.

"H-hey," Dawson croaks out. Hope sparks in his chest, flickering out just as quickly when his gaze falls on Cal's hand, still holding onto the damned papers. He needs to act quickly.

Dawson scrambles onto his knees, keeping his expression open and honest. "Cal, I'm sorry. I should've told you, I just didn't know—"

"Stop," Cal says, sounding utterly broken. "Don't ever apologize to me, Dawson." It's a relief when Cal walks to the bed and sits down, only inches away from him. "I'm the one who should apologize."

Dawson swallows. This is what he's always wanted, for Cal to realize that what he did was wrong. So why doesn't he feel any relief?

"It's okay."

"It's not okay, Dawson." Cal's tone brooks no argument. "Nothing about this is."

"You don't even remember any of it," Dawson argues feebly.

The smile Cal gives him is so sad and devastated, it makes it hard to breathe. "But you do." His gaze drops to the papers. Then he offers them to Dawson. "Here."

Dawson takes them with a frown. What's he supposed to do with them?

His heart comes to a staggering halt when he looks down, Cal's signature is scribbled on the bottom of the first page. And the next. And the next.

"W-what?" Dawson stutters, feeling as though all the air has been sucked out of his lungs.

"This is what you wanted," Cal says gently. "And me being in an accident shouldn't change it." He lifts his hand, hovering over Dawson's. He hesitates before finally touching him, as if expecting him to balk. "You're a wonderful, loving person and I know you wanted to help me because..." He chuckles self-deprecatingly. "That's who you are. You always try to help. But I think it's time you start taking care of yourself first."

Dawson shakes his head so fast his vision spins. "I don't want this." He tries to give the papers to Cal, but he pushes his hand back.

"Yes. Yes, you do," he says firmly when Dawson wants to argue. "This is proof."

"That was before!" Dawson says, the volume of his voice rising as panic squeezes his throat. "Things have changed. You have changed. We both have."

"You're right. And I know what I have to do." Cal licks his lips and gestures at the papers. "I didn't understand everything. Actually, I understood very little, but I want you to have whatever you want. The apartment, the money. It's yours."

Dawson blinks, and wetness slides down his cheeks. Cal might've as well reached into his chest and crushed his heart. "That's it? After everything, you're just going to leave? I don't want the stupid apartment Cal, or the fucking money."

Cal averts his eyes. "Dawson..."

"No!" He tosses the papers aside, uncaring where they land. "You said we are happy. You said—"

Cal grips his arms, trying to make him stay still. "Dawson. Listen to me."

Shaking his head, Dawson fists Cal's shirt, his eyes filling up so quickly that everything is a blur. "Please."

"You're the most important thing in my life. The only important thing," Cal says, voice filled with pain. "When I woke up in that hospital, I didn't remember anything. I didn't recognize the sound of my voice or the feeling of my own body. I looked in the mirror and saw a stranger." He cups Dawson's cheek in his warm, soft palm. There's the barest hint of a smile at the corner of his lips. "But then I saw you and I knew...I knew I'd do anything to keep you safe. I knew in my heart I was supposed to protect you. And now, I've learned that this whole time, you needed protecting from me."

"Cal..."

"You are *everything* to me," he says with ardency that shakes Dawson. "So I need you to do this for me, okay? One last thing." His hands tremble when they cradle Dawson's face, so gentle, like he's something precious and fragile. "I want—I *need* you to be safe. I need you to be *happy*." He holds Dawson's gaze. "Even if it's not with me."

Even if it's not with me.

Words lodge in Dawson's throat. He wants to tell Cal it can't be anyone else. There's no one else he wants to take silly pictures with, paint bad art with, watch rom-coms with, go for walks on the beach with. He wants to tell him he can't imagine his life without burnt pancakes or pink towels, without breakfast in bed and arguing over donuts.

Now that he knows what it's like, he can't imagine a life where he's not completely, utterly, hopelessly in love with the man in front of him.

He wants to tell Cal all this, but then Cal starts to move away, to leave, and all those thoughts go out of the window.

He fists Cal's shirt, holding on so tight he hears the fabric rip.

"It is."

Cal closes his eyes, shaking his head. "Dawson..."

"It is."

He pushes into Cal's space and cups his face, smiling at the feeling of Cal's scruff against his palms. His fingers dig into the back of Cal's neck, not allowing him to look away. Dawson needs him to look at him, to see, to understand. To believe.

"It is with you." His grip tightens when Cal opens his mouth, no doubt planning to argue. "With you." He feels a sense of victory when

Cal's eyes well up. It's a terrible thing to feel—he doesn't want to cause Cal pain—but if it means he's getting through to him, he'll gladly take it.

"You said you wanted me to be happy."

"I do," Cal says, voice cracking.

"Good. Because this is it." He presses their foreheads together, shivering when he feels Cal's breath fan over his lips. "You and me. This is it. You're *it* for me, Cal."

He barely breathes for the next several seconds, afraid that if he so much as exhales too loudly, the spell will break. When he feels Cal's hands on his hips, he gets ready to fight, to hold on if Cal tries to push him away. But that never happens.

Cal doesn't push him away. He grips him tighter, pulls him closer, shaking under the weight of Dawson's body. And then, finally, he nods.

And everything inside Dawson unravels. Every emotion Cal made him feel over the past two months, every moment he wanted to be closer, to let himself be free but didn't, it all snaps.

He attacks Cal's mouth, there's no other word for it. He latches himself onto Cal like he's a breath of air after years of drowning, the only thing that can save him.

Cal doesn't respond right away. Dawson can feel how hard he's fighting to hold back, to not give in. Well, then. If he won't listen, then Dawson will have to show him.

He moves until he's straddling Cal, caging him between his legs and holding his head in place, pouring every emotion, every promise, every memory into each kiss, each brush of lips and each shuddering breath.

He can pinpoint the exact moment when Cal breaks. He makes a sound that slices right through Dawson's heart and wraps Dawson in his arms. His mouth yields to Dawson's as he carefully kisses him back, like he still doesn't believe that he's allowed, that this is what Dawson wants.

He does want it. God, does he want it.

He's not sure if it's the conversation with Ash, or the heated argument with Olivia, or the possibility of never having this ever again, never having Cal again, but he senses a shift inside him, something that's lain dormant for a while, slowly rising to the surface, so inconspicuous and shy he hadn't even noticed it.

No, that's not right. He has noticed it. Ached for it. Got so scared he pushed it back down and tried to ignore it.

He can't ignore it now. Doesn't want to. He's done running.

"Cal?"

Cal trails his lips down the column of Dawson's neck and hums in acknowledgment. Dawson gives a full-body shiver at the sensation, his breath coming out in pants and his cock filling with blood.

"I want..."

"Anything," Cal promises, pulling a breathless laugh out of him. If it were anyone else, Dawson would shoot back that no one should make promises they don't mean, they shouldn't use words like anything, or forever, or always.

But it's not anyone else. It's Cal, and god help him, Dawson believes him. More importantly, he wants to believe him.

"I want you."

Cal rains butterfly kisses along his jaw, making Dawson's head fall back and his eyes roll heavenwards. He moves his hands to Cal's shoulders, gripping them tight when he feels like he's about to sway and lose his balance.

"You have me," Cal says, and it's so...innocent, so oblivious.

A giddy feeling fills the space between Dawson's ribs. "No," he says, realizing his mistake when Cal stills, his kisses stopping as well. His eyes are filled with panic when he pulls away and looks at Dawson, his lips parting, likely in an apology.

Dawson fits his palm over Cal's mouth. "Don't. I didn't mean it like that," he explains in a rush. "I always want you. Here, by my side. That's a given." He licks his lips, suddenly nervous. He hadn't thought he'd feel like this again. "I *want* you." He chuckles when Cal's forehead only furrows uncomprehendingly. Removing his hand from

Cal's mouth, he leans forward to replace it with his lips, his body sinking into Cal's at the utter feeling of *right*. "Make love to me."

The confused expression in Cal's face doesn't disappear right away. Dawson can almost hear the cogs turning. He can't help but smile, because it's so Cal, always trying to analyze everything.

He knows when it all clicks for him, because Cal sucks in a sharp breath, his fingers twitching on Dawson's sides and pupils dilating. And yet Cal doesn't move, never the one to take the first step.

That's fine with Dawson.

He has no idea what strange force overtakes him, but he reaches for Cal's hands and, holding his gaze, guides them lower until Cal's fingers curl around the hem of Dawson's shirt. He can tell when Cal gets the memo, because his chest begins to rise and fall rapidly, and when he shifts, he can feel the firmness of Cal's erection pressing against the inside of his leg.

In the back of his mind, a small, weak voice whispers that this should be scary, this shouldn't feel good. But all it takes is one look into Cal's eyes, one brush of his knuckles against the skin of Dawson's stomach as he cautiously moves his shirt up, and that voice disappears like it was never there. The voice doesn't matter. It was there to protect him, but he doesn't need it anymore, hasn't for a long time.

The shirt rides up Dawson's stomach, Cal's touch leaving a path of goosebumps behind before he stops, looking at Dawson askance. Dawson's mouth is suddenly dry and he only manages a nod. Cal swallows, nervousness rolling off him in waves as he starts tugging the shirt up. Dawson raises his arms, aiding the way, and Cal's breath hitches. Dawson allows himself a quick, silly smile when the shirt is pulled over his head.

A blush creeps up his neck when Cal's gaze roams over his naked skin. The desire he can see in his face fuels his own, and he impatiently paws at Cal's shirt. His hands are surprisingly steady as he works each button open, taking his time even though a part of him wants to hurry up, to feel the heat of Cal's body against his.

He pushes the shirt off Cal's shoulders, running his hands down Cal's arms as he does so.

Cal shivers, his nipples pebbling under Dawson's touch. Dawson bites back a smile, drunk on the knowledge that he's the one doing this to Cal, the one affecting him like that.

He sobers up a bit when he gets a full view of the healing scar running down Cal's abdomen. He's seen it countless times, but for some reason the sight of it now makes his chest ache.

He almost lost Cal that day. It feels like a lifetime ago, despite it being just a couple of months. It's crazy to think about how much has changed since then.

"I'm sorry," Cal says, lowering his chin. "I know it's not pretty."

It occurs to Dawson he must be staring. Instead of saying anything, he shuffles backwards, squeezing himself into the space between Cal's legs and lying down on his front, so he can kiss the scar.

Cal gasps, his abs contracting. Dawson places a few more kisses along the scar, then looks up, finding Cal watching him with a stunned expression.

"I don't care about your scars, Cal. They're not a bad thing. They're a reminder."

"Reminder? Of what?"

Rising up, Dawson braces himself on Cal's shoulders and kisses him, sighing happily when Cal instantly opens up for him.

"That we got a second chance."

"A second chance," Cal repeats, as if trying how the words taste. "A clean slate."

Dawson smiles. "Yeah, Cal." He runs his hand through Cal's hair. "A clean slate."

For a short, blissful moment, Cal returns the smile, then it's gone. "I don't deserve a second chance, Dawson."

"Yes, you do."

Cal winces. "But I—"

"No," Dawson says, grabbing a fistful of Cal's hair and tugging gently so Cal has no choice but to look at him. "You do deserve it, Cal.

And you know what? I don't care if you believe it or not. Because even if you didn't deserve it, I do. I deserve to be happy." Wow, Ash would be so proud of him. "Right?"

"Yes," Cal says quickly. "Always, Dawson."

"Then that's it. I deserve to be happy. You make me happy. If you want me to be happy, you need to stay. It's that simple. Okay?"

Cal's whole body sags, knowing he lost. Dawson would feel bad about running him into a corner like this if he wasn't so freaking relieved.

"Okay."

The dejected way he says it has doubts creeping into Dawson's mind. "But I want you to be happy too, Cal. And if this isn't what you want, if…" It hurts to think about it. "If *I'm* not what you want—"

Cal's lips are on his in an instant, warm and forceful as they forbid him to say another word. "Everything," Cal mumbles, winding his arms around Dawson's waist. "You're *everything* I ever wanted."

Dawson laughs, giddy with happiness. The emotional overload is enough to bring fresh tears to his eyes, but he stubbornly blinks them back. He doesn't want to cry now. He doesn't even want to talk. He just wants *Cal.*

He drags his hands down Cal's chest and stomach, drunk on the way Cal reacts to him, the way he shivers under the lightest touch and how he stops breathing when Dawson's fingers graze the skin just above his waistband. He holds impossibly still when Dawson starts undoing his jeans, the sound of the zipper opening unnaturally loud in the quiet. Then Dawson's knuckles graze the length of Cal's cock, and Cal lets out a sound that seems to come from the deepest part of his chest.

"Dawson…" It's spoken like a plea, one that Dawson desperately wants to answer.

His initial plan to take things slow, not just for Cal's benefit but for his own too, flies out the window. He shuffles backwards and hooks his fingers into Cal's jeans.

"Lift."

Cal looks at Dawson, at his hands, eyes unfocused like he's coming out of a haze. He digs his palms and heels into the mattress and lifts his hips. It's only an inch or so, but it's enough for Dawson to drag Cal's jeans over his hips, then work them off all the way, leaving him in his underwear.

There's something heady about seeing Cal like this, spread out and letting Dawson do as he pleases. Roaming his eyes all over Cal—from his dark, lust-filled eyes and heaving chest, to his sheet-gripping hands and hard cock—sets Dawson's insides on fire.

"Don't move," Dawson orders as he slips out of the bed. He keeps his eyes fixed on Cal as he slides his fingers behind the waistband of his joggers and starts pulling them down. Self-consciousness rears its head—Dawson didn't bother putting on his underwear after the shower—but it doesn't last long. He can feel Cal's gaze like a physical caress, touching every inch of skin, and suddenly he needs to feel it for real.

It's a miracle he doesn't trip in his hurry to get the joggers off and climb back into bed.

"Sit back against the headboard," he tells Cal, who only blinks at him like Dawson is speaking a different language. God, it shouldn't be this adorable. Dawson repeats himself, smiling as Cal clumsily shuffles backwards until he's leaning against the pillows. His hands are clenched into fists by his sides and his cock strains against his dark-blue boxer-briefs.

A rush of power sweeps through Dawson's veins. He doesn't even care how desperate he must look as he crawls towards Cal and straddles his thighs. It's different than before, the skin-on-skin contact heightening everything, and when Cal's large hands land on Dawson's naked hips, it's all he can do not to whimper. He dives forward to feel Cal's lips on his again, moaning into the kiss when his cock presses against Cal's, one layer of fabric the only thing separating them. That one layer has suddenly become very annoying.

Dawson breaks the kiss, and Cal chases after him, making him laugh when he gets Dawson's chin instead.

"Gimme a second," he says, pressing an apologetic kiss to Cal's mouth. Cal grunts out a complaint, but waits, slumping against the pillows with a huff. Dawson grins like a loon as he works Cal's underwear off, nudging him to lift his hips.

Cal all but crushes Dawson to his chest afterwards, kissing the living daylights out of him. There's no trace left of the guilt-ridden, reluctant man from only minutes before who was afraid to so much as touch Dawson. He kisses Dawson like it's their last night on earth, like this is all they have. It's not. It's just the beginning.

Dawson rocks his hips, needing to move, needing...more. More of this, more of Cal.

"Cal?" he says in a shaky voice, letting his head fall back when Cal kisses his neck, then sucks a bruise above his collarbone. Warmth spreads through the place where Cal's lips are and travels through Dawson's whole body, gathering low in his belly and making his cock jump. "Cal."

"Hm?" He doesn't stop raining kisses on Dawson's skin. Damn, is he supposed to focus?

"I need to...need to move a little." Not that he wants to. He wants to stay like this, in Cal's lap and in his arms, being kissed like he's never been kissed before.

Cal stops, and even though Dawson asked him to, he can't stop a whine that forces its way out.

"Are you okay?" Cal asks, so easily worried.

Dawson chuckles. "Yeah. More than okay." He strokes Cal's hair, leaning in to give him a reassuring kiss. "I just need to get to the nightstand." Cal's nightstand, to be precise. Thankfully, they're close enough that he doesn't even have to get out of Cal's lap. He only has to lean sideways and stretch out his arm to reach the top drawer.

Warmth gathers in his cheeks when he realizes what kind of position he's landed in, nearly sprawled across Cal's lap with his ass on display. He ignores the sudden bout of self-consciousness, rolling his eyes at himself. With what he has planned, he can't afford to be self-conscious.

Cal looks like a lost puppy when Dawson slides back into his lap and holds up the half-empty bottle of lube he just fished out.

"It's to uh...aid the way," Dawson explains awkwardly, feeling like a virgin all over again, although Cal's cluelessness is kind of calming.

"Aid the way for..."

His face aflame, Dawson laughs. He can't stop it, the situation utterly ridiculous. Cal's confused face is all kinds of endearing. So endearing that Dawson has to kiss him. He just has to. He drags his lips across Cal's, flicking his tongue out to hear Cal gasp. Feeling brave—and also quite horny—he whispers, "I want to feel you inside me."

It takes a few moments for the meaning to sink in, but Dawson can tell when it does. Cal's fingers dig into his hips, bordering on painful, and he lets out a shuddering breath.

"I don't... I don't really know what to do."

Dawson's heart swells in his chest, almost too big for it. He doesn't know what he's doing either, but he won't say that. Instead, he kisses Cal again. "I'll show you."

Putting on a confident exterior that's completely incongruous with how nervous he is, Dawson flicks the bottle of lube open, meaning to squeeze some on his fingers, but he changes his mind at the last minute. He looks at Cal's hands still gripping his hips like he's afraid to let go, and a surge of desire to feel those fingers inside him overrides everything else.

"Give me your hand?"

Cal lets go of Dawson reluctantly, letting him take his shaking hand.

Dawson coats Cal's fingers with the lube and guides them between his ass cheeks, their gazes locked the whole time. He gasps when Cal touches his hole, more so from the coldness of the lube than anything else. Cal's eyes are wide and helpless as he waits for Dawson's instruction.

"Start—" Dawson's voice wavers, and he clears his throat. "Start with one. I...I don't relax easily, and it's been a while since we..." What's with not being able to finish a sentence, Jesus! "Just...go slow."

Cal's throat bobs as he swallows. "I don't want to hurt you."

Dawson's vision blurs, and despite his best efforts, a tear slides down his cheek. A shaky smile appears on his lips and he presses his forehead to Cal's. "You could never hurt me."

Cal lets out an anguished sound, but his hand stays where it is. "Dawson..."

"I trust you," Dawson says, feeling more words climb up his throat, begging to be released. He doesn't try to fight them, not when he feels them to the marrow of his bones. "I love you." He rakes his hand through Cal's hair, smiling at his bewildered expression. "I love you, Cal."

Cal's lips tremble when he says, "I've always loved you."

It doesn't make sense, it *can't* make sense, but...Dawson believes him. More tears escape as they kiss again, slow and earth-shatteringly tender. Dawson shudders when Cal's fingers start to move. He nearly forgot what they were about to do. Now that he's reminded, he can't wait.

He doesn't breathe as Cal drags the tips of his fingers through Dawson's crease, drawing another shudder out of him. Then, with excruciating slowness, he presses one finger against Dawson's opening, hesitating for a couple of seconds before pushing it in.

For a second, Dawson is scared he won't be able to relax after all, but he needn't have worried. His whole body lights up from the point of contact, sending tingles through his limbs which he feels all the way to his fingertips. If this is what it feels like now, he's not sure he'll survive what follows.

"Dawson?"

"Keep going," Dawson says breathlessly. "Please, keep going."

Cal does keep going. He slides the finger in and out, torturously slow, but it's a sweet kind of torture, one that has Dawson craving more*moremore*. He's never felt so desperate in his life.

Is this what it's supposed to be like?

Knowing it's too soon but growing impatient, Dawson moves his legs further apart, really settling on top of Cal's thighs. "More."

Cal gives a jerky nod. A second later, he's pulling his finger out and circling Dawson's opening with two. He watches Dawson's face closely as he applies pressure, his expression solemn and intense.

Dawson holds his breath, trying not to tense up against the sting that's sure to follow.

But there's no pain. Cal's fingers slide into him easily, lighting him up from the inside. A pleasant feeling of fullness spreads through his pelvis, bringing more tears to his eyes. Not wanting to alarm Cal, he closes them, putting his hands on Cal's shoulders as he gives himself over to the sensation, letting himself really feel it. He whines when Cal withdraws his fingers before sliding them back in.

"F-fuck." He grinds against the fingers. "God."

"Is it... Is it good?" Cal asks, drawing a punched out laugh from Dawson.

"So good." Dawson licks his lips, his breath catching when he sees the way Cal's watching him. "Another."

Cal hesitates. "But you said—"

"I know what I said." He lets his head drop to Cal's shoulder, drawing in a deep breath until Cal's scent fills his nose. "I underestimated how much I want you."

Those turn out to be the magic words.

Cal tilts Dawson's face up so he can plant a bruising kiss on his mouth, thrusting his tongue in and making Dawson keen with want. Simultaneously, he pushes inside with three fingers, brushing Dawson's prostate and driving him dangerously close to the edge.

This is crazy. Never in his life has Dawson felt like this, paralyzed with all-consuming want and feeling like he would die if Cal stopped touching him now, but also knowing he'll come if they don't slow down. He's never come untouched, either. Didn't think it was possible.

He trembles while Cal gently fucks his ass, biting down on his lip in hopes the pain will stave off his rapidly approaching climax. When he's not sure how much longer he can hold back, he reaches back to grasp Cal's wrist. Cal instantly stops.

"Now. Need you now."

It's a testament to how far gone Cal is that he doesn't try to argue. He nods frantically and withdraws his fingers, wiping them on the sheet before his hands return to Dawson's hips, steadying him as he rises up on his knees.

Reaching back, Dawson finds Cal's cock with a shaky hand, smiling when Cal's eyes widen almost comically. He shifts until the head of Cal's cock slides between his cheeks and rubs it against his entrance, hoping to see more of that wide-eyed look.

He gets his wish; Cal's head thunks back against the headboard, a guttural groan escaping him.

Dawson's hole pulses in anticipation, his cock spurting precome and leaving behind a trail where it's pressed against Cal's stomach. His thighs shake like he's run a marathon, and he knows he needs to do something before he embarrasses himself.

Relaxing as much as he can, he angles his hips and lets gravity do its work. At least that's the plan. It doesn't quite work out because Cal holds him tight, forcing him to slow down instead of just sinking down on his cock. It's a little annoying, given Dawson's predicament, but also unbearably sweet. God, he loves this man.

He wants to tell him again, the words on the tip of his tongue. They never make it out because all the air leaves Dawson's lungs as Cal's cock fills him inch by inch. It's not because of pain, not at all. There *should* be pain, there always is, quite a lot of it too.

Not this time.

Cal fits inside him like they were made for each other, like Dawson is only his to take.

"Are you okay?" Cal asks, sounding like each word takes monumental effort.

Dawson gives him a dopey smile. "I'm perfect."

Cal gives him a look that can only be described as loving. "Yes, you are."

It's such a cheesy line, and Dawson wants to laugh. The sound begins to form in his chest, but it comes out as a sob.

Cal's expression absolutely shatters. "Daw—"

Dawson throws himself at Cal, as much as is possible in his position, kissing him frantically and sloppily. Cal lets out a grunt of surprise, but it doesn't take long before he's kissing him back, outright devouring him and god, Dawson wants to be devoured, wants everything from Cal.

A string of moans fills the space between them, and it takes Dawson an embarrassingly long time to realize they're coming from him. At some point, he has no idea when, he started moving, rocking his hips and riding Cal's cock. Cal's hands are gripping his hips like a lifeline, urging him on as Dawson lifts up a couple of inches before sinking back down. Each time Cal fills him, an electric current shoots up Dawson's spine, every single nerve in his body tingling.

He picks up the pace, relishing the burn in his thighs and the way his body shakes with exertion. It feels insanely good, but he needs more, way more. Letting go of Cal's shoulders, he reaches for the headboard for better leverage. The movement forces him to lean forward, changing the angle, and the next time he sinks down, Cal hits his prostate dead on.

Dawson wails, gripping the headboard hard enough to hear it creak, and works his hips even harder, even faster, desperately looking for that angle that made him see stars. Every time he gets it right, his whole body jerks like he was electrocuted. His cock drags against Cal's stomach with each pump of his hips, the combined sensations propelling him to the edge with alarming speed.

"Cal. Cal." He's not asking anything. He just needs to say Cal's name, loving the way it feels rolling off his tongue.

Cal whimpers, burying his face in Dawson's neck, his parted lips resting against Dawson's overheated skin. He runs his hands along Dawson's spine, making him arch into the touch. One arm wraps around Dawson's waist, holding him tight, the fingers of his other hand threading through Dawson's hair.

It makes it harder to move, but Dawson doesn't care. He lets go of the headboard, wrapping his arms around Cal and working his hips as much as he can. The buildup is slower like this, but incessant, and it doesn't stop even when it finally peaks. Instead of a wave crashing against a cliff, it feels like a high tide, rising steadily until it reaches the shore.

Cal comes first, muffling a cry into Dawson's neck that will forever be seared in his brain. It's almost as if Cal's pleasure sets off Dawson's own, his orgasm hitting him out of nowhere. The gentle waves ripple through him one by one, seemingly never-ending. It feels like he's coming for ages, his mind foggy and his body weak. He slumps against Cal like a sack of grain, wanting nothing more than to close his eyes and drift off while Cal is holding him, kissing loving words into his neck. Another part of him wants to stay wide awake, to cherish this moment for as long as it lasts.

Cal clings to him like he has similar thoughts, his face still tucked into the crook of Dawson's neck. "Is it—is it always like this?" He sounds utterly wrecked, some of the aftershocks still running through him. Dawson can feel them in his own body.

"No." He wraps his arms around Cal tighter and just...holds on. "It's never like this."

Chapter 26

DAWSON WAKES UP ACHY and alone. Cal's side of the bed is already cold and there's a sweet smell coming from the kitchen. His stomach grumbles in response. The smoothie yesterday was barely sustaining.

He heaves himself up and makes a face when a certain part of his body protests. It's been a long time, so he's sore, but in the best way. It's a reminder of last night, of being held in Cal's arms and kissed to within an inch of his life. His cock is clearly on board, growing to full mast from the semi he woke up with, but Dawson's too drowsy to do anything about it.

He gathers the strength to brush his teeth and take a quick shower, ignoring his erection that just can't seem to take a hint. Bracing himself, he switches the knob to cold, hissing as the water becomes progressively cooler until his teeth chatter. It works, though, his erection flagging and Dawson finally starting to wake up.

Back in the bedroom, his gaze falls on divorce papers lying abandoned on the floor. Suddenly, he's not hungry anymore, the realization of how close he was to losing Cal twisting his stomach into knots. He marches towards the papers, tearing them in half before dumping them in the bin.

He throws on a fresh pair of boxer-briefs and yesterday's clothes and heads to the kitchen. He comes to a stop when he sees Cal, a frying pan in one hand and a spatula in the other, his blue shirt stretched taut over his broad shoulders.

The memory of what those shoulders felt like under his hands, strong and steady as Dawson held onto them, is enough to make his cock give a valiant twitch.

Stop it, you nympho.

He must make a noise, because Cal stops what he's doing and turns around.

"Good morning," he says, holding the spatula awkwardly in the air.

What a weirdo, Dawson thinks affectionately. "Morning." He makes his way over. "Pancakes?"

"Not quite." Cal nods towards the plate next to the stove stacked with what seem to be perfectly shaped—and hopefully edible—crepes.

"You made crepes? And the kitchen's still standing?" He looks around to check if anything's burned down.

Cal gives him a flat look. "That was uncalled for. I'll have you know I watched a YouTube video for common beginner mistakes to avoid." He pauses and looks away. "Also, this is the second batch. I burned the first one."

Dawson barks out a laugh. He feels warm on a visceral level and doesn't try to fight it when his feet carry him to Cal. He wraps his arms around Cal's middle and presses tight against his back.

"You're very sweet." He inhales Cal's sweet scent mixed with a trace of fabric softener.

Cal's back grows rigid. He drops what he's holding and places his hands on Dawson's, gently coaxing him to let go. Then he turns. "We need to talk."

A ball of lead drops into Dawson's stomach. He tries to calm himself down. It's gonna be fine. He got through to Cal yesterday—he can do it again.

"Can it wait until after breakfast? I'm famished."

After a second of hesitation, Cal relents. "Yeah."

With a relieved sigh, Dawson helps him carry the plates and condiments to the table, despite Cal's protests. Now that his stomach is onboard again, he slathers his crepe in raspberry jam and chocolate sauce, his mouth filling with saliva.

He moans around the first mouthful. "These are amazing. You're getting the hang of this."

Cal's blush is the most adorable thing ever. "Maybe next time I'll try donuts." Donut, who strategically put himself between them in hopes of bribing out food, lifts his head, ears twitching. Cal chuckles, reaching down to pet him, but Donut thinks it's food and licks his hand instead. "No, not talking about you."

Everything about this—the breakfast, them eating together, Cal baby-talking the dog—it's all so domestic, so peaceful. It's Dawson's dream come true, and hell will freeze over before he gives it up.

"Wanna move to the sofa before we start?" he asks when they've polished off their plates and Cal is watching him expectantly. "Because this kind of feels like an intervention."

Cal's expression becomes pinched. "I'd rather not. I need to think straight and I can't do that when I'm close to you." He says it like it's something to be ashamed of, to be so affected by another person. Maybe Dawson should feel bad about it, but he finds the admission flattering, and more than a little arousing. Also, more than a little relatable.

"You shouldn't say things like that, or we won't get much talking done," he says, the implication heavy in his tone.

"Dawson," Cal says, like a warning. A reprimand.

"Sorry. I'm nervous. You're not going to leave, are you? You promised—"

"I'm not leaving. Not unless you ask me to."

Dawson relaxes a little, but the relief is short-lived.

"You should," Cal says. "You should ask me to leave."

Instead of going off the rails like he's tempted to, Dawson takes a deep breath and tries to recall the conversation with Ash. Tries to explain it in a way that will make Cal believe him, truly believe him, and make him give up on the idea that Dawson is somehow better off without him.

"Maybe I should," he agrees. Cal's shoulders sink. "But that's not going to happen."

Cal chances a look at him and shakes his head. "How can you do this? After everything I've done, how can you even look at me, let alone..." His voice cracks, and Dawson is out of his chair and kneeling in front of him in a flash, his hands on Cal's knees.

He waits until he has Cal's full attention, then waves at the table. "Because of this."

Cal's brows furrow. He looks at the table. "Because of...crepes?"

"Yeah, Cal. Because of crepes," Dawson says, letting affection bleed into his voice until it's dripping with it. "And French toast and pancakes, even the burned ones. Because of dick paintings and Lady Gaga. Because of pink towels and your sugar obsession. Because of Donut." On cue, Donut whines, nudging his cold, wet snout against Dawson's hand. "Yes, you." After he scratches Donut's ear, he turns back to Cal. "Because you're *you*, Cal."

He struggles to read Cal's expression which is somewhere between wary, hopeful, and terrified. But then his whole body sags, as though he's finally done fighting this, and Dawson feels the relief in his bones.

"It was not a dick painting," Cal deadpans, and Dawson wants to laugh, his body vibrating with it, but he senses that Cal is just trying to deflect.

So he goes on.

"You're asking how I can do this? I don't know how *not* to do it. I don't know how to look at you and not think how much I love you and how much I want to spend the rest of my life with you." He can feel himself getting choked up, so he pushes on before he breaks down and starts crying. Again. "And I know that you probably think I'm ignoring red flags, pretending that the past never happened, but that's not the case. Maybe in the beginning, when you came back from the hospital, I was trying to shove those disturbing thoughts into a box and dig a very deep hole for it. But I open that box whenever I talk to Ash and now...now there's nothing in the box anymore. I remember everything, but it doesn't scare me anymore."

"It scares me," Cal admits, so quietly Dawson almost doesn't catch it. "I don't even remember it, but it scares me to death."

God, I love you so fucking much.

"And that's exactly why you *don't* have to be scared. Before, you'd never have cared, you'd never have apologized or regretted what you did." Cal ducks his head in shame, only proving Dawson's point. "See? You're not *him*, Cal. Whoever the man I spent the last six years with was, he wasn't you."

Cal releases a shuddering breath. "You're making it really hard to argue." He makes it sound like a complaint.

"Then don't."

Cal nods, and reaches for Dawson, cradling his face between his palms. "I swear, I'm going to spend the rest of my life proving that I'm worthy of you."

Dawson surges up to kiss him, his heart soaring with happiness. "Just keep making crepes and we're good." One more kiss, and then he rises to his feet, his knees creaking. "I'm at the shelter today. You want to come with?"

Cal shakes his head. "I think I'm going to pay Ellis a visit."

"Isn't he at work?"

"I have my card to let me in."

Oh boy. "Don't be mad at him. He just did what I asked him to."

Cal doesn't look convinced. "We should still talk."

Ah, well. You win some, you lose some. Dawson will owe Ellis the best dinner of all time.

"Okay. I'm gonna get ready." He groans when Donut brushes against his leg. He'd completely forgotten about him. He's the worst dog dad ever. "Shit. Could you walk Donut before you go? I don't want to be late."

"Already have," Cal says. "But I'll take him again later."

Dawson can't help it. He kisses him again. And one more time after that. "Love you."

Cal caresses his cheek. "Love you too."

Chapter 27

AFTER CAL'S UBER DROPS him off at the office building, he rings Ellis' number.

"Cal?"

"Hey. I'm downstairs. Are you free?"

"Downstairs? As in here? In the building?" Ellis asks, sounding alarmed.

"Yes."

"Jesus," he breathes. "Can you call next time?"

"I'm calling now."

"That's not—" He cuts himself off and groans. "I'm at a meeting. Come on up, Amanda will let you into my office. Can you wait half an hour?"

Since he's already here...

"I can wait."

"Good. Do you have your card?"

"I do." He fishes the card out of his pocket. "Which floor is it?"

"27th. I'll let Amanda know you're coming," Ellis says and hangs up.

Cal can't blame him for being short with him. He is ambushing him after all. It serves Ellis right for keeping such important things from him. But he's not here to argue with Ellis about what he should or shouldn't have done. He just wants to talk.

Entering the lobby, Cal gives the place a sweeping glance. If he was the workaholic that everyone claims, something here should ring a bell;

but so far, nothing. He heads towards the lifts, swiping his card and pressing the button for the 27th floor.

The lift is slower than the one in his apartment building, and when the doors open, a blond woman in a pantsuit is waiting for him.

"Hi," she says, flashing him a grin.

He steps out. "Hello. Amanda?"

"The one and only." She studies him with interest. It's not hard to guess what she's thinking.

"You used to be my PA."

Her grin widens. "Correct. Now I'm bossing your equally neurotic brother around."

"Shouldn't he be bossing you around?" Cal doesn't know much about running a company, but he thought he understood that.

Throwing her head back, Amanda laughs. "Oh, honey."

Did he say something funny? He doesn't dwell on it, following Amanda when she beckons him down the hallway. She leads him to the very end, then uses her card to open the door with Ellis' nameplate on it.

The office isn't as big as he'd expected, but it's neat and bright, the large window in place of a wall giving it plenty of natural light.

"This is nice." So, this is the place where he was spending most of his time instead of being with Dawson? What was he thinking?

Amanda chuckles. "I'd say so. It used to be yours. Tickles your memory?"

He takes the room in, waiting for something to click. "Not really, no."

"Hm. Fascinating." She gives him a once-over. "Not gonna lie—you've been the main source of gossip here lately."

Not surprising. "That's fair." He looks Amanda over. From their short interaction, he got the impression she's rather straightforward and isn't trying to handle Cal with kid gloves just because he doesn't remember things. "Can I ask you something?"

She opens her palms. "Shoot."

"Was I a good boss?"

She snorts. "Before or after you had your coffee?"

At the mention of coffee, Cal's stomach rebels. "Was there a difference?"

"Oh yeah," she says, snickering, then shrugs. "You were fine. We got along, at least. You were pretty generous with Christmas bonuses, but acted like a dick when things didn't go your way."

"Oh." That's actually much nicer than what he'd expected to hear.

Amanda pats his shoulder. "I have to make some phone calls. You gonna be okay here?"

"Yes. Thank you."

"Holler if you need me."

Cal acknowledges her with a nod before she disappears, closing the door behind her. He makes his way around the meticulously organized desk. God, Ellis is a neat freak. He flops down into the chair, spinning it around to face the window. The view is nice. Not as nice as the one from their apartment, since their apartment overlooks the ocean, but still. Cal checks the clock. If he knew he'd be waiting, he'd have brought his e-reader.

Thinking of what he can do with the time, his thoughts inevitably steer towards Dawson and last night. God, last night...

The reaction of his body is instantaneous. His skin flushes hot and he needs to undo the top button of his shirt, even though the air in the office is quite cool. His lips start to tingle, remembering what it felt like to kiss Dawson so passionately, so thoroughly. Remembering what his skin tasted like, and how much he wanted to taste him everywhere.

If he closes his eyes, he can still feel Dawson, the weight of him as he straddled Cal, gyrating his hips and taking Cal to heights he never thought possible.

All the while Cal lay there like a log, doing absolutely nothing to make Dawson feel the same pleasure he felt. Although Dawson seemed to enjoy himself, it wasn't Cal's doing. It's just...Cal didn't know what to do. He followed his instincts, and at first it was easy, but once Dawson took charge, he was lost.

Maybe there's a manual?

With renewed hope, Cal consults his best friend—Mr Google.

He types *'How to make love?'*

The very first page tells him he needs to make his question more specific.

'How to make love to a man?'

This time, the results are a bit more accurate, but not what he needs.

'How does a man make love to a man?'

It turns out that Mr Google doesn't know everything because the results are almost identical to the previous one. The only thing he gets are articles telling women how to make love to men.

He tries one more time, utilizing the word Dawson once called him for listening to Lady Gaga.

'Making gay love'

The results are completely different this time. For one, there are no articles. Instead, all the links seem to lead to videos. Curious, Cal clicks on the first link called *Passionate Love Making Gay Porn Videos.* Once the page loads, he nearly drops his phone.

Well...that's...

He did *not* expect that. Did not expect to see naked men doing...all kinds of things. In all kinds of positions. And are those handcuffs?

On the other hand, a visual will definitely be helpful. Maybe he should watch one or two? Just in case.

By the fifth video, it's clear he has a *lot* to learn. Damn, he had no idea some of these things were physically possible. Maybe they're not for him. The pinnacle of his flexibility is bending down to tie his shoes. But there's still stuff he could do.

One thing in particular catches his attention. He's not sure what it's called, but he saw it in the previous video too, and his pants have been quite uncomfortable since.

This video is better, the two men taking it slower, giving Cal more time to take in the details. The man currently spread out on his stomach on the bed also looks a little like Dawson—a similar build and hair just a shade darker. The resemblance makes Cal's dick throb, especially when the other man—his hair dark like Cal's—settles himself behind his partner, grabbing both his cheeks. He massages them gently, pressing a kiss to each, then spreads them.

Cal swallows, gripping the phone as he imagines himself in the dark-haired man's place. He imagines doing everything that the men do, imagines telling Dawson to spread his legs wider so he can have better access. Imagines pressing a kiss to the base of his spine before sticking his tongue out and running it down his crease. Imagines the sounds Dawson would make as Cal licks him at the center, swirling his tongue around his opening. He imagines—

The office door flies open.

"Sorry for being late. The meeting went a bit—" Ellis comes to a halt, his eyes like saucers, and he slams the door shut. "Are you watching porn?!"

Cal pauses the video, putting the phone down and crossing his legs. "It's for research."

"Research."

"Yes.

"Can't you do 'research' at home?" Ellis asks in a hiss.

"I was bored."

"Bored."

"Why are you repeating everything I say?"

Ellis throws his hands up, his voice a pitch higher. "I don't know! Maybe because you show up announced—"

"I called you when I was downstairs.

"—and watch porn in my office, where anyone can hear you! I don't want to be explaining this!"

"Did you hear anything from the outside?" Cal asks.

"That's beside the point!"

Cal sighs, realizing how disrespectful he's being. This *is* Ellis' workplace. "Sorry."

Ellis runs a hand over his face and spreads his arms. "Well, I'm here. Is everything okay? How did it go with Dawson yesterday?"

"We had sex."

Ellis stares at him. "Uh...okay. I was kinda hoping you'd talk it out first."

"We did. Twice, actually. This morning too."

"And? All good?"

Not really, but he promised Dawson. "All good."

"I'm happy to hear that." A small smile flashes across Ellis' lips before the corners turn down. "What do you need from me? Came to rip me a new one?"

Cal shakes his head. "I need to talk to someone who knew me before. To...understand why I did what I did. What kind of person I was." At least now his erection is sufficiently killed. He was wondering how he'd get out of the office without alerting everyone to his situation.

"My lunch break isn't long enough for that but...sure. I can do that." Ellis levels him with a look. "If you promise me not to beat yourself up about what you learn."

That sounds delightful. "I'll do my best. I promised Dawson."

"Good." He nods towards Cal's phone on the desk. "I'll probably regret asking this, but what's with the porn?"

Cal heaves a sigh. "Yesterday was amazing. I'm just not sure I did it right."

"It's pretty easy to tell if you did it right or not."

Is it? If Ellis thinks it's easy, maybe he can tell him what to do. "Could you teach me?"

"Teach you what?"

"How to have sex."

Ellis takes a staggering step back. He closes his eyes, pulling a deep breath in. "There's so much wrong with that sentence, especially when spoken to your brother."

"But—"

"Let me make it clear that we each play for a different team. I sleep with women. Dawson very much isn't a woman."

Cal thinks back on the videos he watched. "But the principle is the same. You still need to—"

"No. *Hell* no!" Ellis steps back until he's pressed against the door. "I'm not talking to you about gay sex."

"But—"

"Lalala, I can't hear you!" Ellis screams, covering his ears.

Cal huffs. He'll have to make do with the videos after all.

If he doesn't count the few times Ellis visited him at the hospital, this is the first time Cal's spent time with him, just the two of them. Under different circumstances, he would even enjoy it. Hopefully, after they get this conversation over with, that will be it. No more diving into the past, just as Dawson said.

Cal already knows the basics about his family and childhood from Dawson, but it's different to hear it from someone who was there, someone he grew up with.

When Dawson told him about the tight ship Cal's dad led and about his mom walking out when he was a kid, it left him rather cold. He didn't know these people and couldn't quite summon an appropriate reaction.

Listening to Ellis gets a reaction out of him alright, but only because he can tell how affected Ellis is by all that's happened. Part of him almost wants to reach across the table and hold his hand, but he doesn't think it would be appreciated.

"I'm not a shrink," Ellis says. "And I have no intention of defending you. No way. But honestly, looking back at the way we were raised? It's not quite surprising you turned out to be...you know."

"You turned out fine."

Ellis laughs, but there's no humor in it. "You have no idea how fucked up I am, Cal."

Cal has a hard time believing that. "Are you an alcoholic?"

Ellis lifts a shoulder. "I enjoy a drink or two."

"But it's not an addiction."

"No."

"Have you been in a relationship?"

"Not a serious one."

Cal wants to point out how Ellis likes to avoid answering a simple yes and no, but doesn't. "Have you hurt any of your partners?"

Ellis looks at him. "There have been times I was a jerk."

"But have you hurt them? Intentionally. Repeatedly."

Ellis sighs. "No."

"Then you're not nearly as messed up as you think you are."

"I have my issues."

"Doesn't everyone? You might not be perfect, but you're a good person. You were there for Dawson and you didn't even know him that well. You took care of my screw-ups, dealt with the police and the company and never asked for anything."

"You're family," Ellis says, fidgeting and avoiding Cal's gaze. It reminds Cal of Dawson, and how he always looks uncomfortable when faced with a compliment.

"Based on what we just spent nearly an hour talking about, it's clear that blood doesn't mean much. I was terrible to you our whole life. Our mom walked out on us and our dad was a controlling asshole." A morbid thought crosses Cal's mind. "You might be right. Someone was bound to turn out like him. I'm just glad it wasn't both of us."

"There's no one at this table who's like him."

Cal smiles at the hidden meaning in Ellis' words. "I hope so."

The conversation steers more towards small talk territory, but it's surprisingly pleasant. Cal might be the only one who lost his memory, but it feels like they're getting to know each other properly for the first time. It's like Ellis said—they were never close.

"Read any interesting books lately?" Ellis asks with a sly grin.

"I started reading *Me Before You*, but couldn't finish it after Dawson told me it doesn't have a happy ending."

"I thought you were only into fantasy."

"Mainly, not only."

"Why are you reading hetero stuff, by the way?"

"Huh?"

Ellis gives him a curious look. "You like dick. Why are you not reading about two men instead?"

That's...actually a brilliant idea. Why hadn't he thought of that before?

"Any recommendations?"

Ellis seems to choke on air, and he pulls in a few gasping breaths before he speaks. "Uh, no? Ask your husband. You're on the same team."

"Team?"

Closing his eyes as if in pain, Ellis says, "Gay, Cal. You're both gay."

"Oh. There are teams for that?"

If Ellis' reaction is anything to go by, that wasn't the right thing to ask. He mumbles something about marbles. "Let's talk about something else before I lose my mind."

"Okay. How is the new apartment? Have you settled in yet?" When he talked to him a few weeks ago, Ellis was moving again.

Ellis relaxes after that, telling Cal about his new place—which he bought this time, since Cal had made it clear that he has no intention of going back to work—and complaining about how everything on the Coast is pretentious and snail-paced. They don't get to talk about much else, because Ellis checks his watch and swears, getting up in haste.

Not wanting to get him in trouble, Cal lets him go, albeit reluctantly. All this time he's been focused on Dawson and repairing their relationship, but now he thinks that he could do more. Maybe he can still save the relationship with his brother. Or, more accurately, actually have one for the first time.

Cal checks the clock. He still has time before Dawson gets home, and now that he's not under strict supervision, he might sneak some hot chocolate and a donut in.

He orders an Uber to *Lost and Ground*. It's still lunchtime, so the place is busy, but Gabe waves at him excitedly when he spots him approaching the counter. The line is quite long but moves quickly, and soon it's Cal's turn.

"Look who the cat dragged in." Gabe gives him a sunny smile. "Where's your better half?"

"Working." *Better half.* He likes that expression.

"Ah, I see." Gabe waggles his eyebrows. "Thought you'd sneak out and get a dose when he's not keeping a tight leash on you, huh?"

Cal smiles sheepishly. "Yeah, but I didn't come straight here, I was with my brother. Ellis is now running the company, so I don't have to." He feels really selfish for dumping everything on him, even if Ellis said it was okay. He seemed stressed today. True, he always does, but having to move interstate and find a new home definitely added to it.

Cal must have said something strange, because Gabe looks at him with slightly wide eyes.

"Ellis," he repeats slowly. "Tall, dark, and broody?"

Cal chuckles at the description. "Um, yes? That would be my brother."

Gabe lets out a small groan and laughs. "I should've known. You're practically twins."

"Not really..." They do have the same hair and eyes, almost the same height, but Ellis' features are a little sharper, his face slimmer, and he shaves. Works out more, too, if his shoulders are anything to go by. Cal definitely needs to start exercising more. "You've met him?"

Stupid question, but Gabe, the saint, doesn't point it out. "He's popped in for a coffee a time or two."

That shouldn't be surprising. Ellis mentioned his apartment is nearby; it makes sense he'd find the cafe at some point.

"Anyway, what are you after?" Gabe holds up a finger. "Wait. One hot chocky and one donut?"

"Yes, please." He's really predictable, isn't he?

"To have here?"

Cal looks around, the place swarming with people. He doesn't like people. "I'll take it away." The weather is nice. He might walk home instead of calling for a ride again. Stay on the beach for a bit.

"Sure thing."

Gabe grabs his donut, then scribbles his order on a takeaway cup, passing it along to Zeke.

Once he's paid and got his items, Cal moves out of the way so he doesn't hold up the line. He exchanges a few words with Zeke, who's too busy pumping out drinks to chit-chat.

Once Cal has his hot chocolate and donut, he waves goodbye to Gabe and Zeke as he walks out. Adjusting the takeaway cup to take a sip, a black scribble catches his attention, and he smiles. Gabe left him a message! He's never done that before.

If you don't like your story, rewrite it.

His smile slips. Gabe's message is disturbingly fitting to Cal's struggle. It also reminds him of Dawson's insistence that they should start from scratch. They've been writing a new story this whole time, but that doesn't erase the past. Except...Dawson said he doesn't think of the past anymore. There was nothing in his eyes that suggested he wasn't telling the truth. And Cal believed him, he did. He does believe him. So, why is it not enough? Is it always going to be like this? Will he always feel so damn helpless and guilty?

A sudden need to see Dawson overtakes him. He checks his phone. Dawson won't be home for at least another hour.

Cal looks at his full hands. Well, he can't show up with all this anyway, Dawson would let him have it. He'll just have to wait and try not to spend the whole time thinking of Dawson and last night.

He doesn't have much hope.

Chapter 28

"I'm home!" Cal announces when he gets back to the apartment an hour later. He doesn't get an answer from Dawson, but Donut comes barreling towards him from the bedroom, butt shaking and tongue out.

Cal drops into a crouch, laughing when Donut all but flies into his arms. "Hello, you. Miss me?" It's always surreal whenever Donut is being nice to him, especially after he made it his life mission to terrorize Cal. It would seem that bribery did the trick, despite Dawson's protests. It's almost worth Donut's toxic gas. "Where's your dad?"

Donut pants happily and takes off, running back to the bedroom. Chuckling, Cal follows him, finding Donut sitting down in front of the closed bathroom door. The sound of the shower reaches Cal's ears, and he smiles proudly. Donut actually understood him.

"Good boy." Cal scritches behind his ear, getting a gust of dog breath in his face as Donut starts panting again. Cal huffs, dropping down so he can use both hands. His heart melts at the happy sounds Donut is making before he flops onto his side and shows his belly. "Well, aren't you demanding?"

Too busy being Donut's personal scratcher, Cal must have missed the shower switching off. He jumps when the bathroom door opens and Dawson steps out in a cloud of steam.

Wearing nothing but a towel around his waist.

Dawson staggers back with a startled yelp, bumping into the door frame.

"Fucking Christ." He clutches a hand to his chest—his very naked chest, droplets of water rolling down his skin. "You gave me a fright." He tries to scowl but ends up laughing when he takes in the scene in front of him. "Am I interrupting?"

Donut chooses that moment to roll over and waddle towards Dawson to lick his freshly showered feet.

"Thanks for that," Dawson quips, then looks at Cal. "Thought you'd be home before me. I almost texted you."

"Why didn't you?" Cal stands up, forcing his eyes to stay on Dawson's face instead of ogling him like a pervert.

Dawson shrugs, licking his lips. "I didn't want to come across as needy. You don't have to report to me whenever you want to do something."

A sense of dread settles in Cal's stomach, chasing away all the warmth that started building inside him.

Is this something he used to do to Dawson? Demanded to know where Dawson was when he wasn't at home?

A citrusy scent hits his nose when Dawson takes a step towards him, his brows pinched with worry. "Hey. Something wrong?"

"No," he lies. There's plenty wrong, but he made Dawson a promise. He's not going to ruin it by digging into the past when he said he wouldn't. "How was your day?"

Realizing how close they are, he walks towards the bed to sit down. He needs some space. He can't think with Dawson so close to him, practically naked.

If Dawson finds his behavior strange, he doesn't show it. "Well, I got peed on, hence the early shower." He chuckles, and Cal gives an obligatory laugh. "Everyone's asking about Donut. I had to show them pictures. Again."

At the sound of his name, Donut lets out a whine, tilting his head.

"What if we took him for a visit some day?"

"I don't know about that," Dawson says. "He could freak out and think we're taking him back. He liked the staff, but..."

"Oh. I didn't think of that."

"It's okay. It was a good idea. So, how did it go with Ellis?"

"He wasn't happy I barged in on him, but we went out for lunch. It was...nice. A little weird, but nice."

"Look at you, hanging out with your baby bro," Dawson says with a laugh.

Referring to Ellis as his brother doesn't feel natural, but he hopes that in time, it will.

"It's strange to think about him like that. He's so..."

"Put-together? Serious? Responsible?"

"Mature," Cal says, a little annoyed. Why does hearing Dawson name Ellis' character qualities suddenly bother him?

"Same thing," Dawson says with an eye roll and goes to the dresser. "What about the office? What did you think? Did it, you know, feel familiar?" There's something strange in the way he says it.

"No. Not at all. Not even when I met my assistant."

Dawson seems to relax, and he rummages through the drawer until he pulls out a pair of black joggers. Cal tries to enjoy the unrestrained view of his exposed skin while it lasts.

"Amanda? Is she Ellis' PA now?"

"You know her?"

"We've met a couple of times. She's nice."

"Yeah. A little intimidating, though."

Dawson laughs. "Yeah, she's got the vibe."

"Is it true that she was the first one notified about my accident?"

"Uh, yeah," Dawson says, eyes on the floor. "She called Ellis, and he called me."

A surge of anger fills Cal's chest. Not at Dawson, never at Dawson, but at himself. His expression must give him away, because Dawson puts away the clothes he picked and starts towards him.

"Let it go, Cal. Or it will eat you up."

Yeah, that ship has sailed. "I hate him," he bites out. "The guy who did all those things."

Dawson watches him, his eyes getting a little glassy. He sticks out his hand, palm up. "Give me your phone."

Cal does, a little confused. He watches Dawson's thumbs fly over the screen, doing who knows what. He hands it to Cal when he's done. "There. Now if anything were to happen, I'll be the first to know."

Cal's heart flutters, overflowing with the love he has for this man. His husband.

"Thank you."

Dawson smiles. "You're welcome. You can't have Amanda sorting that stuff out anyway, if you're not going back."

"I'm not," he confirms, just in case Dawson is still wondering about it.

"You'll have a lot of free time now. Maybe you can finally kick-start your career as a future best-selling author."

"Very funny."

"I'm serious! One step at a time, and before you know it, it's there."

"One step at a time and you're having an exhibition of your art," Cal shoots back.

"Ouch. Guess I walked into that one."

"Yup."

They both chuckle, and the conversation stagnates after that. Cal finds himself greedily taking in Dawson's body now that there's nothing to distract him. The memories of last night suck him under, making it difficult to refrain from pulling Dawson into his lap and ravishing him right there.

He *always* wants to touch Dawson, and he'd been doing just fine managing those urges and improper thoughts. But then last night happened, and every single thread Cal had on his self-control snapped like someone cut through them. Now it's torture whenever he so much as looks at Dawson. To have him stand here, right in front of Cal, all but naked and smelling like delicious dessert, is temptation without mercy.

Cal's face must show it all, every sinful thought, because Dawson smirks, an endearing blush spreading over his neck and cheeks, and asks, "See something you like?"

What a ridiculous question. Cal almost laughs. "I like everything about you, Dawson. I thought that was obvious."

For a moment, he fears he said something wrong again. Dawson stares at him, open-mouthed and wide-eyed. His blush darkens, his chest rising and falling faster than before.

"Fucking hell," Dawson utters, then he's ripping the towel off and climbing into Cal's lap.

"What—"

Dawson takes his mouth in a kiss that exorcizes every rational thought—not that there were many to begin with—leaving only the most primal instincts behind. Having Dawson naked in his lap while he's still fully dressed does something to Cal, making his blood boil and his skin tingle wherever they're touching. Even so, he'd rather be naked as well, to be able to soak up every ounce of heat radiating from Dawson's body.

Dawson rips his mouth away, panting into the space between them. "You can't expect me to keep my cool when you say shit like that." His pupils are blown wide, and he's breathing heavily, gazing down at Cal like he wants to eat him up.

I did this to him, Cal thinks. The thought is addicting.

"Sorry?" he says, not meaning it in the least.

Dawson snorts. "No, you're not." He surges forward, the next kiss less savage but more desperate.

Cal wraps his arms around him and opens up, moaning when their tongues slide against each other. He could easily spend his whole life just kissing Dawson. Maybe he can. They're writing a new story, after all.

Dawson withdraws again, his eyes narrowing. "Why do you taste like chocolate?"

Busted. "Well..."

"Have you been to the cafe without me?"

"Maybe?" He gives Dawson his most innocent look.

Dawson huffs, shaking his head. "Menace." It's hard to take him seriously when he proceeds to suck Cal's soul out with his kisses, or when his fingers impatiently start working Cal's shirt open, pushing it off his shoulders like the fabric caused him some major offense.

"Fuck." The word comes out as a hoarse gasp. He moans when Cal's hand wraps around his length, and he presses open-mouthed kisses along Cal's jaw and chin. "What are you doing to me?"

You're one to talk. "Making love?" Tightening his grip, Cal gives Dawson's cock a firm stroke. God, he hopes he's doing it right. He's rewarded with a soft whimper and fingers digging into his shoulders. Reassured, he does it again, finding a rhythm that has Dawson rolling his hips into Cal's fist.

"Yeah. Yeah, you are." Another moan, louder than before, and then Dawson's glazed over eyes find Cal's. "Get lube."

Cal's movements stutter. "Isn't it too soon?" He didn't miss Dawson's subtle wince this morning when he walked into the kitchen.

The smile Dawson gives would light up a dark room. He gently brushes Cal's hair back, cupping the back of his neck. "I'm good, Cal. We took it nice and slow. I'm all good, I promise. And I want you."

It's hard to argue when Dawson is looking at him with heat that could rival the sun, and his cock is hard as steel in Cal's hand, throbbing under his touch. And there is, of course, the obvious fact that he's straddling Cal naked, all but offering himself up to him.

Cal never said no to him. He's not sure he ever could. He certainly can't now.

"I want you too. Always." He wouldn't know how to stop.

Dawson makes a noise in the back of his throat, like a wounded animal, before he's on Cal—his lips, his hands, his scent—clinging to him so tight there's no telling their heartbeats apart. Cal could drown in him—fuck, he wants to drown in him. Become part of Dawson just as Dawson is part of him.

They're so lucky to have been given a second chance. *Cal* is so lucky. He's never been so glad to have lost his memories. If he had one wish, he'd wish for them to never come back.

He slides his hands under Dawson's thighs, still slightly wet from the shower. Planting his feet firmly on the floor, he begins to stand up and promptly falls back when Dawson lets out a cry of protest.

"Whoa! Are you mad?!"

"I want to carry you. Like people do in the movies."

Dawson stares at him with disbelief. "You're not carrying my 68 kilo ass anywhere anytime soon."

"But—"

"No buts. I'm not calling you an ambulance and explaining to them how you got hurt."

"I've been exercising," Cal says, aware he's pouting.

Dawson sighs, kissing him apologetically. "I know. And I promise, when you're all healed up, I'll let you carry me up damn Everest. Bridal style. But not now."

Cal can live with that. "Deal."

Dawson shakes his head fondly. "I should really cut down on your Netflix time."

"You watch it too."

"Yeah, but unlike you, I have common sense."

"That was mean," Cal grumbles, pretending to be hurt.

Dawson's teeth sink into his lower lip. He ducks his head, looking up at Cal through the dark fan of his eyelashes. "It was, wasn't it?" A shy smile grows on his lips. "Let me make it up to you." His gaze locked with Cal's, he removes himself from Cal's lap and slowly, so slowly, sinks to his knees between Cal's legs.

If this happened yesterday, Cal would have no clue what Dawson is doing, but his short educational session in Ellis' office has given him quite a clear idea.

"Dawson."

When he watched the videos, he imagined doing this to Dawson, wanting to find out what kind of sounds he could draw out of him simply by using his mouth.

But seeing Dawson on his knees—*for him*—leaves him at a complete loss. Well, maybe not a complete loss. His body seems to have opinions on the current development. He feels his jeans tighten around his groin, all his blood rushing in the same direction.

"Tell me if you don't like something," Dawson says and starts undoing Cal's jeans.

Cal swallows a hysterical laugh. As if he could ever not like something Dawson does.

He watches, speechless and hardly breathing, as Dawson gets the fly open and hooks his fingers in Cal's underwear, giving it a tug. Cal bites back a moan when the fabric rubs over his cock, fully hard and only inches from Dawson's face. He has to grip the edge of the mattress for support.

Dawson's expression is a mixture of nervous and aroused when he glances at Cal before he leans forward, his breath gusting over Cal's sensitive cock. Then it's not just Dawson's breath, but his wet, hot lips wrapping around him in an imitation of a kiss.

The sound that comes from Cal isn't even human. It's something broken, and desperate, and for whatever reason, it makes Dawson's face light up in delight. He gives Cal a grin that's just short of feral and dives back in. Except this time, he opens wide and swallows Cal down, half of his cock disappearing inside Dawson's beautiful, talented mouth.

Time ceases to exist. Dawson's lips are tight around him, his tongue slick and hot and absolutely sinful as it works Cal over. Sometimes he pulls up for a breath, but then he's back at it, slowly taking Cal apart. Each time he sinks down on Cal's cock is pure bliss, and whenever he pulls back, his cheeks hollowing, it's all Cal can do to keep still, to not thrust into his mouth like he never wants to leave it.

Dawson does something particularly wicked with his tongue, and one of Cal's hands shoots up, threading through Dawson's hair. The need to touch him is overwhelming, and he pets Dawson's hair, his thumb brushing the soft skin behind Dawson's ear.

A whimper leaves his throat when Dawson suddenly pulls off. His lips are obscenely red, his eyes hooded.

Cal snatches his hand back. "I'm sorry. Did I—"

Dawson shakes his head. "It's okay. You can touch me. Just...don't hold me in place. I have a shitty gag reflex."

Sagging with relief, Cal's hand reluctantly returns to Dawson's hair. He loves the feel of it, so silky and thick, and always smelling like citrus.

His head falls back when Dawson takes him in his mouth again, setting up the same leisurely pace as before. It's the sweetest kind of torture, leaving Cal hovering on a precipice that could drive him mad with want. His thighs tremble when Dawson rubs his palms over them, one hand stroking the skin of his inner thigh and the other finding his hip.

Dawson pulls off with a particularly powerful suck, his lips brushing over the head as he fixes his dark eyes on Cal.

"Good?" he asks, voice absolutely wrecked. There's a glint in his eye that tells Cal he knows all too well what kind of effect he has on him.

"Incredible." Now that Dawson's mouth isn't driving him to the edge of sanity, his mind clears up a bit. "I want to do that to you." He wants it more than he wants to feel Dawson's mouth again.

Surprise fills Dawson's features. "Yeah?" Cal nods eagerly. "Okay. Um...maybe like this?" He gestures at the position Cal's in. "Or I can lie back, but it's harder if you have to lie on your stomach."

"Like this is perfect." He couldn't care less, but whatever gets Dawson's cock in his mouth faster works for him.

They rise to their feet, Cal shedding the rest of his clothes. He guides Dawson to sit at the edge, then bends down for a kiss. He means for it to be quick and chaste, but Dawson makes a noise that sets something inside him off, and then he's plundering Dawson's mouth like a starving man.

He's already out of breath when he finally pulls away and drops to his knees, imitating their previous position. Dawson seems half-gone already, but he sobers up a little when Cal's fingers curl around his erection.

Uncertainty makes Cal's stomach clench. "I'm sorry if I'm not very good. I watched some videos, but they weren't very detailed." Maybe he can just replicate whatever Dawson did to him? Not that he remembers much; he was too lost to the sensation to focus on the mechanics.

"Just be careful with the teeth and—wait. Videos?" Dawson blinks at him slowly, his eyes going wide. "You mean you watched *porn*?"

"A little. Ellis came in and he yelled at me."

"You watched porn in Ellis' office?!"

He thought Ellis was overreacting when he found Cal like that, but judging by Dawson's reaction, he might've been wrong.

"I was waiting for him to finish a meeting. I couldn't stop thinking about last night and wanted to make sure I did it right."

Dawson's mouth opens and closes, then he lets out a bark of laughter. "I think that's one of the most disturbing, sweetest things I've heard."

"I'll tell Ellis you said that."

Dawson's answering chuckle transforms into a soft moan when Cal presses a kiss to the tip of his cock. It's hot and a little wet, and when Cal's tongue darts out, he tastes something bitter and sweet. His eyes slide shut—he knows he should probably keep them open to gauge Dawson's responses, but he can't help it.

Praying that this is going to be one of those things he can wing by letting his muscle memory take over, he parts his lips and takes Dawson as deep as he can, wanting to feel him everywhere. He can't take all of him, but it's okay because Dawson is perfect in his mouth, stretching his lips in a way that feels strangely satisfying.

Cal starts bobbing his head, hollowing his cheeks when he pulls up just as he saw Dawson do. It earns him a beautiful moan, and Dawson buries his hands in Cal's hair, giving it a tug. Cal answers with a moan of his own, the sensation of having his hair pulled sending sparks through his scalp and down his spine. Dawson shudders, as though he likes hearing Cal enjoying himself.

"Yeah. That's...that's good. Fuck," Dawson stutters out, his thighs tensing and relaxing sporadically. So, Cal does it again, making every sound under the sun as he sucks Dawson's cock. The bitter-sweet taste spreads across Cal's tongue, making his own cock throb.

"Cal, I'm close. You have to...have to slow down."

He doesn't want to. He could listen to Dawson's desperate, wanton sounds forever. But Dawson keeps pulling on his hair, harder now, trying to get him to stop.

He pulls off regretfully, licking his lips to chase the remnants of Dawson's taste.

Dawson's face and neck are flushed, his lips bright red like he's been chewing on them. He cups Cal's jaw and leans down to capture his mouth, the kiss slow and tender, but it rekindles the fire inside Cal all the same. Everything about Dawson does.

His thumbs stroke Cal's cheekbones, and he smiles; a shy, precious thing. Then he's letting go and moving up the bed until he's resting against the pillows. He keeps one of his legs bent, letting it fall to the side.

He grins. "Do I have to start without you?"

Cal has never moved so fast. He's still dizzy from bringing Dawson pleasure with his mouth, but seeing him like that, all spread out and waiting for him, calls out to Cal's most primal part. There's another part that would love to see Dawson touch himself, but that's for another day. Hopefully.

Getting lube from the nightstand, he joins Dawson on the bed, kneeling by his side. He looks so open and trusting, and it has Cal's protective streak awakening with a vengeance.

He wants to ask if Dawson is sure, but what comes out instead is, "You're stunning."

Dawson gives a nervous laugh and runs a hand over his face, as if trying to hide. "Shut up."

"No." Not a chance.

He squeezes some lube onto his fingers and stretches himself out alongside Dawson, propping up on one elbow so his other hand is free. "Stunning," he repeats, kissing along Dawson's collarbone and up the column of his neck as he slowly brings his hand between Dawson's parted legs. "Beautiful." He touches Dawson there, between his cheeks, spreading the lube around his entrance before pressing in with one finger. "Perfect," he whispers against Dawson's lips that just opened on a gasp. He kisses his mouth and his face, anywhere his lips can reach while he works him open. He adds a second finger when Dawson starts pushing down onto his hand. "Mine."

Dawson makes a sound like a sob. It sets off alarm bells in Cal's head, but before he can draw back and put a stop to everything, Dawson's nodding frantically and whimpering, "Yours."

Cal has to kiss him again. He has to. He's sure he'll die otherwise.

Dawson's back arches when Cal adds another finger and his legs fall open further.

He gazes up at Cal, looking half-drunk. "Are you? Mine?"

Cal lets his forehead rest against Dawson's, eyes closing. "Always, Dawson."

Dawson lets out a shuddering breath. "Okay, that's enough. I'm ready."

Cal can't summon the will to protest. He needs to be inside Dawson, feel him as close as humanly possible. He fits himself into the space Dawson has created for him and stretches out on top of him, containing him with his body.

Dawson's eyelids flutter, his legs spread wider.

Cal guides himself in, watching Dawson's face for any sign of pain, but doesn't find any.

Dawson's mouth falls open on a silent moan, his chin tipping back and exposing his throat. Taking it as an invitation, Cal runs his lips and tongue over the soft skin while he continues driving his hips forward in small, rocking thrusts until there's no further to go.

"Dawson?"

"Hm?"

"Are you okay?"

Dawson laughs, and it jostles his whole body, causing him to clench around Cal's cock and make him see stars.

He loops his arms around Cal's neck and gives him the sweetest smile. "Never better."

This man will be the death of him, Cal's sure of that. And he doesn't even mind.

His lips descend on Dawson's as he gives the first, experimental thrust. He swallows Dawson's moan, and does it again, and again, setting up a steady rhythm that has his eyes rolling back into his head. Dawson clings to him for all he's worth, face buried in Cal's neck and muffling his moans against Cal's skin.

All too soon, Cal's arms start to shake, the muscles of his abdomen burning. Sweat beads at his temples even though he hasn't done anything too strenuous.

Dawson lifts his head. "Cal?"

"I'm fine," he grunts through clenched teeth. This is ridiculous. He should have more stamina than this. He's been doing his planks and push-ups! And what about all the swimming?!

Dawson pushes at his shoulders. "Let me get on top." He gives him a stern look when Cal opens his mouth to argue.

Defeated, Cal straightens up and sits back, withdrawing from the heat of Dawson's body with a grimace. He allows Dawson to manhandle him until he's lying flat on his back, head propped on a pillow. He tries to sit up when Dawson throws a leg over his hips and straddles him.

Dawson holds him down with a hand at the center of his chest. "Stay." He rises onto his knees and reaches back to grip Cal's cock, the position not unlike yesterday. His lips curl in a mischievous grin. "Just lie back and take it." He takes Cal's cock in one smooth glide, eyes firmly on his.

Cal just lies there, gripping Dawson's hips.

And takes it.

"How's that?" Dawson asks, both hands on Cal's chest as he slides up and down, up and down.

It takes a moment for Cal to find his voice. "The view is rather phenomenal." While he feels bad for having Dawson do all the work, he can't deny it's heavenly. Like this, Dawson is a vision, one set on driving Cal out of his mind with want.

"Yeah?" Dawson looks way too pleased. An idea glimmers in his eyes. "Just wait until..." He comes to a stillness, Cal's cock buried all the way inside him. He takes his hands off Cal's chest. "Okay, just so you know, this is something *I* saw in porn and always wanted to try. It's supposed to feel really good."

He watches in a daze as Dawson leans back, bracing himself on Cal's thighs inches above his knees. If the view was amazing before, now it's magnificent, Dawson's whole body on display.

And then Dawson starts moving.

Something about this position allows Cal's cock to reach impossibly deep, making him choke on an inhale.

Dawson's muscles ripple as he works his hips, his hard, flushed cock bouncing against his stomach. Suddenly, he lets out a strangled cry, and Cal knows he must've found what he's been looking for. Whatever it is, it makes him go completely unhinged, riding Cal's cock until his legs quake and sweat rolls down his chest.

The heat that's been building up in Cal's belly turns into a scorching flame. He manages to let out a raspy "Dawson" to warn him.

Dawson's next moan is the loudest yet. He nods, chest heaving as he gazes down at Cal. "Yeah. I'm right there with you." He tips his head back, exposing the beautiful stretch of his neck littered with red marks Cal has left on him.

A surge of possessiveness rushes through Cal's veins. *Mine.*

He wraps a hand around Dawson's leaking cock, stroking in tandem with his movements.

"Cal!" Dawson's hips stutter, thrusting into Cal's grip before sinking all the way down Cal's length. "Oh fuck. Fuck. Cal."

A few seconds and another call of Cal's name later, Dawson's cock erupts in Cal's hand, his release splashing across Cal's fingers and stomach.

Seeing Dawson like this, lost to pleasure and chanting Cal's name has him hovering on the edge, and when Dawson clenches around him, he tips over completely, filling Dawson up.

Panting, Dawson flops down on top of him, Cal's cock still buried inside him.

"Ow," Dawson groans.

Cal's arms are around him in an instant. "Are you hurt?"

Dawson huffs, sending a gust of breath over Cal's skin. "My thighs are burning. No running for me tomorrow."

"Sorry."

"Hm, not at all." He rolls his head so he can look at Cal. His content smile soothes all Cal's worries. "I like seeing you under me."

Cal likes it too. He likes everything, honestly.

Dawson makes a face when Cal's softening cock slips out of him.

Cal can sympathize. He trails one hand down Dawson's spine, over the enticing curve of his asscheeks, dipping his fingers between them. Dawson shivers when Cal rubs his slick rim, Cal's spent cock twitching when he feels his come leak out.

"That calls for another shower," Dawson mumbles, nuzzling Cal's chest.

"In a minute." He traces lazy circles around Dawson's opening, loving how it makes him whimper and squirm.

"Hmm...alright." Dawson blinks up at him, looking bashful all of a sudden. "What are you thinking?"

"That you're amazing and I love you."

There's that blush again. Cal can't get enough.

"I'd say it's just the post-orgasmic haze talking, but...same." Dawson intertwines his hands and rests his chin on them so he can look at Cal.

Cal's gaze catches on Dawson's wedding ring and a strange sensation spreads through his gut. There's something wrong with that ring—with what it represents—even though being able to call himself Dawson's husband is the biggest privilege he could ever dream of.

An unbidden thought pushes to the forefront of his mind. The words are out of him before he can consider them.

"Marry me."

"What?" Dawson says with a nervous laugh.

Cal doesn't take the words back. They feel right. "Marry me."

"Um…" Dawson purses his lips, humor shining in his eyes. "That ship has sailed, honey."

Cal's heart flutters at the endearment, but can't afford to dwell on it now. "That was different. That was before…" He can't say it. "*Before. I'm not the same person you married. I never will be. But I still want to be your husband.*"

Stunned speechless, Dawson just looks at him, baffled but… Is that longing?

"It wouldn't really count, officially," he murmurs, averting his gaze.

Cupping his face tenderly, Cal tips his chin up so Dawson has no choice but to look at him. "It would count to me. To us."

Dawson licks his lips. "You're serious."

Cal nods, removing his own wedding ring before doing the same for Dawson. He leaves them on the nightstand and clasps Dawson's left hand between both of his, kissing the tips of his fingers.

"Will you marry me?"

Dawson's eyes fill up with tears, one of them spilling over when he blinks. "Yes," he whispers in a broken voice, surging up to take Cal's lips in a frantic, sloppy kiss. "Yes."

Cal's eyes burn, so he closes them, kissing Dawson back with all he has left. "I'll be so good to you, I promise."

He'll never take this for granted. He'll cherish every day together like it's their last. He's going to make Dawson the happiest man on earth.

"And I to you."

"That's all you have been, Dawson," Cal says, meaning every word. He's been in love with Dawson from the start, but every day he falls a little deeper, a little more hopelessly for him. "One more thing. What was your name before you took mine?"

Dawson's brows draw together in a cute little frown. "Winters."

Winters. It's beautiful, like everything about Dawson. "I want to take your name."

"What?" Dawson laughs. "Cal, that's really sweet, but...your name is connected to the company and—"

"I don't care." He strokes his knuckles over Dawson's jaw. "Cal Winters sounds better anyway."

"Technically, it's Caledon Winters."

Cal's body locks up with aversion. "No."

"God," Dawson says, shaking his head and chuckling. "Ellis will flip his shit. First you refuse to come back to work, then you watch porn in his office, and now you want to marry me again and shed your name."

"He'll get over it. You'll just have to invite him for dinner again. What?" he asks when Dawson's smile falls.

"Nothing."

"It's something."

Dawson hides his face in his hands, groaning. "It's...really bad, especially if I say it out loud."

"Say it anyway."

"Just..." He gives Cal a look that's guarded and apologetic at once. "I never thought I'd be so happy about a car accident."

"Well, I don't remember it, but...I'm happy for it too." *A clean slate.*

Dawson giggles. "We're a pair, huh?"

"Yes." Cal pulls him up for a kiss. "We are."

Chapter 29

AFTER THEY FINALLY ROLL out of bed and take a shower, they venture into the living room, only to find Donut sitting on the sofa and giving them a look of such disdain that even Cal feels bad. To make it up to him, they take Donut for a long walk on the beach, buy him a bag of treats, then spend the rest of the day watching movies with Donut sandwiched between them.

They don't bother putting on pajamas before going to bed—a fact that Cal is very, very grateful for when the morning comes.

Because Dawson is beautiful when dressed, and magnificent when not.

But naked and with his body softened with sleep, he's otherworldly. And he's all Cal's.

Inhaling the scent of Dawson's shampoo, Cal presses a kiss behind his ear, loving the small little hum Dawson makes. He trails his lips down the side of Dawson's neck, fascinated with the way his skin pebbles under the touch even when he's asleep.

Cal's cock has been hard and pressed against Dawson's lower back since he'd woken up, but he doesn't pay it any attention. He has more important things to take care of.

Like take Dawson apart.

He skims a hand over Dawson's chest, grazing his nipple. It draws a sleepy whine from him, so Cal does it again, a few more times for good measure, filing every single reaction away. He plans on utilizing the information *a lot.*

Moving his hand lower, he rubs it in circles over Dawson's lower stomach, his knuckles brushing Dawson's swelling cock.

Dawson squirms, letting out a loud yawn. "Hmm... Cal?" he says sleepily. It's unfairly adorable.

"Good morning," Cal mumbles against his nape, flicking his tongue out to get a fleeting taste of Dawson's skin. God, he tastes good. Smells good. Cal wants to ravish him.

"Morning." Dawson cranes his neck to peek at Cal over his shoulder. Amusedly, he asks, "What are you doing?"

"Devouring you," Cal says, pressing himself against Dawson until there's no space between them. His cock drags over Dawson's cheeks, but he ignores it again and wraps a loose fist around Dawson's cock.

Dawson's hips give an involuntary thrust, and he moans. "Um, Cal?" Cal hums to let him know he's listening as he continues showering Dawson's shoulders with kisses. "That sounds...really good but...I'm actually a little sore after, you know. Yesterday and the day before."

Cal stills and pushes himself up so Dawson can see him. "I wasn't going to do that."

"Oh." Dawson blinks in surprise and licks his lips. Intrigue lights up his eyes. "What were you going to do?"

"Can I show you?"

"Uh, yeah, sure." He looks down the length of his body. "What should I..."

"Like this." Cal nudges him until Dawson is flat on his belly, all that beautiful skin on display. "Lift your hips for me." Remembering something he saw in a video, he grabs a pillow and slides it under Dawson's hips.

Dawson wiggles until he's comfortable and rests his cheek on his folded arms. "What are you up to?" he asks with a smirk.

"Something I saw yesterday."

"Yest—In porn?!" Dawson pushes up on his forearms, his expression turning alarmed. "Cal. Very few things in porn are realistic. Most of them wouldn't even work, let alone feel good."

Is that true? But the men in the video—porn—seemed to enjoy it a lot.

"Can I give it a try? And you tell me if you like it or not?"

Worrying his lip, Dawson finally nods. "Okay." He flops back onto his belly and burrows his face in his arms. "Saw it in porn. My husband is crazy," he mumbles.

Smiling to himself, Cal nudges Dawson's legs apart and settles between them. He doesn't jump straight in, as much as he's tempted. Instead, he takes his time exploring Dawson in a way he hasn't had a chance yet. He drags his palms from Dawson's ankles and up over his calves, chuckling when he finds a ticklish spot behind Dawson's knee.

He rubs Dawson's thighs, marveling at how his skin is so silky compared to Cal's. He holds his breath when he reaches Dawson's ass cheeks, remembering what it felt like to slide between them and bury himself in the heat of his body.

"Having fun?" Dawson asks with amusement, watching over his shoulder. Despite his lighthearted tone, his face is flushed and his eyes hooded. He's affected more than he's letting on.

"Yes." Cal slides onto his stomach and places a kiss on Dawson's tailbone, then drags his lips down over his cheeks. He grasps each cheek in one hand and pulls them apart. It's no wonder Dawson is sore; his hole is red and a little swollen, and it flutters when Cal leans in to kiss it.

Dawson's breath hitches. "Cal?"

"You're so beautiful."

"Um, thanks? But—" Dawson bucks when Cal flicks the tip of his tongue over his entrance.

"Not good?" he asks, disappointed. He'd really hoped Dawson would like this. He hasn't been able to stop thinking about doing it to him.

"N-no," Dawson chokes out. "I mean, I don't—you've never—we've never done...that."

Oh. What a waste. "I should've watched more porn."

Dawson barks out a laugh. "That's not—oh my god." He trails off into a guttural groan when the flat of Cal's tongue licks a long stripe between his cheeks. Cal does it again, slower, gaining confidence now that he's sure Dawson doesn't hate this. In fact, he sounds very far from hating it.

"C-Cal." He lets out a sob that shoots straight to Cal's cock, making him grind against the sheets. "Fuck."

Cal spreads his cheeks wider, eager to find what other sounds he can extract from Dawson. He circles Dawson's rim before pushing inside with his tongue and nearly comes back up with a broken nose because Dawson's whole body jolts off the bed.

"Holy motherfucking shit. Stop laughing!" Dawson cries indignantly, but doesn't do much to stop Cal. Cal's never heard such language from him, and he doesn't know what to do with the rush of power it gives him.

"Relax, Dawson."

"You rel—ahh, god." He grips the pillow and buries his face in it, his knuckles turning white.

It only spurs Cal on.

He runs his tongue through Dawson's crease, doing it over and over until Dawson's swearing becomes unintelligible, until he can only muffle his sobs into the pillow and his ass is dripping with spit.

"I-I'm gonna—Cal—"

He sounds absolutely wrecked, exactly like Cal wants him.

Cal redoubles his efforts, pulling out every trick he saw in the porn vid until his tongue grows tired and his jaw aches. He doesn't stop, determined to bring Dawson to the pinnacle of pleasure first.

He's been so focused on Dawson he hasn't noticed his own building need. The drag of the sheets over his cock is heavenly, and he rolls his hips into the mattress in tandem with the sweeps of his tongue.

Dawson's body locks up a few seconds before he lets out a desperate sob and chants Cal's name, a series of violent shudders sweeping through him. His hips jerk against the pillow and then he stills, going completely boneless.

Feeling Dawson's muscles tense and relax under his hands and mouth, Cal grinds into the mattress two, three times, before his cock pulses and spills against the sheets. For a few seconds his vision whites out, and when he can see again, Dawson hasn't moved an inch.

"Dawson? Are you okay?" His voice is hoarse, his jaw aching, and he's never felt better in his life.

Dawson mumbles something Cal doesn't catch, but he considers it affirmative.

"I take it that porn isn't completely unrealistic, then?" he asks with a smirk, kissing Dawson's cheeks where his hands left an imprint.

Dawson turns his head, his eyes narrowed into slits. He looks a wreck, his lips red and puffy from being bitten on, and droplets of sweat are clinging to his forehead.

"Don't be so smug. It doesn't suit you." He starts to roll over. "Let me help you out."

"No need."

"Huh?"

"I finished when you did."

Dawson gapes at him. "Seriously?"

To prove it, Cal shifts until Dawson gets a clear view of his softening cock and sticky sheets. They'll definitely have some laundry to do later. Totally worth it.

"I loved seeing you like that, loved knowing I was making you feel good."

Dawson huffs. "That's an understatement."

"Does that mean we can do it again?"

"Uh, yeah." Dawson laughs, tapping his chest. "No complaints here."

"Now?"

"Now?!" Dawson shrieks and shakes his head firmly. "No way."

"Why not?"

"Well, I..."

"Are you in pain?"

"No..."

"And you liked it?"

"I did, but..." He glances at his cock which is already plumping up again. He *likes* the idea. "I just came."

Cal shrugs. "So?"

"I..."

He maneuvers Dawson until he resumes his previous position on his belly and wastes no time pulling Dawson's cheeks apart and diving straight back in.

Dawson cries out, instinctively pushing back against Cal's face, making him grin manically.

"See?"

"Cal..."

"Let me. Please?"

"Jesus," Dawson groans. "You're insane."

"Is that a yes?"

"Yeah," he says quietly, spreading his legs and canting his hips. "Yeah, okay. But if I die, I'll go full poltergeist on you."

Cal doesn't understand that reference. "I can live with that."

Dawson doesn't die, but he does black out.

Cal makes a mental note to watch all the porn in the world.

There's something Cal's been thinking ever since they did the Paint 'n' Sip thing. Dick painting aside, watching Dawson wield a brush was a magical experience, one that Cal's dying to witness again, preferably very soon.

Which is why he's on his way to the post office after getting a notification yesterday that his parcel has arrived.

The parcel isn't heavy, but it's bulky. Calling an Uber to save himself the trouble of dragging it home, Cal checks the time. Still at least 45 minutes before Dawson is back from his therapy appointment. That should be enough.

It takes him a while to get the whole box across the lobby to the lift, shuffling it across the floor, then doing the same after getting it into the apartment. He drags the box across the living room to his former home office. Originally, he planned on asking Ellis for help dismantling or removing the desk, then decided to leave it because Dawson can still make use of it.

If he actually likes the surprise, that is. There's a good chance he won't be happy with Cal's idea, but that's a risk Cal's willing to take. Because if there's just the slightest chance Dawson *will* be happy about this, it's worth it.

Cutting the box open, Cal starts pulling out the contents—five smaller and five bigger canvases, similar to the ones Dawson used for his art before. Ten fitting frames, in case Dawson wants those too. 500ml bottles of acrylic paint (Mr Google says this brand is one of the best), a set of watercolors and a pack of brand new brushes. He hadn't ordered an easel, because he found Dawson's old one in the storage room. Yeah, he did a little sneaking around, so what? Hopefully, Dawson will understand.

After setting everything up as neatly as he can, he huddles on the sofa with Donut and a book, waiting for Dawson. He spends five minutes rereading the first page, too anxious to pay attention. Thankfully, it's only another five minutes before the lock turns, and Donut shoots off the sofa like a rocket to greet Dawson. Cal listens to Dawson sweet-talking him, before walking over to the sofa and bending down to give Cal a kiss.

"Hey, you. What are you reading?"

Cal sets the e-reader aside. "Nothing yet. I was about to start," he lies. "How was the appointment?"

"Good, good. Wanted to punch Ash by the end, but that's how it usually goes." He chuckles. "Does Donut need to go out?"

Cal bites his lip. He was so jittery about setting everything up that he forgot. "Yes. I'll take him in a minute. Can I show you something first?"

Dawson's eyebrow quirks up, and he grins. "Show me something. Another sex position you want to try?"

Cal feels his face getting warm. "No." He doesn't watch *that* much porn.

Dawson laughs. "Shame. What is it?"

"It's in the office."

Luckily, Dawson follows him without question, stopping in the doorway when his gaze falls on the set-up.

"What..."

Cal jumps in to hurry and explain, before Dawson gets upset. "I know I took some liberties. I know I should've asked, but I wanted it to be a surprise. If you don't like it, I'll get rid of it. Donate it or something. But I'd like you to consider it.

"You said you don't do this anymore, but I saw you the other day. I saw how you got lost in the process even though you were painting something so simple that they teach it to complete beginners. You deserve to experience it again. As often or as little as you want. I just want you to have the option if you ever feel like picking up a brush again. And you don't have to. You never have to if you don't—"

Dawson strides over with purpose, cups the back of Cal's neck and draws him into a kiss. His lips tremble against Cal's, but he doesn't stop kissing him, clinging onto the kiss like it's his only source of air.

His eyelashes are wet when he pulls away. "Thank you. I don't even know what to say. Just...thank you."

Cal wipes a stray tear from Dawson's cheek. "You don't have to say anything." He hesitates. "Does that mean you like it?"

Dawson gives a watery laugh. "Yeah, Cal, I do. I love it." He throws his arms around Cal's shoulders. "I love you."

He's never going to get tired of hearing that. "I love you too."

Cal wakes with a jolt. It's another of those nights when the horrible memories haunt his dreams. They've been getting worse since he found out the truth, though he hasn't mentioned it to Dawson. He's not planning on it either. It's just something he'll need to get used to. Maybe he should ask for Ash's number. He seems to be helping Dawson, no matter how much Dawson complains about him.

It's already morning, the other side of the bed empty. Cal rests for a few minutes, waiting until his racing heart slows down. It takes longer than usual, his chest tight and aching, as though someone is pressing on it. He forces himself to take slow, deep breaths. It helps only marginally, the tightness persevering. Figuring he'll have to walk it off or something, he throws the covers back and stands up, a bout of dizziness making him sit back down. He tries again a minute later, and it's better this time.

He makes his way to the kitchen, desperately craving a glass of water. He finds that Dawson is already home, leaning against the island, still in his running gear and smiling at his phone as he types. His eyes flick up when he hears Cal approach.

"Morning, sleepyhead."

"Morning." Cal looks around. "Where's Donut?"

Dawson points at the sofa where Donut it spread out, belly up and legs in the air, tongue lolled out. "I tired him out."

Cal chuckles. "I see. Who are you talking to?"

"Olivia. She's asking when we're going to visit."

Cal pulls out a glass from the cupboard, putting it under the tap. His hand shakes, a strange pain traveling from his shoulder down his arm. He raises the glass to his lips and takes a long, grateful sip. His skin flushes hot and cold, sweat beading on his forehead. Is he coming down with something? He hopes he won't pass it onto Dawson.

"As far as I'm concerned, we can go whenever. It all depends on your shifts at the shelter."

"Well, Christmas holidays start in a couple of weeks. Maybe we could go then."

"Sounds good."

Cal throws back the rest of the water, then braces himself against the counter when his vision swims. It clears up quickly. He turns around to tell Dawson he'll have to go lie back down for a bit, and freezes.

Seeing Dawson like this, in this position, bent at the hips as he leans his forearms on the island...

Something's not right. Something is very, very wrong.

Before he can find out why, a sharp pain pierces through his skull, making him squeeze his eyes shut as images, horrible images, flash in front of him. Then the pain moves, ripping his chest apart and constricting his lungs. There is ringing in his ears, drowning out everything else.

He stumbles, feeling a dull pain as he crashes to the floor. Dawson's voice calling out his name reaches him, though it sounds like it's coming from far away.

"Cal! Cal, what's wrong? Cal!"

There's barking, loud and frantic. Something wet touches his face.

Donut. Their dog.

When Cal dares open his eyes again, Dawson's terrified face is the first thing he sees. He can't even tell if it's real or not, but Dawson's lips move, forming the shape of Cal's name, so it must be. Dawson starts to get smaller, as if something is dragging him away. Cal tries to reach for him, to save him, but it's too late.

Then everything goes dark.

Chapter 30

HE KNOWS HE'S AT the hospital, but it's different this time. The walls are the same depressing white, the monitors beeping over each other like he remembers, but something's not right. The whole room feels as if a shadow has fallen over it. He can hear voices, likely from the hallway, but they sound distorted. There's a buzzing sound in his ears which gradually transforms into static, not painful but annoying.

He feels pressure against his left side. His body is cold except for his left hand, and when he looks, his heart stutters in his chest and all the noise dies down. It's quiet and calm, and Dawson is there, holding Cal's hand, his head resting on Cal's thigh, eyes closed. His face is serene, but there are trails of dried tears left over on his cheeks. He looks so vulnerable and soft and—

Memories slam into Cal like a tidal wave.

The apartment. Dawson in the kitchen, smiling as he types on his phone, resting against the island.

Except he's not typing and he's not smiling. He's crying, begging. *"Please Cal, not like this."* And then—

Oh god.

Dawson's face covered in blood, bruises littering his cheeks.

Caledon standing over Dawson with a clenched fist, holding a bottle of whiskey in his other hand.

Caledon gripping Dawson's hair as he pushes his face against the counter before—

"That looks like quite an epiphany you're having there."

Cal's head snaps up, searching for the voice.

"Sienna," he breathes, confusion battling with fear when he sees her sitting on the bed next to him. How did he not notice her? More pertinently, how can he see her?

"Hi, stranger," she says, her teeth flashing in a dangerous grin. "I'm hurt. Are you not happy to see me? I missed you."

This isn't right. She can't be here. Not unless...

"Are you here to take me?" Hopelessness overtakes him. This isn't right. He and Dawson, they didn't have enough time—

"No."

A heavy weight lifts off his chest.

"One of the patients?" he guesses. Hospitals were pretty much the only place his and Sienna's paths ever crossed.

She smiles. "No."

Cal frowns, his confusion growing. That's not possible. She has to be here to do a job. If she's not here for him or a patient, then—

"No." He tries to squeeze Dawson's hand, but his body won't listen to him. Why won't it listen?

It's not really your body, is it?

"Please, not Dawson. Please don't—"

"Cal," she says patiently. Her smile is gentle, comforting. Not something one would expect from a harvester. Not something Cal would expect from her. "I'm not taking anybody."

"How are you here, then?" Cal shoots back, distrustful. "Harvesters can't go wherever they please."

She just keeps smiling. "They can't, no."

That doesn't make sense. There's no way she can be here, if not to harvest a soul.

Unless...

"Who are you?" A realization is sinking into the edge of his consciousness. It's the only explanation, but it can't be.

"I'd let you guess three times, but I'm pretty sure you've already figured it out, being the smart cookie you are," she says, managing to sound smug and approving at the same time.

Oh god. All those times their paths have crossed, and he had no idea who he was really talking to.

"I don't understand."

"I know," she says, sounding almost apologetic about it. "Excuse the cryptic mood. I have a penchant for suspense and drama. Comes with the job." She winks. Then her expression changes, becoming softer. Kind. "I'm here to see how you're doing. Check if you're okay."

If she knows what's been happening to him—as he suspects she does—then she must know how ridiculous she sounds.

"I'm far from okay. Dawson, he..."

Fuck. He can't even think about it without being sick.

"I would've expected you to feel relieved," Sienna says. "Until now, you thought you were the one who caused him all the pain. Now you know it was never you."

How does she know? Has she been following him? Keeping an eye on him? Is she here to take him back where he belongs? That's not fair. He isn't a harvester anymore. He has a life with Dawson, a home, a *dog*. He can't leave—

"Cal, calm down. You already had a cardiac episode." She snickers. "Whatever is going through that head of yours, it's wrong."

Why doesn't it make him feel better?

"It doesn't matter that I know," he says, going back to their original conversation. "Dawson, he thinks...he thinks he fell in love with his abusive husband."

Sienna turns to look at Dawson, cocking her head as though she's studying an interesting animal. "He seems fine with that to me."

"Nothing about this is fine."

She shrugs, and it makes Cal want to scream—at her, preferably. He manages to quell that urge, getting a hunch it wouldn't end well.

"Maybe you should take him as an example and leave the past in the past, especially when it doesn't concern you."

"Dawson concerns me, so I'm not just going to sit here and pretend everything is fine. Why are you smiling?" He's basically growling at her and she looks so nonchalant. That fits. What does Death have to get worked up about?

"No reason. Are you going to tell him?"

"I have to." He wouldn't be able to live with himself otherwise. He looks at Dawson's beautiful face, his chest aching with longing. Dawson is right here, but he suddenly feels so far away from him. "He won't believe me, but I can't have him think that I..." He takes a deep breath. "He deserves to know."

What happens when he tells Dawson? Will he even believe him? And if he does, will he want to stay, knowing who Cal really is?

"I can hear you thinking."

"I'm scared," he admits. "I know I have to tell him, but I'm scared. I can't lose him."

"You won't lose him, Cal."

"How do you know?"

She snorts. "It would take *way* more than that to break a soulbond."

"Soulbond?" he echoes incredulously. "There can't be a soulbond."

"Why not?"

"Because I don't have a soul?"

"Then how come you were able to take over a human body?" She giggles at Cal's stricken expression. "Aww, look at you, so confused. It's adorable."

"Sienna..."

She sighs dramatically. "I told you once. You're not like the others. And you *were* my favorite."

That's not very reassuring. "Why? Why did you pick me?" And why is she here now if not to take him back?

She sighs again. "Because, as you can imagine, this gig doesn't exactly allow me to socialize. I guess I was bored. A little lonely, maybe? And I liked watching you become who you're meant to be. You were *so* interesting."

Cal scowls. "You're being cryptic again."

Judging by her infuriating smile, she knows that, and she's enjoying it. "Do you know what makes a soul, Cal?"

"Energy?" he guesses, unsure where she's going with this.

"Close." She smiles. "Love, Cal. The ability to love gives rise to a soul."

"You're telling me I grew a soul because of my feelings for Dawson?" he asks, skeptical. That sounds so far-fetched.

"You mentioned energy. Before you took on a physical form, this body, you were energy too. We all are. Everything in the universe is. And energy can take many forms."

Right. So, falling in love with Dawson turned his sorry existence into an actual soul. A soul like the ones he'd harvested.

And he somehow managed to bind himself to Dawson's soul without knowing it was possible.

"Why are you telling me all this?"

Sienna leans closer to him but never touches him. He's not sure what would happen if she did.

"Because I wanted to remind you why you're here. Why you risked everything for a fraction of a chance to be with Dawson. When things get difficult, when something feels impossible, just remember what you're fighting for." Her eyes move to Dawson, and Cal is surprised to find something like affection reflected in them. "What you two have is something that transcends time and space. And even me." She chuckles. "You'll always find your way back to each other. Yours is a pretty epic story. Maybe you should consider it when you finally write your book." She pats the mattress and gets up. "See you later, stranger."

"Sienna," he calls out to her before she leaves. "Thank you." It occurs to him he won't see her for a long time. It feels like he's losing a friend. Not that they ever were friends, not really. But then why does the thought make him sad?

Sienna just smiles, her teeth flashing. Then she winks and in the next second, she's gone.

Dawson is still there when Cal wakes up, for real this time. His head rests on Cal's thigh, his fingers squeezing Cal's hand. He must've stayed the night. He's going to be so sore today, and tired. He needs to go home and rest, not waste time sitting by Cal's bed. He's too selfless for his own good. Cal loves him for it, but it's exactly why he needs to tell him the truth. No matter the consequences, Dawson deserves to know.

Using his free hand, Cal reaches over to stroke Dawson's hair to gently wake him up. Dawson makes a noise of protest, his brows twitching.

"Dawson. Wake up, sweetheart."

Dawson's eyelids press together tighter before fluttering open.

"Cal?" he says in a sleepy voice, rubbing the corners of his eyes.

Cal's heart clenches. "Hi."

"Cal," Dawson says again, fully awake now. "Oh my god. You're awake."

"I'm awake."

"Fuck." A heart-wrenching sob is torn out of Dawson, and throws himself at Cal. Cal swallows a grunt, willing to take any discomfort if it means he gets to hold Dawson. "I thought I lost you."

"Never," Cal promises, pressing a kiss to his hair. "What happened?" He remembers pain and collapsing in their kitchen. And then, Sienna...

Dawson pulls away, wiping tears from his face. "You had a heart attack. I thought it was because of all the donuts," he tries to joke, but it comes out as another sob.

Cal summons a smile. "It's not?"

"The doctors said it's likely linked to you having had a major surgery and a history of cardiovascular diseases." He shakes his head, framing Cal's face with his hands. "You had me so scared, Cal. I really thought that was it this time. Please, don't do this again."

Cal catches his wrist, thumbs rubbing over Dawson's pulse point. "I'll try my best."

Giving him a crooked smile, Dawson leans in to press their lips together.

Cal closes his eyes, chasing Dawson when he starts pulling away. He needs to make it last, make every kiss count. He doesn't know which one will be the last.

Dawson must sense something is wrong because he pulls back. "Hey, what's wrong? Are you in pain? Do you need—"

"No. I'm okay."

"You sure? You're acting weird."

"Weirder than usual?"

"Well..." They both laugh, and Dawson kisses him again. "It's fine. I kind of like you weird." He smiles. "I love you."

Cal blinks back tears. "Dawson, there's something I need to—"

The door opens, and a doctor walks in. He comes to a stop when he sees them. "Oh, hello, gentlemen. I can see someone is awake." He smiles. "I'm Doctor Moore. How are you feeling, Cal?"

"Fine. A little dizzy."

The doctor nods. "That's perfectly normal. Mind if I do a quick check?"

"I should probably wait outside, get out of your way," Dawson says, starting to rise.

Cal catches his hand. "Don't go." So much for wanting Dawson to go home and rest.

"I'll be right outside," Dawson reassures him. "I'm not going anywhere. Also, I promised Ellis I'd keep him updated after he left."

"He was here?"

"Yeah. I called him right after I called an ambulance for you. He wanted to stay, but there was no reason for both of us to be here."

At the thought of Ellis, Cal feels a hollow sensation of loss. He knows that Ellis isn't his brother, but he'd started to feel like one. Is Cal about to lose him now too after they've started rebuilding the bridges between them?

"Tell him I said hi."

"Will do." Dawson gives him a quick kiss before turning to leave. "Love you."

So much for telling Dawson the truth. Maybe it's okay to wait. There's no harm in enjoying a few more moments together, is there?

Cal will tell him when it's time to go home.

There's not much space to enjoy those last moments. Since Cal's heart attack was one of the milder ones, he gets an 'all clear' by the end of the day and is to be discharged tomorrow. Ellis visits again in the evening, coming straight from work judging by his suit. He gives Cal a speech on how important it is to have a low-cholesterol diet and manage stress if he doesn't want to *kick the bucket at fifty-eight like their old man*, then hugs him for the first time. He leaves in a rush after that, like he's embarrassed for showing emotions.

Dawson is there to pick Cal up at 12 o'clock sharp, hugging him so tight Cal feels his ribs creak. He doesn't mind.

The doctors say something about complications post-surgery and genetic predisposition. Cal listens with one ear, too anxious to pay attention. He's given a plastic bottle of something called beta-blockers. Apparently, he needs to take those now, probably for the rest of his life.

"Feels like déjà vu, huh?" Dawson says as he drives them out of the hospital's parking lot.

"Not really," Cal admits.

"No?"

"I know who I am this time." He's just not sure if it's a good thing. A part of him wishes he hadn't remembered anything. Ignorance *is* bliss.

"Hm. It's a good thing you didn't lose your memory again," Dawson says with a chuckle.

Cal is quiet for the duration of the drive, his stomach threatening to turn itself inside out.

"Hey, are you sure you're okay? You're unusually quiet."

A tentative smile pulls on Cal's lips. "Are you saying I never shut up?"

"Cal," Dawson says solemnly.

Cal takes a deep breath. They're a block away from their apartment.

"I need to talk to you about something."

Dawson shrugs. "Yeah, sure. But can it wait until we get home? There's someone who missed you."

"Donut missed me?" Cal finds that hard to believe. Donut has warmed up to him somewhat, but miss him?

"Oh yeah. Kept whining all night long. Had no one to bully."

"Ah. I can believe that."

When they get to the apartment, Donut is already waiting at the door, barking his head off and bouncing up and down.

"There he is!" Dawson laughs. "Look who's home!"

Dawson wasn't lying. Donut barely pays him any attention, forcing his way towards Cal and attempting to jump into his arms. Chuckling, Cal drops into a squat and lets Donut assault him with stinky kisses.

"Yes, yes, it's me. I missed you too. Hi."

"This needs a picture," Dawson says, pulling out his phone and snapping a photo. "Aww, look at you two. So cute!" He shows Cal. And yes, they look cute. They look happy.

Which makes all of this so much harder.

Cal rises to his feet. "Dawson? That thing I need to talk to you about..."

"Hm?" Dawson looks up from admiring the photo. "Oh yeah. Go ahead. I'm gonna start on lunch. What would you like?" He turns around and heads to the kitchen.

"Anything is fine," Cal says, though there's no way he could eat now.

"I looked up low cholesterol recipes while you were at the hospital. How do you feel about salmon? I never asked if you like fish now."

"Dawson."

"Come to think of it, I could—"

"I remember."

Dawson turns around. "Remember what?"

This is it. This is the moment. Cal can still turn back, he doesn't have to tell him. He can keep the secret. He can still have Dawson.

But it would be a lie.

"Everything. Who I...who I was before the accident."

Color drains from Dawson's face. "What?"

Cal goes on before he loses resolve. "The memories came back in flashes after I collapsed." He clenches his hands so they don't shake. "I'm so sorry, Dawson. If I'd known, I'd have told you in the beginning. I swear, I had no idea."

"What are you talking about?"

He takes a step forward, considering it a small victory when Dawson doesn't immediately take one back. "I know this will be hard to believe. But I need you to listen to me, okay? I'm not who you thought I was. I'm not your husband. I'm not the person who put you through hell. I'm not even human."

"You're not human," Dawson echoes, voice flat.

"I mean, I am now, I guess. But before, I was a harvester, or what people would call a reaper. My job was to collect souls when it was time for them to pass on. And Caledon, he was assigned to me. I followed him around until it was time for him to go. But when I saw those horrible things he did to you, I couldn't just stay away. I should've, but I couldn't. So, when his time came, and I reaped his soul...I took over his body. I didn't know if it would work, if his body was strong enough to contain me, but I had to try. I had to try because I fell in love with you."

The last few words are barely legible, his voice quakes so bad. The silence that follows is deafening, and it takes one look at Dawson to know everything is over. There's no coming back from this.

Cal lost him.

"Oh my god," Dawson says, and this time he does take a step back. "Oh my god."

"Dawson." Cal tries to go after him but freezes when he sees contempt in his expression.

"Why are you doing this? What are you playing at?"

"I'm not playing at anything. I would've told you sooner if I'd remembered, but I didn't until—"

"Stop it," Dawson says. "Just stop it. Are you listening to yourself?"

"I know how this sounds—"

"Do you?" Dawson hisses. "Because it sounds like you're either deliberately messing with me, fucking with my head like you always used to—"

"I'm not—"

"—or you actually believe the stuff you're saying and that's..." He laughs, but there's nothing nice about it. "That's a whole new kind of fucked up. If you're trying to make yourself feel better about the shit you did by fabricating some make-believe story about reapers and body possession or whatever, then forget it." He turns away, but not fast enough for Cal to miss the tears spilling down his cheeks.

"I considered not telling you," Cal admits shamefully. "I did, but it would be wrong. I know you told me a million times to let the past go but...I can't. It's selfish, but I couldn't stand the thought of you thinking that I was the same person who hurt you so badly."

Dawson spins around, anger flashing in his eyes. "Well, you are. You are that person, Cal. I told you to let the past go because *I* did." He points a finger at his chest. "I made my choice because I believed you'd changed. Everyone warned me not to trust you, not to let you in, but I did. You know why?" He doesn't wait for a response. "Because I fell in love with you. And I thought, after you learned the truth, you'd own up to it. But what you're doing now? That's fucking low, Cal. If you think you can blame your mistakes on a ghost story, think again."

Bile burns the back of Cal's throat. He swallows, forcing words out. "What can I do to make you believe me?"

"You can stop lying, that's what you can do."

He isn't getting anywhere with this. There must be a way to prove he's telling the truth.

He'll hate himself after this, but he has no other choice.

"I was there when Caledon hurt you after you told him you wanted to get a job. He was drunk again, and he hit you. There used to be a glass table here." He points in front of the sofa, where a wooden coffee table sits. "You fell on it and it shattered. After, you hid in the bathroom. You were crying, trying to wash blood off your face."

"Stop it," Dawson grits out, pain flashing across his face. It's almost enough to shut Cal up.

"I was there the day you went to visit your sister. I was there when you came back and he—"

"No."

Cal holds his gaze. "I was there when he drove into that street sign. I was at the hospital when you and Kieran came in. And the next day you came by yourself, before Caledon died."

Dawson's eyes turn hollow, his shoulders slumping as if all the strength left him.

"I can't do this," he says, voice small and weak. "I can't be around you right now."

He stalks past Cal towards their bedroom. A minute later, he walks out with a backpack slung over his shoulder.

"I'm staying with Kieran," he informs Cal, striding towards the front door. He stops halfway, turning around. "Donut, come here."

Donut, who's been sitting at Cal's feet the whole time, doesn't move.

A muscle in Dawson's cheek jumps. "Donut," he says, sounding desperate. "Leg."

Donut lets out a whine, looking up at Cal. Blinking back tears, Cal crouches down to pet him.

"It's alright, little one. Go to your dad." He nudges Donut towards Dawson, but he refuses to move, licking Cal's hand. "Go."

Donut whines pitifully, but finally starts in Dawson's direction. He stops several times, turning to look at Cal before continuing to walk. Dawson clips the leash to his collar, giving Cal an unreadable look.

"Don't forget to take your pills," he says—always thinking about others no matter how mad or scared he is—and opens the door.

"Dawson."

Dawson stops but doesn't look at him.

"Whatever you decide, *whenever* you decide, I'll be here."

Dawson leaves without saying a word.

Chapter 31

"WOULD YOU FINALLY TELL me what the fuck happened?"

Kieran was frantic when Dawson showed up on his doorstep, a backpack in one hand and Donut's leash in the other, unable to form full sentences.

"I told you."

Kieran demanded Dawson tell him what's wrong, then picked up his baseball bat and threatened to 'kill the fucker' when Dawson wouldn't tell him. So he spilled. Kinda.

Kieran didn't say a word when Dawson climbed into his bed like it belonged to him and hid under the covers, sobbing into Donut's soft fur.

That was three hours ago. And Kieran is pissed.

"You told me he remembered. But what did he do? He must've done something, or you wouldn't be freaking out like this. You always knew that him getting his memories back was a possibility."

But that was back when Dawson was scared of him, when he planned to stay only until Cal got on his feet, then pack his shit and leave.

That was before he fell in love.

"He remembered, and then he tried to make excuses for how he'd treated me." He doesn't give Kieran details. No need to repeat the ridiculous story.

Where did it all go wrong? Cal was so apologetic, so miserable when Dawson told him why he'd wanted to file for divorce. He felt so guilty he would've left if that's what Dawson wanted. He promised Dawson to spend the rest of their lives making it up to him.

Dawson should've known it was just lip service. He's always been so fucking gullible, and he only has himself to blame.

"Jesus Christ," Kieran expels a breath. "What a dick."

"Yeah." He waits for Kieran to say something else, but he doesn't. "Aren't you gonna tell me 'I told you so'?"

Kieran gives him a look of pure confusion. "Why would I do that?"

"Because you'd be right?"

"Wow. Don't you have a high opinion of me," Kieran says saltily.

"That's not—"

"I don't give a shit who was right and who was wrong. I give a shit that my best friend is hurting, and I have no way to help him."

Dawson's miserable heart melts a little. "You're here when I need you. That's all that matters."

"Yeah, yeah. Smooth-talker." They both chuckle. "But I don't get it. Even though he remembered, he could've pretended he didn't. Why tell you?"

Dawson is too tired to think. There's no point. He's wasted so much time in the past six years trying to get into Cal's head, to understand why he'd acted the way he had, why he'd done the things he had. He shouldn't have bothered. Cal's mind is a mystery, and it's probably better it stays that way.

"I guess I'd have figured it out sooner or later if he started acting like he used to."

"Yeah, maybe," Kieran says. He doesn't sound too sure.

"Is it really okay for me to stay?" He always comes running to Kieran when things go south.

"Dee, as far as I'm concerned, you might as well move in here."

Dawson scrunches his nose, thinking of the state of Kieran's apartment. "I think not, but thank you."

"Rude," Kieran says. "Seriously, stay as long as you want. Just make sure the dog doesn't shit anywhere."

"It wouldn't make this place look any worse."

"Hey!"

"Dawson, it's been three days. You can't be holed up here the whole day."

"Eh ot," Dawson says through a mouthful of Fruit Loops, Donut curled in his lap. He grabs the remote, pressing play to watch the next episode of *Stranger Things*. He really needs to get Cal to start watching it—

Fuck. He did it again. He can't even watch stupid TV without thinking about him. Worst of all, he can't stop checking his phone.

God, he's pathetic. No amount of therapy will make him right in the head.

"Uh, yeah, you are," Kieran insists, the pain in the ass he is. Is it wrong of Dawson to want him out of his own home already, so he can wallow in his misery?

"I walk Donut four times a day."

"Yeah, the only time you get out is when your dog needs it. You need to get out too. You need the sun and fresh air. People are basically plants."

The mention of plants makes Dawson think of cacti, and of Cal's cactus-dick painting.

And there he goes again.

"Seriously, Dee. Get out. Go to the cafe. Say hi to Gabe and Zeke. Just chill a little."

Chill. Right.

"I could bump into Cal." Which is something he'd never had to worry about before, because Cal had no idea about Dawson's little getaway. Except Dawson made it *their* little getaway now.

"Text Gabe to ask him if Cal's there. And even if you bump into him, it's a public space. You have nothing to worry about."

After Kieran leaves, Dawson watches three more episodes before Donut begins demanding his attention.

"Wee time?"

Donut barks.

"Yeah, okay."

Dawson's spine pops as he stands up and stretches his arms overhead. Jesus, Kieran might be right. Dawson's ass has already left an imprint on the sofa.

His phone vibrates in his pocket, causing his heart to skip a beat. His fingers twitch with the impulse to reach for it and pick up. He lets it go to voicemail, then finally dares to look at the caller.

He can't even hide the disappointment when Ellis' name glares at him from the screen. Fuck. Ellis. Has he talked to Cal? Or has he been trying to reach him and Cal wouldn't pick up?

He gets his answer when Ellis sends him a text.

Ellis: *Hey, how are things? I've been messaging Cal but he sounds weird. Is he okay?*

Fucking perfect. Another thing to worry about. How does he explain this to Ellis? Actually, why should he? Why can't Cal talk to his damned brother and tell him what he did?

Dawson opens a new chat with Gabe's number. He does need to get out. He can't stay here closed in with his racing thoughts.

Dawson: *Hey. Has Cal been in today?*

Gabe: *Last time I saw him, he was with you. Everything ok? Did you lose your husband? xD*

Aaand there he goes. Fucking crying again. Because he did, didn't he? He did lose Cal. One day, everything was perfect, and the next...

"Come on, Donut." He grabs Donut's leash, clipping it to his collar. "Let's see our friends."

Donut's been to the cafe enough times that he remembers the way. Despite his small size, he all but drags Dawson down the road, short of choking himself on the collar. It's hard to say if the enthusiasm is because of Gabe and Zeke, or because of the doggy biscuits Gabe started to bake when he learned of Donut's existence.

Dawson hesitates before pushing the door open, giving the shop a sweeping glance. It feels like ages since he's been here by himself, taking a break from life. Now it just makes him feel lonely. At least he has Donut.

Gabe is behind the counter, chatting animatedly with a customer, as is his habit. Dawson goes to take his usual seat, but Gabe spots him, his ever-present smile widening when he notices Donut's there too.

"Dawson, hey! We were just talking about you."

The person Gabe's been talking to turns, flashing him a smile. "Hi. Fancy seeing you in the wild," Ash says, his eyes lowering. "This must be the famous Donut. Hello, there."

At the sound of his name, Donut's tail begins to wag and he pulls on the leash. Dawson goes with him, so Ash can get some obligatory pets and scratches in. The scene is cute, but Dawson can't even appreciate it anymore.

After all this time, it shouldn't surprise him that Gabe instantly picks up on his gloomy mood. He rounds the counter, giving Donut a quick scratch before turning his attention to Dawson.

"What's wrong?"

Instead of words, a wrecked sob escapes from Dawson's lips.

Gabe's eyes widen, and even Ash looks up.

Fuck, this was a mistake. He shouldn't have come here. Of course, Gabe would notice. Of course, he would ask questions. What the hell is Dawson supposed to tell him?

"Oh, Dawson." Gabe pulls him into a tight hug. For such a small person, he's deceptively strong, and the physical contact draws another embarrassing sound out of Dawson. "Here, sit down." He leads Dawson to a table far from everyone else. Thankfully, there are only a few customers, and nobody is paying them attention.

"I'm sorry," Dawson says when they sit down, and hides his blotchy face in his hands. "God, this is embarrassing. I didn't mean to come here and lose my shit."

"It's not embarrassing," Gabe says. "And you're welcome to lose your shit. We got you."

Dawson forces a wobbly smile. He's not used to this, to letting himself break in front of people. Kieran is his best friend and not even he has seen Dawson at his worst. Ash has seen a lot, but Dawson never cried in front of him, never let himself be that vulnerable.

"Is this about Cal?" Ash asks, never one to beat around the bush.

A self-deprecating laugh forces its way out. "Am I that obvious?"

"No," Ash says, regarding him with sympathy. "I just have a hunch for these things."

Dawson huffs, suddenly grateful Ash is here. He's not his therapist right now, but unlike Gabe, he knows things about Dawson no one else does. Although it makes him feel vulnerable, it also gives him a sense of security.

"What happened?" Gabe asks. "Why were you asking if Cal's here?"

"Because I didn't want to bump into him." He ignores the little voice inside his head saying that's not really true. "He...he had a heart attack. Spent two days in the hospital."

"Shit," they say at once. Gabe follows it with, "Is he okay?"

"Yeah. He went home three days ago."

"Okay..."

Right. Context.

"His memories came back."

Gabe gapes at him. Even Ash seems taken aback, which happens...never.

"How's that possible?" Gabe asks. "It's been like...two months, no?"

"I don't know. But he remembers now."

He doesn't know anything anymore. The doctors had stressed that the brain is unpredictable, and the statistics don't tell you everything, but he'd disregarded it. He'd pushed it to the back of his mind and, with each day that passed without Cal regaining his memories, he'd sunk further into blissful ignorance.

"What else? There's something else," Gabe says, cocking his head as he studies Dawson, making him fidget under the scrutiny.

Whatever. He might as well tell them. He'd end up confessing everything to Ash anyway. He has a feeling he'll need him more than ever from now on.

"He said...stuff. Nonsense stuff." A fresh wave of anger fills his gut. "Made up this story that he's not the real Cal, that he's..." He gives an incredulous laugh. "A reaper, or something, and that he took over Cal's body when he was in the hospital after his accident. And some other stuff. I packed a bag, took Donut, and got out of there. No reason to stay and let him manipulate the fuck out of me because he can't handle the truth." He looks at Ash. "You were right. People don't change."

Instead of patting him on the shoulder and giving him a gentle but truthful *I told you so*, Ash stares at him with an unreadable expression which slowly transforms into a thoughtful one. He opens his mouth but gets interrupted.

"Oh. Oh!" Gabe taps the table, eyes like saucers as he stares into distance. "So *that's* what that was."

"What was what?" Ash asks before Dawson can.

Gabe almost tells him, then seems to remember Dawson is there too. He holds up a finger and gives him a pinched smile. "Can you give us a sec?" Without waiting for a response, he slaps Ash's arm and mouths something. They hurry off behind the counter, far enough that Dawson can't hear. He tries to read their lips, but can't see much. Gabe's hands fly through the air as he explains something of *utmost importance* to Ash, who seems more stricken by the second. Ash looks over at Dawson, perplexed, and his lips shape around words that Dawson can read even from a distance: "Holy shit."

After another minute of the heated discussion, they return to the table, that baffled expression still on Ash's face.

Gabe interlaces his fingers, his cheeks puffing up before he expels a sharp breath. "Dawson, this will sound crazy, but hear me out, yeah?"

Dawson scoffs. "Crazier than a reaper taking over a dead guy's body?"

The following silence isn't very reassuring, and neither is the look Gabe exchanges with Ash.

"Have you considered the possibility that Cal was telling the truth?"

Is that a trick question? "Um, no?"

"I think you should."

Dawson laughs, of course he does. Because Gabe is joking, right? *Right?*

"Are you being serious?"

"Hear him out," Ash says, his unusually solemn expression giving Dawson pause.

"There are things you can't explain with logic," Gabe starts. "With science, sometimes, but not always. That doesn't mean they're not real."

"Like your superpowers?" Dawson quips. He doesn't intend to be mean, but what Gabe is saying is ridiculous.

Gabe gives him a knowing smile. "Like that, yeah."

"You can read people, Gabe. So can any good psychologist." He nods towards Ash. "And you know how to make them feel better, because you're a kind, empathetic person. It's amazing, but it's not magic."

Gabe doesn't look offended, just tired, like someone who had to explain something a hundred times over. With a deep sigh, he raises his hand and slowly, giving him a chance to move back, he puts it on top of Dawson's.

A feeling of absolute weightlessness and peace envelops Dawson, making him feel like he's floating. He almost expects to see himself levitating when he looks down. He's not, of course he's not, but the tranquility that fills his body could easily make him believe it.

It's over in the next second—Gabe has stopped touching him

"Could a regular empathetic person do that?" Gabe asks. A golden hue passes over his eyes, like a flicker of candlelight.

"What was that?" Dawson demands, his heart hammering against his sternum. Gabe's touched him before and it always felt good, but this was something utterly different.

"Magic," Gabe says with a small grin. His eyelids begin to droop, and he looks exhausted all of a sudden. "I'm sorry. I try not to do this without consent, but you were being stubborn.

"I have...empathic abilities." He gives Dawson space to react, but when nothing happens, he goes on. "There's more to it. Remember the first time you brought Cal here? After he was released from the hospital?" Dawson nods, speechless. "I talked to him. There was something about him I couldn't put my finger on. And for a moment there, we touched, and I...I didn't understand what I felt. I'd never felt anything like it. But whatever it was, it wasn't bad, it wasn't malicious." He holds Dawson's gaze. "But it wasn't human either."

A buzzing sound fills Dawson's ears. "I—I don't..."

"I felt how much he cares for you," Gabe prowls on. "You're on his mind constantly, Dawson. Whoever this man is, he's not the person you knew. He's worlds better, and he loves you so much that I can feel in my bones when you two are around."

"He's telling the truth," Ash takes over. "I've never met Cal, but I know Gabe. He's the real deal."

"How do you know?"

"I'm not the only one with superpowers," Gabe says ominously.

"Another time," Ash says when Dawson looks at him for explanation. "I think you should talk to Cal."

"*Now* you're advocating for him?" Dawson bristles. After spending each session pointing out Cal's flaws and throwing them in Dawson's face for him to confront, he wants Dawson to believe him?

Ash shakes his head. "Do you remember the second time you came to see me?"

He remembers it very well because of how monumental it was. "Which part?"

Ash gives him a look like knows what Dawson's thinking. "You said you were so happy you couldn't bring yourself to care about what anyone else thought. You said that when you are with Cal, you can be yourself. You said he makes you feel safe. Is it really so unbelievable that he might not be the man you thought he was?"

The question strikes something inside Dawson. He spent the first couple of weeks after Cal woke up trying to explain away how someone can be a completely different person without their memories. How someone so intense and vicious can end up being the gentlest person on the planet. Hell, Dawson even joked about the old Cal being kidnapped by aliens because there was no plausible explanation to any of it.

Cal's little ghost story isn't plausible by any stretch of imagination, but what other explanation is there?

Some of the stuff Cal had said rushes back to him.

"Can people hear you when they're comatose?" he asks Ash.

"What?"

"Cal said something about the hospital. About me and Kieran...going into his room." Dawson was so upset and confused his brain didn't even process it. "Could he have been aware of what was going on around him even when he was sedated?"

In the movies, people whose friends or family have been in an accident and aren't conscious are always told to keep talking to them, that they can hear them on some level. Maybe that's how Cal knows? Was he subconsciously aware of Dawson and Kieran's presence?

"Possibly," Ash says, very reluctantly. "Just because the conscious part of your brain is on vacation doesn't mean the whole thing shuts off. Kind of like when you're sleeping."

That's not good enough for him. He needs to know for sure.

"I have to go." Dawson pushes his chair back, giving Donut's leash a gentle tug.

He has questions for Cal. And Cal had better have really good answers at the ready.

Neither Gabe nor Ash try to convince him to stay, but Gabe catches up to him when Dawson is already outside. He hands him a folded piece of paper and squeezes his hand, warmth trickling up Dawson's arm.

"What is it?"

"I don't know," Gabe says. "I'm just a messenger." With that, he disappears back to the cafe.

Steering Donut in the direction they'd come from, Dawson unfolds the paper.

Fresh tears run down his face as he reads the words.

If it isn't happy, it's not the end.

Chapter 32

THE THIRTY MINUTES IT takes Dawson to get home from the cafe isn't nearly long enough to prepare a speech, and whatever he does manage to put together falls apart once he steps out of the lift on their floor. He stands in front of the apartment for what might well be hours, fiddling with the keys in his hand.

Donut's growling whine is what finally propels him to action. It takes him four tries to unlock the door, and his stomach swoops when the familiar scent of the apartment washes over him. Cinnamon and sugar.

"Cal?"

There's no answer, the apartment eerily quiet.

Dawson's heart sinks. Is Cal even here? He said he'd be here when Dawson decided to come back. Has he left after all? The apartment looks meticulous, it's hard to say if anyone's been here in three days.

Stop catastrophizing. He might've just gone for a walk.

Donut's nose twitches as he sniffs the air. He lets out a bark and starts marching on the spot, his tail swishing from side to side.

Leaving his shoes at the door, Dawson continues into the apartment, letting Donut guide him.

He finds Cal stretched out on the sofa, fast asleep. He looks exhausted and like he hasn't shaved in days.

And he's hugging the plushie Dawson had won him to his chest.

Willing his treacherous heart to calm down, Dawson comes closer, wanting so badly to touch him, but refraining. "Cal?"

Cal doesn't so much as stir, but then Donut barks again, and Cal's eyelids flutter, opening slowly.

"Dawson?" he blinks, looking around, disorientated. He scrambles up into a sitting position once his gaze falls on Dawson, suddenly wide awake. "You're home. Or..." His whole body sags. "Am I dreaming again?" His expression is crestfallen, and how fucked up is it that Dawson's instinct tells him to go to Cal and make him feel better?

That's not what he's here for. He wants answers and he's not leaving without them.

You don't have to leave at all.

"You're not dreaming," he says simply. He lets go of the leash when Donut starts towards Cal, jumping straight into his lap.

Cal lets out a choked laugh, putting the plushie aside so he has room for Donut. "Hello, little one. Hi. I missed you too." He allows Donut to slobber all over his face, rubbing his spine.

Dawson looks away. "Have you been taking your pills?"

Cal looks like shit. If he were to have another episode when no one's here...

"I have."

Thank god. "Have you been eating?"

"A little," Cal says. He pats Donut and stands up, watching Dawson dejectedly. "Did you come to get the rest of your stuff? Because you don't have to," he says in a rush. "You don't have to move out. Keep the apartment if you want. I don't care—"

"Shut up," Dawson says, pinching his eyes shut. "Just...be quiet." He can't fucking do this when Cal is being such a fucking martyr. He's not sure he can do this at all. He can barely look at him without wanting to feel those arms around him, for fuck's sake.

He runs a hand through his hair and takes a deep breath, reminding himself what Gabe and Ash told him.

"So, you're a reaper, huh?"

Cal hesitates before answering. "Yes."

"And you took over Cal's body when he died."

"Yes."

"You do realize how nuts you sound, right?" Dawson demands, his anger making a comeback. A part of him had hoped Cal had done some self-reflection and owned up to his past.

Cal's shoulders slump. "Yes."

"And you still insist this is true."

"I know it's—"

"Just answer yes or no."

"Yes."

Right. *Right.*

So, Cal claims to be a reaper.

Gabe claims to be some ultimate-level empath, and Ash... Who knows what Ash is, except an irritating ass who Dawson has a strange affection for.

Clearly, Dawson's life is an episode of *Supernatural.* The only thing missing is a witch or a demon.

"How did you know Kieran and I were at the hospital? In your room?" he asks. "Did someone tell you? The doctor? One of the nurses?"

Cal shakes his head. "No. I was there."

"You were comatose."

"Caledon was." When Dawson just looks at him blankly, he continues. "The doctor gave you a few minutes to visit him. When you were there, you said: "I don't know what to say." The day after, you talked to him. About Ellis—you said that you liked him, that he was nice. And then you said, just before Cal started crashing: "I wish I'd never met you.""

"How do you know this?"

That's not possible. Dawson knows fuck-all about how the subconscious works, but there's no way Cal could hear something so clearly and remember it in such detail, especially after months without his memories.

Cal looks him straight in the eye and, in a voice Dawson's never heard, he says, "Because that was the moment I ripped his soul out."

Dawson takes a step back, blood rushing in his ears. "I can't...I thought I could do this, but I can't." He struggles to take a proper breath. It feels like there's not enough room in his lungs.

"Dawson..." Cal whispers. He looks like he wants to go to Dawson but doesn't know if he's allowed.

"You wanna know the most fucked up part?" Dawson laughs bitterly. "I want to believe you so fucking badly. No matter how insane you sound, a part of me is begging to get onboard with whatever you say because the past three days were a hundred times worse than the past six years, and I missed you. So. Fucking. Much."

There. He said it. Could he be any more pathetic? There's not enough therapy in the world for him.

Then Cal twists the knife. "I missed you too. I can't tell you how much." His eyes are shiny, like he's about to cry. Dawson's never seen him cry in his life. "But if you never want to see me again, I'll understand. I'll let you go."

"You'll let me go," Dawson repeats flatly.

Cal lets out a frustrated sigh, showing Dawson his palms. "This wasn't always the plan, Dawson. I thought that if I removed Caledon from your life, that would be it. It would be enough, knowing you were safe from him. But I got selfish. Greedy. I spent weeks following Caledon around, but you were all I cared about. Not him, not my job. You. I was there whenever he hurt you, and I tried to reach out, to tell you it would be okay. That you'd soon be free of him. Of course, it never worked. We can't communicate with the living. But I liked to imagine you could hear me."

Dawson's skin prickles with goosebumps, Cal's words awakening something he's forgotten about.

"Say it again."

Cal hesitates, unsure. "I liked to imagine—"

Dawson shakes his head. "No. Before. You tried to reach out and tell me what?"

Cal's brows furrow in thought. Very slowly, he repeats, "That it would be over soon. That you'd be free."

That's it. Right there.

"Soon."

Cal nods. "Yes."

Oh god.

Oh god.

He has heard that before. He has *felt* it before, dreamed about the soothing deep voice and the promise it carried. Is that...is that what it was? Has Cal been with him all along? But that would mean...

"You said he makes you feel safe. Is it really so unbelievable that he might not be the man you thought he was?"

Dawson looks at him. *Really* looks at him—the man he's spent months with, made love with. The man who'd made him pancakes and held him when he was in pain. The man who promised him forever, but who would let him go if that's what Dawson wanted.

Because he loves him.

"You hate coffee."

Cal blinks owlishly. "Yes?"

"You watch Disney movies and read corny vampire fiction."

"You put pineapple on pizza. You're the last person who can judge me," Cal retorts, and that touch of defensiveness almost makes Dawson smile, which in turn makes him cry.

"You can't do laundry for shit, and your cooking attempts are hit or set-the-kitchen-on-fire-miss."

Cal takes a step forward. "Yes, but I'm working on it. I promise."

Dawson stays where he is. "You wash the dishes and make me breakfast in bed."

Cal nods earnestly, taking another step. "I'll make you breakfast every day for the rest of our lives if you let me."

Dawson's heart flutters with hope. It's a dangerous thing to feel, but he's helpless to stop it. "You love donuts and listen to Lady Gaga."

Another step. "I like Taylor Swift too."

"You love me."

"With everything I am," Cal says, like it pains him to admit it. "I loved you even when I didn't know who I was."

"I fell in love with you thinking you're someone else."

Regret and guilt fill Cal's features. "And now? Could you love me now when you know the truth?"

Dawson laughs. He can't not laugh because Cal couldn't have asked a more ridiculous question. "I already do. Maybe more than I ever did."

Cal stills, his hands twitching at his sides. A single tear escapes from the corner of his eye "Can I hold you? Please?"

Dawson's tears keep coming, like a never-ending waterfall. He manages to nod, and in the next moment, he's cocooned in Cal's strong, *safe* embrace. Nothing's ever felt this good.

Cal's arms tighten around him, and his shuddery exhale fans over Dawson's neck. "I missed you so much. Both of you."

"We missed you too." Dawson breathes in Cal's scent, feeling all the tension in his body bleed out as his mind quiets, replaced by a sense of calm. "I'm sorry for leaving. I just—"

Cal pulls away to look at Dawson, drawing a noise of protest from him. "No. Don't apologize. You did what you had to do." He cradles Dawson's face in his hands, wiping the tears away. "I'm just so happy you came back. For a moment I thought it was over."

"For a moment, I did too." It wasn't a moment. It was *days,* but they felt like years. Fuck, Kieran deserves a fruit basket for nagging Dawson to go out. And Ash and Gabe too. "But then someone very wise reminded me that we haven't finished writing our story yet."

"Who?"

"Gabe."

"Oh. How did he know it wasn't over already?"

"It couldn't be. It wasn't happy." Reaching into his pocket, Dawson pulls out Gabe's message, handing it to Cal. He smiles at Cal's confused expression. "If it isn't happy, it's not the end."

Chapter 33

"IT's GONNA TAKE ME a while to come to terms with everything. Just be patient with me, okay?" Dawson asks when they are lying in bed that night, facing each other with Donut stretched across their entangled legs.

Fuck, he missed sharing a bed with Cal. Missed his comforting presence and the heat of his body. He even missed the little snoring sounds Cal sometimes makes, so cute compared to Kieran's earthquake-inducing snores.

"Anything you need," Cal says. He raises a hand and tucks a stray strand of hair behind Dawson's ear.

Dawson shivers, catching Cal's wrist and keeping his hand there before he can withdraw it.

Cal gives him a tender smile and cups Dawson's face, stroking his thumb back and forth over his cheek.

It's hard to focus on talking when Cal is being like this, unbearably sweet and attentive, but Dawson forces himself anyway. "Can I ask you...about stuff?"

Cal hums an affirmative.

"How old are you?" He doesn't know why it's important. It probably isn't—he's just curious.

Cal's eyes sparkle with mirth. "A few eons, give or take. But don't tell your sister."

"Um, did you say eons?" That's one hell of an age-gap.

It's kind of hot.

"I don't know for sure," Cal amends. "Time doesn't really exist where I come from. It's fluid. One could say I've been to the future too."

That makes sense. Dawson's seen so many movies about time paradox and time travel, it gets more complicated each time. But his little human brain struggles to grasp the concept.

"Yeah? What is it like? Do we have spaceships? Flying cars? Has Australia sunk into the ocean?"

Cal grins. "Maybe we should restrict *your* Netflix time."

Dawson pouts at the vague response, but Cal doesn't budge.

Moving on, then. "Can you tell when someone is going to die?" He's surprised that Cal actually answers him.

"No. As I said, time doesn't exist...there. There are no dates, no marks in a calendar. You are assigned souls and you follow them until it's time."

"How do you know it's time?"

Cal ponders it for a moment. "You feel it. It's instinctual."

Not very specific, but Dawson can't blame him. Their worlds have different rules. He's grateful Cal is talking to him about it at all.

"You said time doesn't exist, but you also said you followed C—uh, you followed *him* for weeks."

"By human standards, that was probably accurate," Cal says, his eyes growing sad. "You can say his name, you know."

"Doesn't it bother you, though?" It's strange to refer to both of them with the same name. Maybe Dawson should come up with nicknames.

"It probably should, but..." Cal shrugs. "Not really. It feels natural. It feels right."

Huh. "What's your name? Non-human one."

Cal averts his gaze, like he's ashamed. "I didn't have a name. Not that I remember."

"Oh." That's...sad. But maybe you don't need a name when you're going around the world and, well, reaping souls. "Do you know where the souls go?"

"In Caledon's case? Hopefully to hell." The last part comes out as a growl.

Wow. Dawson has had many hateful thoughts about Cal—Caledon—throughout the years, but even those fade in comparison to the pure loathing in Cal's voice.

"Did it hurt? When you took him?"

"I made it hurt," Cal says, his eyes hard and cold. It gives Dawson chills because it feels like he's getting a peek behind the curtain, a peek at the real Cal. "Usually it's quick, a snap of the fingers. But I took my time." He strokes Dawson's hair, regret twisting his features. "I'm sorry I couldn't step in sooner. I wish things hadn't happened the way they did."

Blinking back tears, Dawson says, "You're here now. That's all that matters." He doesn't want to think of the past anymore. It serves no purpose, other than holding them back.

"What happens to you when you die? Will you go back to being a reaper?" Why does the idea bother him so much? It's not like he'll care about anything once it's his time too.

"No. My place is with you, Dawson. I'll follow you anywhere."

"That's low-key stalkerish, but I like the sound of it," Dawson jokes, trying to deflect from how much Cal's words are affecting him. Cal would sweet-talk him into an early grave if given the chance. "Why me? You'd been doing this for 'eons', so why me?"

Cal gives him a look as though Dawson couldn't have asked a more ridiculous question. "You have no idea, do you?"

"Uh, no? That's why I'm asking."

Cal strokes his hair, his soft gaze roaming over Dawson's rapidly heating face. "I wish you could see yourself the way I see you," he says, sounding sad. "There's a whole world inside you, Dawson, and it's waiting for you to discover it."

"You're talking like you can see my soul." Dawson chuckles, all this attention making him squirm. Something in Cal's face gives him a pause. "*Can* you see my soul?

"Not the way I used to," Cal says, sounding disappointed. Dawson is stuck on the *used to* part. "The physical doesn't mean much where I come from. I could see you, your body, but it was just the surface. But your soul..." He closes his eyes, a tender smile appearing on his lips for a second. "It shone so bright, despite everything you've endured. It was calling out to me." His fingers stroke the bridge of Dawson's nose, the outline of his lips. "I can still see it. It's just different."

"How?"

"It shines through you. I don't mean just your body, but *you.* Your actions, your words. Every time you help at the shelter, every time you cook for us. When you laugh. When you paint. When we make love." He brushes their lips together, and Dawson can't hold back anymore.

He surges forward to capture Cal's lips, rough and unapologetic. He needs Cal's kisses more than he needs air right now, feeling himself grow more desperate the more they kiss. He can feel Cal smile against his lips, taking everything Dawson's giving him.

Dawson is dizzy when they finally pull apart, needing actual air now. Stupid human body.

Cal kisses his pout away. "You're beautiful Dawson, inside and out. There's nothing, *no one*, like you."

Dawson lets out a groan. "You seriously need to write a book."

"Why?"

"Because you just about killed me with words. Others should have the same honor."

"No," Cal says, smiling. "No, those were just for you."

Dawson wiggles closer until they're flush, needing to be completely surrounded by Cal. He can't suppress the sigh of pleasure when Cal wraps him in his arms.

"You said you wished things didn't happen the way they did," he whispers into Cal's neck, lifting his head so Cal can see the sincerity in his eyes. "I'm glad they did. I wouldn't change the past. Not a single thing. All that pain was worth it because it led me to you. Or you to me. I could never regret that. I'd do it all over again if it meant I get to love you. Have a life with you."

Cal's Adam's apple bobs. "I just…" He clears his throat. "If I'd found you sooner—"

"I might not have been ready. Things happened the way they had to happen. I had to know what love isn't to learn what it is."

A ragged exhale escapes Cal's lips. "And what is it?"

"It's this." He takes Cal's hand, bringing it into the space between them and over his heart. "It's us."

Chapter 34

"WHY ARE YOU LOOKING at me like that?" Dawson asks, his hackles up. That all-knowing look always puts him on edge.

Ash grins, lifting a shoulder. "I'm just waiting for you to say what you've been psyching yourself up about."

Smartass.

Dawson crosses his arms over his chest. "Does this thing you and Gabe have run in the family?" At least, Gabe isn't obnoxious with his, uh, gift.

"Interestingly enough, it appears to be contained to the male side of the family," Ash admits, but doesn't elaborate further.

So. Obnoxious.

Dawson caves. "So, what is it that you can do?"

"Read people really well."

"Clearly." Dawson sighs, getting to the point since Ash is being mysterious and shit. "I think it'd be best if this was our last session."

It's been over a week since Cal's big identity reveal—or more precisely, since Dawson had come to terms with it—and also the first session with Ash since then.

And...yeah, it feels a little weird. How is he supposed to dive deep and talk about his *feelings* when the fact that his fiancé is an out-of-this-world entity hangs over his head? It feels so petty. Unimportant.

Ash has been incredibly helpful—and annoying—during the last couple of months, but after everything Dawson's learned lately, Ash doesn't feel like his therapist anymore, and Dawson doesn't feel like his patient.

"Agreed," Ash says without missing a beat.

"Yeah?"

"Oh yeah. It's time. We've finally figured out what's wrong with you. Nothing, surprisingly." He winks when Dawson rolls his eyes. "Also, and I'm speaking only for myself, I'd like us to be friends."

Dawson quickly hides a smile. He was hoping they could be friends. Ash is like an annoying older brother to him.

"Not sure about that. You're kind of a dick."

Ash makes a thoughtful face. "I can't deny that."

"Good." He lets the smile slip out this time. "I'd like to be friends. Let's do a trial period of three months."

"Three months, huh?" Ash pretends to consider it. "I better be on my best behavior during that time."

Dawson snorts. "Yeah, I won't be holding my breath."

"Smart." Ash crosses his legs and leans back. "Now that's sorted, tell me more about the big, bad reaper doing house chores. I'm dying to know."

Dawson laughs.

Yeah, they're going to be just fine.

Donut greets him at the door as if Dawson's been gone for a month instead of an hour and a half.

Dogs... How had Dawson lived so long without one?

"Hey, little devil." He pats Donut's side and calls out that he's home. There's no answer. "Where's your dad?"

Donut snorts. He pushes past Dawson so he can get to the door, then looks up meaningfully.

"Of course," Dawson says with an eye roll. When he opens the door, Donut attempts to squeeze through. Dawson snatches him by the collar, tugging him back. "Nuh-uh. No dogs allowed. Don't give me that look. I won't be five minutes. You can wait that long."

Donut gazes up at him in betrayal, but Dawson isn't swayed. He pushes past him and slips out, then makes his way to the rooftop.

As he expected, Cal is in the pool and there's no one else around. Dawson sits on a sunbed, content to just watch him for a bit.

Cal is fast. He's really improved over the past few weeks, and apart from being unable to lift anything too heavy just yet, no one would be able to tell he's had major surgery. Some time soon, he might even try his hand at surfing.

It makes Dawson wonder how much his body will remember and if there's anything left of the *other* Cal. He's not sure how he feels about that.

Cal finishes a lap, coming up for air. He rubs water from his eyes—Dawson really needs to tell him about a magical thing called goggles—and his face lights up with a smile when he notices Dawson.

"Oh, hey." He swims towards him, propping his forearms on the edge of the pool. "Sorry, I lost track of time. How was Ash?"

"Full of himself, as usual." He goes to sit on the ground in front of Cal. "I told him this was our last session."

"It was?" he asks, surprised.

Dawson hasn't mentioned it to him because he wasn't sure about it until he sat down in Ash's office.

"I feel like I've milked it as much as I could. I mean, I started going to him because I wanted to understand my feelings for you. In the light of recent events, I think that mystery is solved."

Cal's eyebrows slowly climb up. "Is that right? And what are your feelings for me?" he asks suggestively.

Dawson glimpses a sparkle of mischief in his eyes and slaps his hand. "Stop fishing for compliments. I'm not inflating your ego any more."

Cal catches his hand before Dawson draws back. He kisses Dawson's knuckles, making him blush. "Want to join me?"

"I didn't exactly bring a swimsuit."

"No one is here."

Dawson stares at him in shock. "I'm not skinny dipping!"

"Keep your underwear on," Cal says like it's no big deal. The exhibitionist. He lets Dawson go and pushes himself off the edge, just floating. Waiting for him.

Ugh. Why is everyone in Dawson's life such a pain?

"I swear, the things you make me do…" he grumbles as he starts taking off his shirt and jeans, leaving only his undies on. At least he had the foresight to wear something dark today. He makes his reluctant way to the pool and throws his legs over the edge, sucking in a breath when the water turns out to be colder than he'd expected.

Sweeping his gaze around one more time to make sure no one is there to see them, he slides into the pool, submerging himself completely.

When he comes up, Cal's grinning face greets him.

"You did it."

"Yeah, because you were being annoying."

"Hmm." Cal floats towards him, treading water as he grabs Dawson by the waist. "How much can I get away with by being annoying?"

Dawson squints. "Do not try to find out."

Cal's grin turns feral, and he grasps the back of Dawson's thighs, hoisting him up until Dawson has no choice but wrap his legs around Cal's waist unless he wants to get his nose full of water.

"Whoa!" He gives Cal a stern look. "You shouldn't really—"

"Relax. I can't get hurt. You barely weigh anything in the water." He covers Dawson's mouth with his before Dawson can protest. "I've always wanted to do this."

"You and your movie obsession," Dawson chides, trying not to smile like a dork.

"Are you complaining?"

"I haven't decided yet."

"Maybe I could help you make up your mind," Cal says huskily, kissing Dawson again. He cups Dawson's ass and rocks their hips together, drawing an unmanly squeak out of him.

Dawson is already half-hard, the light friction and Cal's touch all he needs to feel blood rushing to his cock. Jesus. It's only been two weeks since they touched like this, but his body is reacting as if Dawson has been depriving it for years.

He might've been depriving it for the past week, though. Whenever he and Cal had gone to sleep, all wrapped around each other, Dawson wanted more, craved it on the basest level. The timing hasn't been right, though, so he's refrained from pursuing anything. Cal must've sensed his reluctance because he never gave an indication of taking things further, giving Dawson all the time he needed.

Fuck, Dawson loves him so much.

And he wants him. Now.

"Okay, okay, we need to slow down," he gasps out when Cal grinds their erections together, his fingers shy of slipping between Dawson's cheeks. "Public space."

Cal makes a noise of complaint but listens. "How about you go downstairs and wait for me? I'll get a few more laps in, then join you."

A few more laps? Is he for real?

On the other hand, maybe that's a good idea. It will give Dawson time to calm down at least.

"Yeah, okay. See you in a bit?"

Cal gives him a long, sweet kiss that has his toes curling. "Yes."

Dawson's dripping when he climbs out, his dick creating a big enough tent that five people could camp under it. Great. Now he can only hope he's not gonna run into anyone in the lift.

Using Cal's towel, he quickly dries off just so his clothes don't get completely soaked when he puts them on. He looks over his shoulder, but Cal is already doing another lap. Unbelievable.

Dawson hurries downstairs. The cosmos must be warming up to him because he doesn't bump into anyone. He ignores Donut's judgmental look when he sees the state of him.

"Stop it. I'm just a man. I have needs."

Donut snorts and walks away. Rude.

Dawson peels off his wet clothes and heads to the bathroom. He never liked the smell of chlorine, always reminding him of toilet cleaner.

He makes quick work of showering, not wanting to risk Cal walking in before he's done. He scrubs himself clean, using the grapefruit shower gel he knows Cal loves. It's probably overkill, but he brushes his teeth as well even though it's only three o'clock.

He negotiates putting on a pair of joggers, but upon realizing they'd end up on the floor within minutes anyway, he sticks with a towel around his waist. Checking himself in the mirror, he lets out an embarrassed laugh. His face is flushed, his pupils so blown they nearly overtake his whole irises.

He looks debauched, and they haven't even done anything yet.

He feels like a virgin all over again as he trots to the bedroom, perching on the edge of the bed and waiting for Cal to walk through the door. Anticipation thrums in his veins, making his cock throb and harden further without a single touch. Not even as a teenager was he so easily riled up, geez.

Hours later—okay, there's a chance he's being a little dramatic—Dawson hears the front door creak and click shut. His fingers twist in the sheets, heart threatening to beat through his ribcage. Then the bedroom door opens and...

Donut barrels in and throws himself into Dawson's lap.

Dawson yelps, shielding his private parts. "Donut, no! Ow, careful with the jewels!" A rumbling laugh reaches his ears. "It's not funny," Dawson pouts, grabbing Donut and depositing him on the floor.

Cal just keeps grinning. He's put his clothes on and his hair is wet. Dawson suddenly feels very under-dressed.

Which his dick seems to like.

He gulps as Cal approaches, no longer grinning. There's heat in his gaze and tension is rolling off him, so intense Dawson can physically feel it. He stops in front of Dawson, his stiff cock level with Dawson's face, and just looks at him. He must've showered upstairs because he smells fresh, not like the pool, and droplets of water are dripping from his hair and soaking the collar of his shirt.

Raising a hand, Cal tilts Dawson's face up with two fingers under his chin and bends down for a deep, slow, toe-curling kiss. Dawson grabs him by the neck, opens up for him, letting Cal's taste overtake his senses. He moans into his mouth when Cal flicks his right nipple, then rubs his thumb in circles over it.

Fuck. At this rate, Dawson will be glad if he lasts five minutes.

A pitiful whine escapes from him when Cal pulls away, only to drop to his knees. His eyes bore into Dawson's as he reaches for the towel around his waist and slowly, so painfully slowly, unwraps it, leaving Dawson completely exposed. He lowers his head and, gaze never steering away, takes the leaking head of Dawson's dick into his mouth.

Dawson's lips part on a silent moan, the sound caught somewhere in his throat. He flops back on the bed as Cal's mouth descends on him, taking him deeper. Cal hums, the sound reverberating through Dawson's cock and through his whole body.

"Fuck, Cal."

Cal must take that as encouragement, hollowing his cheeks and sucking Dawson cock so hard he nearly levitates off the bed. Then he pulls off, hooks his hands under Dawson's knees, and pushes his legs up. Before Dawson can process what's happening, Cal's mouth is on his ass, tongue circling his rim.

Dawson slams his hand down, gripping the edge of the mattress and holding on for dear life as Cal eats his ass out like he's done it a million times, not just the two, producing noises that make Dawson blush to the tips of his ears. God bless the porn industry.

When Dawson is dangerously close to coming untouched, Cal releases his legs.

"Wha—" Dawson starts to ask, his mind fuzzy.

Cal rises up and, without preamble, whips his shirt off. The joggers come off next, ending up in a pile on the floor.

Dawson takes a greedy eyeful, roaming over Cal's muscles, chiseled from swimming, and landing on his hard, flushed cock.

Dawson's hole clenches at the sight, heat spreading through his pelvis. He moves backwards and, acting on instinct and desire, turns onto his belly. He throws Cal a look over his shoulder, hoping he'll get what Dawson wants.

He's rewarded with a groan and a look of pure, unadulterated lust. Yeah, Cal gets it alright. Dawson watches as Cal marches towards the nightstand to get lube, then climbs on the bed and kneels between Dawson's spread legs. He braces himself on his hands either side of Dawson and presses a kiss to his sweaty neck.

"Like this?" he asks, voice rough with arousal.

"Yeah."

He used to hate this position. It was degrading, disempowering, making him feel like a toy.

It's nothing like that now.

There's nothing degrading about offering himself up to Cal as he drags his lips over Dawson's shoulders. Nothing disempowering about the intensity of Cal's desire for him. He doesn't feel like a toy when Cal slicks his fingers and brings them between Dawson's cheeks while whispering "You're beautiful" into his ear in that sinful voice. And when Cal fingers him open, torturously slow and sweet, it's all he can do not to rock against him, beg him like a slut to fuck him already.

Not that he would mind being a slut for Cal. Only for him, though.

Some of his desperation must rub off on Cal, because his patience seems to have run thin. He slides a third finger inside Dawson, pumps them a few times and pulls out. Dawson gasps at the feeling of emptiness, but it's short-lived.

The head of Cal's cock drags along his crease, slick with lube, and presses against his hole.

Cal kisses his ear. "Ready?"

"Uh-huh."

He whimpers when Cal's cock sinks into him, filling him up perfectly. He clenches around Cal, pulling a hiss from him. He does it again, intentionally this time.

"Dawson," Cal warns.

"What?" Dawson feigns innocence.

"You know what."

"Oh, this?" He clenches again, Cal's hips stuttering, his cock dragging over Dawson's prostate. They both moan.

"Stop it."

"Why? What are you gonna—Ah, shit!"

Cal draws back, pulling out almost all the way, and thrusts in. Chuckling at Dawson's reaction, he does it again, setting up a rhythm that has the bed creaking and Dawson crying out in no time. He lets out a particularly loud wail when Cal's cock hits the spot inside him *just* right.

Cal freezes. "Dawson? Did I—"

"Don't fucking stop!" Dawson sobs, rocking back against Cal, wanting to feel him deeper.

"Oh. Sorry," he says, amused. He covers Dawson's back, caging him in, and drives into him.

The pace is different now, languid and almost decadent, Cal's cock sinking in all the way before pulling out, then filling Dawson up again. It's intense in a way that has Dawson shaking and babbling within minutes, his pleasure skyrocketing.

Cal gradually slows to a stop and runs a hand down Dawson's side. "Could you turn over? I'd like to kiss you."

Oh, yes. Kissing. Kissing is good.

Dawson mumbles a yes, biting his lip when Cal pulls out of him. He flips onto his back, nearly swallowing his tongue at seeing Cal so disheveled. Cal descends on him instantly, taking his mouth in a fierce kiss that has his head spinning. He spreads his legs when he feels Cal between his cheeks again, and, grabbing Cal's hips, he guides him in. A relieved sigh escapes him when he's full again, and he wraps himself around Cal like an octopus, holding on.

Cal gathers him in his arms, rocking into him in gentle waves as he kisses him thoroughly. The combined assault on Dawson's senses has him soaring high and fast. A part of him wants to slow down, make this last as long as possible. He has to remind himself there's no need to stall. This is far from the last time he'll have Cal like this. There will be so many times. So many more. They have the rest of their lives for it.

"Cal."

"I know."

Dawson clings on tighter when the pressure inside him builds, seconds away from unraveling. He doesn't stand a chance when Cal grabs his legs and pushes them to his chest, the new angle changing everything.

Cal's cock drives into him four more times before Dawson cries out, ropes of come landing between their stomachs. Cal fucks him through it with sinful rolls of his hips that make Dawson's legs shake and his cock dribble out whatever is left in him. Then Cal shudders, his movements stuttering, and he spills inside Dawson, whimpering into his neck.

Dawson kisses his neck, his limbs too jelly-like to move.

Jesus. Christ.

"Are you alright?" Cal asks.

Dawson would laugh but it requires too much energy. "Peachy."

Cal chuckles, kissing Dawson's brow as he starts to pull out.

Overcome with a sudden surge of strength, Dawson locks his legs around him. "Wait. Can we stay like this for a moment?" He's not ready to let go yet, feeling too raw.

Cal settles back on top of him, threading his fingers through Dawson's hair. "Anything you want."

As Dawson lies there, basking in the afterglow with Cal's comforting weight on top of him, something occurs to him, making him giggle. How has he not put it together before?

"What's funny?" Cal asks.

Dawson hums, stroking Cal's back. "Do you like making love with me?"

Cal's expression grows incredibly fond. "Yes."

Dawson grins. "More than you love donuts?"

Cal ruins it. He purses his lips and actually *considers* it. "I'd have to think about that."

"Ugh, you ruined it! You're the worst," Dawson complains, trying to wriggle away when Cal tickles his side.

"Ruined what?"

"I just realized my life is like a movie."

Cal tilts his head like a curious puppy. "In what way?"

"I mean, an actual movie. A favorite of mine too. Can't believe I never put it together before."

Interest sparks Cal's gaze. "What movie?"

"I'm glad you asked." Dawson slaps his flank, letting Cal slip out of him. "Come on. Let's clean up. It's time for you to meet Joe Black."

Epilogue

2 Years Later

"You'll walk a hole in that floor if you keep that up," Cal says affectionately, sipping his champagne. The bubbles feel good on his tongue, making it taste much better than plain wine.

"Just let me pace dramatically, will you?" Dawson grumbles.

As endearing as it is to see him so nervous that he has to pace back and forth, it also breaks Cal's heart. Dawson has no reason to be nervous. He's incredibly talented, and people are going to love every single piece at the exhibition.

Eventually, he does stop and takes a big gulp of his champagne, fingers tapping against the flute. "What if no one likes it?"

Oh dear.

Cal closes the distance between them, winding an arm around Dawson's waist and kissing his temple. "We've been here for half an hour. Have you seen anyone leave?" Because Cal hasn't. Instead, more people are pouring in every minute.

Dawson gives their surroundings a tentative glance. "I don't think so?"

"Me neither. People don't stay for stuff they don't like."

Dawson purses his lips. "I don't like it when you're being a smartass."

"You married me. I'm pretty sure you do like it."

Dawson pouts. "Not when it's directed at me."

Cal is about to call him on the lie—or kiss him, he hasn't decided yet—when Gabe's voice interrupts.

"Aww, look at you two lovebirds!" He swaggers towards them with a cheeky grin, looking like a different person when wearing a dress shirt and well-fitting dark jeans. The only other time Cal's seen him all dressed up was for the wedding.

"Kind of you to show up," Dawson scolds as he opens his arms for a hug, a bit of champagne splashing over the rim of the glass when Gabe crashes into him.

"Sorry, I got a bit, um, sidetracked." He chuckles sheepishly and goes to give Cal a hug as well.

"Sidetracked, my ass," Dawson grumbles. He looks around. "Where's your boyfriend?"

"Trying to find parking."

"You could've just walked."

Gabe laughs, waggling his brows. "Easier said than done, if you know what I mean."

Dawson makes a face. "I do and I hate it. Please stop."

Gabe giggles. "So, how was the honeymoon?"

"Dee!" Olivia runs toward them, barreling against Dawson's back and hugging him from behind. More champagne splashes out. "This is so fucking beautiful, I have no words. I'm so proud of you!"

"Mommy said a bad word!" Chloe yelps, her and Leia's eyes wide.

Olivia waves them away. "I'll put a dollar in the jar when I get home." She looks at Cal. "Thank you for making him do this, Cal. He never listens to me. How did you convince him?"

"French toast."

"Holy shit," Gabe chokes out at the same time that Olivia cries, "Oh my god, eww," her face turning green.

Why eww? What's wrong with French toast?

"Jesus, no!" Dawson steps in, looking horrified. "He made me actual French toast!"

"Well, that's disappointing," Gabe says.

"Is there another meaning for French toast?" Cal asks him.

"Well..."

"Gabe," Dawson says in a warning.

Gabe seals his mouth shut, but Cal can see him smiling.

"How's your book coming along, Cal?" Olivia asks, her color back to normal.

"It's good."

"Any closer to the finish line?"

"It's already finished," Dawson tells her, earning a look of betrayal from Cal. "He's just scared to send it out for editing."

"If I send it out for editing, other people will read it."

"That's...kind of the point?" Olivia says, confused.

She doesn't understand. No one does. Maybe Dawson does a little, but that can't compare. His art is breathtakingly beautiful. Cal's writing is...not.

"What is it about?" Gabe asks. "You never said."

Cal smiles, glancing at Dawson. "Soulmates."

"Oh, I love that! Can I read it?"

"No."

Dawson laughs, pressing himself against Cal's side. "Give him a break. He gets teased enough by me."

"I do."

"You know I love you," Dawson says, taking his hand. He presses his lips together, looking nervous again. "Guys, could you excuse us for a sec?"

"Please don't have sex in a public place," Olivia begs, scrunching her nose.

"Sex," Chloe repeats, then Leia joins in.

Dawson gives Olivia an unimpressed look. "Really?"

"What? They'll have to learn, eventually."

Dawson shakes his head. "Anyway, we'll be right back." He steers Cal away.

"You should totally have sex in a public place!" Gabe calls after them, making Dawson flush bright red.

"Why did we invite them again?" he asks.

"Because we love them."

"Not right now, I don't love them."

"Where are we going?"

"You'll see." He gives Cal a shy smile. "I have something to show you."

"I've already seen all the paintings," Cal reminds him, but lets himself be led wherever Dawson wants him.

"Not this one, you haven't."

Dawson leads him to the other room, and they stop in front of a painting Cal decidedly hasn't seen before.

It's him. Dawson painted *him*. Kind of.

The painting has a supernatural quality to it. The right half of Cal's face looks normal. Dawson even managed to get his eye color spot on. The other half, though...

The left side of Cal's face has no skin. It's just a human skull, blended perfectly with the rest of his face. Someone who doesn't know their story might find it morbid, but Cal gets it. He gets what it symbolizes.

"It's incredible. Although, I should tell you reapers don't actually look like skeletons," he says with a chuckle.

"That's not you," Dawson says, smiling softly. He steps towards the painting and points to the right side—the human side. "This is you. This is how I see you."

"Oh." He hadn't expected that. "So, the other side is..."

"Yeah." Dawson's gaze drops to his feet, and he rubs the back of his neck. "It's not for sale, but I wanted to include it anyway. It's...it's important to me."

Cal prompts him to look up with a finger under Dawson's chin. "I love it. I love *you*."

Color rises to Dawson's cheeks. He blinks rapidly, flicking Cal's hand away. "Stop it."

Cal grabs him around the waist, pulling him in. His smile feels too big for his face. "Nuh-uh. Never." He kisses Dawson, pulling a soft, delicious sound out of him.

"What am I going to do with you?" Dawson wonders when they break apart.

"I'd say you could marry me, but that ship has sailed."

"Hmm. We'll have to think of something else." Dawson bites his lip, his gaze uncertain as he peers up at Cal. "How about kids?"

"Kids?"

Dawson nods. "Would you have kids with me?"

Cal would have anything with him, no question about it. But does Dawson really think Cal is fit to be a father? He's still figuring out how to be a human. Being a dog dad is hard enough.

Dawson, on the other hand... There's so much love in his heart, of course he wants to give it to somebody. Cal can't selfishly keep him all to himself, not when he knows what a privilege it is to be loved by him.

"Would you have kids with *me*?"

"I'd have anything with you," Dawson says, taking the words right out of his mouth.

And who is Cal to stand in the way of what Dawson wants?

"Okay."

Dawson blinks, stunned. "Okay?"

"Yeah." He strokes a hand through Dawsons hair. "Let's have kids."

Dawson surges up and kisses him. "When?"

Cal brings their lips together and whispers, *"Soon."*

What's next

Should Our Hearts Catch Fire (Book 2)

Ellis has been looking for something for as long as he can remember. It was never important, though. There's been expectations and rules laid out for him since he was born.

It doesn't matter that his dad isn't here anymore to remind him how inadequate he is compared to his big brother: not as smart, not as driven, not good enough. Never good enough. The only thing he's good for is being a cash-cow and ironing out other people's messes—like having to take over the family business, because his brother dear somehow managed to lose all his memories. Just great.

But that's his life.

It all changes the day he crosses the threshold to an unassuming cafe across the road and meets the local barista. Gabriel is insufferable, cheeky and looks at Ellis like he knows all his secrets.

Ellis swears to never go back, but something about that place keeps drawing him in. Every time he steps in there, he feels more like himself. A little more alive and far less lost.

He has no idea what he's looking for but sometimes, when he's in Gabriel's shop, it feels like he might have found it.

Also by Amithia

Novellas

UNRAVELED
UN/TAMED

The novellas are available for purchase on my website only.
If you'd like to receive a free copy of UNRAVELED, you can sign up
to my newsletter.

About Author

I'm your regular anti-social weirdo who loves to escape reality by getting way too invested in the lives of fictional dudes, be it through reading or writing.

I was born and raised in the Czech Republic. In 2019, I ran away to Brisbane, Australia, where I made camp and have no plans on changing that. In real life, I'm a physiotherapist, and a coffee and sugar addict. In my other (way more interesting) life, I'm a sap who can't survive without two (or more) boys in love and a proper happily ever after.

I like my boys to be imperfect and a little broken. I like seeing them being put back together. I love slow burn, the kind of love that's flawed but pure and lasts forever. I like that inexplicable pull that transcends reason and time. I also may or may not have a weakness for 'trashy' romance, cliches, idiots in love and characters whose toxic inclinations would make a therapist run for the hills. Whatever my wandering soul craves in the moment.

To stay updated about my upcoming releases, visit my website **https://amithiraine.com** and join my newsletter, or follow me on social media.

Printed in Great Britain
by Amazon